Robert Day

The Collected Short Stories

ROBERT

The Collected Short Stories

DAY

SERVING HOUSE BOOKS

2020

SERVING
HOUSE
SHB BOOKS

*For Kathryn Jankus Day (aka "The Wife" in Western Kansas patois)
and Crosby Kemper (a charter member of the Mutual Admiration Society)*

CONTENTS

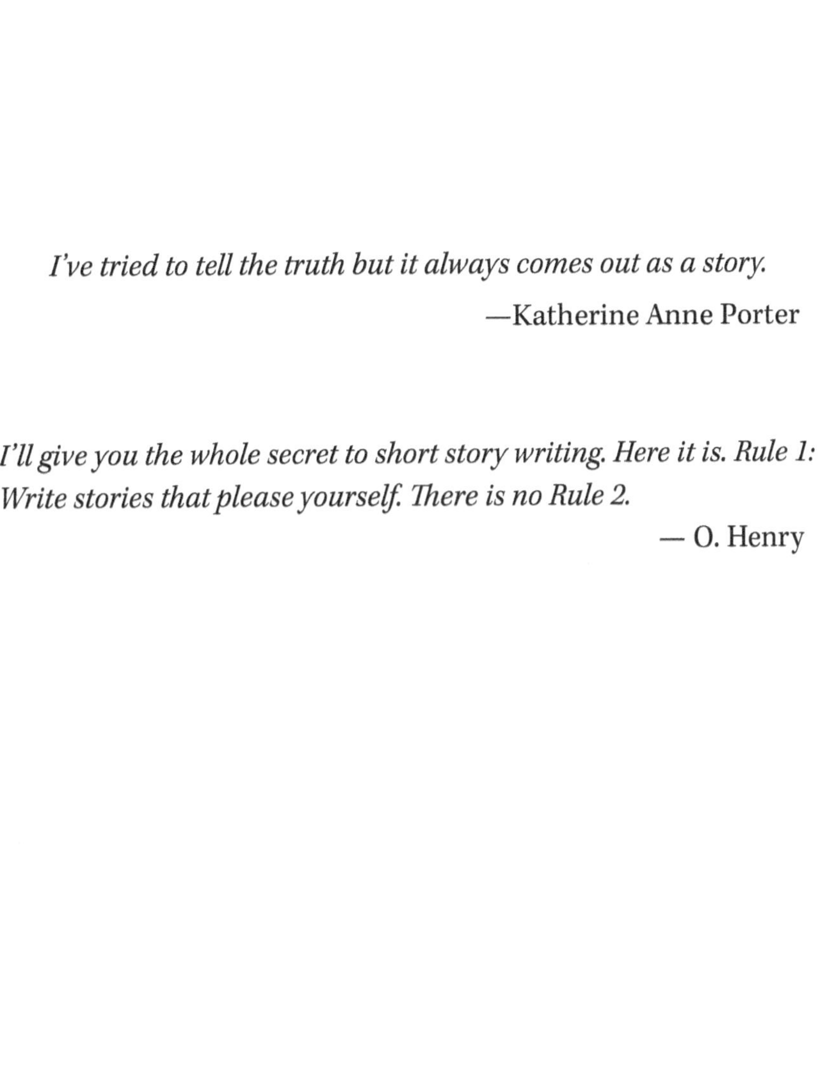

I've tried to tell the truth but it always comes out as a story.

—Katherine Anne Porter

I'll give you the whole secret to short story writing. Here it is. Rule 1: Write stories that please yourself. There is no Rule 2.

— O. Henry

Preface: Becoming a Writer

I began writing not unlike the kid in the short story "Free Writing." First, notes left to girls of my dreamy life—Heather Kirk, Sherry McPherson, Nancy Fulton—hidden under rocks near Shafer's Pond in Paint's Pasture (where they languished unread). Then later I wrote a "What I Did Last Summer" account for Mr. Schwartz, my teacher.

I claimed I had gone to Paris, as I had seen the flyers for *An American in Paris* at the Dickinson Theater. Our parents had told us we were too young to see the movie, so instead my mother dropped us off at the site of a traveling circus where for a quarter each we got to see a hermaphrodite, a rather flaccid penis drooping out from her side. It was not the kind of story you wrote for Mr. Schwartz. Or told your mother.

As to Paris, instead of watching the movie I looked up the city in various photography books at the local library and got myself there with ease: I liked especially the Seine, which I paddled down in the small flat-bottom boat Tom and I used to fish at Shafer's Pond: past the Louvre and Notre Dame, going under various bridges whose names I tossed around to impress Mr. Schwartz.

Mr. Schwartz wrote that he didn't believe I had gone to Paris over the summer but that my account was amusing. He also observed that I seemed not to understand "point of view," that sometimes I was writing in the first person, and other times in the third person. I had no idea what to make of that. Then he wrote that he had been to Paris once and with my account he enjoyed going back. With that praise I became a fiction writer: not that I knew that then, but I knew something. I know it now.

The stories in this collection represent about six decades of writing. Over time some of them have grown the "claws and wings" of novels, as Vladimir Nabokov put it. But they were stories first.

At the University of Kansas I took a course titled "Narration and Description." Not that I knew what those terms meant, but I was curious to find out. It was taught by "Staff."

What I found out was that I could not contain myself with those two categories, and in an early submission I branched out into scenes. My teacher (a Miss Staff) did not reprimand me for this, but pointed out that "scenes" typically had two "unities": one of time and one of place. I had no idea what she meant. But since I had not been scolded, in my next submission I not only had a scene but also introduced two characters who talked. Meanwhile, the other students were dutifully writing narration and description: *We walked from our dorm to Strong Hall where our class met and along the way we saw the cars on Jayhawk Boulevard.*

Once again my teacher stepped in and pointed out that even though I was now writing "scenes," I could also incorporate the features of our course: How did my character get to where he was? And what did he see along the way? Then there was again that nasty problem of "point of view" and how I seemed to mix first-person present tense with omniscient and limited omniscient. What a mess!

In spite of not knowing what she was talking about, I kept going.

I suppose somewhere in the course files for the University of Kansas, a "Narration and Description" is listed, as well as who among the "Staff" was my teacher. Thank you.

—Robert Day

Part One

Women

The Mystery of Women

Long ago and probably not far away, I was invited along with a few other Midwestern writers (all men) to a symposium on our writing. Each of us gave a short reading followed by questions (Q&A, as it is called in the trade): How do we get the ideas for our stories? Do we write in longhand or on a typewriter? (It was that long ago.) Do we rewrite? (One of my fellow authors quoted Saul Bellow's remark—"Writing *is* rewriting"—and I quoted Nabokov, who said that his pencil points outlasted his erasers.)

Then someone asked me what I would be writing next. Would it be a sequel to *The Last Cattle Drive*? No, I said. I am thinking of writing about women. The remark surprised me. And it must have surprised the audience because there was a moment of silence. Then: What about women? The question was asked by one of the few women in the audience.

I think women are more interesting than men, I said in response. They have the most secrets: from their husbands, from their children, from their lovers, even from themselves. And there I stopped and thought about what I had said, and how it seemed true.

What followed over time are the stories of women in this section of my collected short stories.

Edith at the Eighth Street Tavern

Back in the early 1960s you could go into Lawrence, Kansas, on Saturdays and get a beaver dinner, potato salad, and draft Coors for a dollar. You could do this if you were not a university student or if you knew Edith, who ran the Eighth Street Tavern. If you didn't know Edith, you might not get a beaver dinner, but you could at least get a beer and sit in one of the booths along the wall. The beavers were given to her by the men who trapped the rivers around Lawrence.

Beaver is dark, rich, oily meat that tastes something like roast beef, but nothing like it at all. Edith would serve it on white paper plates, the kind you can no longer buy. They were thick as cardboard but that did not stop the beaver grease from soaking through onto the long painted wooden bar where you had to eat. Edith would not budge from behind the bar; you could take your beer to the booths but not your beaver dinner. She wanted to watch you as you ate.

But when you were done, you had to go and sit at one of the booths to finish your beer because there were others who had not eaten and were waiting. Edith would mop up (redistribute) the circle of grease that had soaked through the thick paper plates and then wave the rag at whoever she decided was next. It wasn't first come first serve at Edith's. But then nobody knew what it was.

All of this is not a joke. Although it is true you could not get beaver dinners year round. You could only get them in the Winter Months. When that began you didn't exactly know, except that when you went inside the Eighth Street Tavern one day to have a beer, there would be old men with orange Grange hats on, eating at the bar, and then you knew the Winter Months were upon you. The rest of the year there was nothing whatsoever to eat at Edith's. Not even peanuts. Only tap Coors. Which is now so rare and popular in the East but which is like milk in Kansas.

One of the men in the orange Grange hats was likely to be "Original" John Smith, who trapped beaver on the Wakarusa and who was in love with Edith. Edith was between fifty and sixty. Smith was the same age. In a voice that sounded like James Stewart, Smith would tell Edith that he loved her. Everybody at the bar would laugh and tease Edith and tease John Smith. Only Edith and John Smith knew that Smith wasn't kidding. But over the years they had never said anything about what they knew. John Smith was married. Edith was not.

It is 1963. The Winter Months are upon us. John Smith is at the bar, near the end by the door. The window out onto Eighth Street is steamy, more steamy than usual, and small beads of water are forming at the top, or near the top, of the window and flowing down, leaving a clear line for a moment before the line steams up again and your attention is drawn to another line come to life. Edith boils the beaver meat before she bakes it, and one way you can tell the Winter Months are upon you is if the windows of the tavern are steamed up. But this is not always a surefire way. Today it is.

"Does John Smith love Edith?" Clarence Wiggins says from the other end of the bar, bringing grins to a line of men hunched over their food. Edith has banished Tom Burke from the bar as he has finished and replaced him with E. K. Drieling, who came from western Kansas a year ago and taught the river men a few things about how you trap beaver when the water is low in the creeks.

"John Smith loves Edith," says Jimmy Stewart in his "Original"

John Smith voice. He is eating slowly, picking around in his food, pushing large lumps of potatoes into the beaver grease. "That's true," he says. "That's very true. Edith, now don't I love you?" Edith says he does.

"You know what I love about you most?" says Smith, spacing his elbows on either side of his plate and rubbing his greasy fingers into his palms.

"Is it my money?" says Edith, handing Drieling a full plate of food and a glass of beer.

"No. I have more money than you do. That's what you love about me," he says.

"That's true," she says. And it is. But there isn't anything greedy in it. The others at the bar laugh except Drieling, who has just taken a bite of food and his mouth is full. He is also kind of new to all this and doesn't quite understand that the same scenes played over and over give everybody amusement.

"What I love about you," says Smith, "is that you paint the bar every year." She does. Light grey. A shade lighter than the floor, which she also paints every year, but nobody notices the floor like they notice the bar. It is a long bar and low enough for a man to feel tall at. The stools are high, have arms on them, and spin all the way around. She paints the bar and floor in the summer, on a Sunday morning, so that it is ready for use when Monday comes. If it is rainy that Sunday, she does not close the tavern on Monday so that the bar and floor have time to dry completely. She opens. And all through the year you can see the circles that the glasses have made in the almost dry paint that first Monday. Of course, the floors are rough, as walking on them pulls the paint a bit, but nobody notices that. The circles will be on the bar until the next year when Edith will paint them out, along with the jackknife cuts that mark how many beers a man has drunk during a particular contest or how many times Jimmy T. Hallmark says "Bat Shit" during an evening, or how many times Buffalo "small bladder" Chip Wilson has to visit the john. But each year the light grey paint flows into all the cuts and mars and nicks and gouges and scratches of the bar and makes it new again. Or nearly new, for the men take great pleasure in discovering in the newly painted bar faint evidence of last year's marks. Or the year before that. Some claiming they can find the gentle dents made five years back. They rub their fingers where they had made their marks, testing to see how long it will be before they can't be found.

"That's what I love most about you," says John Smith.

"Are you finished or just resting?" Edith says to Smith as he leans his head into his hands and props his face above his dinner. Edith is an impartial dictator of who sits at the bar Saturdays during the Winter Months. "If you're done, you know what you can do," she says. "We'll make hash outa what you got left there. Or give it to Jack-Off."

He is the cat. Who is seldom seen but is usually asleep where the beer cooler's motor warms the floor under the bar. He only comes out when the tavern is nearly empty and sleeps on the bar chair nearest the can, the chair that does not turn at all so few people want to sit there. Besides, it is by the can. On Sundays, when Edith opens the front and back door to let the tavern air out (summer and winter) for the afternoon, Jack-Off ventures out into Eighth Street. He is the most canary yellow cat anyone has ever seen.

"I'm just resting," says John Smith.

"He wants to look at you," someone at the bar says to Edith. "That's why he's eatin' his food slower than a possum."

"Possums ain't slow eaters," says Drieling.

"Bat shit they ain't," says Hallmark.

"I saw a possum eat a mouse in one bite," says Drieling. "Out on the Smoky Hill."

"Everything got to eat fast out there 'less a tornado come along and suck them up," says John Smith.

"I watched a possum one whole afternoon," says the fellow who first claimed they were slow eaters, "trying to eat a bunch of livers some fisherman had left there on the bank. He couldn't get it done. I was up on the K-18 bridge. After a while I shot him. Got him in the head, too."

"You dally over your food all afternoon like that," Edith says to Smith and points a finger at the man who had just told the possum story, "and you'll get shot just the same." All the men laugh hard.

Edith has a gun. A single-barrel twenty-gauge shotgun Tom Kincade gave her one spring ten years ago, after some hoods from Kansas City came in and bashed her in the head with an iron pipe and stole a hundred and forty-two dollars from the cash box. It was a Friday night, after midnight. Taverns in Kansas close at midnight, and although they can lock the doors and let the people who are drinking finish their beers, Edith doesn't do this. She has everybody out by midnight. She likes running the tavern, and she doesn't want to get to not liking it by having people around there until two in the morning, nursing a warm beer and pleading with her for another. Or stocking up on beers just before closing and then selling them back and forth to one another, the price jumping the later it gets. She doesn't want that so she doesn't have it. But she does stay a while after she's run everybody out and has a beer herself as she cleans the tavern before she goes upstairs to the apartment where she lives. She still was downstairs, in the tavern, halfway through her beer, when she heard a pounding at the front door.

"If that's you, John Smith, you can just as well go home," she said.

There was no answer. John Smith had been unusually talky that night, and there were times when she thought the other men in the bar might in fact catch on that he really did love her. She hoped not, but then she thought that perhaps they had when Smith said that after everyone had left, he was coming back and that he'd see her up the stairs to her apartment in a big hurry.

"I said you just as well go home," she said to the pounding at the door. She didn't know what was to come of this. If they had met when they were younger, she might have let it take its course, but she was getting too old to be taking on another woman's man. She had been young once and missed her chances, and she had come to think that the punishment she must impose upon herself for that was to miss her chances the rest of the way. Still, in spite of herself, she wondered if she had put away the ironing board that morning or was it smack in the middle of the living room, its ragged cover telling on her neglect. The pounding grew louder and the door rattled. If he was silly drunk, she'd be disappointed. She'd send him home for sure if he was drunk. She killed her beer and went to the door.

The hoods hit her square in the forehead and, as she was going down, smashed her in the right ear. She was bleeding from the mouth and both ears when John Smith found her in the doorway about twenty minutes later.

She told the police she could hear the hoods talking behind her. As they left, she opened her eyes to get a good look—but she could not see out of them. Then she couldn't remember.

It was a week before they'd let anyone in her room at the hospital. John Smith came to see her and brought some Russell Stover candy. Tom Kincade brought her the gun, broken down into two pieces and wrapped in a blanket so that it didn't look like a gun. Chip Wilson painted the sign on the door: I HAVE A GUN AND I CAN SHOOT—Edith.

After a month she came back to the tavern. On Sundays Kincade taught her to shoot the gun so the sign wouldn't be a bluff.

Two years later she shot a Mexican from Topeka in the heel—well, pretty much up and down the whole back of his left leg just after he had robbed the liquor store up the street and the owner, Tom Jenkins (whom she hated), began screaming like a baby right in the middle of the robbery. Edith ran out on the sidewalk and got the Mexican going away. She told the police she was going to ask Kincade for a gun with two barrels—that way once they were down she could finish them off before a crowd began to gather.

She is smiling as she tells John Smith she is going to shoot him for being so poky. Other men are getting finished now, and the ones sitting at the tables who have not eaten are getting places. So it doesn't matter. Good. She doesn't like to be fair when it comes to John Smith. Still, if he doesn't eat his beaver meat when it is warm it won't be much good. At least not until it becomes stone cold and you can cut it up into small chunks.

"Eat your food," Edith says. "Or I'll send you to the tables anyway." John Smith downs his beer.

"Let me buy you a round," he says to Edith. The men laugh. Edith never drinks at anyone's expense. Not that she drinks much on her own. Only a beer with a meal, like now, or another one during the day. And of course the one at night when she and the cat are cleaning up.

"I'll fool you all," she says in a crisp voice and goes over to the tap and draws a beer down the side of the glass. Out here they don't put heads on the beer. The foam is as thin as November ice, and you can see clear circles of golden beer at the top of the glass.

"You owe me a quarter," Edith says to Smith as she takes a sip. The men are silent for a moment and then they laugh as one.

"See what all this loving comes to," says one of them. Laughter. Edith comes toward Smith, sipping her beer as she walks.

"Don't I get wholesale price?" Smith asks. "That's about a dime, now isn't it, Edith?" He is digging in his pockets and like so many men he doesn't think to stand up to get his change but rather points his leg out and bends his wrist and hand into his crimped jean pocket.

"A quarter from you, money bags," she says, putting the beer rather squarely down in front of him. He is confused.

"It ain't for me," he says.

"I know that. A lady just drinks with a man what buys her a beer." Amid the laughter there are catcalls, whistles and whoo-eees. John Smith has dropped his quarter on the floor, and Edith is peering over the bar to watch him pick it up.

"See what it comes to," someone says. "All these years of pushing the point about loving Edith—now he's lost himself. Can't keep ahold of his money."

"Here's your quarter, now," John Smith says. Edith has settled herself on a stool she keeps at that end of the bar.

"Maybe I better have another one myself," John Smith says as he looks at his empty glass.

"Now's a fine time to tell me just when I got myself all settled. You just share mine." More catcalls and one long whoo-eee.

"Why don't you two make a toast?" Chip Wilson says from the doorway of the john.

"I believe I've got him bluffed out," says Edith. "I don't believe he can drink, much less talk."

"You gotta have two glasses to toast," says Smith in a sour way. "Besides, I'm not making no toasts. That's for sure." Edith looks at him straight on.

"How come you don't threaten to stay around and see me upstairs anymore?" she says frankly, drinking her beer in gulps. Low whistles. No whoo-eees.

"If it's true Kincade gave you a double-barrel shotgun, you got your answer right there. I know better than a Mexican to come prowling around here at night," Smith says. He takes a gulp of Edith's beer.

"I don't know about that," Edith says. "I hear some tomcat noises in the alley now and then. I don't guess that would be you out there trying to get my attention. Now, would it?"

"That's not my style," Smith says. "I come through the front door."

"I'd leave it unlocked," she says, "but I guess you'd rather bust it down." Whoo-eees. She finishes the beer and waves in mock disgust at Smith as she twirls off the stool and back to the beer tap in the center of the bar.

More men are coming in the tavern and standing around. She gets them beers and shoos off the men at the bar who are finished eating. John Smith takes some last bites and leaves of his own accord. He gets another beer with the wave of men who have just come in and then goes over to a booth where Wilson, Wiggins, and Drieling are talking about what the new Clinton dam will do to the Wakarusa.

"I'll put an end to beaver and rats," says Chip Wilson. "No question about that."

"Just so some rich lawyers from Kansas City can go water-skiing," Smith says.

"I'd like to shoot me one of those water-skiers," says Wiggins. "Put a 30–06 on him and that would be the end of water-skiing there at Clinton. Bet your life on that."

"Just pump a few rounds into the fancy outboard. That's all you'd need to do," says Drieling.

"Maybe," says Wiggins. "But you plug one of those lawyers right when he's skiing and that'll put an end to the matter right then and there. Then shoot up the boat just to put the scare into the rest of them."

"Maybe we should just mine the lake," says Smith. They laugh. "Wouldn't that be something. Just like when you'd blow up frogs in the pond with cherry bombs. Ever do that as a kid?" They all had.

What would they all do when the dam dries up the Wakarusa

and there is no more trapping along the river? They didn't know. There had been plenty of beaver and rats this year. Big beaver, too. Edith would have enough meat for a long winter. If she could freeze some, they might have these Saturday dinners into March. But it would all come to an end when the government finished the water-skiers' lake.

The afternoon fades into evening. It is getting brutal cold outside. Up in the corners of the large front window where it isn't calked well, the air is frosting the inside of the pane. The tavern is thinning out. There is no more meat left. Only potato salad, which the men can eat at the booths if they wish. They have to come to the bar to get it, though. John Smith brings back four plates for his table.

Dinner time is slow for the tavern. The men go home for supper no matter how much they have eaten at Edith's. Finally, there is just the Smith table, a few men at the bar, and two fellows who have just come in and who are drinking beer in the back booth. Edith comes over to John Smith and asks him if he thinks the two might be university students. She doesn't want them in here if they are. Smith says he doesn't know one way or another. She lets them stay, and when Drieling leaves she draws herself a beer and then joins Smith, Wilson, and Wiggins. Wilson excuses himself for a moment. The cat comes out from under the bar and leaps into the end bar stool. Wilson returns.

"Times are changing," Smith says to Edith as she sits down. "How come you don't run those two out?" He tosses his head toward the back booth. "Used to be if you just had a thought they might be students you'd run them off. Getting soft?"

"Maybe," she says. "Some of them ain't so bad, I guess."

"I don't know about that," Wiggins says. "I saw in the paper one of the girls up there went and made a dress out of the flag. Wore it, too. That's what the picture's about. Standing smart-assed right in front of the war memorial."

"Not that she don't have something good to wear, either," says Wilson. "Her old man's probably a doctor or lawyer in Kansas City and lives in one of those fancy ranch houses in Shawnee-Mission."

"Her old man's probably the one you shot off his water skis," says Smith to Wiggins. They all laugh, even Edith, who doesn't quite understand.

They are silent for a moment, drinking their beer. The door opens. It is someone from the tavern going out.

"Did you see?" Smith asks Wiggins. "Was it snowing out?"

"No. Supposed to?"

"I guess so," says Edith. "Six to eight inches."

"I better get along if that's the case," says John Smith. He drinks off his beer.

"You can have the beer you bought me back," says Edith, looking into her glass. There is a pause.

"I better not pass that up," he says and laughs by himself. Wiggins is lighting up a pipe and grins through the smoke. Without a crowd there is no one to play to, and Smith seems foolish laughing out loud like that.

They all drink another round, and then Wiggins and Wilson say they must leave, and do. Yes, it is snowing after all, Wilson says, as they go out the door and hold it open so Smith and Edith can see out into Eighth Street and see the snow falling into the street with such speed and thickness that neither of them can spot the shops on the other side. The door closes and leaves them both sitting on the same side of the booth. Edith moves to the other side. The young men in the back booth leave.

"How things going?" Smith says idly.

"Not bad. I can't complain. I paid the building off last year. Putting a little away." Smith looks into his beer.

"It's a good thing you do here, Edith. Feeding men so cheap as this during the winter."

"I don't pay for the beaver. They give it to me."

"It's either that or let it lay. Nobody wants to mess with it but you."

"You having a good year?" she asks him.

"Not bad. Lost a few traps to badgers early. But you gotta expect something like that. I guess I don't get down the river as quick as I used to. Don't get out as often or up as early either. Age."

"I do pretty much the same day's work," Edith says. "Except cooking winters wears me so. At least this year."

"It's a good thing you do, Edith," he says. He looks in his beer again. It is half empty. The cat readjusts itself on the stool.

"You want another?" she asks.

"I guess not," he says. He doesn't even finish what he has and gets up to leave.

"I might stop back later on," he says at the door in his Jimmy Stewart voice. "If this snow don't get too deep." The door closes behind him.

The snow begins to gather on the streets. Eighth Street is not busy, and so the snowplows won't get to it right away. Edith thinks if nobody comes back by nine she'll close and go upstairs and watch television. Too soon it is nine.

She opens the front and back doors to let the cold air sweep through the place and clean it out. The snow is a pelt on the ground now. The curbs are gone, the snow has muted all sharp edges. The cat comes forward to peer outside and then dashes back under the bar, his tail high in the air. In a moment the tavern smells like the outside and is nearly as cold. Edith closes both doors and locks them.

While she is drinking her beer and picking up the ashtrays and mopping off the tables and the bar, she thinks she hears something at the door.

"Is that you, John Smith?" she says in a voice not loud enough to be heard if it is. It is just the wind. She checks the door three more times before she turns off all the lights, save the naked bulb in the kitchen that shines throughout the tavern when all the other lights are out. As a last thought she makes a sign and hangs it in the front window:

CLOSED CAUSE OF WHETHER. AM UPSTAIRS. E.

Twice during the evening she thinks she hears someone at the tavern door, and she pokes her head out of her apartment window into the snowy air to look down into the street. Each time there is no one there. Around midnight the snowplow finally comes by. She watches it build ridges of snow up against the curbs, blocking the alley off. After it goes up and down the street, the snowplow turns onto Massachusetts Street and goes south. Eighth Street is silent again, save for the odd sound falling snow makes, which we all know but cannot describe.

We All Have Our Stories

The Good Blue Shirt

"I think you give the wrong impression," she said. "And I think you do it on purpose." Irunea was tired of Rob's dinner table stories. In fact, tonight she was tired of all Rob's stories—but it was the one about Tallulah Bankhead that he had told this evening at the Carys' that irritated her the most. And she knew exactly why. None of this "vague uneasiness" that her friend Leslie was always talking about when it came to her husband Turner. U.S. (that was Turner's nickname) had made her "vaguely uneasy" at the Howards' last weekend when he'd brought up a matter of Bill Clinton. Or U.S. was making her "vaguely uneasy" these days just being around the house. There was so much of him. What Irunea didn't like about Rob's stories was that they made him seem self-important. As if he had once known Tallulah Bankhead. Or as if they had once known someone who knew Tallulah Bankhead.

"What impression?" said Rob.

"That we knew her," said Irunea. "And we don't even know anybody who knew her. Ever. I don't know where you got that story. It's the way you tell it."

"Al Tapon told it to us when we were all in Greece," said Rob. He was putting away his ties like he was supposed to, but he was about to hang his good blue dress shirt on a peg instead of using a hanger.

"I don't remember," she said.

"You were sick," Rob said. "I think that was the time you were sick from the shrimp and had to stay in the hotel room. It was a rough day for you."

"It's the way you tell it," she said.

"How's that?" he said. He had changed into a pair of sweat pants from the athletic team he was on in college, and a t-shirt from a bike trip he and U.S. made across the state every year.

"Well, you never say we didn't know her."

"Why should I?" he said. "I don't say we were there. I just tell the story the way Al did. How could we know her? She's long dead. We're not that old. We've never lived in New York. We don't play bridge."

"It just seems pretentious."

"Darling, you just don't like the 'fuck' in the 'Fuck Betty Crocker' line," Rob said as he went downstairs to watch television. After he was gone, Irunea hung up his shirt properly.

Sentences. Stanza. A Few Lines Even.

Irunea and Leslie were members of a book club that met every month on a Sunday afternoon. It had become the rule of the club that each member had to memorize a short section of the book the group was reading and be able to recite it sometime during the gathering. A small paragraph would do. Even a few sentences. If the book was poetry, a stanza was fine. A few lines even, as when Irunea had memorized:

> *O, learn to read what silent love hath writ:*
> *To hear with eyes belongs to love's fine wit.*

The idea to memorize a passage had come from a local author they'd invited one Sunday when they had discussed his novel. He had been able to quote a number of sections from his own work, and at the next meeting Leslie had continued the practice by quoting a sexually explicit description from the Sebastian Faulks novel they had read that month: "The skin was young and new and almost white, with its patterning of little marks and freckles that he tried to taste with the tip of his tongue." And she went on from there, and everyone knew the passage themselves, if not by heart.

Leslie had an excellent memory and was able to recount quite long passages, sometimes with dialogue. But Irunea had difficulty and was always practicing, and even then she'd rarely get it right (she'd recited "...to read what secret love had writ"). Not that the exercise was to be a test of memory, they all agreed. It was just a way of getting into their heads some small part of the book that was important to them, which in turn would lead to a way of talking about the book itself. It was a system of keeping them "on message," as Leslie would say.

Over time, Irunea had decided the best way to get her passage right was to recite it to Leslie sometime before the meeting. Usually, Leslie would stop by Fridays on her way home from work and the two of them would have a glass of wine and go over the week behind them. If it was a Friday before Book Club Sunday, that's when Irunea would try out her recitation with Leslie checking her memory against the text.

"*Destroy therefore all your knowing and feeling of every kind of creatures, and...*"

"*Creature,*" says Leslie. "*Singular: creature.*"

"*...creature, and especially of yourself. You're thinking of all other...*"

"*...thinking and feeling...*" says Leslie. "Must not forget *feeling* in this book."

"*...thinking and feeling of all other creatures depends upon your awareness of yourself, for when you have overcome that, all other creatures can easily be forgotten.*"

"*On* for *upon,*" says Leslie, "and you've got it." She hands the book *(The Cloud of Unknowing)* back to Irunea, closes her eyes and recites: "*If you will actively apply yourself to practice this, you will find that when you have forgotten all other creatures and all their words—there will still remain between you and your God a pure awareness and feeling of your own being."*

"Is that your passage for Sunday?" says Irunea.

"No. It is what follows yours."

"You memorized it just now?"

"Yes."

"How do you do it?"

"I write it out in my head," says Leslie. "I see it being typed in, and it is there. As if on a computer screen. Try it sometime." Irunea said she would.

Ohio Street

Irunea and Rob and U.S. were all in college together. Rob and U.S. had an apartment on Ohio Street and in those days Irunea dated U.S.—not Rob. Rob was dating a girl from high school; Irunea never knew who. Then one Friday night when Irunea was late getting back to the dorm and was locked out because of curfew, she walked down to the apartment. She thought U.S. would not be there, because he had told her he was going home for the weekend and not to bother to stop by. But maybe Rob would be there and let her stay, and that way Irunea would not have to "Take a Late" and get another letter from the Resident Assistant. Much later—it was almost morning—U.S. came into the apartment with a girl. But by then Rob and Irunea were in bed together.

When you are young, you do things and don't even think about them. Not in advance, anyway. They don't seem right or wrong at the time, you just do them. When you get older, you do the same, only not as often. It all becomes sections in a story about yourself that you have in your head and that demands to be read now and then even if you don't want to. Like when you had to take a test in college. This is what Irunea had come to believe.

Even after Irunea had *left* U.S. for Rob, she continued to *see* U.S.

now and then: *As if they had never finished being lovers; as if there were a natural length to their relationship that had to run its course and unless it did, she would be forever thwarted in her heart, and thus unfinished in her soul.* It was a sentence from a book their club had read some time ago and that Irunea had memorized, but had not recited to either Leslie or the group. She hadn't felt *unfinished* until she'd read that passage. Still. And why in her mind did she call what she did with U.S. *seeing him*? Even now.

The White House

"And so," says Rob, "the guy sitting next to Sybil Burton doesn't know he's sitting next to Sybil Burton. He's come in late because he's with the White House and those guys are always late to dinner parties. So he doesn't know who he's sitting next to. But his wife does. She's across the table. And of course the whole 'Big Deal' with Richard Burton and Liz Taylor has hit the press. This is when they're filming *Cleopatra*. So this guy from the White House says: 'Don't we all think Liz is going to get him?' He means Burton. And this guy's wife goes from white to red like stripes on a flag. And everybody at the table doesn't say a thing. Not a thing."

Bike America

"Do you think women talk about sex?" says Rob. "Not think about it. Talk about it." It was late in the day with a bright sun yellow in the west.

"Leslie doesn't," says U.S. "At least not to me. Although..." And here he stopped.

"I mean to each other," says Rob. "Like men are supposed to talk about sex in locker rooms."

"Or on bike trips," says U.S.

"Exactly."

One of the rules of Bike America is that you ride single file, and that you do not talk. Even over your shoulders. That way accidents happen. U.S. and Rob should know. They are the co-captains of this year's state ride, and so they were the ones who gave the safety presentations to those who were new to the event. But as they are bringing up the rear of the line of riders, at least they aren't setting a bad example.

"Why do you ask?" says U.S.

"I've been thinking about the difference between men and women," says Rob.

"Why bother?" says U.S.

"Women can't tell stories," says Rob.

"Neither can I," says U.S. "I wish I could. Like you."

"Let's make a list," says Rob.

"Women can't read maps. Women don't remember jokes. Women use more toilet paper. Is that enough?" said U.S. "Women change their mind for no good reason."

"I'm serious," says Rob.

"Why?"

"Because Irunea is all over me about my stories. The one I told the other night about the guy asking Queen Noor's daughter what her father did for a living."

"I thought that was very funny," said U.S. "But the one I like best is the one about Tallulah Bankhead. Standing there in the doorway after all that racket in the kitchen with flour all over her. And those people at the bridge table who thought they were all going out to dinner with her afterward like they usually did, but no, Tallulah was going to cook instead. I wish to hell I could tell it like you do."

It was the last thing U.S. ever said.

"This Is My Beloved"

The Friday before the Book Club Sunday (when Rob and U.S. were on their bike trip), Irunea and Leslie decided to have dinner together at Irunea's house. As usual, Leslie stopped by after work and the two of them drank a glass of wine while Irunea practiced her passage, a stanza. She got it right on the first try. This month's book was by a poet named Lyn Lifshin. The woman who chose it said Lifshin was the most popular poet in America. Irunea didn't much like the poetry, and in fact it had made her realize that for some time now she hadn't much liked anything they'd been reading. Maybe that was her fault.

Irunea had decided she was going to ask Leslie what she thought of Rob telling those stories of his. The ones with famous people in them. Like the one he told at the Showens' house about Queen Noor's daughter. Or the one he told last week when they had all had dinner together so Rob and U.S. could plan their bike trip.

Of course Irunea knew that U.S. and Leslie didn't think that she and Rob knew anybody from the White House, but Rob was going to tell that story all over the place now that he'd told it once. And it embarrassed her. Leslie was standing by the counter that separates the kitchen from the dining room. Irunea was in the kitchen itself fixing a pasta dish.

"We all have our stories," Leslie said. "I tell mine. You just don't tell yours."

Irunea looked out the window for a moment and wondered if that was true. The afternoon had been warm and sunny, and it still was. She was about to say they could eat on the patio when Leslie went on:

"I was always very sexual. I knew it from about the time I was fourteen. I had this boyfriend named Johnny Bullard who kept pawing me front and back, mainly front, and I knew I wasn't supposed to like it and slap his hands, and all those things you were told to do by Miss Taylor, but it felt really good to have his hand on my body even through my clothes, and at night I would put myself to sleep by thinking about what it would be like to be naked with Johnny Bullard and how he'd touch me all over. I even wrote him letters about it, but I never mailed them. I must have used the word 'breast' ten times in twenty-five words. It made me quiver just to write it."

"Who was Miss Taylor?"

"She was the headmistress of Bayonne," said Leslie. "That was the day school where I went. Did you go to boarding school or day school? I forget."

"I went to public school."

"Then my brother came home from college with a copy of *Ulysses*," said Leslie, "and there was a bookmark in the back where Molly Bloom talks about everything and ends up saying *yes, yes* all over the place."

"I've never read it," said Irunea.

"Have you read *Lady Chatterley's Lover*?" said Leslie.

"No." Irunea was lying. And she knew the passage Leslie was thinking about. Both the first part of it, and later when the gardener or the stable man—or whoever he was—says something like "it wasn't there for you." Irunea poured them both another glass of wine.

"Well, I did. And I read *Peyton Place* too. And then I read *This Is My Beloved*. And after I read *This Is My Beloved* is when I decided I would take my clothes off for Johnny Bullard and let him look at me and touch me wherever he wanted to. Only by then it wasn't Johnny Bullard, it was Steve Bourg. Do you know *This Is My Beloved*? It's a poem. A long poem. It was thrilling. It was like having tiny words all over your body."

And here Leslie quoted quite a long and explicit passage in such a way that it occurred to Irunea that Leslie might very well have recited that very passage to Steve Bourg. One night? One afternoon? In a car? Down by a river on a blanket? In her bedroom with her parents away for the day? Maybe even to U.S. It was not something Irunea could do.

Then, just as Leslie finished reciting, Irunea remembered again that she did not know the story of how Leslie and U.S. had first met, because when asked about it, U.S. would only say they "met in a volcano," which Irunea took as some kind of code between the two of them, and as some kind of signal that neither of them wanted anyone to know anything about. All of which bothered Irunea, because U.S. knew how she and Rob had met. And now that Irunea imagined that Leslie was reciting a passage from *This Is My Beloved* that she'd once recited to U.S., Irunea said something without thinking:

"Did you know that U.S. and I were lovers? In college. He was my first lover." And then she said other things as well.

Babette's Feast

The only story U.S. ever told was the one about *Babette's Feast* and how he and Leslie had once been invited to a large dinner party that included friends-of-friends, so that not everyone knew everybody, but that the foods and wines had been in the movie, which at least most people understood.

The story was that there was this guy there who didn't know about the movie and didn't know very many people at the party and so kept asking to meet Babette. Most everyone thought he was joking, but Leslie didn't think so, so she went up to him and said she was Babette. And this guy was quite impressed and thanked her for inviting him and wondered if she would give him any of the recipes for the dishes they had. He also said it was nice of her to include so many clergy. This was the place in the story where U.S. would say that he had dressed up as one of the clergy, and so had a few other men. Anyway, Leslie says of course, she'll be glad to send this guy some of the recipes, and they exchange addresses, and Leslie sure enough sends him some recipes, but the recipes have some kind of sexual innuendoes to them out of books that Leslie was always reading. And this guy writes back and thanks her, but doesn't say anything about the recipes.

No matter how many times he told it, U.S. would never get the laughs out of it that Rob did when he told it—and Rob and Irunea were not at the party.

The Phone Is Ringing

There are some things you do without thinking, and it is only later that you give them more thought. And when you think about what you have done—what a stupid thing you have said: how you agreed to meet U.S. again, and what forbidden and explicit things you said to him that afternoon, and he to you; how you walked past a woman on the street you knew without greeting her; what a dumb observation you made about politics to the host at a dinner party; how you changed your mind at the last minute about...and what a fool you felt yourself to be for having done so; what silly shoes you wore to a reception at the club; or, again, what a stupid and rash thing you said for no good reason—you know (at least at this stage in life you do) that all of these moments will be lying in wait for you when you are in bed at night thinking about what to think about in order to get yourself to sleep.

This is what Irunea had come to believe. And she had come to believe that in very old age, on the very night that she was going to die, every thoughtless and ill-considered thing she had ever done would be there in the pages of her mind as she was trying to imagine better things: the smell of mint; a yellow café in France where she and Rob had once had lunch; the first time she read *Franny*; how, at Ohio Street, U.S. would come up behind her and what he smelled like. And how he touched her that first time.

It was no doubt Leslie on the phone. It had rung insensately twenty minutes after she had walked out, leaving her copy of Sunday's book on the counter. And it had rung again an hour later. And now again, toward midnight. Never mind. Irunea was not going to answer it. Maybe in the morning. For now she would think of the quiet there always was in the house when Rob was gone, a quiet that did not exist even when he was downstairs watching his television where she could not hear it; nor hear him even—except in a vague way—when he came to bed. It was the absence of Rob that would put her to sleep. And it did.

"Who is there?" she said when she heard the door open.

"Me," said Rob. "I have bad news."

Two Conversations That Did Not Take Place at the Reception After the Service

"I just want to say that what I said the other night was not true."

"Then why did you say it?"

"I don't know. I've thought about it, and I can't tell you any reason why I should say such a thing except reasons I might make up that would sound good. But in fact I don't know why I said what I said. None of it was true."

"Thank you for telling me that."

Nor was this said:

"I think you should know something."

"What?" says Rob.

"U.S. and I were lovers in college."

"Not that I didn't know."

"He was my first lover."

"I could have guessed."

"We've kept seeing each other."

Even though Irunea had tried to put herself to sleep two nights in a row by writing into her head what she would say to Leslie and Rob when the time came, as well as what they might say, she did not say anything at all. And now she wished she had not memorized any of it because it meant that the three of them would always be characters in her mind in such a way that she could not write out.

This from the Past

After U.S. had come into the apartment on Ohio Street with another girl and found her with Rob, Irunea would not make love to Rob in the apartment. It didn't seem to make much difference to either Rob or U.S., or even the new girl (who only lasted a few weeks), but it did to Irunea. In fact, it wasn't until Irunea left the dormitory the next semester and got herself a place on Fourteenth Street that she would have anything to do with Rob. Or with U.S. again. But that was later, and this was now. And there were reasons. Bored with Rob? Bored with marriage? A memory of lost time? A way of showing U.S. he had been wrong?

But of course they were not reasons. They were summer blankets and sometimes the cabin of a friend's sailboat. Once a car. Some inflatable tarp one night on an athletic field. Mostly the prop room of the community theater that Leslie was involved with and to which somehow U.S. had gotten the key.

But never at either of their houses, and never at a motel, and not even once in St. Louis when Irunea was there because of her mother and U.S. was there on business, and they both knew it, but did not call one another. Were these her stories? The ones she did not tell.

And there was the last time, just the other day, before U.S. and Rob left for the bike trip, and she had come into the prop room and U.S. was wearing a mask and asked her to name the movie it reminded her of, and she said *Breakfast at Tiffany's*. And she was right.

Then, sensing him behind her as she had turned away to unhook her bra, having already taken off her blouse, she said: "I don't like this." And that was the end.

When the World Was Young and the Death of Bird Four

The Rushing of Seasons

Their tax man told Anne the only safe ("safe": he repeated the word: "safe!") way to deduct even part of their yearly July and August trip to Paris was for her to make "French Paintings," with "French titles," and "French subjects." Like nudes. Or cheese and fruit on tables. Or wine bottles on tables: *Chèvre Avec Femme*, Anne thought. Brie with legs. Nudes with legs. Wine with legs. On tables with legs. Herself with legs.

"Write the titles on the back of the paintings," he said. "It might be better if you write them in French, even if you have to get someone to help you. Think of your painting as a document for the IRS. If you sell one, take a picture of it. Document everything. That way you'll be safe. Document everything. Tell Roy. He'll understand."

On the way home she stopped at the farmers' market to buy strawberries for dessert that night. They were being shipped from North Carolina and expensive, and not all that good.

"'Seven francs a kilo,'" Roy said, looking at the strawberries.

"What?" Anne said.

"It's a Sinatra song my parents used to listen to," he said. "Something about strawberries costing seven francs a kilo."

"I don't know it," she said.

"What did Tax Ted say?" Roy said.

"That I should paint Paris at night. Then to be safe, title it 'Paris at Night.'"

"Then take a picture of it?"

"Yes," she said.

"I told you so," he said. "What else?"

"That we'd probably be audited for last year, and that we'd probably have to pay. Both interest and penalties."

"I doubt that," Roy said. But he frowned. Then he began to look for the bruised or green strawberries in the carton, taking them out and setting them aside, saying:

"You should wait for the local ones to come in. Don't rush the season. Everything in its own good time."

What to Do with Bird Four?

What to do with Bird Four while they were in Paris? Last year Bird Three died. The year before, both Bird Two and the cat died. The year before that, Bird Two made it through, but their first year in Paris Bird One had died. Roy said he expected to open up the *International Herald Tribune* and read of mass pet deaths in America. At least Bird Three had died while they were home.

Anne's mother had given them their first canary (named "Yellow") the year before they started going to Paris. Joy-filled, her mother would say when she came into their house.

"They make a place so joy-filled. Besides, canaries were used in your grandfather's mines to detect some kind of nasty gas. Put them in the basement to detect radon. Isn't it radon in basements these days? Leave the bird in your studio overnight to see if it dies. But don't tell me. I don't want to know about dead birds. And have Roy build you a studio above ground. He's got the money."

One summer day when Roy was cleaning the cage, Yellow flew out and was gone.

"I wonder what Doctor Freud would say," Roy said. Anne said

she didn't think it was very funny. Her mother said she'd get them another "Yellow."

"No need to change names if you don't change species," she said to Roy. "Anne's father and I had four toy boxers all named Max." When she brought them the second canary is when Roy started numbering them.

"The least she can do is take care of them when we're gone," Roy said.

But Anne's mother wouldn't. So the first summer they arranged for a college girl down the street to house-sit. Late one night in Paris the phone in the apartment they'd rented rang and Bird One was dead: Sorry. Really.

"Belly up," Roy said the next morning. "So Yellow Radon Bird One went belly up. I hope Co-ed Connie didn't try to grind it down the garbage disposal."

A year later, the same girl called the Paris apartment at about the same time to reassure them that Bird Two was doing just fine: How was France? It's very hot in Washington. But the house was cool because we've kept the air conditioner going. Did they mind if her boyfriend stayed a few weeks? He was studying modern Europe in college and knew all about Paris and the war and how Hitler kept asking *Is it burning? Is it burning?* The plants were fine. Really. The bird was fine. Really. The cat is awesome.

The third summer, Bird Two died; by then they had hired a cleaning lady to water the plants and feed both the bird and the cat. Roy asked the neighbors to watch for House-Emptying U-Haul Trailers, or columns of smoke rising through the roof, or streams of water coming down the driveway. Everybody said everything would be fine. Go to Paris. Have fun. The cleaning lady didn't call about the death of Bird Two; it just wasn't there when they got home.

"At least she cleaned the cage," Roy said. It was the neighbors who told them the cat had been run over by a Rive Gauche van.

You know, the new caterer that everybody is using. We didn't want to spoil Paris by calling about a dead cat. It was painless. We buried her by your apple tree.

Her mother promised that she would give them another canary for Anne's birthday in October. But she said they must take better care of them. Two dead birds in three years, not counting the one that flew away. Not much joy in that. As for the cat, her mother didn't like cats. They were sneaky: You didn't feed the dead birds to the cat did you?

"Please don't bother about another bird, Mother," Anne said.

"What's the bother?" said her mother. But Anne's birthday came and went with no bird. In fact, no gift.

"Don't ask," Roy said. "It's a blessing." Her mother gave them Bird Three for Christmas, but it died the next day.

"I tell you Bird Three is belly up," Roy said to Anne, as she was taking a shower. "Maybe there's radon in the living room."

"I don't want to hear about it," said Anne, not turning off the water.

"Let's just have it stuffed. Your mother will never know," Roy said. "We'll find an old Montovani album and crank up the turntable when she comes in and she'll think it's the bird singing. Montovani is so joy-filled."

A week later her mother gave them Yellow Bird Four. The previous bird was "defective," she said. The replacement bird was free. It was the advantage of dealing with the local pet store. They stood by their birds.

The Car Is on the Table

"Do you want to go to Paris again this year—or not?" Roy said from the couch in the living room where he has settled down with *Newsweek*. There was an edge to his question. In previous years when Anne had expressed even the most reasonable restraint about leaving the house—the cat, the bird, the…what?…the routine?—Roy had become impatient with her in just the way she could now hear.

"I do, but I don't want to worry," she said. She had expressed this reservation before, and she wondered if he'd say: *You said that last year. And the year before that. Here I go and arrange the business so I can take off for two months in order for you to get a little of Paris under your belt for your painting, and you worry about birds and cats and the washing machine hoses breaking. We could stay home and build a swimming pool and save money.* But he didn't say anything.

It was as if restraint were growing inside her, not a spiritual or psychological thing, but more like bones or fat or blood vessels or organs. A full-body X-ray would show a spare organ somewhere between her heart and her pelvis, dark and quivering. What is that? a doctor says. Restraint, says the nurse without hesitation. She puts a hand on Anne's head.

Anne had been the one who suggested Paris. It would be good for them. Good for their marriage. A change of pace. A way of putting their lives back together. That kind of self-help thinking. Roy's business—his company drilled "test holes" for road and bridge builders—had done quite well in recent years and as a result he could split the duties with his partner, George, who was "into boats." Two months' vacation (August and September for themselves; October and June for George and Sally), plus the security of a fully funded retirement plan, were just two perks test holes had provided them: a Stretch Volvo (Roy's phrase here), quota colleges for the kids, business-class tickets on flights to France, a yard man to go with the cleaning lady, "power shopping for the wife," the backs of paintings as documents for the IRS—it was all adding up. Strawberries out of season.

"We could let the kids use the house," he finally said. "They might enjoy the change, and they'd take care of it. Cut the grass. It would be a cheap vacation for them." He got up from the couch and walked into the kitchen where she was sitting at the table, cutting the green and white out of the strawberries.

"They have their own homes," she said.

"Well, then?" he said, the edge out of his voice. He put down *Newsweek* and studied the car ad on the inside cover. "George Will was good this week. Better than what's-her-face last week. She wobbles. George never wobbles." He sat down.

"I don't know," Anne said. "I don't know what to say."

"*Le voiture est sur la table,*" he said.

"You just said the car is on the table," she said, thinking of the time he tried to buy some tickets for the train to Versailles, but had—according to Fredericka—ordered two seats of stomach bile. He pointed at the picture of the car in the *Newsweek* advertisement.

"I know what I said," he said. *La*, not *le*, she thought to say, but did not.

Socrates Is a Man

People with fewer choices live better lives. It was the kind of thought she could not test on Roy. Not that he wouldn't talk about ideas ("topics," he called them), it was that they had to be impersonal: distant, listed. Served like restaurant fare. Or off the "S.S. Lists" (Saturday/Sunday Lists) he made for himself: The nature of screen doors. The value of riding lawn mowers. The essence of "pressure-treated" wood. Or—to give Roy his due—more general topics from George Will's column: the dinner special tonight might be what the Christian Coalition is doing to the Republican Party. A topic for talk. Not an idea to be tested through. *People with fewer choices lead better lives. Roy would cut it to the bone: You have fewer choices when you have less money? Do you want to be poor? Will you be happier poor? You'll have fewer choices.*

Life for Roy was not a matter of choices, but a matter of arranging for choices. When you had two, or three, or four options, you could go to work on them. If Anne didn't want to accept George and Bella's invitation to spend a weekend at their beach house in Delaware, that was fine. What then?—asked not in anger. Not in disappointment. Just: What then? The movies? The concert at the college? A walk? Nothing? Nothing was fine with Roy as long as nothing was decided on. Something could come of nothing: *Let me know.* Then he'd head out to mow the lawn, or tinker with the car, or run some errand in the nearby shopping center, as often as not coming home with a specialty bread for dinner that night, or flowers for the table. And as full of good cheer in his own fashion as her mother was in hers: *I thought you might enjoy some daisies. The bread is still warm. What's cooking: chicken, wanna neck? I know a small Bordeaux.*

But for Anne, a life of lists and topics and choices was growing more than vaguely dissatisfying. It reminded her of college logic and how over-and-done-with-it those Monday-Wednesday-Friday 10:30 syllogisms had seemed to her (in spite of the talk-until-dawn crush she and her roommate Sara had on Professor Gassette). *"All men are mortal"* led in two quick steps to the death of Socrates, complete with Professor Gassette's chalk-line coffin lid drawn over the conclusion.

Was that all? Life in major and minor premises? And then the line on the blackboard. What about the way she felt? What had become of the premises of what was to become of her? What about happiness? What about movies where she cried? Where was the premise that was Roy? And two children? And Paris? Her father's death? What about the Uccello painting with all its baby-faced soldiers she had seen projected in her art history class in the very same room the hour before logic? What conclusions have there been since the death of Socrates? What lines drawn on what blackboards? What about lean, handsome, worldly Professor Gassette and his hint of an accent? And the way he'd put his right hand on the top of his head when you'd ask him a question. And how his long fingers would disappear into the black boil of rich hair as he'd lean toward you with the answer: *The conclusion of the syllogism is the ultimate truth of its premises, Miss Johnson. Do you understand?*

She did not.

The Apartment in Paris Was a Gift

"I sometimes wondered," Fredericka says, "how I'd feel about meeting you again."

"I never did," Roy says.

"Sweet of you to say," she says. Then Fredericka says something Anne cannot hear from the bedroom.

"I didn't mean it that way," he says. "It's just that I don't think about meeting people from ye olden college days. I do think about ye olden college days, however. I think about the time we..."

"I don't," Fredericka says.

"Maybe that's the difference between men and women," he says.

"I don't believe in the differences."

Anne hears a pause between them. Outside there is the noise of the traffic, and from farther away a loud cheer. Maybe one of the street theater acts has come to an end on Pont des Arts: a mime dying; a diver off the bridge into the Seine; the man (or is it a woman?) on stilts doing a falling bow.

"Jane tells me you're a trapper in Kansas," Roy says.

"Not really," Fredericka says. "Something like that, though."

"And a Communist."

"Not really," she says. "But something like that."

"What are you then?" he says.

"What do I know?" she says. There is another pause. Anne wonders if Fredericka is smiling, and if so, is there irony in it? If there is a sfumato to it? She doesn't know her well enough to know. She hears them talk on, but not about much. Then she falls asleep.

The apartment in Paris was a gift. They could use it July and August as long as they paid the cleaning lady and the electric bill. Roy's sister Jane had married a French lawyer and they had settled on Place Dauphine in the late '70s. In the summer they went to the Dordogne where they lived—if the pictures on the dressers were any indication—in a château roughly (as Roy put it) the size of the Chevy Chase Club.

Anne spent her Paris days making paintings on a portable Italian easel; Roy spent his reading the *International Herald Tribune* and crime novels, and "scouting restaurants" for the evening meal: *It is my calling to walk the boulevards of Paris in search of a meal and a bottle of vino,* he'd say as he'd head out in some direction or another, more often than not coming back late in the afternoon with a discovery just as if he'd come back from the shopping center with a warm loaf of bread: *Tonight we dine at Le Caveau du Palais, which, if you will notice, is just across the park. A Bulls throw from here.*

"*Boules,*" said Anne, whose French improved with each visit, but who noticed little such movement in Roy's: *Où est la café. Où se trouve la Louvre. Le fleur est sur la table.*

Place Dauphine had a catch: Roy's college girlfriend had been—and still was—a good friend of his sister's and used the apartment on her summer wanderings throughout Europe. Not so much to live in, Anne was assured (and reassured), but only to "park herself and a few of her things now and then." Fredericka would be in the small bedroom off the kitchen. She had her own key. And while she was more than a bit of an eccentric what with her politics and her writing and her pilgrimages, she would not be any trouble.

Anne did not want to give much thought to what might or might not have transpired between Roy and Fredericka twenty some years before. During her marriage there had been a woman in Roy's life to concern herself about. Jealousy had bled her dry. Something in her died: all the usual clichés in spite of them being the usual clichés. Trust was trashed.

When they met Fredericka in Paris that first summer, Fredericka made it a point to be especially pleasant and courteous to Anne. No, she would not be staying long, just a few days, then she'd be taking the train to the Dordogne to visit Jane; then on to Spain by bus.

"I know Paris pretty well," said Fredericka to Anne, "and my French is decent. So if you'd like to use me as a walking *Plan de Paris* before I go, let me know. I'd enjoy it."

Anne thanked her, and while she fully intended to take Fredericka up on her offer, she never got around to it. Instead she walked to the Louvre and looked at the Uccello she had seen in the art history class the hour before Socrates and his syllogisms.

The second summer (and the non Death of Bird Two) Fredericka returned to the apartment with a political Frenchman and the two of them sat up all night in the kitchen talking French about what Anne imagined was the socialist agenda in Eastern Europe (a scene out of *Reds*, Anne thought, even as it was going on). The third summer Fredericka came before and after they were in Paris. And last summer the three of them drank too much wine one night in the apartment and said some things to each other they should not have.

Are We Going to Paris? A Topic for Conversation

"Did Ted really say something about being audited?" Roy said at dinner.

"No," Anne said.

"Why did you tell me that?" he said.

"I was upset," she said.

"'Upset'?" he said. "Why?"

"I don't know," she said. "Let it drop."

"Are we going to Paris this summer?" he said. "I'd like to know, because if we're not…"

"I don't know," she said. "I don't think so."

"Why not?"

"You don't much like it, so why should you care?" She could feel something going on inside her. What was it?

"I like it," he said. "You're a grump this evening. *Le fleur est sur la table.*"

"Have you heard from Jane if Fredericka will be there?" she said.

"I have not," he said. "She probably will. What difference does that make?"

"It wasn't such a pretty scene last year," she said. "I'm surprised we get to use the place at all if she told your sister what happened."

"Blood is thicker than water," he said. "Or wine. We were all drunk."

"Speak for yourself," Anne said, although with less velocity than she felt entitled to.

"It wasn't her business to butt into my life," said Roy.

"Or mine?"

"Yours either."

The next week Bird Four died.

When the World Was Young

"When you think about him, what do you think about?" says her roommate Sara one night.

"I think about his black hair," Anne says. "I think about his green eyes. I think about his voice. His accent."

"I think about him making love to me," Sara says.

"I don't think about *that*," Anne says.

Her roommate's full name was Sara Johnson. Johnson was Anne's last name as well. They had fun telling people they were sisters. The following year, Sara transferred. Or dropped out. Anne never knew which. They hadn't kept in touch over the summer, and their names and their crush on Professor Gassette aside, they had pretty much gone their separate ways in college. Still, something left Anne when Sara left.

"I think that one day he'll invite me to his apartment along with other students to have dinner," Sara goes on. "I pretend to be sick and he takes me to his bedroom and I lie down. He puts his hand on my head to see if I have a fever. When he touches me I tell him I'm not sick at all."

"What does he say?"

"He says he understands. That we'll have to wait until the other students go home. He'll tell them he's going to take me to the infirmary himself."

"What happens next?" says Anne.

"Sometimes I imagine one thing," says Sara. "Sometimes other things. Before I go to sleep at night is when I imagine being with him."

"Do you make love?"

"Yes," says Sara.

"Does he talk to you afterward?"

"Yes," says Sara.

"What about?"

"I haven't imagined that yet," says Sara. "But I will. After the first time we make love I ask him if we can make love again, and he says yes. Don't you imagine what it is like to make love to men?"

Anne does not. Anne does not answer. The two sit for a moment. Then Anne asks Sara if she imagines what she will do with her life. With her life after she graduates.

"I want to go to Paris and be a boulevardier," Sara says.

"With Professor Gassette?" asks Anne. She doesn't know what Sara means.

"Oh no," says Sara. "Just because we make love doesn't mean I'm going to marry him. I'm not going to marry anyone. When I am in Paris I want to be by myself and sit in the cafés and imagine the apple trees. Just like in the song."

"What song?"

"'When the World Was Young.' Don't you know it? Do the apple trees still blossom in the breeze? When the world was young. My parents play it on their Hi-Fi all the time."

"I've never heard it," says Anne.

"What do you imagine you will do?" says Sara to Anne.

"Marry Professor Gassette," she says. And laughs. "If you don't want him."

The Heart of Montaigne

"I understand you're a painter," Fredericka says.

"Yes."

"A good one, I understand."

"Thank you," she says. "Roy said you skin animals. That can't be true."

"It is not," she says. "In the winter I buy skins from trappers. I have a route I make with my truck through Western Kansas, Eastern Colorado, and Southwestern Nebraska and I buy pelts. Then I sell them to a dealer in Kansas City. It's a business and I get material for my stories. I'm a writer of stories."

"Should I know your name?" Anne asks.

"No," Fredericka says. "I use a man's name. I write wildlife stories for men's outdoor magazines. I'm Fred Whitebread when I'm a man. They think I'm part Sioux." She thumps her chest. Anne laughs.

"I'm not sure I believe you," Anne says.

"I also write stories about France," Fredericka says.

"Not for men's magazines," Anne says.

"No," she says. "More for myself. Myself and the tax man. And the few literary magazines that will publish them."

"The tax man?" Anne says.

"If I write a story about France I can deduct my trip here. My politics aside, I'm compos mentis enough to know I live in a capitalist country. Do you do that with your paintings?"

"I don't know how to," she says.

"Look into it," Fredericka says. "You probably have more to gain than I do."

"I'll ask Roy," Anne says.

"Do it yourself," Fredericka says. There is a pause between them.

"Are your stories about France true or fiction?" Anne asks.

"They're fiction. But then so are the ones I write for outdoor magazines. Fred Whitebread and I just don't tell the male editors."

"I see," says Anne. "Where are you going when you leave Paris?"

"I always make a pilgrimage to Montaigne's heart," she says. "It's buried in a church not far from where Jane lives in the summer. His body is elsewhere. Do you know Montaigne?"

"No. Only the name. I think from college."

"He was a very great writer," says Fredericka. "He asked the right question."

"His heart is in a church?" says Anne.

"Yes," says Fredericka. "Buried in the floor in the church in Saint-Michel-de-Montaigne. I stand in the church with the swallows and talk to him. We have a heart-to-heart." She smiles.

"That's terrible," says Anne. They both laugh.

Anne, Is That You?

The death of Bird Four set her free in some way she could not—even later that summer when she was in Paris by herself and thought about it—fully understand. And that sense of freedom had come upon her immediately: Upon looking into the cage and seeing the bird dead on its side, small gnats on its eyes. He's dead, she said out loud, although no one was in the house. She took it to the sink and ground it down the garbage disposal.

Nothing else had had quite the same effect. Not when the children went away to college. Not when they emptied their rooms to get married. Not when she walked out on Roy five years ago after her clichéd jealousy had gotten the best of her and she moved into the small furnished apartment she had rented months before and kept all summer long until finally she packed herself up one Sunday while he was fishing at the lake (or humping Tina) and left. Not when she "spilled her guts" (Roy's phrase) that night in the apartment in Paris.

"Mother?"

"Anne? Is that you?"

"Yes."

"What's wrong? You don't call unless something's wrong."

"The fucking bird died."

"Don't swear, Anne. Your father didn't raise you to swear. Maybe it was the radon."

"It died on the back porch."

"Maybe there's radon on the back porch."

"No, Mother. It just died."

"I'll get you another one."

"Please don't."

"I'll bring it over this afternoon."

"I'll kill it myself if you do."

"Anne!"

Were lists premises? Were choices conclusions? Were topics shadows? What is left when restraint leaves?

It Is Two Days Later

"I'm going to Paris by myself," Anne said.

"What am I supposed to do? Water the plants for two months? Talk to your mother? It doesn't sound like fun to me. I might as well stay at work."

"There is always Tina," she said.

"I thought we were over that," he said.

"Are we?" she said.

"Is that what this is about?" he said.

"No," she said.

"Is it about Fredericka?" he said.

"Yes," she said. "No."

"Then what?" he said.

"I don't know," she said.

"Well, maybe you better know before: one, you start telling me you want to leave for two months, and two, you throw old horse turds in my face. That fucking bitch started all this last year. That's what I think." He walked out of the house and went somewhere.

What Did She Know?

Could she use the apartment without Roy? What would she say to Fredericka if they met again? Would she be pleased? What about money? What would her mother say? Why was Montaigne's heart not buried with his body? Would Roy be at home when she got back? What would happen to her if he was not? Should she go back? Could she talk to Fredericka about that? What difference would it make if she didn't paint cheeses on tables with wine titled in French? Do people with fewer choices live better lives? What would the children say? Would her French continue to improve? Would Roy go back to Tina? Why did the faces in Uccello's painting seem childlike? And where did he get that red? Would she go to the restaurants Roy had scouted? Why had Fredericka said what she said that night in Paris? Would she find Sara Johnson in a café? What would she do about the painting that was growing somewhere in her body like a light: She is baby faced in red on horseback riding away from a crowd of mothers and husbands and yellow birds toward the front of the canvas and onto the Île de la Cité. Is Professor Gassette still a premise somewhere: his black hair and his green eyes the same as when the world was young? What was the right question? What did she know?

Words Make a Life

He Could Fix Anything

My father was tall, taller than I am. He grew old gracefully, my mother would say. He had red hair that stayed red until his fifties, then went only slightly gray. His hands were large, but his fingers were long and delicate. He might have been a pianist. When he smiled (which was seldom, but not because he was an unhappy man), you had a sense he was enjoying himself immensely, and in ways he chose not to explain. "Nothing, my dear," is what he would say to my sister when she'd ask. "Nothing at all."

"He's pleased to have fixed something at the garage," my mother would say.

At work he wore blue bib overalls (that had a plethora of pockets), no cap, and steel-toed work boots. In the left-hand breast pocket of his overalls, he kept his pens and chalk markers, two tire gauges, and a pencil magnet.

He was a neat man who, when not bending over an engine, stood straight and walked straight. His tools were cleaned and his workbench set in order each night. The floor was swept, and the nuts and bolts and washers and cotter pins that had fallen onto it were put into a bucket and sorted into coffee cans on Saturdays between pumping gas.

There was a shower in the garage that he would use before he walked home in clothes he kept clean for supper. At home his fingernails were never dirty. In the mornings, he would walk back to work in the same clothes, put them on hangers and change.

On Saturdays, he would bring home his overalls, and my mother would wash them on Sunday along with his "travel outfit."

When explaining a car's problem to a customer—whether it was the engine or the brakes or the transmission or the cooling system—my father would spread his arms full length if the matter was serious, less so if it was not, and hold his hands apart in front of him if the solution was simple. Changing a tire that was out of round to correct a front-end wobble was simple. A new front-end suspension required the full width of my father's rather long arms. As he explained what needed to be done and how he would do it, my father would bring his hands together (sometimes pausing for a detailed digression about where he was going to get the tie rods and why he might not need to change both of them), until his hands met at a clap of the job completed. He would smile. He could fix anything.

When he died the bucket had been sorted.

Our Mother

"You'll need a dictionary," my mother said before I went to college. "Pick three words a day, even if you think you know them. But not in ABC order. That way you won't get bored. Open the dictionary, find a word, learn it, then write it on a slip of paper. Like a bookmark. Do you know what *domain* means? You need to make up for the words you missed. *Plethora*?"

She was referring to a grade school year when I was a sickly child with a case of acute tonsillitis that resulted in earaches, high fevers, and many days absent from class.

"Words make a life," she'd say while washing the evening's dishes. "Do you know what *countenance* means? *Atonement*?"

A Short History of Blanks

I design books: *Gutters* and *case backs*, *rivers* and *verso*, *quarto*, and *signature* are the nomenclature of my trade. Or were when I started. *Format* and *galley proof.* I understand I am un-hip, as if I were to use *Hi-Fi* instead of *stereo*—which I do. *Mono*, I am told by Lillian, my sister's late-in-life daughter, is a disease. It used to be music as well: the kind that came from the lid of a forty-five record player: "Memories Are Made of This."

At first I worked at Hallmark here in Kansas City. Now I freelance. My Plaza apartment is my office. The Country Club Plaza, Kansas City, Missouri. Mr. and Mrs. Bridge's domain. Calvin Trillin slurping a frosty at Winstead's.

Over the years I have spread into many rooms: computers and scanners and light tables throughout. Tastefully throughout.

At Hallmark I designed "favorites": 20 Favorite Sonnets by Shakespeare. 100 Favorite Love Poems. 50 Favorite Words of Wisdom. 100 Famous Quotations by American Women. I also designed "paths": 50 Paths to Wisdom. 25 Paths to Bliss. No one ever suggested 50 Ways to Leave Your Lover.

I was not cynical about such work then, nor am I now. If my book buyers want their wisdom "famous" and flush left in purse-sized octavos, who am I to judge? We all have our paths.

These days I design address books. I design recording calendars, sometimes called *agendas*. I do not design memoirs (fictional or not). I design exhibition catalogues: *A Painter's Room of One's Own.* I design coffee-table books: *Joyce's Paris. Small Hotels of Italy. A Place in the World Called Seville.* And once, a small duodecimo for autographs.

Among my favorite projects have been two Abecedarians. One was for painting: *M Is for Matisse* (with a lovely black-haired young woman in an afternoon pose). A second was for writers whose pictures appeared like a watermark behind their letters with their text at the bottom. C: "It was said that a new person had appeared on the sea-front: a lady with a little dog."

I also design *blanks*—books with empty pages for memoirs to be written or diaries to be kept. Or not. I am Mr. Tabula Rasa of Kansas City. And many other cities as well.

I like what I do. There is a pleasing philistine sensibility about a well-designed, large-format book that features the flora and fauna from the French Impressionist period. The philistine sensibility is not in the book but in the plush homes and apartments where Monet's *Water Lilies* or Fantin-Latour's *Still Lives* languish. I test my designs against the horizontal of coffee tables, not the vertical of bookshelves.

"Did you do this?" My sister asked me when she and Gerhard had me for dinner not long ago. I specify that the publishers not include my name in the credits.

She showed me a coffee-table book that featured paintings of women in New York museums: *Madame X* from the Metropolitan, a Vermeer from the Frick. Picasso's *Two Nudes* from MOMA. Others. I had been inspired by an old *Playboy* photo series: The Women of Rome (they were riding topless on Vespas); The Women of San Francisco (they were hanging out of both their blouses and the cable cars on which they rode).

"Not that you always fess up," she said.

"It's one of mine," I said. "Fess up" is what our mother used to say when trying to find out who spilled orange juice on the kitchen counter.

"Lovely," she said. I keep it out.

My sister's diary, an early blank of mine (a garden motif with flowers), also in the living room that night, was (I took a peek) blank: Hours without alphabets. Days without words. Impatience without patience. It was sitting next to a book of mine on the gardens in Tuscany, but since Elaine did not ask about either, I said nothing.

On whatever coffee table I am, I want to be featured, even if anonymously. My aim is to be number one on the bestseller lists of unread, stacked books in the magazine homes of America. *The Gardens of Tuscany* in an agreeable arrangement with *The Women in New York's Museums.*

The Text of Spark Plugs

The week before I left for college, I took my secondhand Ford to the garage so we could change the oil and rotate the tires. My father was there even though it was past closing. Sometimes he would work until my mother called him to come home or sent me to get him; other times he would go back to work after supper. In summer, when he came home late, he'd get himself a beer and sit in a webbed lawn chair beside a pedestal-mounted blue glass globe. We could hear him talking to himself into the evening. Once, returning from the pool where I was a lifeguard, I sat with him.

"You're a strange kid," he said to me.

I didn't know what to say.

"Your mother likes you," he said after a moment.

I thought this was my father's way of saying he liked me, too.

"I've got a new set of plugs," my father said from above the car while I was in the pit draining the oil.

I could tell by the sound of his socket wrench that he was taking my old ones out. Not that I had asked him to, although they needed changing.

"Thank you," I said.

"New wires too," he said.

"I can do that," I said.

"Points."

"Sure. Thanks."

"Dwell."

"Not necessary. But thank you. I can help you with the Studebaker before I go," I said.

"When you come back," he said.

Then there was the quiet you get among mechanics. The sigh of a stubborn bolt coming free. The small thud when a nut hits the floor. The roll of a washer like a coin. Closed-lipped grunts and groans that formed a patois—not that I knew that word then, nor was it among my mother's words. Finally, my father, again, from above:

"Don't disappoint your mother."

"I'll try not to. I have my dictionary."

"I mean with women."

"Yes."

"Do you know about women?"

"Some."

"I didn't think so."

"What should I know?"

By now the oil had been drained, and I had put on a new filter. I climbed out of the pit and found the oil cans and a metal spout. The car took five quarts if you replaced the filter. When I finished filling the crankcase, I stood by the fender. My father was bent over the engine putting the spark plug wires in place.

"What should I know?" I asked again. "About women."

"If they break you can't fix them like cars," he said. He replaced the distributor cap, and wiped his hand with his shop rag.

"I see," I said.

"But then we can't be fixed either," he said.

He put out his hand, and I shook it. I noticed more than a small tremor among his fingers and something odd about his eyes as he looked at me.

It was my mother who told me years later, after he had died, that my father once loved another woman. It was my sister Elaine who told me that our mother had once loved another man.

"But it was before they were married," she said, as we were driving back from visiting their graves.

"For them both?"

"I don't think so. But they knew. They must have told each other."

"Atonement," I said.

"Yes."

Dinah Shore

When my sister was young she looked like Dinah Shore. She could enter a room with the same television-show skirt flourish, which she would make to the amusement of those who understood her parody, our father among them. And like Dinah, my sister could sing silky torch songs: "A Small Hotel," "Dancing on the Ceiling," "The Way You Look Tonight."

These days she has about her a Joanne Woodward countenance. She said she was hoping for a Grace Kelly face as she aged (modesty is not one of her virtues). I think Joanne Woodward suits her better. Recently she has reverted to Dinah, singing "My Funny Valentine."

"Are you thinking of someone?" I asked her.

"Yes."

"Do I know him?"

"No."

Like me, she is tall, at least taller than our mother, but not as tall as our father. Unlike the matrons of her society, she is lithe.

I think a man other than her husband would find her winsome as she is. I wonder if she has lovers—or has had lovers. Should a brother ask?

She wears little makeup, has auburn hair with touches of gray, stands straight, and walks with ease; bright, alert, I have seen her suppress a smile at something up ahead during one of our walks through a nearby park: a lady with a dog pulling her toward a wing-clipped goose. Always when we see old men sleeping on benches.

Once, when a man I didn't know passed us on a sidewalk.

Talking

After I graduated from college, and after my father had died, I lived with my mother for a summer, while lifeguarding at the local pool as I looked for full-time work.

One evening when I came home, she was sitting in the front lawn by my father's globe. Both chairs were out. I sat in my father's chair.

"I talk to him," my mother said.

The evening was summer in that fullness that says there is no other season. We were quiet for a moment.

"He talked to himself," I said.

"He said he talked to you before you went to college. Something about women."

"Yes."

Again: quiet.

"Did Elaine have to...?"

"Yes."

This time the silence between us was longer.

"I'm not going to tell him," my mother said.

The Studebaker

It was a maroon convertible. Two door. There was a joke in those days that you could not tell if a Studebaker was going forward or backward because the front and the rear were streamlined.

My mother and I were alone in my father's garage. The Studebaker was there, parked as if ready to go.

"We had to sell it to get you out of the hospital," my mother said. "We came home from the University Medical Center with you on the bus. Your father walked to the garage until he made a deal with Bob Snow on a car. But that was for me to drive. He never gave up walking to work. He said it was good practice for poverty. I never told him about the money."

"What money?"

"Your uncle Conroy sent me money. He was a doctor by then."

"To pay the medical bills?"

"For a car."

"The Studebaker?"

"No. The Studebaker was gone. We'd see it driving around with the top down, and I got so I couldn't look when it passed by. Your father courted me in that car. He was so pleased when he bought it back and you two restored it. But..."

My mother seemed to have lost track of what she was going to say. She went over to my father's workbench and looked at his tools, touching some of them. We had sold the garage and everything in it to pay for his medical bills, the Studebaker (for a second time, I had just learned) included. My mother got a work rag and dusted the hood.

"What car did you buy with Uncle Conroy's money?" I asked.

"Your Ford."

"I thought that was a trade. Something about work father was doing for the used-car dealer in town."

"It wasn't enough," she said. "I put in a hundred from Conroy. And when your father bought back the Studebaker as well. Only then it was money I'd saved."

"Did he..."

"Both times he thought he'd gotten a good deal. Why not let a man think that? Good deals are important to men."

"It runs," I said.

Its top was up. I unhooked the latches and pulled it back. I opened the passenger door. I turned the key, but not so far as to crank the engine. Ignition lights came on. I pumped the brake.

"I don't want to," my mother said.

"You sure? I can take you for a drive."

"I've been sitting in it now and then. I'd rather leave it at that," she said. "But keep the top down."

A Portrait of Our Mother

She had gray hair from as long as I can remember, a wide forehead and pale blue eyes. Her arms were short, and in contrast to my father, she walked with a slight—a very slight—stoop, more a bending forward as if to get where she was going by putting her head in that direction.

A traveling one-armed painter my father hired one year did a portrait of her as her Christmas present.

The woman in the painting seems a little sad. At least sadder than when we were growing up, but not as sad as after my father died. I can think of no portrait of a woman from any period of art history that resembles it. The one-armed painter got the eyes right, the forehead, and hair. If she could speak out of it, she would say: *The quintessential me. More for the word than for the fact.*

"May I have it?" My sister asked as we were cleaning out the house.

"Yes."

"When did you realize it was mother?" she asked.

"Not long ago. And you?"

"Not until now."

My Turn

By the time my father and I had finished refurbishing the Studebaker, he was too weak to drive. Once after lifeguarding, I stopped by the garage, parked the Ford, and took the Studebaker the rest of the way home, honking as I came up to the house. My father was sitting by his globe. My mother came out of the kitchen, wiping her hands in a dishtowel. We helped my father get in front, and she got in back. I drove up and down the streets of our neighborhood, past the garage, then across the street into my high school's parking lot.

"My turn," my father said.

I got out and helped him around to the driver's side. My mother joined him in front. The top was down. Off they went. My mother waved her hand in the air.

I walked to the garage and drove my car home. When I got there the Studebaker was in the driveway, but my father's chair was bereft.

I Am Lady Open

*The Story of Fox News, Angry Ivan, Sir Robert Shrink Wrap,
West Jesus Land, Kansas, and The Rest of America*

My name is Sallie French, but everyone calls me Lady Open. I spray-painted it on both sides of my Datsun 260Z. On the hood as well. A very old model I got from this man who lived with me until I shot him in the foot with a .25 purse pistol. Took the tip of his Great Toe off. Clean off. Then he moved out. He's just down the street in a doublewide parked at his sister's that she and her husband lived in while they built a house. She's a saint to take him in. I owe her. But then she owed me, so we're even. Only one day I need to return the purse pistol. His name is Ivan. Her name is Carol Jane. She's a nurse. Al's her husband. The man who named me Lady Open is George.

I always wanted a Z-car because of that joke about the snail. I can't remember jokes but Ivan could. He used to be full of jokes before he took early retirement from driving a road grader for the county. You could never empty him out. You got to like a man who treated you to a good joke. I did. But these days, after he's watched a shitload of Fox News with his buddies at the Cottonwood Coffee Shack, he's pretty jokeless. You got to think twice about something that robs you of your sense of humor.

Women can't run wood stoves, read maps, or remember jokes, Ivan used to say when I'd ask him to tell the snail joke again. You're right, I'd say. Just tell the joke. It's not like I'd put Joan Rivers on the Z-car, and then I'd be dead.

There is this snail, Ivan says, who wants to buy a Datsun 260Z. But instead of a Z on the side…And then I'd remember the rest of it, but I'd let Ivan go on so he could be pleased with himself. Like I said, he's the one who bought me the car. I'll give him that.

What I do is open things for people. Cans. Bags. Anything shrink-wrapped. Most of what you buy these days is tough to open. Especially for the old, though some of my folks are not all that old. I'm not that old myself. Men give me the once-over when I'm out and about. Or shopping at Food Bonanza. George did.

I have my folks as I call my clients. I have my route. I have my days. Mornings, mostly, so you can get on with your life. I also come out at night if there's an emergency, which sometimes there is with medicine tops, and once with Listerine. This woman forgot about it when I stopped by the morning before. She has this thing about her teeth because she says a friend of hers died from gum disease. The week before I had to open a value pack of dental floss and make sure they were all started so she could floss ten times a day.

The problem with Listerine is first of all they sell the big bottles in packs of two and you have to cut off the plastic wrapper that holds them together. She can do that with a steak knife. Next, you have to cut the plastic wrapper off the top. She can't do that. Then it has this big top that you push in from the sides to open it. The top is black, so you can't tell where to push unless you know. And even then it's tough. I left it unlocked but she turned it the wrong way and, click, it locked itself up again. Everybody's a little mental about something, and if you go through an economy pack of dental floss and a large bottle of Listerine every week, it's more than your teeth that are giving you trouble. Anyway, that's an emergency. I don't charge extra for an emergency. Not for my regular folks.

What's to open besides medicine tops and Listerine? Cans of all kinds, even the ones with pull-tabs. Gelato ice cream if it's got a plastic wrap around the top. I use the scissors in my Swiss Army Knife.

This one man buys only Dark Chunk Chocolate Gelato, and to make life easier he gets them by the dozen and I open them all and he puts them in his freezer. I tell him he ought to meet the dental floss woman because if she ate Dark Chunk Chocolate Gelato she might not worry so much about her teeth—but maybe that would make it worse. Anyway, I tell her about him. No more cats. No more dogs. No more men, says the dental floss woman. No thanks, says Dark Chunk Chocolate Gelato. If they lived together I would open for both of them at the same price.

Most of my folks are by themselves. No kids around to help. No grandkids. Not all that many in Cottonwood who haven't left for Denver. Eight Man Football at the High School. We're not as beat up as Bly or Blaze, but we got empty houses not to be sold because nobody's coming to town to buy. More of us pushing up soapweed than riding to cattle. Still, I got enough business and might could have more.

There is this guy who buys bones for his dog that are shrink-wrapped. His wife says they're nasty. That's her word. Nasty. The same with the suet cakes for the birds. I'm on his side because it seems to me she might help out, living off his retirement as they are. But no. Nasty is nasty, is what she says when I come by. It's shrink-wrapped that's nasty, if you ask me.

I work in the garage on his workbench. Only once did she come out and then it wasn't to help, but only to say why did they have to spend good money hiring me. The damn dog didn't need bones and the birds could live off bugs just fine. Now the workbench was nasty from all the nasty work I was doing, which I figured meant I was nasty too. I kept opening bones and suet cakes but I thought to myself, I'd be pleased to lend her husband my .25 purse pistol if he ever wanted to shoot her in the foot. Just thinking about it starts me trying to remember that joke Ivan told about a man's wife who bothered him while he was currying his horse and the horse kicked and killed her, but I can't get it to come. I call her Lady Nasty.

There are two men who have me open wine for them. One has bottles with corks and a girlfriend younger than he is. I can only hug her, he tells me when I open two bottles for an evening they are having together. I come late to light the candles even though I guess they could do that. I'd like to have candles on the table when coming to dinner. Sure. And hugging is fine even at my age. Maybe better, to tell the truth. Now that Ivan's gone, no more men in my house. I've had my fill. I'm emptied out.

The other guy buys wine in boxes with bags inside them. You have to pry open the tab on the front of the box, then pull out this spigot that has this tiny piece of tape to pull off. It's not that his hands are bad, he just can't see well enough to do it. I stop by Fridays. By then the old box is pretty much drained, so I rip it open and squeeze what's left into a peanut butter jar. Then I open the new one. A box lasts about a week including the peanut butter jar. He tells me his daughter is in California these days, but she might come visit. I doubt it. She's the one who sent him a Food Bonanza Coupon for a case of Smart Water. Talk about something hard to open. He's Mr. Box Wine to me. The other guy is Mr. Bottle Wine.

This one woman who is now dead had me open DVDs for her. They'd come in the mail and she couldn't get them open because they are shrink-wrapped. Then you have to push some kind of button in the middle of the DVD to get it out. Once I taught her, she could do it herself.

One day she asked me to go through her ballpoint pens and throw away the ones that didn't write. She put me at her kitchen table with a pad of paper to try out the pens and a trash can underneath for the bad ones. Out of a hundred and twenty-eight, seventy-six didn't write. Well, some worked, but badly, and she said that fifty-two would probably last her the rest of her life. She was right about that. Anyway, she's the one who got me started sorting ballpoint pens for my folks. By now I've got most everybody good to go. No extra charge.

The reason Carol Jane owes me is because of Al. He's getting dried out and fixed mentally. It's been a while and it's going to be a while more. Not that he drank that much but on weekends. All weekend. Nobody thinks he's coming back from the state mental ward. Ever. He's the reason I have my .25 purse pistol. Carol Jane gave it to me from what was left of the guns Al had bought. Maybe fifty or more. Carol Jane didn't count.

Not that Al was a hunter. He just got to hearing voices in his head that he was going to lose his guns even though he didn't have any guns. So he started buying them. And he didn't get the idea from Ivan or Fox News. He wasn't retired. He didn't work for the county. He was the assistant manager at Food Bonanza and I'd see him putting out cases of cans and wearing a headset with a black button in his left ear and mike attachment coming around to his mouth.

Then one day he came home with a rifle. Carol Jane asked him about it but he didn't say anything, just put it against the wall in their bedroom. Then the next day he brought home three shotguns. We have a Buck Dynasty gun store which is some kind of rip-off from a television show I don't know who would watch. It sells anything you'd need to kill anything that's alive. It's full of camouflage clothing, heated boots, deer stands for what I don't know because we don't have a lot of trees out here. Bows and arrows. Racks of guns. Cases of pistols. All kinds of dead animal heads on the wall from what the men have shot. I remember this man shot a big buck right in Cottonwood as it was walking through the park.

It made the paper with a picture of him giving the head to Buck Dynasty. I was in there once with Carol Jane when she sold back Al's guns all at half price. I told the owner his store should be called Buck Nasty, but he didn't think that was funny.

Two days after Al brings home the shotguns, he brings home half a dozen pistols. Revolvers like in John Wayne movies. Big handguns our Badge and Bullets cops wear around town that shoot these huge shells by just pulling the trigger and then it loads another automatically. Bang. Bang.

When Carol Jane asks Al about the guns, he doesn't say anything but points to his left ear. Then he gives her a small pistol for her purse. That's what she gave me. It's a .25 automatic, she says.

We have Home Health out here, and other kinds of government services for the old and crippled up. But most of my folks aren't that old. They just need to have things opened. And sometimes filled. George has me put razor blades into this Schick injector he uses. He told me his father gave it to him. He's about the oldest of the folks I got. He was the one ahead of me at Food Bonanza with a four-pack of Ocean Spray cranberry juice and asked the checkout girl if she'd cut off the plastic rings that held the bottles together and the girl says, we don't do that. I said I would, and I took out my Swiss Army knife and cut the bottles free. You are Lady Open, says Mr. Cranberry Juice. Here, I say to the checkout girl, you can at least throw this away, and she says, I don't throw away trash for anyone. My guess is she was a blood relative to Lady Nasty. Anyway, George is how I got my start. I think he was sweet on me from then on.

Some of my folks do get Home Health. Nurses checking in on them if they've had a fall. For shots. Carol Jane is a nurse for that. We've got diabetes in the men from eating too high on the hog. And glazed donuts at the Coffee Shack in the morning so full of grease you could wring them out into a puddle. That's Ivan for you. Not me. I'm into apples and oranges. The Coffee Shack is where the men with less than nothing to do meet every morning with Fox News telling them what to think. Nothing's funny by the time they're heading home. Ivan especially.

We've also got the Sunset Shuttle for folks who have a hard time driving from the country into Cottonwood. Or even around Cottonwood. To Blaze to see relations. I don't do rides. But I'm glad the county does. Ivan thinks it's just a waste of money. That's all the government does, he says, is waste money. Flushes my tax dollars into a cesspool full of no-good Washington bureaucrats whose job it is to pump it down the sewer line to the lazy colored in Cleveland. Talk about a government shooting itself in the foot. And with my money.

When he goes on like this, I tell him I'm going to shoot him in *his* foot, even though it's his mouth that should be duck-taped shut. He listens to Rust Limpball on the truck radio coming home from Fox News. He tells me its Rush Limbaugh. I know it's Rush Limbaugh, I say. You're just being smart-assed, he says.

Last week when I stopped by, George had fixed me lunch. Usually I put him in the middle of the morning run, but he called to say better toward noon. Sure. When I got there he had me open a packet of greeting cards. They were shrink-wrapped. I had to be careful not to cut into the cards. For jobs like that my Swiss Army knife scissors are too big. I got these tiny shears you use to cut your toenails. They were Ivan's. He had half a dozen all over the house because he was always cutting his fungus-filled toenails and leaving the clippings where they fell. Now that he's one toe short he doesn't need so many clippers, so I kept a pair. No more Ivan, no more fungus among us. Out the door with one, into my vacuum cleaner with the other.

After I opened the cards, George handed me packets of nuts his daughter had sent him from a Southwest Airlines flight. I get those from other clients. The packets have this place marked where you are supposed to rip them open, but nobody can do it. I can't do it. So I use my Swiss Army Knife scissors and George puts the nuts into a bowl. There were four or five packets. You'd think his daughter would come and see him from Denver now and then, but no. She sends him Southwest Airlines nuts.

I've never been on an airplane but I got to wondering if I might get a job on Southwest Airlines opening their nut packets. I wouldn't charge anything to ride along. Just as long as it was round trip so I'd be back in Denver the same day. But Ivan said the government wouldn't let me on the plane with my Swiss Army knife. Maybe.

After he puts the airline nuts in the bowl, George says come into the kitchen, I've made us lunch. And he has. With flowers on the table and a meal all laid out on matching plates he's put on a tablecloth with matching napkins. There were glasses and a pitcher of something red in it.

The lunch was a soup you buy in containers at Food Bonanza and a salad as well, all made up. He had these packets of salad dressing and he says, you'll have to sing for your supper, and asks me to open the salad packets and I do. Then he pours us both what's in the pitcher. Cranberry juice. It's good for your bladder, he says, then raises his glass, and I pick mine up as well. Soup to nuts, he says.

One day when Ivan gets home from Fox News, he starts in on socialism. I can't even stop them from giving me Medicare, he says. That's socialism. Next year the government is going to make me a socialist.

How about instead of shooting you in the foot, I say, I shoot you dead the day before your Medicare card comes? It's not funny, he says. Socialism isn't funny. You being smart-assed isn't funny. And then he goes on about how the government gave some university a grant to study why people laugh. Or how they laugh. Or the way they look when they laugh. They wouldn't use you for a subject, I say.

You tell me one thing the government has ever done that's any good, he says. Hire you, I say. I didn't work for the government, he says, I worked for the county. I tell him that if he'd get his Fox News buddies to dig his grave and stand so he'd fall face down into it, I'd shoot him the evening of August 27, which is the day before he turns sixty-five. His Fox News buddies would have to fill in the hole. Free. But if his Fox News buddies want the same deal when their times come, there's a charge. No free deaths from Lady Purse Pistol. Bang. That's not funny, he says. This is serious. Socialism is serious.

I charge ten dollars a call. It pays my gas. I get gifts. Tips. Leftovers. Re-gifts. We have a Women-in-Need and sometimes one of my folks will have a box for me to take there saying, go through it first for anything you'd like. Most of us have too much already. Cottonwood has three self-storage units and they are full so there is talk of building another. If they do, there will be more self-storage units than bars. Times are changing when that's the case. We're dying out and leaving storage-unit stuff behind. Mostly I never need a re-gift or what's in the Women-in-Need box. Ivan would want it all. He became his own self-storage unit. I hate clutter and he was clutter all by himself with that crap he hauled into my house. I should have known better.

It took him a month to get it all out, limping around as he had to after I shot his toe off, first him bumbling about with a crutch, then with a cane. He'd get his Fox News buddies to help, but if you sit on your ass three hours every morning eating glazed donuts and pissing and moaning about the government, you haven't got much piss and vinegar for work. Now I'm started just thinking about it. What makes me angry is Ivan being angry. That's no way to live.

More and more is coming on the market that's tough to open. I just bought some frozen fish at Food Bonanza in a big plastic bag. It has a picture of a pair of scissors in the upper-right-hand corner, so I know I'm supposed to cut there. Then there is a symbol like a zipper I don't understand, but since the package is still not open after I cut it the first time, I cut it there as well. Two cuts to get a piece of frozen catfish from about half a dozen inside, each shrink-wrapped to boot. And "farm raised," I see it says. What kind of catfish is "farm raised?"

After I cut the package a second time, I think maybe I was supposed to unzip it, but now I've cut the zipper off even though there wasn't a zipper, but something else. And when I look at it, I see they wanted me to unseal it then reseal it, so I try that even if it's no longer attached to the bag, because I think maybe I should practice for my folks. It doesn't work. Well, after I put it flat on the kitchen table and use my thumb, it sort of works. Finally, I got my catfish out. It's shrink-wrapped so tight that I have to use a box cutter and trim it all around. What madness is this, all for a piece of catfish? I'll tell my folks I've got enough to share if they want the "farm raised" kind.

Carol Jane says I'm into the learning curve. After a while it gets easier. She also thinks I should start a franchise. I'm not sure what that means. Begin an Internet site with Lady Open's Ratings for The Rest of America, she says. Like I have a computer.

The truth is, I didn't start opening with George at Food Bonanza. I started with crayons at the preschool here in Cottonwood. I was a teacher's aide. It was a pleasure. I opened crayons and pencil packs and packets of drawing paper for the kids. The pay wasn't much, but enough if you live alone and are careful. When Ivan moved in, he said I didn't have to work. So I quit. That was a mistake. But he said if I wanted something to open, I could open his XL Hershey's

Special Dark Chocolate bars. He'd have me buy them by the value pack. Sure, I said, just to be nice.

There is this Easy-Open place on the back, but it isn't that easy to understand, and even when you do, it's not easy to use. In fact, I didn't even know it was there for a long time and kept cutting the bars open at the XL end with my Swiss Army scissors until one day I turned it over. When I finally opened the chocolate bar top to bottom on the back, Ivan ate the whole thing at once. Then, after he retired, it was glazed donuts in the morning and Hershey's Special Dark for lunch until I stopped being nice. Otherwise, how much fun was that going to be for Carol Jane when they cut off the rest of his toes with diabetes and he's limping around her double-wide going blind even though she's a nurse for that.

After Al bought thousands of dollars' worth of guns at Buck Nasty, his checks starting bouncing. That's when Carol Jane had to go to court to get him committed. Not just sent to Happy Hope to dry out, but to the state mental ward. I had to say I heard how Al talked about the voices in his head. More than once, the judge asked? Yes, I said. Two or three times Carol Jane had me over, usually just before Al would get home from work bringing in more guns. Did you ask Al why he was buying guns? asked the judge. Yes, I said. All the time, Al was in the courtroom turning his head up and down and back and forth like he was trying to pick up some signal from outer space.

What'd he say? asked the judge. He said Jesus told him the Russians were coming to take away his guns, I said. Anything else? asked the judge. No, I said. I was a little worried about Jesus talking to Al because we've got more than our share of Jesus out here. There are big signs on all four sides of town and some in town saying Jesus Is Real, plus twice as many churches as bars and storage units combined. For all I knew, the judge might have been hearing

Jesus in his head. What goes around, comes around. Carol Jane says that in The Rest of America we are called West Jesus Land, Kansas. She might know, as she lived there before she moved here.

The judge looked down at some papers and then over at Al, who was still turning his head this way and that. Then he asked Carol Jane if she had anything to say. She said she didn't have the money to pay for all the guns, and that Food Bonanza would give Al medical leave and insurance if the judge would send him to the state mental ward. So ordered, said the judge.

Even after Ivan's Fox News buddies moved him out, there was stuff left over. So I had them put it in the garage I've got for the Z-car, where there's enough room on the west side. Then it took me two more days to get the place back like when I had it to myself. I don't see the use of a man you have to clean up after unless they are bringing home wages, and then it's a close call. Carol Jane says that when Al got put away she missed talking to him. Not that they talked about much, but it was something. I don't miss that with Ivan, angry as he was about nothing he could do anything about. Like the Fox News men at the Coffee Shack are going to repeal Obamacare because they got a sugar jag and a caffeine talking high. Some of them can't even button up their barn doors from what I saw of them helping Ivan move out. Not that any stallions were about to get loose.

George always seemed to have something for me to open. Usually I just stop by my folks once a week to see what they've got. Sometimes I get a call when pills come in the mail and they're worried about running out, but mostly I put them on a schedule, Monday through Friday. I've got ten, down from a dozen when the woman who had me toss pens died, and after what happened to George. Not that I know what happened to George. Well, I do. I do.

One day he wasn't there. It was about a week after he'd called to say he needed me to open a four-pack of yogurt, and could I stay for lunch? He'd been doing that about twice a month since when we had cranberry juice. Lunch was always something good, and usually it had something I could open so he could say you'll have to sing for your supper. One time he had me pat him on the cheek. My father's Schick Injector, he says. Thank you. You're welcome, I say.

After lunch he asked me to help him sort through keys. He wanted to throw away what didn't work anymore. Old cars. Changed locks in the house. But mainly he was looking for the key that opened a drawer where his wife kept her jewelry. He thought he'd give it to his daughter after all these years. Maybe she'd come to get it. You'd still be Lady Open, he says. Sure, I say.

The most difficult jobs I have are with what's shrink-wrapped. Dog bones from the pet section of Food Bonanza that Lady Nasty's husband buys. Shrink-wrapped DVDs. Shrink-wrapped cheese, the kind that woman who died on me couldn't get off with a knife and stuck herself in her hand. And when I tried, I stuck myself as well. By now the cheese had two holes in it, so I could peel it off. Next time, she said, let's try my hair dryer. I'll practice at home, I said. And I did it on a holiday nut ball one of my folks gave me and all that happened was that it melted the plastic into the nut ball and ruined it.

I may be Lady Open here in West Jesus Land, Kansas, but there is a guy in The Rest of America who is Sir Robert Shrink Wrap. Talk about a man who needs to be shot in the foot every day of his life. If somebody doesn't stop him, he's going to shrink-wrap anything that's loose and not in cans. Apples. Baked potatoes. Sticks of butter once you get inside the box. Pears. I like pears. Go ahead, Sir Robert, shrink-wrap pears. And while you're at it, shrink-wrap bananas too. How about light bulbs? They'd be easy in those cartons. But like the butter, keep the carton and shrink-wrap the bulbs. Eggs. Same deal. Shrink-wrap the eggs one at a time but keep the carton. Not even Ivan's toenail fungus clippers could get it off. And no doubt I'd pop the bulb and soft boil the eggs with my hair dryer.

Carol Jane says in The Rest of America they shrink-wrap boats before they put them away for winter. I doubt it, but maybe so. I wouldn't open a boat for somebody mental enough to do that.

I'm trying to think what it's like to be George with his daughter gone to Denver and not coming back, and his wife dead from that car wreck years ago, and here he is having me to lunch a couple of times a month. I know what that's about, but I don't know what it's like to be George. Gossip has it he got a pickup load of insurance money from his wife's death as the milk truck was to blame, but money's not a wife. My guess is he's past even hugging, not that I mind.

This last time he took me by the hand as we went into the kitchen. He told me he'd written his daughter in Denver about us, the one who sends him Southwest Airlines nuts and stuff. That's when he showed me his wife's jewelry and said I could have a string of pearls, but I thought better about it and he seemed a bit sad that day at lunch. It was a week later that I got one of those cards I'd opened for him and it said he was in Denver, but he'd rather be in Cottonwood with me singing for my supper. His handwriting had the shakes to it.

One day Ivan came home from Fox and Rust to say guess who shot himself in the foot today, and sure enough it was some senator from The Rest of America who said that the government should try to stop the mentals from buying submachine guns to mow down kids in grade schools. That's gun control, Ivan says. I say, how about we give the kids submachine guns before they go to school and everyone will be safe? Hand them out on the morning bus. Gun control isn't funny, Ivan says. Socialism isn't funny. The government isn't funny, he says.

If you think about it the way I do, Ivan shot himself in the foot after I told him plenty of times that I'd do it for him if he didn't shut up. That's what's not funny.

Carol Jane claims that in The Rest of America they have a saying that a woman needs a man like a fish needs a bicycle. I don't own a bicycle. I don't want a bicycle. For sure I don't want frozen catfish you can't open except with box cutters. If I wanted a man, I'd rather him ride a horse than a bicycle. And catch us fresh catfish out of the Whitewoman like Ivan used to do, taking me with him after work summers or on weekends. It was a pleasure. Sometimes what they say in The Rest of America doesn't make any more sense than Rust Limpball.

Another day Ivan came back from the Coffee Shack with how people cheat on food stamps, and on the way home Rust Limpball filled him to the brim with a government study on why people scratch itches. Then he goes, there was this woman senator from back east who shot herself in the foot by saying everybody should have Medicare. Not just folks over sixty-five. That turns the whole country into socialists. We'll be like France. Who wants to live like we're in France? I could shoot the whole country, I say. The French aren't funny, he says. My last name is French, I say. You're not funny, he says. You're just smart-assed. You're not Lady Open, you're Lady Smart-Assed. Paint that on the Datsun. That's when I decided to shoot him in the foot.

These days I get some pleasure being alone. More so just talking to myself inside my head about my folks, how I help them out, why I am Lady Open, my Z-car, the woman who died after I tossed out all those pens. George. I think a lot about George and how he got me re-started opening things and how he became sweet on me. I can't think what to do about him. The card had a return address.

The other day I went by his house and there was a Men-on-the-Move van and a car with Colorado plates with a U-Haul trailer. It looked to me as if they were done so I drove off. Some things are better not to know about. I haven't been back by. Nobody else on my route is on the way, coming or going. Carol Jane says the house is up for sale.

I'm thinking maybe I shouldn't have shot Ivan in the foot. What was the point? It wasn't like I was getting even with him for being who he was. And to be fair, he hadn't always been angry. We had some good times. Better to save the foot shooting for Sir Robert Shrink Wrap. Who am I to shoot the man who gave me my Z-car? Doesn't that make me Lady Angry? I don't want to be Lady Angry. I want to be Lady Open.

Carol Jane says it was the only way to get Ivan out of the house, and she was probably right about that. But the rest of it, Rust and Fox News, the Coffee Shack glazed donuts grease balls going on about socialism, what did it matter to me? When Ivan came back from the Coffee Shack I could have left to see my folks.

After I drove by George's, I drove by Carol Jane's. Ivan's truck was there, parked by the doublewide. I slowed down, but didn't stop. Maybe I should have. Maybe not. I wonder if he opens his own Hershey bars. I might could be of use to him even if he's no use to me. What am I to think about my thinking? If I had stopped, I could have returned Carol Jane's purse pistol. I drove home.

I'm getting new folks. One woman had me over to open battery packs for her. Also, her son had new lights and ceiling fans put in her house and they don't use a switch but a remote, and that's what needed the batteries. But she couldn't open the remote to put them in. And while I was there, would I open the place for the batteries on the remote. Life was better with on-off light switches, she says. The same for television. I put her on my route.

Another new client got my name from the man who's married to Lady Nasty. She feeds birds from bags with this strip you are supposed to pull to open it. She can move the bags but can't get the strip to work. It's like the Southwest Airlines nuts—sometimes I can get it to work, but sometimes it takes my Swiss Army knife. At least it's not shrink-wrapped.

The week after I drove by George's, Mr. Box Wine man called to ask if I'd open his Smart Water bottles. The whole case. Sure. I had to study them awhile but finally I got it. Not like they made it easy. You have to unlock the top first, then flip a small lid. He tells me his daughter was watching Doctor Pill on television and people his age should not get dehydrated, so she's going to send him a gift coupon at Food Bonanza for a case of Smart Water once a month. Let me fix you lunch afterward, he says when I'm done. I need to keep going, I say.

Now that Ivan is gone, Carol Jane thinks I should have Lady Open House parties where I charge a fee to teach people how to open packages. Like Tupperware parties, she says. Even get a franchise for Swiss Army knives and sell those along with the lessons. That's where I could make my money.

But I don't want people in my house because they'd be clutter all by themselves, and with no-fungus-among-us-angry-Ivan stashed in her doublewide, I like the peace to my life. No bicycle. No man. Besides, I like to visit my folks. There's a pleasure coming into their houses, a pleasure in opening what needs to be opened, a pleasure in leaving knowing I've been helpful. Plus there's a pleasure in the coming and going in my Datsun 260Z while I try to remember the snail joke. There was this snail…Why should I give up all that to sell Swiss Army knives? This is not The Rest of America. This is Cottonwood, Kansas. West Jesus Land, Kansas.

When I shot Ivan in the foot I had him step outside so I wouldn't put a hole in the floor and then he'd bleed all over the carpet. It was my house he'd moved himself into. That was my fault but I didn't have to pay for it more than once, and Ivan was once enough.

I need to show you a leak in the outdoor spigot, I say. I don't fix plumbing, he says. Just come and look to tell me if it's something simple. So he steps outside and I have my .25 purse pistol in my back pocket and I come up to him from the side and shoot him through his ratty sneakers that he won't take off coming into the house even if they are full of mud. I aim for the right great toe and hit it so that it takes the tip off to the end of the fungus. A .25 purse pistol is not what you need to shoot the whole great toe off, but for the tip it works just fine.

You stay right where you are, I say. What the fuck was that about? he says. Fox News, I say. And that's when Carol Jane drives up because I had told her I'd need her at 1 p.m. sharp to fix Ivan enough so we wouldn't have to take him to the hospital where they'd report a gunshot wound to the sheriff. Either that or Ivan could say he'd done it to himself, but I didn't want to take any chances. Carol Jane takes off his sneaker and you can smell it a yard away. Bury that, she says and pours alcohol on Ivan's toe. By now he's on the ground oinking like a stuck hog. He'll live, says Carol Jane. Good clean shot. Bullet wounds are sterile. Then she bandages him up and puts a toe guard on and bandages that, saying, you're coming with me. We pull him off the ground and load him into her car. You don't get to keep the 260Z, he starts in yelling. It's in my name. Carol Jane props his foot out the window. Off they go and his head is shaking back and forth and he's yelling at me about me being Lady Smart-Assed plus something more I don't know what. I just stand there.

What's to yell back? How about, if you don't watch out I'll send Sir Robert Shrink Wrap to do a number on your head? How about,

I'd still be willing to shoot you before you become a socialist if you take your sneakers to the grave.

But nothing smart-assed came to mind. I'm standing there watching him with his foot out the window, all the time yelling until just before he's out of sight I see him pull his foot out of the window and onto the dashboard. It made Carol Jane's driving wobble. I don't say a thing.

Maybe it was knowing that when I went back into my house there wasn't going to be any anger, not even me being smart-assed. Maybe it was thinking about George. And the pearls he tried to give me, and how he seemed sad I'd said no thank you. Maybe it was Mr. Box and Mr. Bottle with their wine, and how Mr. Box Wine was starting to get sweet on me. Or that woman who had me sort through her ballpoint pens. Maybe it was knowing that for sure I was going to return Carol Jane's purse pistol, driving it back in my Z-car with the windows down, the breeze in my hair. Or knowing how I've beat Sir Robert Shrink Wrap here in West Jesus Land, Kansas. Maybe it was thinking I'll go back to work as a teacher's aide. Or the pleasure of me not knowing the snail joke, but trying to find it in my head by myself as I went along. There was this snail...

Whatever it was, it was something. I am not Lady Smart-Assed, I said to myself. I am Lady Open. I am real. And then out loud when I walk into my house, I am Lady Open. I am real.

It feels good.

The One-Man Woodcutter

Clayton made me promise I'd tell his story. This is it. He's dead. That's part of the story. How he died and all. Cutting wood. This big rotten tree limb that broke out and killed him down on the Whitewoman. How I found him. Why he was called the One-Man Woodcutter. I'm the widow.

Not that I want to tell about it. But he made me promise. He was always making me promise something. Don't give more than a dollar at church. Promise to fix me bierocks for supper on Saturday. Don't tell those women in Cottonwood anything about us. Not your sister about Casey. Nobody about Casey. Promise now! Casey's our daughter. She's dead too.

They're always telling you what to do. That's all a promise is. Just telling you what to do. I don't much like it. When he was dying, he'd come to now and then and have me promise something else. Change the oil every three thousand miles. Put the screen over the flue pipe in the spring. Give the welding tools to Tony. He loaded me with a pickup full of promises. I think he died before we got him to the hospital, but they never told me one way or the other. When I finish his story, I'll do things my way.

We live in Whitewoman County. In Bly. Not that anybody'd know about Bly. There's not much left. Tony works on the Cody ranch between here and Blaze. He's a hermit. Lives in a hut on Big Oxbow just off the river. They call him Flatshot. He's our son. Casey's buried in Denver. That was years ago. Why she's buried in Denver and not here in Bly. I must have promised him that fifty times. Maybe I'll tell. Maybe I won't. I'm thinking about it. I'd like to be rid of it, I can tell you that much.

What Clayton did before he cut wood was weld. He had his shed on the highway north of Bly with his tools and torches and iron in it. He'd go there every day but Sundays and be home around dark, filthy to the bone. Before he'd come inside, I'd have him bathe in the canning house where he'd rigged a shower because I made him. You can't have them in your clean house all nasty and shedding dirt like they're a dog in summer. I don't let Levi in whatever the time of year, why should I let in a dirty man? Levi's the dog. He sleeps outside in the back of Clayton's truck. Even now, he's there.

When Clayton got the first layer off, he could come in. I had this robe in the canning house for him. And slippers. I had things arranged. Then he'd shower inside a second time. On Saturdays he'd give me his work clothes to wash. They'd be so full of grime and burn holes and dirt I'd put them in the Kenmore by themselves. Then I'd run it through once empty to wash the tub out. At least everything would be clean for Jesus on Sunday. Not that Clayton went to church or had much to do with Jesus. My sister Ellen and I are Lutherans. Missouri Synod Lutherans. Clayton made me promise not to bury him in the church cemetery but out of town in the country cemetery with the pagans.

"You think Clayton will be going with us to the service Sunday?" Ellen says.

She knows better because her Albert didn't go to the service either. Ellen and I talk back and forth here in Bly, feeding our birds.

"You think Albert will be popping out of the ground for dinner?" I say back. It's not as mean to say as it sounds.

"If Clayton goes to service, Albert will be to dinner," my sister says.

How Clayton got so filthy every day was that welding shed of his. It had this dirt floor. There was scrap in piles. Bird droppings coming off the rafters. Half of Whitewoman County blowing through the cracks when the wind was up. Cats leaving of themselves. Grease on everything. Sparks flying so fast Clayton didn't even know I was there when I'd stop by to tell him one thing or another. Or the last time I went there. To tell him Casey died.

The Pastor Harrison had tracked me down in Cottonwood because the sheriff had called him. I drove back along the highway to the shed. It was winter, and it was blowing snow off the ground from some weather we'd had the week before. I could see there were no trucks but Clayton's parked out front. Levi was in the cab.

Sometimes when I'd go by in the mornings on my way to Cottonwood I'd see trucks and rigs in front. I'd see Clayton welding on a piece of machinery, the men standing around waiting for him to get done. At least I knew where he was. And he always brought his money home, I'll give him that. The bottle hadn't gotten him either. Thanks be to Jesus.

The time I stopped to tell him about Casey, Clayton didn't know I was in the shed, and I didn't make any noise or come around to where he could see me, or let Levi out of the truck as a sign. I just stood there until he saw me. Maybe ten minutes. He upped his welding helmet and looked at me, and he knew there was trouble. The way we looked at each other.

After I told him about Casey he shut the shed door, snapped the lock, and never went back. It didn't make sense then and it doesn't make sense now. We'd get people coming by the house with welding to do, and he wouldn't do it. Just say no and shake his head. The phone would ring about some job and he wouldn't do it. With spring coming and planters and stock trailers and branding chutes needing work, they'd have to take their jobs to Cottonwood, and the man there cost twice as much and wasn't half as good. The shed sat empty. Still does. I don't wonder what happened to the cats. They didn't come to Bly. I shoot cats to keep them off my birds.

When we got back from Denver, Clayton didn't do anything for work. Not a thing. Only, cut wood the rest of that year to keep us warm. Made me turn off the floor furnace. Cleaned out the flue pipe for the Riverside and got it fired up. I never thought I'd have to use that wood stove again. It seemed like going backward. Here we had a good floor furnace that didn't make a mess, and the co-op delivered the propane. Now I had ashes to clean up and the dirt he'd bring in with the wood. And bugs as well. What a mess. He cut wood all that winter.

Then the next year he cut more wood than we needed. Said he had to lay in two years' supply. Then he went past that. All the time cutting and stacking wood. With him not welding, we lived on what I made cleaning houses in Cottonwood. It's what I've been doing all these years. I'd use the money as savings or for myself and the church. But with Clayton only cutting wood we had to live on it. That's not what I had in mind. I'm getting old. I want a soft life here at the end, with not so many worries as when we started out. I want to be warm in winter, but not with wood.

"What's with Clayton?" says my sister when she sees he isn't going back to the welding shed, and the yard is filling up with stove wood.

"Something to do with Casey," I say.

"How she died?" says my sister. She wants to know, but I haven't told her.

"Just that she's dead," I say.

"I'll pray for her, only don't tell the Pastor Harrison. He says we're not to pray for the dead. That's what the Catholics do."

"OK," I say.

"Men are strange," she says. "Albert was strange."

"Yes." She was helping me with my bird feeders.

I've decided I'm going to tell about Casey. Why she's buried in Denver. I've decided not to keep that promise. Only I'm going to tell it later. I want to figure out what part comes first. There are two parts. How she lived. How she died. I have to think about it. Maybe telling about Clayton like I promised, it will come to me how to tell about Casey. We'll see.

Clayton wouldn't sell the wood he'd cut. Even after we had more than two years' supply. He'd just cut it and split it and bring it back to Bly. I'd see him head off in the mornings with his truck and his log splitter hitched behind, and his gas cans for his chain saws and the chain saws themselves and Levi all in the back bouncing out of Bly toward the River Road. He'd have packed himself a lunch and a jug of water for himself and one for the dog as well. He'd be gone past sundown. When he'd come home he'd have a pickup full of wood to unload and stack. Which he'd do. Even if he did it in the dark. He worked headlights to headlights. I'll give him that. Do it all, do it now. That was one of his sayings. He was a quiet man. Tall. Grew a beard after Casey died. It came out white.

He'd get just as dirty cutting wood as when he worked in the welding shed. Worse. Only he wouldn't shower in the canning house. Turned his head no when I told him to. Maybe you could talk him out of no when he'd say it, but not when he'd turn his head. He'd strip to his underwear in the backyard and shake out his jeans and work shirts before he'd come into the mudroom where he'd get the rest of the way naked. In winter he'd have on long johns. At least he wasn't so dirty naked. I'd wash his clothes Saturday night, the same as before. Clean for Jesus on Sunday. Not that Casey being dead or cutting wood all week brought him closer to God.

"Good thing Mrs. Harvey moved to Denver," my sister says. She's talking about Clayton getting down to his underwear in the backyard and how Mrs. Harvey was always looking out for something to spread around the church. She's with her daughter now which is one stop before the old folks' home. The Raisin Ranch, Clayton used to call it. Promise me you'll not put me in the Raisin Ranch. Promise now.

"Can you see Clayton from where you are?" I ask.

"If there's enough light."

"Can you tell he's near naked?"

"Not so," says my sister. She's probably telling the truth.

We own most of Bly. When he was in a good mood, Clayton used to say we were Mr. and Mrs. Donald Trump of Bly, Kansas. We own it because everybody's moved out, and before they'd go, Clayton'd buy the house dirt cheap from what he'd saved by himself and whatever lots they wanted to sell. Some people would sell the lots but keep the house in case they lost work wherever they were going. Denver mostly. Kansas City and Wichita as well. The Hustons went to Manhattan. Not New York Manhattan, but Kansas Manhattan. Nobody comes back. By now we own thirty-nine lots and seven houses. Most all the town. I guess I'm the widow Donald Trump of Bly, Kansas. What we don't own my sister does. More or less.

When we'd buy a house, I'd clean it. To keep the mice out, Clayton would find a black snake. They're better than cats. Mostly there wasn't much furniture, only sometimes chairs and broken tables. Televisions. They get left behind when people move. I'd haul the junk to the dump and put the house in some kind of order, only mainly it was just empty space. I like a house when it's empty. There's something about it.

After I was done cleaning, we'd drain the water and lock the door. Always I'd put curtains up so nobody could look in. It just seemed better that way. Maybe word got around about the houses being empty, but nobody wants to live in Bly. We got dirt streets and bad water. Nobody ever wanted to buy one of our houses. No matter how neat they looked. Not that they were for sale.

Clayton stacked his wood on our lots. You could see it on the ten lots we've got to the south of us, and you could see it elsewhere.

On the lots where we owned the houses so it looked like someone was living there. On the three lots we own west of my sister's that go right up to the graveyard. On the lots next to the few houses we don't own. The whole of Bly got filled with Clayton's wood.

He'd stack it between trees with lodgepole pine laid down so the wood was kept off the ground. And he always stacked it in a rick so the air would come up and cure it over time. Clayton cut nothing but ash. No cottonwood. Ash. Maybe fifty cords of good split ash before he started trading it. Real neat. The whole of Bly was as neat as my house.

After a while his wood was the main thing about Bly. That and wild turkeys that must be a flock of fifty by now. Also cats people drop off. They'll be in the trees in the mornings after the coyotes come through at night, and I can shoot them better then. I use a .22. It's Clayton's Marlin, but I bought my own shells. Long rifle hollow points. He didn't know about me shooting the cats. Or about me shooting the unworthy birds coming to my feeders. Starlings mainly. For them I use bird shot. Ellen shoots unworthy birds as well. Neither of us shoots the squirrels even though if you don't put out corncobs they can eat you out of house and home. Once our shooting brought the sheriff to Bly.

"What'd Leo want?" my sister asks. She had gone up to the church to do some typing for the Pastor, and when she came back she saw the Sheriff leaving.

"Told him I was just shooting cats," I say.

"Somebody call in?" she asks.

"Yes, but he won't say who."

"Wendy Thomas," says my sister. She's probably right.

Beyond what we own, the rest of Bly is down to five lived-in houses, unless you count the Stevensons south of town camped out in the old school building. But I don't count them because first of all they're not from around here, and also I don't think they're married. My sister says they do drugs. For sure they raise rabbits because the rabbits are all the time getting out and Levi is all the time killing them so I find a dead rabbit half-chewed in the backyard when I put the clothes on the line. The Stevensons never ask about it though. You'd think they would, but they're trash. He doesn't do any work that I know of.

"They keep a light on all night in that old garage behind the school," says Ellen. "I think he's growing drugs in there. Why else would you not turn off a light?"

"None that I can think of," I say.

"I fed three cardinals this morning," she says. "And my nuthatch came back."

"Did I hear you shoot?"

"Bluejay," my sister says. "Dead."

We buy our birdseed in bulk at the co-op when I go to Cottonwood to clean houses. The same place we get our shells. The rest of us in Bly are related, my sister and her dead husband being the next of relations to me and Clayton. At least to me. The others are shoestring relations to Clayton. That would be Tom Jenkins and his mother-in-law, Wendy Thomas, who lives with him since his wife died. Wendy's always got a gripe about something. She's Episcopalian. They think they've got more manners than other Christians. Then there's Ed Earl Thomas who's not directly related to Wendy Thomas. He's always been a bachelor and is retired from the county roads. Next to him is Mrs. Watkins who claims she lived in three sod houses before she had a frame one. She's a liar. There are days when I think she's dead she sits so still on her porch. I remember when she smoked a pipe. She doesn't have religion and is proud of it. She'll see when she's dead. The devil will smoke her in his pipe. Up near the graveyard there's only my sister, whose Albert is dead five years by now. Some say she shot him, but she didn't. He shot himself and it was an accident. He's buried here in Bly. So is Clayton. In the church graveyard. Not in the county cemetery like he asked for. It's the first promise I didn't keep. You got to start somewhere.

"If he's not in the Great Beyond like he always said he wouldn't be," says Ellen, "then what difference does it make to him where he's planted? Same with Albert. It's us that's living, and us that knows they're buried with the blessing of Jesus."

"It does make me feel better," I say.

"Death is for the living," says my sister. "And besides, if Clayton is with the Lord, he'll forgive you for what you've done. They teach them that in heaven."

One Sunday afternoon someone from Cottonwood was driving through Bly and came to the door.

"You the man with all this wood?"

"I guess," says Clayton.

"What you want for a pickup load?"

I'm in the kitchen but I can hear.

"I don't sell it," says Clayton.

"It's not cottonwood, is it?" says the man.

How he could say such a thing shows he's from town. You can tell cottonwood from ash a quarter section away.

"Ash," says Clayton.

"How come you stacked it like you did? Crossways. If I get a pickup worth, I don't want it cross-stacked like that but laid out flat. And piled high. What would you want for such a load?"

"It's not for sale," says Clayton.

"Why not?" says the man. "Looks to me like you got plenty."

When I don't hear Clayton say anything for a long time, I go look. They are on the sidewalk that leads to our front gate. That's when I see the Buick and the wife in it, and I know that they are from down the street of a house I clean in Cottonwood. I know something else about him, but even after they leave I don't tell Clayton. Never did.

"I'll pay your price," says the man.

I see he's backing toward the gate like he thinks Clayton might be a quart low. He probably knows the story about Albert shooting himself, as it made the paper in Cottonwood. Maybe he thinks we're all a quart low here in Bly. Guns going off now and then. People not married to each other living in the old school, a light on all night. Wood all over town. Maybe he knows Tony's our son. Maybe by now he's heard stories of the One-Man Woodcutter working the Whitewoman all by himself, even in summer with only his dog in the truck. I can see Levi's killed another of the Stevensons' rabbits, and he's chewing on it in front of the Buick.

"I'll make a trade," says Clayton just as the man turns through the gate.

"What?"

"I'll make a trade."

"What kind of trade?" says the man from the other side of our fence.

"What you got?" says Clayton.

I'm not happy about what I'm hearing. We don't need anything in trade. That always comes to junk. We need money. More money than I make cleaning houses in Cottonwood, or once a week for that Cody homosexual living by himself in Blaze. We need money, I've said that to Clayton. I let a month go by with him not going back to the welding shed, but when the bank account was getting thin and me taking my cleaning money straight to Food Bonanza for what we need, I told him he ought to get back to welding. But he wouldn't say anything. Just shook his head no.

"Not much that you'd want," says the man. By now he's standing on the sidewalk next to his Buick. He looks at Levi eating the rabbit.

"Think on it," says Clayton.

"Who was that?" my sister says later that afternoon. Clayton is walking the lots checking his stacks. He does that Sundays. The houses, too.

"Somebody from Cottonwood," I say.

"What'd he want?"

"To buy the wood."

"Clayton selling?"

"No," I say. "Says he'll make a trade."

"Just what you need," she says. "Do you know them?"

"I know his car isn't always parked at his house," I say.

"I see."

The part of Clayton's story I'm supposed to tell is how he was on a ship at Pearl Harbor and how he didn't even know what a welding torch was until somebody on December 7th, 1941, handed him one with all the bombs going off and the ship sinking and he was supposed to cut through a metal door so the sailors screaming and banging on the other side could get out. And that's what he did even though he didn't know what he was doing, being even too young to be in the Navy, only he lied about his age. That's the story. But he liked to tell it with the moral of it as well. That you don't know what you can do until you do it.

Clayton never told the story to be a hero. I'll give him that. Only to get to the moral. But he'd put in all kinds of details that I've left out. How everybody was screaming. Blood everywhere. Fire. Water coming in. Men's names, and if they were officers or not. Who died right then and there. All kinds of things I'd see the men around here nod to because they'd been in the war and knew what Clayton was talking about. It was the most he'd talk in one stretch.

He told the story to Tony when Tony came home from Vietnam and lived with us a few weeks before he moved down to Big Oxbow on Cody's ranch. Tony had heard it all before and didn't want to hear it again. He and Clayton had it out about something. I never knew what. Tony came to Clayton's service, though. Not the church service but the burial. I haven't seen him since. He's been by himself to see Casey's grave. That's what I hear. My sister says he was once here in Bly to look at Clayton's grave, but he didn't stop by.

When those sailors got out from behind the door, they remembered Clayton and for years would write him. Not a thank you, but just a note to ask how he was and to say what they were doing. He'd always write back. But whenever they had some kind of reunion, he'd beg off. Clayton made me promise I'd let what was left of them know he was dead. This was one of the promises he got out of me on the Whitewoman after I found him. And a second time in the back of Tony's truck on the way to the hospital in Cottonwood. It wasn't the last promise he got out of me. That was not telling about Casey. But it was the promise next to last. Tell the men I'm dead.

The Sunday after the man with the Buick came to Bly, he came again, only this time with his truck. Not a truck like we've got in the country, but a sweet new-paint-fever truck, all black with arm rests between the seats and a phone plugged into the cigarette lighter and no dents in it anywhere. He must have kept it in his garage. Not once did I see it in front of his house when I was cleaning for this woman up the street. I was putting out feed for my worthy birds when he drives up. Clayton was walking around Bly looking at his wood and checking our houses. When I see the sweet truck and know who it is, I look to find Clayton. But Clayton sees him as well and comes over and they talk for a moment, but I can't hear so I walk over myself just when Clayton looks into the bed of the truck. I can't see what's there from where I'm standing.

"You can have them all," says the man. "Would that be a fair trade for a load of wood?"

"Where'd you get them?" says Clayton.

"In-laws," says the man. "They went to Mexico a number of years ago and brought them back. I won't say they paid much, but they might be worth something now."

I'm trying to guess what might be in the truck. I know I can't stop what's going on, but I'll have my say later. If you get at them afterward, sometimes it will slow them down next time. That's my sister's idea, too. Not that it ever worked on Albert. Which she says is how he shot himself. Being stubborn about keeping a loaded gun in the house when she'd chew on him not to.

"OK," says Clayton.

The man lowers the tailgate, and I can see there are five round metal light wheels, the kind you hang from ceilings. Like wagon wheels, only not as big. They are mainly black. There are sockets in them for light bulbs, and wires coming out of the hub on top. Around where the light bulbs screw in there are metal leaves. Like off a plant. These are green. There are metal brackets that look like vines. They are green as well, only a darker green. I have come up to the truck. Neither the man nor Clayton says anything to me.

"OK," Clayton says again.

I don't understand what I'm hearing. That was just the beginning.

"What'd you get this time?" my sister says. She always comes over after she sees Clayton's made a trade. By now he's made half a dozen. Two months of Sundays. Various folks. Word was getting around.

"The man said they were Hummels," I say.

"Funny-looking little people, aren't they?" she says. "And so many all lined up. The case might be worth something."

We are standing outside because it's warm with summer coming in. I am putting out sunflower pods I get from the Pastor's wife. My sister and I feed our birds all the year; that way we get them to nest here in Bly. Just like Clayton's got his wood stacked all over town, we got bird feeders on the lots as well. I tend the ones at my end, my sister tends the ones at her end. You know how some towns got a sign that says they are a tree town or a flower town, well my sister and I want Bly to be a bird town. We talk about making our own sign but can't decide if it should be *Bly's for Birds* or *Bly, Bird Town USA*. We agreed on a sign that says *Bly Is a Cat-Free Zone*, but we could never get either Albert or Clayton to make it for us.

"They take up less space than the lights we got right at the start," I say about the Hummels.

"There's that advantage," she says. "Where's he going to put them?"

"One house or the other," I say. "I never know. Not until I look when he's gone."

"He still won't sell the trades either?" my sister asks.

"No."

Every Sunday since Clayton died, I've written one of the men on his ship to tell them. At first I'd just write a postcard to save the cost of a first-class stamp, but since Easter I've had more to say about how he died. There are sixteen men on the list that I think are still alive. There were twenty-nine he let out from behind the door. I got four to go. Two have come back with "Deceased" stamped on them. One man's wife, Jane Wiggins Osborne from Wilmer, Minnesota, wrote to say her husband had died in a car wreck because he was half-blind and too stubborn not to drive, even though he couldn't get his license re-upped. She went on two pages about all this and what misery it was to live with Mr. Osborne when he got half-blind and stubborn. It was her letter that got me writing more about how Clayton died. Only I haven't answered her back. I'm thinking on it. Maybe she's the one I'll tell about Casey. I think I will.

Just now I'm writing a letter to a Robert W. Boyd of Old Town, Maine. He's the last one on the list. I've made a copy of it in pencil, and when I get it the way I like, I'll have my sister type it out. She used to be a secretary. In it I've told how Clayton didn't come home one Saturday at noon like he said he was because he wanted to be here to make another trade for the wood. Usually Clayton would only make his trades on Sunday, but this was an exception. I didn't know why.

When Clayton didn't show up after an hour, the man left. I didn't like him, and I didn't like what he had to trade. A collection of Coke bottles with the names of the towns where they were made stamped on the bottom. Also, an old Coca-Cola sign. I knew Clayton would have made the swap, so I was glad he wasn't home.

Then I had a vision. I was cleaning my bird feeder and I had a vision that something was wrong. It was a green-black thing in my mind. The color you get at the bottom of clouds that have tornadoes in them. There was a sound as well, a kind of hissing sound. Not like a snake. Not like anything I've heard.

That's when I got in my car.

The River Road goes along the Whitewoman River from Bly to Blaze, and I knew that's where Clayton had been cutting. About ten miles east toward Blaze I saw his truck. Levi wasn't in the back or even in the cab. I could see where Clayton had been working, but I couldn't see him. Then I heard Levi barking. I couldn't see where he was. Just hear him. Then I found them both.

That's as far as I've gotten in my letter to Robert W. Boyd of Old Town, Maine. It's taken a page and a half, front and back, and I want to end it, but I don't know how much I need to tell about going over the fence and then down the river where I find Clayton with Levi barking over him. And the big dead limb I had to pull off him. Or if I ought to say about how Clayton was awake when I found him, but that he'd pass out. And the rest of it. The blood all over his head and down into his eyes. And Tony coming along by chance and how we loaded Clayton into the back of Tony's truck and took him to the hospital with me riding with him in the bed and Levi chasing the truck until we left him behind and that he didn't come home for two days. In the postcards, I'd just write: "Clayton died not long ago cutting wood. A widowmaker got him.

He wanted you to know." My sister didn't even have to type them. But telling more about how he died takes more than a postcard.

I don't see why Clayton made me promise about Casey. What people don't know, just means they'll make it up. Most of what you hear isn't true. Clayton was all the time saying that to me when I'd tell him one thing or another about people here in Bly, or the women I clean for in Cottonwood. Nothing much is true, is what he'd say. But others make it up worse than me. And if you don't tell them something, then they make it all up. To this day I don't know what people are saying about how Casey died. They never tell you, just like I never tell Stevenson I think he deals drugs and that he's not married to his wife. But in his case I'm right about what I think, so that's not making it up.

Word got around about the trades Clayton made for wood, and before long we had not only those black wheel lights, but a set of mounted wall maps of the world from years ago to now, that case of Hummels, ten Winchester wooden cartridge boxes, three Negro men statues holding out a ring in their hands as if that's where you're to tie a horse, a barbed-wire display with the names and dates of all kinds of barbed wire written below the wire itself, and a set of four saddles arranged in a row on saddle stands, with the first saddle only being the tree and the rest getting more to them so you can see how a saddle is made. Everything a set of some kind, because Clayton wouldn't trade for anything that was just one of a kind or boxes of junk. I'll give him that.

He'd put what he traded for in our houses or, like the Negro men, into the yards. On Sundays he'd walk around Bly looking at his wood and going into the houses to check on his collections. It wouldn't be until later that I'd learn what he got. And then only because after he'd leave Monday mornings, I'd go over to the house where he'd put it and see what it was.

The Sunday before he died, he'd traded for three big photographs of old cowboy bands, all blown up and mounted. Framed real neat. But who wants to look at a picture of the Dodge City Cowboy Band from God knows when? Clayton and me, we never talked about these trades. Just like we never talked about him not going back to work, or how he'd just cut more and more wood all by himself, so that it wasn't long before my sister said he was called the One-Man Woodcutter of the Whitewoman. We never talked about any of it.

"There's something you're not telling me about Casey," says my sister the Sunday after Pastor Wilbur preached a sermon on Casey being such a special girl and how we'll miss her, but that she was with her eternal Father now and that should give us satisfaction. Clayton wouldn't go, even though he knew what the sermon would be because the Pastor had stopped by to grieve with us.

"I can't," I say.

"Can't what?" my sister says.

"Can't tell you."

"Clayton make you promise?"

"He did."

"OK," she says. But she asks me about it anyway every time we visit. Sometimes hinting. Sometimes straight out.

"Clayton let you off that promise yet?"

"No."

"Can you say why she's buried in Denver and not here?"

"No."

Once, Clayton went to Denver by himself. He never told me. Only since he wasn't dirty, I asked him what he did that day. Then he told me. Took Levi with him. Denver and back. Five hundred miles round trip. We didn't talk about it. The next day he went back to cutting wood. The Sunday after that is when he traded for the Negro men.

I'm going to Denver myself. Later this summer. When I get all Clayton's men written. But I need to take my sister so we can share the driving. I'm getting old. I'll grieve one more time at Casey's grave, and that will be the end. Once for both me and Clayton when we buried her. Once for Clayton by himself, and once for me. Then there's Clayton's grave here in Bly. All this death and my own coming along. Everything dying out with nobody left in the country, not even so many in Blaze anymore, and the butane stars we used to see on the farms at night now gone. More people in the graveyards than in church these days. And maybe them buried with something they didn't tell. What secrets should you go to your grave with? That's what I want to know.

Even though Clayton's dead, I still got people from Cottonwood coming out on Sundays to make trades for the wood. I say no to trades. I sell it. He didn't make me promise not to sell it, so I do. I get a hundred dollars a full pickup load, stack it yourself the way you want it and as high as you want. The stacks are going down. We still got turkeys and birds and dirt streets and bad water and sometimes cats in the trees, but we've got less wood. Times are changing.

I'm also selling what Clayton traded it for. I get a few buyers. Antique dealers off the highway come down because they've gotten wind of what's here. I show them around. The Hummels went first. Then one of the Negro men. The wagon-wheel lights are still here. The cartridge boxes got me a good price.

"I want one of those Negroes holding a horse ring," says my sister. "For my front yard." I have been shooting unworthy birds, and she's heard me so she's come up.

"Sure," I say.

"Are they too heavy for the two of us to carry?"

"I think we can manage," I say.

"You want to go to Clayton's grave?" she says.

"Today?"

"I was thinking of visiting Albert," she says.

"Let's move the Negro first."

And we do. I take the ring in his hand and my sister takes his feet. We walk down Middle Dirt to her house and put him at the end of her driveway, next to the cattle skull that's there.

"He looks good," my sister says, backing up to take him along.

"He does," I say. Then we walk over to the graveyard.

I've had another vision. All my life I've had visions. Not many. But some. Right after I got married there was a blue ball at my feet in bed just before dawn, and I guessed it was God, but He didn't say anything, and as the morning came it started to turn pale so I could see the wall behind it, and when Clayton turned on the light in the bedroom to get dressed it was gone. I never told Clayton about it. Or Ellen either. I told Casey, though.

I don't always see things in my visions. Sometimes I just feel them. Even if I don't see anything, I still call it a vision. I think maybe if I stay with it long enough and peer into what I'm feeling, something will show up. This new one is following me.

When I'm walking through town checking on my bird feeders and the houses and what's left of Clayton's wood, it's been at my back. It doesn't scare me. Not like the black-green cloud that told me Clayton was hurt. This is something soft following me. I turn around and try to look into it. But I don't see anything. It's been with me most of the week. I haven't told Ellen. But I told Clayton. At his grave. Not the other day when I went with my sister after we moved the Negro, but yesterday.

"Is that you, Clayton?" I say. I am standing at his feet.

It has been warm in recent days. Not yet hot, but getting there. The wheat harvest is on. That makes the sunsets red. I go to the edge of Bly to watch them. The vision is with me then. When night comes, it leaves. Then it comes back in the morning and follows me, but only when I go outside. It's not with me in the house.

"Is that you, Clayton?" I say again. Levi has found me. He's wet from having been in the creek or somebody's stock tank. When he shakes, it goes over Clayton's stone.

"I'm sorry I put the cross on your stone," I say to Clayton.

"I just didn't feel right not doing it. If that's you following me, give me a sign."

Then I think it's not Clayton, it's Casey. Or maybe it's one of the men from Clayton's ship. Or maybe it's all of them from the ship that he saved but now are dead, and what they're trying to tell me is that he's with them. And Casey is, too. I peer around me to see what I can see.

"Give me a sign," I say.

Levi thinks I'm talking to him and sits down. I can feel the vision is all over me. Front and back and it's rising out of the ground. It feels good. It's like harvest sunsets or a hunter's moon. Maybe it's my own time come to get me. But I haven't been sick. And I've chores to do. Clayton left me his Social Security, but I still clean a few houses in Cottonwood. There's the wood and the trades to sell off. The floor furnace to get the Co-Op man to clean before fall comes. Maybe Tony and I will have time together now that everybody's gone but the two of us. Maybe he'll tell me what happened between him and Clayton. Sometimes I'm tired. But I've got my birds to feed. It can't be my time has come.

"Who's there?" I say.

My sister comes out of her house and calls to me something I can't understand. The vision goes away. Not that I think it's angry, just that it wants to be with me and nobody else.

It's about Casey. I've thought on it. I'm not going to tell. I want Clayton to have that. I don't want him to be the One-Man Woodcutter who died for nothing. Not that I ever understood him. I never knew what any of it was about. Not the promises. Cutting the wood. The trades. How the shed on the highway is still locked, and by now I've lost the key. That he wouldn't shower in the canning house after Casey died. Or why he wouldn't go meet those men whose lives he saved. Why he grew his beard. It's what I just finished writing to Mrs. Jane Wiggins Osborne of Wilmer, Minnesota. That I never understood what Clayton did, but now that he's been dead long enough for me to think on it, I'm not going to tell her about Casey. Not to anybody. Not to Ellen. Only to Jesus when my time comes. But that will be to give me peace even though Jesus knows how Casey died. I'll be with her then. And maybe with Clayton, too. I hope so. Now that he's dead, I hope so. The letter, it took me a page front and back. I wrote by hand and didn't have my sister type it.

It's in the mail.

Chloe in the Canoe

"How'd you get here?" she asked him.

"Who are you?" Harris replied.

They were both standing in the kitchen; he had come in through the back door. It was snowing outside, as it had been for the past week. Off and on.

"They said you couldn't get in or out," she said. "That's what they told me." She was standing at the sink. Dishes were in the water, pans were on the drainboard. Nothing much had been washed yet.

"Where are they?" Harris asked. He took off his coat and shook off the snow. "You might have done that on the porch," she said. "I just finished the goddamn floor."

He kicked the bootjack away from the wall and out where he could use it. "They around?" he asked.

"I don't know," she said. "I don't know where they ever are. I've never been out here before." She paused. "How'd you get here?"

"You can always get through the north gate," Harris said. He pried off his boots and set them on the grate of the floor furnace. "The shelter belt goes along the road there and you can always get in and out that way." He looked at the coffee pot on the stove.

"They drank it all this morning." she said. "And I'm not fixing any more." She picked up a dish towel and dried off her hands and sat down on a chair at the kitchen table. Out the window beside her there was an open space in the trees that circled the house, and beyond that there was a white pasture. A line of cattle was moving north to south across the opening, trotting. Harris sat down on the other chair at the table.

"Where you from?" he asked.

"Dodge City," she said.

"How long they had you up here?" he asked.

"A week and three days now. I was only supposed to be here a week, and then they said we couldn't get out. Much less back to Dodge. Goddamn," she said. She looked out the window. "I said I'd take the bus from town and they didn't have to pay for it. They didn't have to drive me to Dodge." She turned back and looked at Harris. "You work here or what?" she asked.

"From now through the summer," he said. "Blake's my uncle." Harris looked at his socks which were brown from being wet through his boots. He took them off and tossed them on the floor furnace grate.

"If they're wool, they'll stink," she said.

"That thing come on lately," Harris asked.

"It'll come on in a moment," she said.

"I'm surprised they turned it on so early," he said.

"I made them," she said. "Good thing I did, too. Or I would have wound up chopping wood as well as cleaning house." He looked at her and then got up to make some coffee.

All the time he made the coffee she didn't speak and neither did he. From outside they could both hear the sound of a pickup truck, and some men talking. She looked out the window.

"They're feeding those cattle again," she said.

"I see they put up quite a bit of hay," Harris said.

"I wouldn't know," she said. "They haven't exactly showed me around." She tapped her fingers on the table, looked at the dishes, and took a deep breath. "Say, will you drive me out of here?" she asked Harris. "Just to the bus station. If you can get in," she said, "you can get out."

He looked out the window and said she'd have to ask Blake about that. She stopped drumming her fingers.

"I might have made some pretty bad ruts down there," Harris said after a moment. "It was wet underneath the snow, and it might be hard getting back."

"I'm a little tired of being here," she said. "Doing dishes is not exactly what I had in mind."

"They pay you for the second week?" Harris asked.

"Yes, they did," she said. "But I'm still tired of being here." She got up and went over to the sink and began to wash the dishes. "They got me doing these dishes, and scrubbing floors, and doing their washing." She banged the dishes around in the sink and made a lot of noise. "Just like I was a wife or something."

"The place does look clean," Harris said.

"I guess it should," she said. "That's what I've been doing for three days. That and cooking meals." She paused. "They're never here except to eat. At night they get drunk in front of the television. They're not much." She banged a pan against the water nozzle.

From outside they could hear a truck. Harris went to the door and yelled something. He didn't get an answer and so he yelled again, and then they yelled back. Both of them in the kitchen could hear the truck get gunned and the wheels spin in the snow.

"I wish you hadn't called them before I got these dishes done," she said. "That's what I was supposed to do this morning. These dishes." Outside they could hear the truck stop and the truck doors slam. She put the rest of the pans into the water.

"When'd you get here?" Blake said as he walked onto the porch and through the back door into the kitchen. There were two other men behind him, grinning. One of them brought out a pint of Jack Daniels.

"Just a minute ago," Harris said.

"Matilda here fix you some coffee," Blake said.

"My name is not Matilda," she said from the sink. The man with the pint passed it around.

"You can drink when you get those pans done," Blake said.

"Go to hell," she said.

"We got ourselves something of a bitch this time," Blake said. The two other men laughed. "Good to see you," Blake said to Harris.

"Good to be here."

"He got through the north gate," she said from the sink.

The other two men sat down on the floor with their backs against the wall and their feet out over the floor furnace. One of them asked Blake for the pint back, and he passed it to Harris, who took a belt and then tossed it to the men on the floor.

"I hadn't thought of that," Blake said. He scratched his ear. "Cut some ruts getting in?" Blake said to Harris.

"I might have," Harris said. They went over to the kitchen table and sat down.

"Maybe we can get you out sometime soon," Blake said to the woman. One of the men on the floor asked her what was for lunch. She said she didn't know and she didn't give a damn. She hoped to be out of there by lunch.

"No chance of that," Blake said. "We can't do that even if we could get out. Got to feed these cattle, Tammy."

"My name's not Tammy," she said. "I told you what my name was." She had finished doing the dishes. The floor furnace came on and all of them looked at it as it stirred the wet socks. The men on the floor cocked their legs so the hot air would heat their feet. The woman left the kitchen and went to another part of the house.

"Damn whore's getting uppity," Blake said.

"Woman's liberation," said one of the men on the floor.

"She's pretty old," Harris said to Blake.

"I'm pretty old," Blake said. The men on the floor laughed. "I can't fool around with those green apples anymore. I got to have something long in the tooth."

"Why don't you take her back to town?" Harris asked.

"Haven't gotten around to it," Blake said. "We just got the heat on the other day. Willa there wouldn't do her thing unless we turned on the propane." One of the men on the floor said it hadn't been cold at all, and that there was still plenty of wood for the stove.

"I guess there is," Blake said. "We'll go back to using it after she leaves."

"You taking turns with her?" Harris asked.

"It's your turn, if that's what you mean," Blake said. "We stopped fooling with her the end of the week. I think she's got bugs on her."

"She's your Christmas present," one of the men on the floor said.

The heat had dried the socks on one side and Harris got up and turned them over. He checked the coffee but it wasn't done yet. One of the men on the floor passed Harris the bottle saying one way to kill the stink those wet socks made was to have a drink. They passed the pint around and talked about the weather and the price of beef.

"I'll unload my truck and help you guys feed those cattle," Harris said.

"Wait until your boots dry," Blake said. "We might go to town for lunch since there's nothing here. To pick up some booze, too," he said.

"You want to take Ethel there with you?" Harris asked.

"Maybe the end of the week," said Blake. "There's still plenty she can do. It's like having a wife around," he said." "Complete with the bitching."

The men on the floor laughed. Everybody got up and stood on the porch and looked at the snow. They said they'd see each other later.

"Don't stand on ceremony with that fat girl," said Blake as he went to the truck. When Harris went back into the house the woman was in the kitchen standing by the sink.

"What'd they say about taking me to town?" she said.

"Maybe tomorrow," Harris said. He went over to the floor furnace and propped his boots up against the jack so the hot air would blow up inside them.

"That'll shrink the leather," she said. "I'm just telling you."

"I've done it before," Harris said. She went over to the table and sat down and looked out the window.

"Well this is some mess I've got myself into this time. Yes it is. This is some goddamn mess," she said.

"You didn't bargain for two weeks?" Harris asked her.

"I didn't bargain to be no goddamn maid. That's what I didn't bargain for."

"Then don't do it," Harris said. She looked at him.

"Fine for you to say," she said. "But I can't exactly walk to town."

The floor furnace went off. Harris got up and turned off the stove. He checked his boots and socks and moved them from the grate. He poured himself a cup of coffee and stood by the stove and looked at her sitting by the table.

"How come you only work now through the summer?" she asked him.

"I go to school September to Christmas," Harris said.

"Ag school?" she asked.

"Yes," Harris said. "Blake sends me. He sends me for working the rest of the year. It's a good deal."

"It's a better deal than I got," she said. "I should have known."

Harris was about to sit down at the table when he thought to ask her if she'd like a cup of coffee.

"Yes, I would," she said. "I see they drank the pint they promised me when I finished the dishes." She picked up the empty bottle they had left on the table and looked at the label. "At least they drink good stuff," she said. Harris brought her a cup of coffee and sat down.

"Black?" he asked. Black was fine with her, she said.

"The best deal I ever had was at school," she said. She looked into her coffee cup. "It was easy money," she said. "It was when I was living in Kansas City and there was this fraternity in Lawrence that made all the rookies go out on a scavenger hunt before they could join, and…"

"Pledges," Harris said. "They call them pledges."

"That's right," she said. "Pledges. They made the pledges get statues, a raccoon one year, flags—all kinds of stuff. But the one thing they always had to have was a woman sitting in a canoe right in front of their house just as the sun came up." She smiled and took a drink of her coffee. "You in a fraternity?" she said to Harris.

"No," he said. "But I know about them."

"These guys were real swell," she said. "They'd be out on the porch in the dark waiting for the sun to come up to see if the pledges had gotten a woman for the canoe. The pledges didn't have to get the canoe. The fraternity had that." She looked out the window. Harris tested his coffee and it had cooled enough for him to drink it.

"I had that job for years," she said. "Every spring. They'd pay me a hundred just to sit there in that canoe. They'd come in to Kansas City and drive me up and back. I could stay the weekend there at their house, or I could go out to a motel. Either way it was on them. It was like a vacation," she said. "All I had to do for my hundred was sit in that canoe in the dark until the sun came up."

From outside they could hear that far away the truck had started up again. The floor furnace went on and neither of them said anything for a while. The room began to smell of the wool socks and Harris got up and took them off the furnace grate and hung one on the doorknob and the other on the refrigerator handle.

"Blake used to have a wife," Harris said when he sat back down. She was looking out the window. "But she left him."

"He deserved it," she said.

"What's your name?" Harris asked her.

"Matilda," she said. She drank her coffee.

"Maybe they'll take you in tomorrow," Harris said. "I'll ask them to do that."

"Do what you want," she said. "It's my goddamn mess. I guess I can get myself out of it."

He finished his coffee and got up and tested his socks. They were dry enough and he sat back down and put them on. She went over and wiped the dishes. The window by the table rattled as the wind picked up, and outside they could see that it was snowing harder. Harris pulled on his boots but the first one got stuck, and so he had to hop around the house with one boot half on and no boot on the other foot until he found the boot hooks. Then it was easy. By then she had finished with the dishes.

"One spring they didn't come to Kansas City to get me," she said. "I never heard who they got in my place. I had a chance to go to Dodge with this lawyer in an airplane so I went there instead. But he didn't take me back, and one thing led to another so I stayed." She hung up the dish towel in the handle of the refrigerator.

"I'll see if I can't get you in tomorrow," Harris said. "Work the rest of the day and I'll see what I can do."

He went outside to get his gear, and when he came back he tromped mud and snow on the floor. She complained about that and when he came back with a second load, he kicked his boots at the porch step before he came in. He got the dish towel and wiped up his tracks. She was standing by the sink washing out her coffee cup.

"You get your stuff ready," Harris said. "I'll take you to town myself." She looked at him.

"If I go, I'm keeping the money," she said. "For the second week."

"That's all right," he said.

When she came back into the kitchen, she had on a rabbit coat and a red hat that looked like an old-fashioned leather motorcycle helmet. She had forgotten her suitcase and went back into the bedroom to get it.

"They gave me this hat," she said as she came back into the kitchen. "The boys in the fraternity. They gave me this hat. I think it was about the third year I did that job." She put down her suitcase and looked at an angle in the window to see if she could get it to reflect her. She adjusted the hat.

"It's a good-looking hat," Harris said. "You ready?"

"It was the fourth year," she said. "Because that's how long they go to school, and the first bunch that hired me were the leaders by then. When the sun came up that spring they cheered and clapped to see it was me in the canoe. I pretended to row across the lawn. They put all the other stuff they got around the canoe. That was the year of the raccoon. He hissed when they tossed me this hat." Harris wriggled his foot in his boot as if to get it a bit snugger.

"Let's go, Matilda," he said. He looked out the window.

"Chloe," she said.

"What?" Harris said.

"My name's Chloe," she said. "From the song Spike Jones used to play. You ever heard of Spike Jones?" Harris said he hadn't.

"Nobody has," she said. "Or the song either. That last spring they tried to sing it to me: 'Once in love with Chloe, always in love with Chloe.' But that's not it. That's Amy."

"Let's go," he said. "Before Blake gets back."

She picked up her suitcase and went out through the door he held open for her. It was snowing so hard he had to point her toward his truck that was difficult to see with the wind and snow blowing straight into their faces.

Later when Blake asked him what happened to the whore, Harris said since it was his turn, he took her to town.

"I don't want a case of bugs for a Christmas present," Harris said.

They all laughed. Harris passed around a pint of Jack Daniels he had bought in town; they drank and talked about women.

Part Two

Men

Males—Alpha or Not

I think there is a natural tendency on the part of readers to see the male characters in stories written by a male writer (like me) as being part and parcel of the author himself. But Ernest Hemingway is not Jake Barnes; Vladimir Nabokov is not Humbert Humbert; John Barth is not Todd Andrews; and I am not the narrator in "My Father Swims His Horse at Last," "By the Light of the Silvery Moon," or "My Uncle's Poor French."

On the other hand, we do sense that Sal Paradise in *On the Road* is Jack Kerouac and that there is a lot of Truman Capote in some of his short stories (i.e., "A Christmas Memory"). It's a mixed bag: horses and cattle in the same pasture.

For me, fiction is one part previous fiction (authors I have read and ripped off: Jack London, Anton Chekhov, Walker Percy, Mark Twain); one part "real life" (I once worked on a small ranch); and one part Invention (*not* Inspiration). Invention arises from what I am writing, as if my story were its own muse. How this happens I am not sure, but I am sure it happens.

I have looked over my male stories with an eye to finding myself (or at least one part of myself) in them, and in the main they are bereft of their author.

I am rather pleased with myself in this regard.

My Uncle's Poor French

Saturday Morning

When I was a boy, I lived for a year with my Uncle Bert in an apartment over the train station in the village of Lamothe-Montravel on the Dordogne River in southwestern France, not far from Bordeaux. This was during the Korean War; my father had been called back to service (he had seen duty as a Navy pilot toward the end of World War II) and for reasons that were not clear to me at the time, my sister was taken to Oklahoma to live with my paternal grandmother, and I was flown to France to live with Uncle Bert. It was only later that I learned my mother had been deemed "unstable" by the adults in charge of our lives and that was why my sister and I were sent to our respective foster parents. I was ten at the time; my sister was eight.

I arrived in Bordeaux in late summer by plane from Paris. My father had taken leave from his naval base in California and returned to our home in the suburbs of Kansas City a few weeks before shipping out to Hawaii. After a couple of days' stay, and after my grandmother left with my sister, my father and I boarded a triple-tailed TWA Constellation for a flight to New York. My father was himself a captain of TWA Constellations, and it was this position he was forgoing to fly jets off a carrier off the coast of Korea—not unlike, now that I think of it, William Holden in *The Bridges of Toko-Ri.*

All of this seemed quite thrilling to me: my father first in this uniform, then that one. Pictures in *Life* magazine of the plane he had flown in World War II (the Navy Corsair), and then in "civilian life" (the Lockheed Constellation), and now again in Korea (the Panther). My father was a one-man flying machine for peace and war. No one else in Hickory Grove Grade School had a father like mine.

I remember my father and me waving goodbye to my mother in Kansas City as we boarded the flight to New York. We were on the top of the stairs, and I remember how thin my mother looked, and I remember that she wasn't crying. For some reason, perhaps the movies you saw in those days, I always thought mothers cried when their children went off to Boy Scout camp, to visit a grandmother in Oklahoma, or to the Dordogne of southwestern France. My father and I waved. My mother did not wave.

In New York, my father confirmed the arrangements he had made with his airline friends in Paris to meet my plane at Orly and then to put me on an Air France flight to Bordeaux where my Uncle Bert was to pick me up. After that, my father walked me up the stairs onto my Paris-bound night flight to find my seat. He was wearing his Navy uniform, and the bill of his hat was trimmed with gold. Scrambled eggs, he called the design. It's what he got when he reenlisted, he said.

The captain of the plane, a friend of my father's, came down the aisle and shook hands with me. My father and the captain had some discussion about the winds aloft and the route we would take. I was told I would be allowed to visit the cockpit after the plane was airborne. Your father is quite a pilot, the captain told me. You should be proud of him. He tapped my father's "scrambled eggs" and said it was about time. Looking back, I suppose they were in the Pacific together and there was more to the story than I could ever know.

When it was time to go, my father had me follow him to the

doorway where we said goodbye. He not only patted me on the sides of my shoulders—his usual way of saying hello or goodbye—but he shook my hand. That was the first time he'd done that.

Take care, he said. Then he walked down the steps, stood at the bottom for a moment, motioned for me to go back to my seat, saluted, and put both his thumbs in the air. I saluted back.

Through my seat's window I could see my father standing on the tarmac while the engines cranked up, and I could see that he could see me as well. He waved. I waved back. As the plane turned, the prop-wash caused my father to lean into the wind and hold his hat, one hand on the top, the other on the bill. It was the last time I saw him. And he was not my father.

Saturday: Late Afternoon

Uncle Bert's French was poor. I never knew exactly how long he had been in Lamothe before I got there, much less in France, but piecing it together as I grew older, he probably came back to Europe right after the war (he had been, I learned, a sergeant in an outfit that landed well after D-Day and made their way finally to Paris). Because I arrived on my uncle's doorstep, something of a foundling, the late summer of 1952, it would have been six or seven years that he had lived in France. As it would turn out, he'd live there another forty-odd years, and I suspect that the day he died he knew no more than the baguette tails and cheese rinds and dregs of the French he had during the year when we lived together.

I came to know about his bad French because, as a young boy in the Lamothe school, I learned the language quickly. By Christmas, I had become something of a discreet translator for my uncle.

"What did he say? I've bum ears, boy," said my uncle. "A war wound. Too many 155s. Nothing serious. What'd he say?" And here Uncle Bert would take off his black beret, as if that might make it easier for him to understand.

"He said you owe him five francs," I said.

"Five francs it is. And cheap at half the francs."

Along with bad French, Uncle Bert also had the habit, à la Sancho Panza, of mixing up (and making up) aphorisms, a phenomenon I would learn both sooner and later when I'd finally get them straight for myself, at first with the help of tolerant teachers back in Kansas City, and later with the assistance of puzzled editors. Still: "Eating your cake and having it too" is forever tangled, while "A day short and a dollar late" I rearranged by myself not long after I heard my uncle use it. But I never knew what he had mangled when he'd say: "The road of the mind is a twisted branch." Or: "Don't feed the staff of life to an ugly pig." Or: "Flowing beer gathers no foam." And sometimes Uncle Bert would mix and match French and English to get, say: "*Too la monde* likes a cow you can milk through the fence." The world was always feminine to Uncle Bert.

"What does he want now?" said my uncle.

"He says he'll see you again next week," I said.

"That's what I thought he said. Of course. Yes. *Oui. Oui. D'accord. Mais oui. D'accord, à bientôt. Merci. Au revoir. Bon soir. Bonne nuit. Mais oui. D'accord.*" And a final "*Toot Sweet*" as Uncle Bert put his beret back on.

In such conversations my uncle might have used up a good ten percent of his French vocabulary, a vocabulary he doubled and tripled with nods and smiles and gestures and winks, along with the few idioms he knew, often with no regard to the matter at hand. In the end, and taken together, sight and sound, an aphorism here, a cobbled phrase there, plus a *tant pis* French shrug for good measure, my uncle's poor French was plausible in its way: a *patois* of its own.

What was not plausible was his accent: a cross between the East Texas drawl that was his own and something like a high pitched Cockney—the latter laid on ("slathered" might be a better word: it would be his word) because of my uncle's conviction that French should not only *be* "foreign," but *sound* "foreign": Eliza Doolittle cum Slim Pickens ordering *pommes frites* with chicken fried steak. It was not only less than *loverly*, it made a noise that never failed to produce suppressed mirth from those in our village who heard it. Still, I had the sense then, and I retain it now, that Uncle Bert more or less understood what he was talking about in a language he did not know and could not pronounce. Between the two of us we could get on. In fact we did. *Mais oui.*

Uncle Bert was my father's older brother and to even my young eye and youthful sensibilities, they could not have been more different. My father was trim and tall, and had an ease of elegance about him, both in the way he carried himself and how he dressed and talked. My uncle's belly hung over his beltless britches; his shoes were ripped where a big toe had poked out the front end of the left one, and a calloused heel had split the back of the right one; his hair was wild as John Brown's in the great Curry mural my school class had visited the year before I left for France. And instead of a crisp walk like my father's, Uncle Bert walked like his battered, gray Deux Chevaux, which was full of creaks and rattles, with a decided tilt to one side even when it was not turning. My uncle was not yet forty when I lived with him; he seemed sixty. And he affected it.

"I was born to be old," he said to me. "Tell me how to say that in French. Ask your teacher. I'd like to know. I'll memorize it. I've memorized some French sayings since I've been here. Give me age. It is my fate." And then Uncle Bert would wave his hands above his head, palms facing out, in what I came to learn was his all-purpose gesture of exuberance and happiness, something like Anthony Quinn does as Zorba the Greek dancing on a quay. In Uncle Bert's version he'd not only dance with his hands above his head as we'd walk along, he'd wave them out of the top of his Deux Chevaux when it was warm enough to roll the top back, steering briefly with his knees as we motored ahead. His gesture was so much a sign of him that I'd see villagers greet him with it themselves as he approached; and once I saw two men talking on the street in Lamothe and one of them put both his hands in the air and waved them palms out. The other man nodded, and they both smiled when they saw me, and then they made the sign again.

"And while you're at it, learn how to say 'It is my fate' in French," my uncle said. "I'll memorize that as well. You should hear what French I've put to memory."

Uncle Bert not only wanted to be old, he wanted to be old and French. He wanted to be a Dordogne peasant, not unlike the men we would see driving a donkey cart out of the hills behind our village, or walking ahead of their wives on the long trek down the narrow road to Castillon on market days. He wanted to be one of the men we could see through the open doorways of their farmhouses as they took lunch, tearing their bread with big hands, a liter of wine on the table, cursing the clerics and the Parisians. Uncle Bert would be an old French peasant in a black beret pouring the last of his wine into his soup; a man with his own language, which was neither his nor theirs: "*Il trouve le destin*," if that is what he meant.

Sunday

I live in Paris. I have lived here for twenty years. I work for the English-language magazine *France in English*. We recycle articles about France from other magazines: "Gallic, The Oldest Wine," "Elizabeth David: The English Writer on French Cookery," "Mauriac Château Opens as Museum," "Balzac's Paris." That kind of thing.

Our subscribers are the English and Americans who have settled in France and who don't read much French. Some are here in Paris, but mostly they are in the south of France, Provence and the Dordogne. The Ardèche. The Pyrénées-Orientales. I looked at our subscription list the other day to see if we mailed any issues to Sainte-Foy, Castillon, Villefranche, Lamothe: and we do. I did not recognize any of the names, but then I did not live there long enough to meet many people. Besides, I stayed with my uncle, and through him I met mainly peasants.

We have a back page titled "La Résolution" that is a *récit* about France: sometimes about confusion *à propos* language; other times about farewells, bittersweet or otherwise. I am the writer of "La Résolution," a task that is pleasing for me in an ironic way because while I believe in "*La Fin*," I do not believe in "resolutions"—either French or English. When I write "La Résolution," I write in order not to reveal myself. In so doing I am not always true to the facts. It is from these duties I am taking the week off.

I have never married. I suppose that a single man, fully and pleasantly employed, with a long lease on a furnished apartment in the 7th arrondissement, and with a decent palate for *vins fins*, must be in search of a wife. But I am not.

My apartment is a fifth-floor walk-up on rue de Poitiers not far from the Musée d'Orsay. Another floor up I have a small office. It is where I am now with my tabula rasa and my Olympia Splendid 33 typewriter. My friends say that over the years I have gotten stuffy. No doubt.

From here I have a cubist view of mansard rooftops and photogenic *rues*. I can see today's bird market on the Quai du Louvre. I can see Montmartre, or rather half of the dome of Sacré-Cœur, rather like a slice of moon in a Chagall. At night the lights from tourist boats that head up and down the Seine blaze through my windows, creating a strobe-light-disco starry night. I am not so high up that I don't hear street noises. And with the windows open, smell the chestnuts roasted by the small old Moroccan man just across the street. It is all pleasant and pleasing in ways that I cannot explain, even to myself. Perhaps especially to myself—if that is what I am doing.

In summer, Paris gets hot and crowded: but I don't much mind.

I rather like the city when it is filled with a plethora of Mr. and Mrs. Bridges standing in front of the Grand Palais asking directions to the Grand Palais. In winter, the city is not all that cold compared to Kansas winters, and you can again walk in the smaller streets for decent stretches before a taxi honks you off.

And I like the rain. I like coming into my restaurants and cafés and brasseries to get warm and to be recognized. I think the reason I have never married—or even had more than a series of pleasant affairs (and in recent years only with wives who love their husbands)—is because my affection for Paris is persistent, consuming, and easy. When I am tired of it, I shall be tired of life.

I don't say much about myself to anyone at the magazine. As for my lovers, I let them believe what they like. Sometimes I let them think I am a teacher. Sometimes a film critic. I have an Algerian lover who is convinced I am a famous American baseball player who retired to France on "bonuses." Not that she knows what that means, but she lies in bed while I get dressed to go back to work and says in her English: "What will you do with your bonus this year? Why not take me to La Tour d'Argent for lunch? Why not? With such a handsome bonus as you must get."

When I have visitors from the States, I let them believe I am not fully employed—that way they have something to talk about on their flight back. I have never told my sister exactly what I do; however, I once wrote my mother (after she had been "put away") that I was living in our house in Kansas City where I was employed by an insurance company. I went on to write that I was tending to the privet and keeping the house clean and neat for her return.

I had hoped the letter would give her some comfort (and perhaps it did), but somehow my sister found out (probably from the friend I used to post the letter from Kansas City) and wrote me saying that it was a "terrible and unchristian lie" I had told my mother.

I walk to work, which is in the 15th. And back. My café for

weekday evenings is Balzar or Café St. Germain. I take lunch with my colleagues at Le Bistrot d'André with its walls populated by pictures of Deux Chevaux. I take friends who are visiting from America to La Closerie des Lilas so they can say they've been there, and I show them the statue of Marshal Ney and give them a Xerox of Hemingway's passage about Marshal Ney so they know where they have been. I meet my lovers at La Marlotte, where we take the side room instead of the front one, even though the front one is thought to be better. My favorite museums are the Delacroix, the Maison de Victor Hugo, and, perhaps predictably, the Musée Carnavalet. Saturdays, I watch the men play *boules* on Place Dauphine (where I also used to watch Yves Montand watch the men play *boules*). I watch the river from the Pont des Arts. Of course.

When I walk, I look up, only ahead when necessary, seldom at the sidewalk itself. I remember Emma Bovary running her finger along the streets on a map of Paris and wishing she were there— more to get away from Flaubert, I suspect, than from Charles. But as I am the author of myself, every Sunday about one o'clock, I write myself across the Pont Neuf to take a long Italian lunch at Il Delfino. The Prosecco is always cold and crisp. The Barolo firm. The room one step down.

Thus I turn the pages of my life where every day I read it along a breadth of streets and bridges heading roughly in the direction in which I am going. Always what I have seen before delights me more than what, if I happen to get out of my way, I notice for the first time. It is as if the familiar in Paris is new, and the new is, well: *l'étranger*. Over the years, the city has created in me a curious xenophobia: I wonder what it portends. Will I only reread old novels? Watch only old movies? Look at Uccello and Bonnard endlessly? Attend only concerts where they play Corelli? Rewrite the previous pages of my "Résolution" instead of typing fresh ones? Recreate my old rendezvous with old lovers (will they have me?), instead of making new ones in new cafés? *Tant pis*, as my Uncle

Bert might have said (turning the French *pis* into a Texas piss). But maybe not. The streets I revisit still smile on me with the bloom of novelty.

It was to this Paris, to this life of mine, and mine alone, to this singular and tawny and warm October, to this garret above my apartment, that there came two days ago a letter from my sister telling me that our mother has died.

Monday

Summer was short that first year in the Dordogne. By September and school and *vendange*, the weather was cool enough so that my uncle was warming the mornings with a kindling fire in the small fireplace at the east end of the apartment. Later, he would light the *butano*—but only in the mornings and evenings. Otherwise "*Le Train Omnibus*," as he called our home, was cold by day and night. There were times from November through March when, if the sun was bright and there was no wind, it was warmer outside the apartment than inside. I remember more than once putting on my coat to go up the stairs after school.

The food of that winter was *soupe éternelle*, complemented on random nights by confits, various pâtés, and French and Dutch cheeses—all stored along the edges of our windowsills when the weather was cool.

For lunch (I walked home as all the children did), we'd have what Uncle Bert called "*gros croque monsieur*," the recipe for which (as I once published in La Résolution) is as follows: four or five slices of stale bread slathered with olive oil and mustard and doused with *Herbes de Provence*. Top the bread with thin slices of onion (shallots may be substituted if you've recently traded for them at the market), then thin slices of tomatoes, cuts of *chèvre* that is getting more than a little old and thus hard—and thus easy to slice thinly. More *Herbes de Provence*. (Notice the absence of ham.) Put under a broiler (the one we had was part of a very dangerous small propane oven that would from time to time burst into flames and cremate whatever was in it, including not a few *gros croque monsieurs*, and once a *confit de canard* that had come our way) until the cheese melts its way down and around the tomatoes. Serve with cool Montravel Moelleux wine, giving a watered tumbler to any growing Kansas boy who happens to be living with you in your train station. Boy returns to school with a slight buzz about him. Consider it practice for future Paris lunches.

"*A gros croque monsieur* is made *gros* by slivers of layers and layers of slivers of layers," Uncle Bert would say, as he'd slice his ingredients as thinly as possible. He pronounced the *gros* as *gross*, giving it what he thought was its essential French meaning by drawing it out: *grooooss*, and then he'd pat his belly with the same open palms that he'd wave above his head.

"It's the way I'm made. A sliver of confit, a lump of *pain au chocolat*, a sliver of *pâté de duck*. A slice of *pâté d'amande. C'est moi.* They have a saying in France: Never trust a fat man not made of layers because he hasn't lived. No, he hasn't. Not enough to know you don't feed an ugly pig the staff of life. Or that when the bread is stale, the tomato must be ripe, he would say and pat his stomach. Nobody could make *grooooss croque monsieurs* like my Uncle Bert.

As to our other meals, I remember the cupboards and the windowsills of the train station going down to bare over time, and then all of a sudden they were full again. Not with cans and packaged goods as we had in Kansas City, but with small boxes and paper bags and glass jars. Out of these my uncle assembled dinner. Breakfast year-round was *pain au raisin* or *pain au chocolat* or croissants, bought at a discount in the afternoon in the bakery-cum-newsstand that is still there—at least the newsstand must still be there because they take our magazine.

Some nights we had boiled black sausages over rice. Sometimes freshly butchered duck or chicken. Once we had foie gras, and along with it my uncle drank a sweet white wine that I suppose was made by one of the peasants with whom he did business. He let me have a sip. With each taste of his foie gras, my uncle would say: "*C'est une petite sotte. C'est une petite sotte.*" By then I had learned enough French to wonder if he had the goose in mind or if it was a toast to someone I never came to know.

Or maybe I did.

Looking back, I see that Uncle Bert must have been some kind of low-grade black-market trader. I can't remember if I thought that at the time, but I probably did in the way children understand adults for what they are—and then it is settled. Not judged, just settled. In any case, when you are young it is never clear how the adults with whom you live support themselves. And money was not so much in the news those days. I learned later my uncle received a check each month from my father to pay for my expenses, but he never cashed them and it was on that balance—discovered by my Oklahoma grandmother years later—that my sister and I went to college. As for when I was living with him, I always had a few francs in my pocket; I never went without or was hungry. Cold sometimes but not hungry, nor wanting much of anything money could buy. I was privileged in that way. It is my inheritance.

You get used to a different life rather quickly when you are young, at least I did; in fact, my fifth grade Hickory Grove girlfriend and my fifth grade Hickory Grove teacher and my baseball glove aside, living with Uncle Bert in France above a train station in the middle of wine-and-*confit de canard* country seemed not so much a change as continuation. Baseball gloves and soccer balls are pretty much the same thing to young boys. Young boys and girls are pretty much the same thing to one another.

And I liked my uncle. Not in the same way as I saluted my father. But I liked being with my uncle. I liked helping him with his "work."

And unlike my father, my uncle needed help. With each translation I made for him I moved up a notch in my age toward his.

In the mornings between the time I got up and the time I got dressed my uncle would put out the pastries he had bought the previous evening. Before I left for school, there were questions to be answered and a routine to be followed: Had I brushed my teeth? Had my "system" worked? How had I slept? Any bad dreams? He made sure I had my schoolbooks. He checked on my lessons. And more than once he visited the school and talked to my teacher, who, as luck would have it, spoke better English than my uncle's French. I was doing fine, she said: With her help I would develop a splendid accent in the Parisian style. Wouldn't I like to live in Paris someday, she asked me in French.

"What'd she say," asked my uncle. "I'm bum of hearing."

"If I wanted to live in Paris someday," I said.

"*May we,*" said my uncle. "*Tray Bone. Been sewer. May we. Toot sweet.*" My teacher and I smiled. "That way," my uncle said, "he can come to Lamothe and visit me." It was our fate that I never did.

Monday Evening

I have read over what I have written so far in this diary, and in order to be honest with the innocent blank sheets of paper rolling through my Splendid 33, I need to confess that I have not always been true to the facts about some essentials:

My grandmother lived in Texas, not Oklahoma. My mother *did* wave goodbye when I left for New York with my father, but not very directly, nor forcefully. I cannot see the bird market on Quai du Louvre, but I know it is there and I imagine it. I did not see Barbra Streisand at La Marlotte, as I was going to write when I mentioned the restaurant, but at Balzar, shortly after the café was written up in the *Herald Tribune*. I don't much care for Corelli, and therefore would never attend a concert where his music is played. Better

Satie. I do like Uccello. I thought about writing a scene where I spoke with Yves Montand, but I did not, and I did not.

There are other details I have also altered in this transcription from life to text. Why I can't confess them just now, I don't know. Perhaps it is a matter of not wanting to waste honesty on mere facts. Montaigne says: "The man who writes...while sitting in torn breeches should first mend his breeches." Is this what I am doing? What does a blank sheet of paper know? Out to lunch with a lover. This is true.

Tuesday

Uncle Bert's "business" was with the local markets: Sainte-Foy on Saturdays; Castillon on Mondays; Villefranche on Wednesdays. Others on other days. During the school year my uncle would take me to the Saturday market in Sainte-Foy-la-Grande about twenty kilometers toward Bergerac. Even though it was after the war and many of the markets in our area were impoverished, often with not a dozen eggs, nor more than a chicken or two for sale at this stand or that, the one at Sainte-Foy seemed rich—or at least it seemed so to me. I believe it still exists.

By Friday night, the Deux Chevaux (out of which my uncle had taken the back seat and put it into the apartment, where it served as a couch) would be loaded with brown cardboard boxes of uniform size that I know now had been used as wine cartons by the less expensive châteaux who sold their *vin de pays* to the hotels and restaurants in the area. Each carton had the corners of its top tucked into one another to keep it closed. Sometimes these boxes were heavy; sometimes not so heavy. Sometimes I could hear the sound of bottles clinking. Sometimes I could smell food. At times, there was something alive in them. Often I smelled tobacco and I would as well notice that the peasants with whom my uncle dealt smoked American cigarettes. Sometimes in addition to the wine cartons there were boxes with U.S. military markings on them.

"Don't open them now, son," my uncle would say. "I've got them all tucked down *toot sweet* and packed *tray bone.* Just so."

Usually there were ten to a dozen of these boxes and, on some occasions, a few brown paper bags as well. Whatever was in them, they weighed down the back of the Deux Chevaux so that the nose of it pointed more up than down. It was as if my uncle had taken to walking like my father: shoulders back, head high.

At Sainte-Foy it was my job to help my uncle carry the cartons to various tables the peasants had set up along the streets, and—as my French improved—to do the translating. If a box was too heavy for me and my uncle had to carry it, I'd clear the way—especially if we were late and the streets were already filling up. When we arrived at the appointed table, Uncle Bert would greet—and be greeted by—this man or that man, sometimes waving their hands at him palms out: *Peasants tous.*

"*Ça va! Oui. Ça va. D'accord. Oui. Bon. Tant pis. Oui. Très mal,*" Uncle Bert would say, half Texas cattleman, half a character out of Shaw. (And another half Walter Brennan, now that I think back on it.)

My uncle could spread these exchanges out with nods and shrugs for two to three minutes, at the end of which he would first pry back the flaps of the box to see if it was the right one for this particular table and, seeing it was, start up again: "*Beaucoup. Bon. Oui. D'accord. À demain. Après déjeuner. Oui. D'accord. Mais oui.*"

When his business was done (tallies made, accounts settled), my uncle and the peasant would say goodbye by brushing the backs of each other's hands in the custom of that country, after which we would return to the Deux Chevaux to get yet another box; then back to another table to repeat the process. *Mais oui.*

Sometimes Uncle Bert and the peasant with whom he was dealing would step away from the table; and more than once I'd see money change hands in a fold of old francs: peasant to uncle, uncle to peasant, all of it done while the men faced the wall of whatever building ran behind the table, as if they were—as Uncle Bert put it—"making water." Only "making water" by men in the Dordogne in those days was more public than exchanging money.

Our business was usually over by ten and afterward my uncle would take a *grand crème* in the Orange Café, a small establishment a street east of the main square. From there we could see twenty or so tables and stalls of the market itself: Dutch cheese sold at one; *chèvre* and sheep cheese at another; Pyrenees cheese at yet another. A girl about my age guarded a few cages of rabbits and some live chickens bundled together by twine at their feet. Every once in a while she'd pick up the chickens—usually two or three of them together—and hold them aloft, not speaking a word, but just letting the chickens flap and squawk, as if to show they were alive and healthy. I never saw anybody buy her chickens. She never looked at me. Or at anyone directly. She had tiny, delicate ears, and her ears were the first feature of a woman I remember admiring.

There was also on that street a man with a foot-pedal grindstone who sharpened knives and sickles and shears. I liked the smell of the grinding metal. Another man in a large black beret wove baskets while selling what he had woven the previous week. There was an Englishman who sold mohair scarves and sweaters and socks, and that winter my uncle bought me a pair of black mohair socks to keep my feet warm. I wonder what has become of them. He also bought me a dark red scarf. I know what has become of that.

In other parts of the market were fishmongers and sausage sellers. One man sold oysters. There were families my father would have called truck farmers had they been in Kansas. They had beans and beats; tomatoes and potatoes; turnips and onions. In the late summer they had wild blackberries; in the fall they had mushrooms; and, if you knew the right table and who to ask (and how to ask), you could get truffles. My uncle could get truffles.

From one table you could buy very old Armagnac, from another foie gras. Many of the tables that sold farm produce sold bottles of wine as well; some had labels and dates, others did not. One man sold wine out of a barrel from the back of a cart that he pulled into town with a donkey; you could fill your own bottles or jugs, which is what my uncle did. A very fat woman who always wore the same yellow dress sold huge sunflowers well into the fall. Some Saturdays my uncle would buy a bunch as we walked out of the market.

In those days you could also buy *eau de vie*, a clear *digestif* made from plums or pears, among other fruits. One Saturday the *eau de vie* maker himself arrived towing what looked like a small steam engine behind a tractor. It chugged and puffed, and puffed and chugged, and then finally out of funnels in the bottom came the drippings of the *eau de vie* itself. You could take your bottle, fill it, pay him a few francs, and the *eau de vie* was yours. In winter it was my uncle's favorite drink: "my pharmacy," he called it.

"Give me age. It is my fate. Give me my pharmacy to help me with my fate." If he drank more than two glasses, he'd either repeat the French sayings he had put to memory or quote one of his botched aphorisms; if he drank more than three glasses he'd look into the bottom of his glass and say something I never understood, in what language I did not know.

Everywhere in Sainte-Foy there were live animals for sale: chickens and quails and ducks and rabbits, along with litters of kittens to be given away, and puppies as well. One man always brought a goat to the market and hung a sign around its neck of how many francs he wanted for the animal. The goat was old, had one horn, and was blind. Week after week there were no buyers, even though in late August the price around the goat's neck went down. Then one winter Saturday the goat was not there, although the peasant was, and because he was a peasant with whom my uncle did business, I often wanted to ask about the goat, but out of some kind of fear that had no name to me then, but does now, I did not. I had named the goat Yogi.

Just as we'd settle into the Orange Café, Uncle Bert would give me a few francs with instructions to buy us four ("*quatre*" he would say, pronouncing the *re*) *Jésuites aux amandes* from a pleasant-faced, black-haired woman whose pastry table was near the church on the main square. We'd have one of these each for ourselves over coffee (yes, I drank coffee), saving the second round of pastry for Sunday morning, a special day at *Le Train Omnibus* in other ways as well.

But every so often, I was instructed to buy five ("say '*sink*,'" my uncle would say, "'*sink*,' just like what you put dishes in.") *Jésuites aux amandes*. When I would do this, the woman selling them by the church would smile shyly, her face would deepen in color, and she would nod and then wrap up an additional pastry. *Sink Jésuites aux amandes* cost no more, I noticed, than four *Jésuites aux amandes*. However, once, when I was sent to buy five pastries, the woman frowned and looked down and would only sell me four—even though there was a full tray of them. My uncle frowned as well when I told him what had happened.

"Oh well," he said. "Tomorrow's another *ah-jur-dwee*." What comes around goes around. Throw your fish upon the water even if it floats belly up. *Tant piss*." That Saturday Uncle Bert did not buy sunflowers.

Tuesday Afternoon

I see that while I still have corrections of fact to make, more importantly I must do what we editors call "fleshing out"—as if writing were tucking the blood factory of veins and arteries and muscles and fat in and around the skeleton of life. Such metaphors are why writers like myself distrust editors like myself.

Still, because these sheets of paper are both my only audience and my only subject, I need to make myself and my oeuvre about the same size, if not composed of the same "truth." We three (me, my paper, and myself on my paper) are becoming a *ménage à trois* and we must learn to get along in tight quarters, even if there are moments (whole paragraphs of them) when I realize that the *moi* in our mutual *récit* is more sophisticated than the me who is typing it. But that is another problem. First, more flesh:

Back in Kansas City that summer before my father flew me to New York, neither my sister nor I went to our respective new homes very easily. For my part, when our mother told us our fate, my imagination crashed. At that age you don't fear the unknown. Or at least I didn't. I feared what I knew I would lose. The balsa wood model airplane of my father's Corsair that I was building in the basement. My bubble-gum baseball-card collection. The girl who told my fifth grade teacher she "liked me." My fifth grade teacher who told me. My baseball glove. The game of "catch" my father and I played. All of it vanished to a sheet of blankness while our mother trembled. And then cried. My sister ran to her room: I ran away.

I went out the back door with nothing but an intention of fleeing and hiding. In fact, I got a good deal farther than the Mission, Kansas, Crown drugstore, where, in a Norman Rockwell painting, the owner would have treated me to a cherry limeade and driven me home. I went beyond that frame into pastures that still surrounded—at some distance to be sure—the burgeoning suburb where we lived.

A survivalist of sorts I turned out to be. I was two days and one night on the road. I stole some Oh Henry! candy bars and potato chips from the Ben Franklin just down the street from the drugstore. I lifted two warm Cokes from the case sitting next to the Coke machine in the Texaco filling station on Johnson Drive where my father had his oil changed and where, while we'd wait, he'd buy me a cold one for a nickel. I cut across backyards until I hit farmers' fields. I spent the night in an abandoned barn that had, among other things, boxes of old 78 records. I spent the next morning sailing the records out over the barnyard and watching the graceful path of their flight, betting with myself if they would break or not. My mother and a neighbor retrieved me later that day heading west: lighting out for the territories.

Hauled home, I continued my rebellion by not talking. I'd write only notes. No: I didn't care if my father found me not talking. No: I never wanted to talk to anyone ever again: Ever. (I date my use of the colon as a matter of prose style from this period of my life). No: I was not hungry, and I would not eat my peas: Never. No: *Jamais*.

My sister cried. My mother had an attack of "nerves," and for a while she was "confined" and we were taken care of by our Texas grandmother, who had arrived a week or so before. My father arrived a week later, probably as quickly as possible after he learned of the crisis. I remember he got there in the evening, after it was assumed I was asleep. He came in, sat down at the foot of my bed, and seeing I was awake, said that everything would be fine in the morning. We'd play a game of catch. We'd finish the model airplane. He had a new one of his new plane. I could tell him all about where I had gone, and he would tell me all about the Panther he was flying. He squeezed my big toe, and I went to sleep. I dreamt of food.

I see there is a wistful quality to all this as I read it over, as if a squirm of nostalgia has been lowered over these events and changed the light in which they are cast. I especially like that scene where I am tossing old records, precursors to Frisbees, out over the farmyard, more of them *not* breaking—as it turned out—than breaking. But the charm of it all was not present when I lived through it; nor was that charm there anytime in my memory of these events before just now. An unavoidable disparity of life, I suppose. There must be many.

Wednesday

Uncle Bert's apartment was intended for the stationmaster, a rail of a man about my uncle's age. However, through some complicated, and no doubt dubious, arrangement, my uncle had bartered for the rooms, while the stationmaster had moved himself in with his family just across the highway and down by the river. All this had been accomplished well before I got there; indeed, it had probably been done shortly after my uncle had arrived in the south of France. I never really knew. What I did know was that the stationmaster and I would sometimes cross paths on schooldays, as he came to open up the station for the first morning train and I headed for my first class. I would nod; the stationmaster would not. This was our routine. In some way his reticence reminded me of my mother, and so one day I asked my uncle about her.

"She's fine," he said, and then, after a pause, and after considering me in the fading light of the afternoon, "She's better. She's much better."

"Has she been sick?" I asked. I guess I didn't know if having "nerves" was the same as being sick. I am struck on remembering these events at how shy I was in raising these questions. I was, for example, too shy to ask about my father at all, although he had been writing me, his mail always sporting various military codes and insignias, so that each letter seemed to be wearing its own uniform. Perhaps it seemed to me a violation of his final salute and our handshake to inquire after him with anybody but himself. It was our secret bond. My mother was a different matter.

"Yes," said Uncle Bert. "But she is better now. And she will come and see you."

"Come here?" I asked.

"Yes," said my uncle. "But you should write her. Maybe toss in a little of the French you are learning. *Tout de suite. Aujourd'hui.* That kind of thing. *Très bon. Où se trouve. Mais oui. Vin rouge.* I have her address."

"Will my father come?" I asked. Uncle Bert paused before he answered. It was getting time for the early evening train from Libourne to pass through: the one that would not stop at Lamothe, but go on, an express of sorts, to Sainte-Foy.

"*Put tet.*"

"Perhaps?" I had understood from my father that our separation would be firm and long, and would only end when he came back from Korea and I came back from France. It was as if the two of us were going overseas to do our respective duties, and when that was over we'd return to Kansas City and play catch and tell each other the stories of our adventures. The idea that he might come to see me in France seemed wrong: not part of the flight path. My mother might come and see me. But not my father: precisely because he had not told me so. And if you flew the kind of planes my father flew, and wore the kind of hat he wore, and put your thumbs up in the air to say goodbye to your son, you were the kind of father who knew where you were going.

I remember looking carefully at my uncle. I remember it was the first time I had ever "studied" an adult in my life. When you are young you don't quite know what you are looking at when you look into the faces of those a great deal older than yourself. You probably don't even know to look. But look I did, and even now I cannot name who was in my uncle's face. After a moment he turned and stared out the window as if trying to hear the train that was soon to come down the tracks. *Peut-être*, he said, pronouncing it correctly this time.

Then I heard the train. First, the whistle as it passed the crossing at Raffin, then the train itself. And then, before it got to us, you could feel its movement coming into the apartment from the ground up. There was a red coffee cup and a saucer that my uncle used only on Sundays for coffee with his *Jésuite aux amandes*. The rest of the time he kept it on a shelf with books and letters. When the train crossed the road by the wine cooperative, the cup would start rattling in its saucer, and it would not stop until the train passed the far end of Lamothe on its way to Montcaret, Saint-Antoine, and Sainte-Foy.

As the train passed on this particular evening, my uncle turned his head to look at the cup. He waited for the vibrations you could feel in the apartment to stop. He waited for the sound of the train itself to fade down by Montcaret. And when it was again mostly silent, he waited beyond that. And then, speaking less to me than to himself, he said the only complete French sentence I ever heard him utter: "*Nous ne dirons jamais l'essentiel même quand nous en avons la prétention.*" He'd pause between each word so that they were like cards laid out on a table, and while his accent was not improved because of the success of his memorization, his pronunciation was. At the end, he paused again. For a moment I thought he was about to repeat himself, as sometimes he would when he'd have a third *eau de vie*, but he did not. Instead he got up and went into our kitchen to light the butane burner and start our dinner.

It would be early in the following summer, arriving by the afternoon local Libourne-to-Sainte-Foy-to-Sarlat train, that my mother would come to see me. She would come to see me about my father. She would not be better. It would be my fate.

Thursday

There was an owl that lived in the attic above the train station, and my uncle said I could name him, and so I called him Hooter. Hooter would fly out about sundown and head east down the train tracks toward the cemetery into the darkness. Sometimes in the morning I could hear him return, and once I was looking out the window when I saw Hooter bank up and into the hole that led to the attic.

In the summer and fall—or even in the winter and spring when it was warm enough—my uncle and I would sit on the benches that lined the walls outside of the train station and watch for

Hooter to leave. My uncle would measure his one-a-day glass of *eau de vie* against the impending flight of the owl, taking a sip here and then another until Hooter flew, and then Uncle Bert would tilt off his drink. *La Blanche Dame*, my uncle would say of Hooter. I had learned in school that in French colors went behind the nouns they modified, but even though I was my uncle's translator, for some reason I decided not to be his teacher. Maybe it was our bond. *La Blanche Dame* he would say again just when Hooter could no longer be seen. And then we would go back inside and my uncle would begin dinner.

There was as well some other animal that lived in the train station's attic with Hooter because at night we could hear it running back and forth. To myself I named it Bête Noire, because the idiom had struck me as mysterious when I learned it in school. Bête Noire, I remember my teacher saying: it means more than it means. And then she asked me if I understood. *Comprenez-vous? Oui, madame.* I did not.

We also had a cat, a fat white one that my uncle had named Balzac. The families up and down the block just opposite the train station fed Balzac by bringing bones and cheese rinds and other table scraps to a dish we kept just under the roof before you went into the train station itself. Sometimes the stationmaster would bring a mouse that had been caught overnight in a trap set in his office. Balzac would growl and hiss, and while he would eat table scraps from his dish, he would take a dead mouse away. Balzac, my uncle said, was a writer who wore white and had many girlfriends.

In the weeks before Christmas my uncle and I would drive into the hills behind Lamothe and look for the mistletoe that grew in the trees, with the idea of making a little money from the English families who spent the holidays in the Dordogne. Mistletoe was also our Christmas gift to his customers at the markets and his friends in the village, and although they accepted it, I later learned they thought mistletoe more a nuisance in the woods than something prized: They were glad the English in Bordeaux and in the nearby villages were pleased to have it. Even pay for it. When I made a gift of an especially fine bunch to my teacher, she at first frowned, then quickly smiled. *Merci.*

"Mistletoe *pour tous les amis du monde*," Uncle Bert would say, taking his hands off the steering wheel of the 2-CV as we went along and waving them, palms out, now inside the car because it was too cold to roll back the roof. "*Les amis du monde.*"

Uncle Bert had a small ladder to climb up to the lower branches of the trees with an army knife and hack off the mistletoe. My job was to hold the ladder. I remember my uncle saying that what he needed was his Browning Gallery Gun, a .22 he had left in Texas, so he could shoot the mistletoe out of the topmost branches, where it had grown into quite large bunches. Maybe when I went back to America I could arrange for his gun to be sent over. It was the kind you could "disassemble" so it might not be difficult to ship.

"*Toot sweet* I'd shoot myself a *groooosse* bunch. *May we*," my uncle said, aiming his imaginary rifle into the trees and going whap! whap! "That would show them that the best carpenters make the fewest chips. *Mais oui. Comprenenz-vous*?"

"*D'accord*," I said.

"*D'accord!*" he said. "Well, aren't we learning a little French. Don't tell them back in Kansas you got it from your uncle. I was always the hat rack with a head for only the hat when it came to your mother's family. Whap! Whap! The thief always thinks his pants are up in arms. Or maybe it's that his *chapeau* is on fire." And here my uncle tapped his beret and plopped the ladder against a tree. "Never feed an ugly pig the staff of life."

In spring, my uncle's scheme for making money was to paint fences and wooden gates with what he called *noir* oil. Black oil was the crankcase oil from trucks and automobiles, and even though the Dordogne was still very frugal from the war, and thus most people would do such work themselves, there were enough professional people from Bordeaux and Paris and other cities who had family châteaux in our department to be customers of my uncle. For a doctor from Paris or Lyon he'd change their oil. For a lawyer from Bordeaux or Limoges he'd paint their gate with the oil from the doctor from Paris. I liked the smell of the black oil in the same way I liked the smell of the knife sharpener in Sainte-Foy. It was the smell of something being done. Not exactly madeleines, but each to the smells of our own lost time.

"Best to dig fence posts and *noir* oil fences in the spring," my uncle would say as the two of us would brush away. "That way the ground is soft, and the oil soaks into the wood because its pores are open. And it is better to use hot oil than cold. Right out of the crankcase. Mix it with a little fuel oil and that way it will brush on better. Use everything up in the world, but not *tout suite*, so what comes around has time to go around and drop a few seeds along the way. That's very French. We need a little French in everything we do. That way you get some movement in the monkey."

This latter aphorism (a once-a-day favorite of Uncle Bert's) I use to this day around the office as all-purpose sarcasm when there is yet another slitting of throats in Algeria, a bomb blast in Northern Ireland—or when some religious-minded school board in America prohibits the teaching of evolution: There is some movement in the monkey, I'd say, translating my uncle's routine optimism to my routine irony in the flash of an American generation. No doubt it happens in the best of families.

"And don't own anything if you can help it," Uncle Bert would say, usually in front of a large house where we'd be working, or from underneath an expensive car whose oil we were changing. I remember there was not a hint of envy (much less irony) in how he said it. More like breathing than talking. Don't own anything if you can help it. *Dénuement*: A stripping of life to its sensory essentials, if I remember my Gide correctly. I wonder if it leads to *La Résolu-tion*, or keeps us from it.

Thursday Evening

Through my seat's window I could see my father standing on the tarmac while the engines cranked up, and I could see that he could see me as well. He waved. I waved back. As the plane turned, the prop-wash caused my father to lean into the wind and hold his hat, one hand on the top, the other on the bill. It was the last time I saw him.

It has been five days since I first typed this. I typed it again just to make sure. Of what?

Friday

A few years ago I received the following letter from one M. Roget of Saint-Michel-de-Montaigne, the village in the hills just above where my uncle and I lived. The translation is mine.

> Your grandfather [*sic*] died two days before now and we will bury him as he wished in the cemetery in Lamothe-Montravel. There are matters of his estate that must be settled and you should come to Castillon to do so. His death was natural. If you do not wish to come to Castillon to attend to the matters of the estate, perhaps they can be arranged by an advocate. There is a bank account. There are cartons with your name on them in his Deux Chevaux which he put there when he knew he was to die and went to the hospital to do so. I hope I have written you at the correct address.

I got the letter about the same time that one of my lovers stopped seeing me, although to this day I don't know why. She simply did not show up at the appointed time at our usual restaurant. I thought of calling her at her office, but decided against it. As far as I know, she was not angry with me, and had not seen me with another woman (not that she would care). As she was young and had a husband (an American, although she herself was French), perhaps she started a family. Perhaps she was found out—or thought she might be. I used to buy us sunflowers from a vendor just outside the restaurant where we'd meet and then take them back to the apartment, where they'd last a few days on their own. The vendor is still there.

After I got the letter from M. Roget, I asked our magazine's lawyer if he would handle my uncle's estate for me. He agreed and also agreed to bring back the boxes from Uncle Bert's car. I asked him not to sell the car, but if it had been willed to me, to make arrangements with someone in Lamothe-Montravel to garage it—and that he has done. I understand it is in a small barn of the farmhouse just east of the cemetery, which itself is just east of the train station. I send a yearly check for its storage and I notice that it is cashed immediately.

This year I got a letter saying there was an offer to buy the car, but I have not responded. In the boxes our lawyer brought back there was dried mistletoe, an American .22 rifle (the kind that can be broken down by unscrewing the barrel), clothes of mine, a red coffee cup, schoolbooks, and dishes. There were other items as well. I was going to tell my mistress about the contents of the box the day she did not meet me at the café as planned. No, I was not going to do that. I wonder if she has had a child and it is mine. Our lawyer is a woman, not a man.

On the flight over from New York to Paris, the captain invited me to come into the cockpit, and then the navigator in turn put me up into his dome, from which I could see the stars in the sky above us as we flew. I wondered if the stars I saw at home in Kansas were in the same place in the sky as the ones I was now seeing, and I wondered if they would be in the same place when I got to France. Sitting in the navigator's dome I thought I would ask these questions of the navigator or the captain when I climbed down, but then I thought I'd save the question for my father. Nothing in this paragraph is false.

It was just before my mother came to see me that I received the following letter from my father: it was the only one to me that he typed (the capital "B" and the small "r" were broken, while the small "p" would always rise above the line, and now and then there was an extra space between the words, which I took to be the effect of a ship at sea); it was the last letter from him I ever opened.

I have left my father's French just as he wrote it, but on the letter itself I can see my youthful editing: a straight line drawn through my father's mistakes and my corrections, printed in a neat, almost typewriter hand, above it. I remember when I did this I pretended that while the letter might have come from my father, it was my uncle's French I was correcting. When you are young you can pretend to yourself in many ways.

Dear *Fils*,

That is French for "son," but no doubt your French is very good by now. Mine is *trés* poor and no one among the officers is any better. We are at *le mar* again and it will not be long before we will make some sorties. In the meantime we are making practice takeoffs and landings. My Panther plane is a very good one, and I have had a picture of me taken standing in front of it for you so you can paint your model to look just like it when we both get back to Kansas City. I will *assistee vous* in that job when I return from my tour of duty. Write your *votre mare* as I think it will do her *tres bonne* to hear from you. She has been *tres mal* since we both left, and when we get back we both must stay put (no running away for you, no war for me) to help her get better. That is love. I will *ecrive* again when I send the picture of me and my plane.

Votre Pere

Saturday Strobe-Light Disco Starry Night

The beauty of Paris is that it becomes more and more of your life as you go along. It is as if, when you no longer want your life to be the sum of the past multiplied by the present, the city slips inside you and you walk on: more Paris than you. Instead of a Kansas Crown drugstore there is a mime dressed as Aphrodite still as a statue, each evening in July, until she earns enough francs for a small trip to Spain. For someone like myself, this kind of Paris is a great advantage. Each day, I shrink and grow. It is a way to live without resolve.

I never saw my uncle again after I left the Dordogne. He must have lived on in his singular fashion with his creaky and tilted Deux Chevaux and his creaky and tilted French, but I never knew the circumstances. Once, years later, after I had graduated from college and left home for good, he wrote me a letter, a letter that marched through two postal systems and many time zones all the way to Kansas City and then back to France to find me here in Paris: in this small room above my apartment. I have never opened it. It sits on a bookshelf a few feet from where I sit. By now it is twenty years old and the flap on the envelope has become unglued and the corners are crumbling. I can see the letter itself, but not the text.

I also have a letter from my father that he wrote aboard his aircraft carrier a few days before he died. It was waiting for me when my mother brought me back to Kansas City. I can tell by its heft there is a picture in it. It, too, sits on my bookshelf, a row of French books from Stendhal to Gide to Mauriac to Camus to Montaigne to Balzac and my uncle keeping it company.

Have I said (to myself) that part of my college education—and that of my sister's as well—was paid for by my uncle via my father? Have I said that he is the one who, along with the insurance money from my father's death, supported my mother in and out of the "mental" hospital all these years? Have I written about being in the cockpit of the plane and looking at the stars, or is that yet to be done? Am I losing track of both the facts and the fiction of my life? I read somewhere that a powerful memory usually goes with weak judgment.

It's not that memory plays tricks on you (as I am sure mine does), but that sometimes it doesn't. You remember all too well. I am at an age where I am beginning to have too much memory. I feel the heft and clutter of it, as if I'm an apartment too full of possessions. My life is stuffed not with *objets de luxe* but with the less-than-obscure objects of desire from the unaccountable (perhaps "accountable," now that I think of it) acquisitiveness of my mind. I suppose it is the great harvest I myself desired.

And while there are days when I wonder how I got it all up the five flights of the decades of my life, there are more days when I wonder why I bothered. On those days I'd rather have money to count than memories in the brain bank. A treasury bond doesn't have much emotion attached to it, much less extraneous detail—factual or fictional—that has to be rearranged to fit into bookshelves. A Paris apartment with a Midwestern American youth stored in a garret filled with photographs of old airplanes and two baseball gloves, a red mohair scarf, and a red coffee cup is ripe with *memento mori*. It is only here, one flight up, where I achieve something like *dénuement*—and avoid denouement—as if life were but the last page in a general-interest magazine. *Fin.*

Confessions: First: My fascination with the colon was not youthful but recent: I have been reading Dickens: *A murky red and yellow sky, and a rising mist from the Seine, denoted the approach of dark-ness: It was almost dark when they arrived at the Bank.* Second: "Flowing beer gathers no foam" was not an expression of my uncle's but of Balzac's. Third: There is something my mother is going to say in a few pages that I was planning to claim I did not hear. Fourth: The Moroccan roasting chestnuts below my window is a young woman, and I don't nod to her or wave as I thought of writing when I had cast her as an old man. Fifth: That is not a colon in the Dickens quoted above, although in him they flourish everywhere.

But Yogi, the girl with the chickens and the tiny ears, the woman with the sunflowers, the red cup, the records that I flung out over the Kansas pasture, the letter from my father to me in which I corrected my uncle's French, my Algerian lover, *grooooose croque monsieurs*, my dead mother, and *too la monde* there is herein, above and below, and flying out down the tracks at nightfall, or in the attic above: all of it is true, or getting to be true *toot sweet*. Oh, yes it is: Including:

Uncle Bert never said: "We don't talk about the essentials, especially when we pretend to." François Mauriac did, as I learned a few weeks ago when I edited an article for our magazine on the opening of his house as a museum not far from Lamothe. The truth is I could not hear what my uncle said because he had turned away from me as the train was coming through. All these years what I did not know had been said has been a *bête noire* in my movable attic. To scare it off I have put many different sentences into my uncle's mouth for what I could not hear while the red cup rattled and the train went by. Those sentences, spoken in both English and French over the years, I have sometimes blurted out at curious moments: Once, during a pause in a staff meeting, I found myself saying *I am your father's keeper*. And another time, having fallen asleep in my garret, I woke myself by saying *"Ecrasez l'infâme!"*

Also, when walking down rue Dauphine to Sunday lunch I said out loud that *everything would be fine in the morning*. That we'd play a game of catch. And here I tossed an imaginary baseball onto Pont Neuf, all this to, I suspect, the amazement of an American couple heading my way, the man wearing—as coincidence would have it—a t-shirt whose front proclaimed: "Toto...I don't think we're in Kansas anymore" down the left-hand side, while a silhouette of a small dog barking at a black-stockinged Toulouse-Lautrec dancer was on the right. The woman looked at me with some concern as we passed.

One night, after the last train had gone through, and my uncle thought I had fallen asleep but in fact I was looking out the window of the train station, I saw him walking the rails. It was cold and had been cold and was going to be cold. There was something of a moon, but it was not quite full. There were stars.

At first I did not know what I saw. Then I did. My uncle was balancing himself on the outside rail and walking it west toward Libourne. After a while he was out of sight. Then he came back into view on the inside track, first as something moving in the shadows, then as something stepping on the gleam of the moonlight on the rails. Sometimes both his arms were held out, sometimes not. Once, coming back, when he almost fell, he put the right arm out only and held himself there for a moment, and then started up again, this time coming all the way to the platform without the aid of either arm outstretched. He did not come into the apartment right away, but as he did I could hear that he was talking to himself, and I could not understand what he was saying.

Sunday

When my mother arrived in Lamothe-Montravel she told me my father had "perished" when his plane had been "lost" over North Korea. Then much later that night I awoke to hear my mother and my uncle talking about the "wisdom" of telling me what they had not told my father. They decided it was not "wise" to tell me; however, my uncle thought it would be "wise" for me to stay with him and that he could raise me "*comme le fils.*" That was French for "like a son," he explained. My mother said that maybe the matter should be resolved while I was still young. My uncle said firmly, no: That would not be "*sage.*" They would talk to me about going to Kansas City or staying in France in the morning. They would ask me, and maybe they would do what I wanted to do. Maybe not. Above me I could hear Bête Noire running back and forth. Later, Hooter return to the attic. It must have been close to dawn. I also heard other facts of life.

When I was throwing those records and betting with myself as to which ones would break upon hitting the ground, I was also thinking to myself that their flight was like my father's flight: the ones that broke were the enemy planes he shot down. The ones that did not break were my father landing safely on his carrier. But before I left the barn to get "found" by my mother, I threw one last record and I thought as it left my hand, it is my father's plane no matter what happens to it. I could not stop my imagination. The record sailed as the others had out across the abandoned barnyard, catching this breeze and then that one, so that it twisted first one way then another until finally it stalled, sort of nose up and tail down, before it fell to the ground and did not break.

Late Sunday Evening

From the back-to-front seat where my mother settled me on the train I can see my uncle on the platform. Hooter is sleeping. Balzac has been fed and sits beside his bowl. We are taking the early train from Lamothe to Libourne, then another train to Paris, then flying on to New York and finally to Kansas City, where my sister and I will live as best we can with my mother until I go off to college and my sister takes up religion.

As the train pulls away, my uncle does not wave. He takes off his beret and holds it over his stomach. But he does not wave. He does not put his hands in the air above his head. I don't want to look at him, but I do. It was the last time I saw him.

The Billion-Dollar Dream

Arlene Had Left Him a Year Ago

Paul Andrews began putting himself to sleep by fantasizing he had a Billion dollars. Not a million dollars. A Billion. (He always capitalized Billion.) Each night Paul would add more layers to his story: the money had come from a mysterious source who would never reveal himself (or "herself," as Paul rewrote a few nights into his dream). Then, the money could only be used in specified ways. Next, the method of spending the money had to be worked out: Credit cards (without limits)? Checks? Letters of credit? Bank transfers? Cash in suitcases? The stuff of movies and novels. In this way the plot and the characters and settings and the money itself (because it was earning interest) accumulated. At work Paul looked forward to going to sleep.

Arlene had left him a year ago. Their three children were in California.

Lilly Was in Charge of Ordering

The house was too big for Paul. That's what everybody said. "Everybody" was his sister-in-law Janet and Lilly Frame, the small blond assistant manager of Books-and-Joe-to-Go, the bookstore-cum-coffeehouse that Paul owned with Janet and his older brother Lloyd.

"If you live in spaces too big for your 'essence,'" Lilly Frame said, "you cannot be at 'one' with yourself. That is why Marie Antoinette went from the Palace at Versailles to the Petit Trianon. Versailles was too big for her 'essence,' and one assumes she had a very big 'essence,' considering who she was." Lilly smiled, as she usually did after one of her "monos," as she called them. But Paul could never tell if Lilly's smile was amusement at herself or not.

"If you are not contained by yourself, you begin to ooze out of yourself," Lilly continued. "A glass may be half full or half empty. That is not the point. The point is that it is a glass, and it confines water, and the water does not ooze out of itself. If you are everywhere, you are nowhere. And don't tell me about lakes and rain and seas. That's something else." Again, Lilly smiled.

The house in question was a "rancher" that he and Arlene had agreed upon after the birth of their second child. They ordered the plans from a magazine, and the builder put in a few suggestions—but nothing made the house exceptional in either its floor plan or its exterior. It was a long single story with a lot of lawn to mow and a patio for summer cooking. No pool.

There were, however, the two sets of washers and dryers that everybody thought rather ingenious. One set was located in an alcove between the kitchen and the garage, and the second set was located in the hallway at the other end of the house that joined the bedrooms. In this way Arlene could wash the sheets and the children's clothes without lugging the laundry very far, and she could wash the tablecloths and napkins at the other end, where Paul could also wash his work clothes—as long as he wiped out the tub afterward.

"Very well conceived," is what Janet said at the time. She had just gotten her real-estate license. "Very well conceived." Later, after Arlene left, Janet said to Paul: "What will you do with two sets of washers and dryers? The place has curb appeal. You can get a bundle for it. I'll sell it for half the fee."

"Leave him alone," said Lloyd.

Open This Now

At nights Paul would restart his Billion-dollar dream from the beginning by getting notified of the money; then he would "speed dream" to where he had left off the night before. In an early version, a letter had come with Important or Open This Now or Timed Material stamped on it and Paul would have himself toss it in the waste basket. Later in the dream he'd get up in the night for a glass of milk and, seeing the crumpled Important in the trash, pick it out. In some versions he tears the letter as he opens it and has to piece it back together on the counter. Other nights, coffee grounds from the morning have blotted the letter, so that it is difficult to read. But in all versions is his Billion dollars—or at least the letter telling Paul whom to contact to get his Billion dollars, which was not yet the Billion dollars, but only a "large bequest."

After a few nights, Paul began to imagine the letter's text: *You do not know me, or my firm. But it is important that you contact me as soon as possible because we have a very large bequest that is yours.* Paul had the letter signed *Robert Day*, the name of an author who had recently been at Books-and-Joe-to-Go for a reading and book autographing. Later, Paul changed *very large* to *substantial.* To get this far had taken him the first week of what had been a wet April.

Even Now He Did Not Mention the Matter

Although Lilly Frame had for a number of years dated the sales manager of a local spice company, she had never married. She still "saw" her former lover now and then, but it was no longer "heavy duty-duty."

Lilly was "a bit in love" with Paul and had been from when she first came to work at the bookstore. She considered Paul handsome (he was not, by most standards—including his own); she liked the way Paul put his index fingers on either side of his brow when he was trying to concentrate; she thought the paper clip he used to fasten a broken hinge on his glasses endearing. She admired the way he took time to talk to the customers, including the ones who were probably not going to buy anything. He seemed interested in what people had to say—in what Lilly had to say—even though Lilly knew she could be "flaky" at times. When Lilly talked she would put finger quotes in the air around such phrases as "essence," and "monos" and "heavy duty-duty." Or (in her mind) "a bit in love." Then she would feel herself smile, as if that were part of the punctuation.

Lilly could not understand why Arlene had left Paul. But she was impressed that Paul had not said much about it, either about the divorce (which took everyone at the bookstore by surprise), or about what must have gone on before. Even now he did not mention the matter.

"Let me fix you dinner," Lilly said to Paul one afternoon. "You must be lonely with that big kitchen and those two sets of washers and dryers. I make decent paella with real saffron, and I'll put it together at my apartment and bring it ready to serve and I'll clean up afterward. I'll even bring the wine. And flan for dessert. *A bueno?* With the question mark upside down?"

"How sweet of you," said Paul, and let it go at that.

Are You Paul Andrews?

During the second week of his Billion-dollar dream, Paul has the phone ring just as he gets home from work. It might be Janet inviting him to dinner. Or someone selling mortuary insurance. But at the ring just before his recording kicks in, he has himself pick it up. A woman says: *Are you Paul Andrews? Yes.* Then she says: *Just a moment,* and after a few clicks a man's voice introduces himself as Robert Day and says that he represents a client who has a substantial bequest to make to a Mr. Paul David Andrews of 2634 Midi Lane. *Are you that Paul Andrews?*

I am.

Please come by my office tomorrow morning at ten?
I shall.

In the choice between the coffee-stained letter and the phone call, Paul settled on the phone call because he liked the woman's voice, a woman he named Bonita, which, he knew from his college days, meant "pretty" in Spanish. It was also a small "tuna," Lilly had told him.

"I can cook that for you instead of the paella," she had said.

Janet Decided to Find Paul a Lover

Janet was also attracted to Paul, and had been from their college days. "Enamored," she now called it to herself. She liked Paul for pretty much the same reasons Lilly did, although it was also true that she had never liked Arlene and thought Paul deserved better. Janet was glad Arlene was history. Out of the picture. On the coast. Toast.

Janet decided to find Paul a lover. It didn't make much difference if the woman was married or not. Some of her friends had had affairs in recent years: None of them had been caught; all of them confided to Janet that they were happy to have had such men in their lives; all of them had told her they had become better wives ("person" was what one of her friends had said) because of the affairs. None of them rattled on about how they hated to live a lie, or that they felt "cheated" not to have a husband as kind and as understanding a man as was their lover; or that their husband deserved this infidelity because of whatever "poking around" he was probably doing. Nor did any of these women tell Janet they wanted to leave their husbands for their lovers. Janet prided herself on being the kind of woman other women could talk to. She kept their secrets. She had kept one about Paul all these years. Among the women Janet considered for Paul, she settled on Lilly Frame.

"I Love Men Who Take Their Coffee Black"

Paul arrives at Robert Day's office on the top floor of an elegant steel and glass building in nearby Washington, D.C. at the appointed time. He is greeted by Bonita, who is tall, has blond hair (blonder than Lilly's), brown eyes, a bright, wide smile, and a lovely figure. Fifteen years younger than Paul, she nonetheless looks at him as if struck by his presence. Perhaps it has to do with the Billion dollars he is about to get, but Paul decides not to make that so: Bonita will know nothing of it.

"Mr. Day will be with you in a moment," Bonita says as she escorts Paul into a large corner office with windows on two sides, a large desk in the middle (that has nothing on it but a cell phone), and a coffee table with two chairs and a couch. There are framed photographs on the wall. Some Paul notices are of writers too long dead to have been photographed. Dante, for one. But when Paul tries to change the photograph into an etching, it turns into a photograph of Shakespeare. Then one of Dr. Johnson. There is also a glass case filled with autographed baseballs.

" My name is Bonita," Paul has Bonita say after a moment. "It means 'pretty' in Spanish. Not that I am Spanish. But my mother majored in Spanish and liked the name. May I get you a cup of coffee?"

"Yes," says Paul.

"Cream or sugar?" says Bonita. "Both?"

"Black."

"I love men who take their coffee black."

"Aren't you answering your phone messages these days?" It was Janet. She was standing in Paul's kitchen when he came in the back door. He knew she was there because of her white Lexus in the driveway.

"I forget to listen to them," he said.

"I need to know if I can pry you out of this big house with its two washers and dryers over to our big house for dinner on Saturday. I have someone I want you to meet."

"That's very sweet of you," Paul said.

"You can't just leave it at that," Janet said. "I need to know so I can invite her."

"I have someone in my life," said Paul.

"I don't believe you," said Janet. "What's her name?"

"Bonita," he said. "It means *tuna* in Spanish."

"*Tuna. Lobster.*" said Janet. "Be at our house for dinner Saturday at 6 p.m. And wear good glasses, not the ones with the paper clip. What woman can like that?"

"If you say so," said Paul.

It Was the Way Paul Traveled

In college Paul had been a geography major: steppes, tropics, latitudes and longitudes, lava plateaus, time zones, and (his favorite projection) *plate carée.* As he learned the physical organization of the planet, he had studied with equal pleasure its political divisions: countries, provinces, states, and cities. He had not only memorized the names of countries and regions current to his education (such as Ethiopia), but was delighted to learn that Ethiopia had once been Abyssinia, which in turn led him to a novel recommended by an English professor titled *The Prince of Abyssinia*, and from there to a travelogue by a Portuguese priest named Lobo. It was the way Paul traveled. Then and now.

Paul had no desire to visit the places whose names and provinces and regions and capitals and great cities he knew in literary ways: *From Stettin in the Baltic to Trieste in the Adriatic*, he used to say, to see if anyone knew either the man who said it or the line across Europe that the man had drawn in the mind's eye of his audience (and where was that audience?).

When the Soviet Union broke up, Paul was the only one among his friends who could name its constituent parts: from Litovskaja in the north (he preferred the traditional spellings) to Turkmenskaja in the south—just to use the western edge. And well before Yugoslavia broke apart, he could do a freehand diagram of all its states—and its one "duchy," a word he found amusing.

Paul's major professor had encouraged him to go to graduate school. But it was about this time he met Arlene, and she thought there was not much future in Paul becoming a geographer, whatever they did. Shortly after graduation (and marriage), Paul joined Lloyd and Janet in buying the bookstore. It had been a good decision: he liked the book business and he had made a good living at it, putting their children through college, and, of course, buying and maintaining his house. Nor did Arlene have to work.

"A Billion Dollars"

"We have some...well...astounding news for you, Paul David Andrews," says Robert Day as he enters the office. Bonita has left. With a smile. A smile Paul makes different from Lilly Frame's smile. More knowing.

Robert Day takes a seat in one of the chairs by the coffee table. He glances around, gets up and goes to his desk, checks the cell phone, then returns bringing the phone with him. He looks just like the Robert Day who had recently read at Books-and-Joe-to-Go, and for a moment Paul forgot that was the name he had given him.

"We have a client who has made you a great gift."

"Yes."

"Our client wants you to share the fabulous wealth that our client's astute business sense has created. I must—as you probably notice—avoid even a pronoun. Nor can I tell you the nature of the business that generated the money. Even that you are getting the money must remain a secret. Only three of us know."

"I understand."

"Let us just say," continues Robert Day, "that our client wants you to have what will seem to you like an enormous sum of money, but which to our client—while not insignificant—is not the greater share of the net worth."

"How much?"

"A Billion dollars." Robert Day looks at the cell phone because it is making a discrete ring. "Your benefactor on the line," he says.

Later that night, when Paul awoke and did not immediately go back to sleep, instead of Robert Day telling him he has a Billion dollars, he has Robert Day hand him a piece of paper. Paul reads it twice. Bonita comes in and Paul turns the paper upside down on the table. Paul notices Bonita's neck is exceptionally pretty. Bonita smiles. In her smile Paul senses she knows that he has created her, and this makes him uneasy, and he tries to drop the smile from the scene, but before he can, Bonita leaves.

Paul picks the second version of how he gets his Billion dollars, although he does not write out in his mind what is on the paper. He only nods after he reads it. Then Robert Day reaches across the desk and takes it back. A few nights later, Paul has Robert Day burn the paper with a Zippo lighter and put the ashes in a small glass bowl that Paul has Bonita bring into the office so he can look at her neck again and have her smile. However, after Bonita leaves, Paul notices that his Billion dollar paper has not been burned and that Robert Day crumples it and eats it. Robert Day does this on his own and Paul cannot not stop him.

By the end of the second week these scenes seem too much out of movies for Paul's dream, and so he returns to the version where Robert Day simply tells Paul of his Billion dollars, the phone rings on the table, and Bonita comes and goes with her neck and smile.

May I Come Over?

"Do you remember the time we dug the elevator hole?" said Lloyd. "For the new wing of the student center."

They were outside having drinks. It had stopped raining the day before and was in fact warm for April. Lilly had not yet arrived because Janet had asked Paul to come at five and Lilly at six. That way they could talk about the bookstore, and "other things." Janet had not told Paul who was coming. Lloyd didn't know either. But he knew someone was.

"I've heard that story once too often," said Janet. "Not that I wasn't there. I want to talk about the store and other things."

"What *other things*?" said Lloyd.

"Other things," said Janet. "And I've heard that story a billion times."

"I just wanted to say," said Lloyd, "that you won't find kids today who would dig an elevator-shaft hole by hand all night long to earn some extra money to buy books. I can't even get the boy down the street to mow the lawn for ten bucks an hour because he's in the mall on his cell phone. If he were reading Yeats under a tree to his Beatrice, that would be different. Or reciting Poe to the girls: 'Helen thy beauty is to me like those Nicean barks of yore...' We dug that hole for four hundred dollars and split it four ways. Paul, me, Harris, and Baxter. Why we gave Baxter a share I don't know because he was always climbing out of the hole to talk to Dee-Dee. A hundred bucks to work from sundown to sunup. With two pairs of gloves, I still got blisters. And we broke three shovels doing it. You tell me the country hasn't gone to hell when..."

"What other things?" said Paul.

"Your life," said Janet. "And you," she turned to Lloyd, "might have climbed out of that hole once in a while to see me."

That night when he's putting himself to sleep, Paul returns to Robert Day's office and has Robert Day explain the conditions of getting the Billion dollars. First, it must be spent so that no one notices that Paul has so much money. Nor can he tell anyone. Paul can make for himself a life elsewhere where he can be as rich as he wants, but he cannot leave his job—although he can take more time off, go half time, or, after a while, retire early.

Paul must not make contributions to religious organizations. His benefactor is a "Free Thinker" and does not want any of Paul's Billion given to religious organizations no matter how worthy the cause may seem. Paul can make contributions (anonymously) to medical science, to the local college, the SPCA and other charities—but never to exceed a million dollars total a year. Also, Paul needs to consult Robert Day about any expenses over a million dollars. Or maybe it should be ten million dollars.

Finally, Paul is not to invest the money. The firm of Day, Schwartz and Whitehead will do all the investing and handle all the transactions. At present the Billion dollars is earning one million dollars a week and has been doing so for two weeks. Paul must spend both the earnings and the principal. This last stipulation seemed to come from Robert Day very much on his own. Are there any questions?

Just as Paul is about to say no, Bonita comes in with a tray on which are two cups of coffee and sweet rolls. She is wearing a black dress with white buttons down the front. When she leans over to put the tray on the table, she uses her free hand (her left hand on which there are no rings) to touch the base of her neck. She is wearing pearls. She looks at Paul. Just as when Robert Day ate the Billion-dollar piece of paper, Paul has no control over Bonita's arrival, nor what she is wearing. But he likes the pearls.

Then the phone rang. Not in the office of Day, Schwartz and Whitehead, but beside Paul's bed.

"Hello?"

"Hello."

"Lilly?"

"Yes."

"What's the matter?"

"I wanted to tell you something tonight, but I didn't have a chance at dinner. May I come over?"

"Now?"

"Yes."

"Where are you?"

"At the store."

"So late?"

"Sorting books while I got up enough nerve to call you. 'Tinker Bell to Tolstoy.' May I come over?"

"Sure."

"Thank you."

There Was Less to the Eternal City Than Met the Eye

Until he began his Billion-dollar dream, Paul never read travel magazines: their prose was "not in the language"—to borrow a phrase from Lloyd. But more than that, articles on Rome seemed to be missing what was Roman. A magazine story on Piazza Navona would have it populated by leather goods shops and gelato stalls, but after fifteen hundred words and five color photographs there was less to the Eternal City than met the eye.

On the other hand, novels like *Don Quixote* or *Anna Karenina*—or recent ones like *Woman in the Dunes, Heat and Dust, Broken April,* and *Sheltering Sky* were to Spain and Russia and Japan and India and Albania and North Africa something of a projection in words. Cervantes and Tolstoy and Kadare and Bowles were place-names that any decent map of the world should label along with Orwell, Infante, Sillitoe, Márquez, Bely. Instead of a shopping and eating guide to the Via Condotti, travel magazines would do better to reprint Joseph Heller's Roman scene from *Catch-22*.

Paul's book collection was arranged by country and city: The shelf for Africa had E. M. Forster and Lawrence Durrell, among others. Spain had Hemingway, Orwell, Lorca, and Laurie Lee. Paris went from Peter Abélard (recommended by Lloyd) to Émile Zola. Jean Rhys. Elizabeth Bowen. Mavis Gallant.

Because he had arranged his literary world to suit his geographer's world, it did not occur to Paul that he was missing anything by not traveling to the down-and-out flats of London and Paris—much less to the grid of Petersburg. In fact, he seldom went anywhere.

"Philip Larkin, the English poet, rarely traveled," Lloyd had once remarked. "And Dr. Johnson said that grass is green wherever you find it. Or something like that."

She Wondered If They Might Be for Her

Lloyd was a poet and a printer. He taught at the local college. His printing business was in the basement of Books-and-Joe-to-Go. It was a letterpress operation: Chandler and Prices, a Heidelberg Windmill, plus two Vandercooks on which he printed limited-edition poetry broadsides and posters for literary readings. He had made a decent living because he was an excellent printer and because Janet had a good sense of marketing in the world of small-press book collectors.

For the previous few years, Lloyd had been going to the store at night to print broadsides of his own poems: love poems written for a woman not named in the poetry.

Lilly knew about the poems because she found them one day when she was in the basement looking for an additional copy of Robert Day's reading poster that the author had wanted. She returned to the basement and, reading the poems, thought them not very good.

Of the ones Lilly read, all were frank expressions of desire. The poems imagined that the woman to whom they were addressed was responding in erotic ways: unbuttoning a blouse button by button per line, or revealing the *V* of her "essence" in the poem's closing couplet. But as no woman's name appeared in the poetry, Lilly did not know for whom they were meant. When she wondered if they might be for her, she stopped reading them.

You'll See

After Paul began putting himself to sleep with his Billion dollars, he stopped dreaming. He had always been quite a dreamer: wild, sometimes violent dreams with a large dark animal chasing him off the end of a pier until he falls into the water and then drowns to wake. Or dreams where he is endlessly on a rattletrap of a plane flying over water so low that it hits the masts of boats that break through the plane's windows. Sometimes sailors are tied to the masts. Sometimes there are fish that flop on the floor of the plane.

In another dream, Paul is on a series of trains going someplace he is supposed to know, but there is nothing about the landscape (rocks and rills and open plains with few trees) that gives him a clue. A conductor keeps saying: *You'll see. You'll see.* And once Paul heard himself say in the middle of the night: *You'll see.*

"See what?" he had said to what he had said.

"Be quiet," Arlene had said.

Paul would awake from these dreams with the sensation of having survived. When he went back to sleep he would dream of tables of food and wine all set in a meadow with a silhouette of a young woman asking what he wanted most in life. Sometimes the young woman carried a book of poetry out of which she read aloud. When Paul awoke the second time it would be morning, and he could remember the young woman's voice, the food, and the wine—but not the poetry: nor what he wanted most in life.

"Between your talking and snoring, I don't get much sleep," Arlene had said. "I'm going to the guest room."

"What Did That Woman Buy?"

One day at the store, Paul caught a glimpse of a woman who looked like Bonita. She had the same blond hair and the same appealing figure. She had the same neck. For a moment he considered going over and asking if she needed help, but to see that she was not Bonita would be a disappointment. So he went into the office and put things in order for the literary event they were sponsoring that evening: a reading by a local poet. When Paul came out of the office the woman was walking down the sidewalk in front of the store's windows. From that angle she still looked like Bonita.

"What did that woman buy?" Paul asked Lilly.

"An art book on Goya and something else out of the sale bin," said Lilly. "*The Pillars of Hercules*, by Paul Theroux," she said, reading it off the cash register receipt. "They were both last copies. Do you want to reorder?"

"I don't think so," said Paul looking out the window. There was a small silence between them.

"Have you put any more data into your life program about what I said the other night?" asked Lilly.

Paul noticed she did not smile, but instead looked at the floor. Nor had she put quotation marks around "data" or "life program."

There. That Was Done

After Paul got his Billion dollars from Robert Day, and after they worked out the details of how he was to withdraw the money (through a special check card for amounts up to ten thousand dollars; by a direct payment from Day, Schwartz and Whitehead for more; and by consulting Robert Day for expenditures above ten million), Paul began putting himself to sleep by devising ways to spend the money, and on what.

The night Lilly had come over, he put himself back to sleep by purchasing her three apartments in Paris and an English-language bookstore. The main apartment was lavish; the second apartment in the same building was for guests, and a smaller one for a maid.

When that did not put him to sleep, Paul bought the whole building and put the bookstore on the ground floor, and Lilly's apartment became the entire top floor, from which she could see the Seine. There would still be the apartment for the maid, and one for guests, while the other apartments would be for visiting authors who were in Paris—either to give readings at the bookstore or to stay for a longer period of time (a year seemed about right). Lloyd and Janet would have a permanent suite of rooms in the building as well.

When all that buying did not put him to sleep, Paul established a foundation so that the writers who lived in the apartment could charge their meals at the literary restaurants in Paris. Any café or bistro or restaurant that turned up in Balzac, Proust, Baudelaire, Colette, Hemingway, Gertrude Stein, James Joyce, Genet, Jean Rhys and Mavis Gallant would be free to Lilly's authors. They could take their coffee on the first floor of Café de Flore, then get some chocolate at Debauve & Gallais to tide them over until they took dinner at Le Pré Catelan.

Paul calculated he spent ten million dollars for the apartment building (it would need some work and there was the furniture to buy—Janet could help with that—and the bookstore would need a stock to get it going), plus another ten million on the foundation. In all, twenty million. Not bad for a night's work. There. That was done. And so to sleep.

The next morning, while ringing up a book on investing, Paul realized that since his Billion dollars had been earning a million dollars a week, even though he had spent twenty million in Paris the previous night, he had made little headway on depleting the Billion dollars itself. He remembered Robert Day had told him he must spend both the interest and the principal. But what would happen if he did not?

"Is something wrong?" asked Lilly. She had noticed he had been standing with his index fingers on his brow for quite a long time.

"Not really," said Paul.

"I hope…"

"It has nothing to do with you," he said. And in the sound of his voice both Lilly and Paul heard an edge that had not been there before.

That night he decided to fly Lilly and Lloyd and Janet to Paris on the Concorde. Even though the Concorde was now out of service, he would buy one. What would a Concorde cost? Fifty million. Then there is insurance and pilots and maintenance, so there's another million a year. Now he was getting somewhere.

After the Concorde lands in Paris, Paul installs Lilly in her bookstore and establishes her among poets and writers—and in so doing he makes up for the edge in his voice. Which means he can return to Bonita. Which he does, buying her one of Gaudí's buildings in Barcelona and flying her there—also in his Concorde. But not on the same flight with Lilly and Janet and Lloyd. Paul sees these flights off at the airport: first Lilly, Janet, and Lloyd (whom he puts as the head of his foundation, now that he thinks of it); then, two days later, Bonita leaves for Barcelona. Paul is standing on the tarmac watching her board the Concorde when he realizes he might never see her again. He tries to edit out the Concorde into which she is about to vanish. She waves to him. Paul cannot see if she is smiling or not. Then she is gone. Neck and all.

Beware of Great Wealth

"What would you do if you were given a lot of money?" Paul had said to Lloyd the evening Janet had invited him to meet Lilly. It was his way of stalling the talk Janet wanted to have about his life.

"Give it away," said Lloyd.

"All of it?" said Janet.

"Beware of great wealth," said Lloyd. "It is glass that shatters when it shines. And it never fails to shine."

"I'd want an apartment in Paris," said Janet. "Plus a second apartment in the same building so we could have family over. As long as we're into big-money dreams here."

"And maybe even an apartment for a maid?" said Paul.

"Why not?" said Janet. "I'd also buy a place in San Francisco. And go first class. On land and sea and in the air. It's too bad the Concorde has stopped flying."

"Give it away," said Lloyd. "Flee from both abstractions and money."

"Here's Lilly," said Janet as they heard a car drive up.

"Who?" said Paul.

"The rest of your life," said Lloyd.

She Looked at a Half-Empty Bottle of Wine

"Did I upset you when I came over?"

"No."

The store was closed and Paul and Lilly were cleaning up from the reception.

"I think something has changed between us," said Lilly. "I am sad about that."

"There's another woman in my life," said Paul.

"I wondered if there might be," said Lilly. She looked at a half-empty bottle of wine. "Will you share this with me? And talk. I don't mind if we are not lovers, but I would mind if I lost you in some other way. I promise not to ask any more 'provocative' questions."

Paul glanced at Lilly and wished he had not said anything about another woman. Unlike Bonita, Lilly was not pretty to him, but in that moment when she looked at the wine bottle, tilting it slightly to see how much was left, he thought her lovely. What was there to do with that?

What It All Cost

Paul began reading *Flying* and *Yachting*, as well as *Condé Nast Traveler*, *Boating*, and *Millionaire Homes*. And decorator magazines: *Real Simple* and *Connoisseur*. Also magazines from Sotheby's and Christie's; these—and many more like them—from the racks that a vendor filled once a week.

Paul saw what there was in the world to buy, the finest brands, and what it all cost. The *duPont Registry* listed the grand Peppertree Bend Estate, a sprawl of house that seemed to take up most of the 1.69 acres on which it sat: $7,199,000, which (Paul found himself thinking) probably meant he could get it for a flat seven million.

He made lists: Hinckley Sou'wester, $1.8 million; Gulf Stream IV, hangar in New Orleans, $5 million; the library of Montaigne at auction, as well as a wine cellar from an English baron. What would they cost?

Paul could only guess. Montaigne at a million. Fifty cases of Bordeaux pre-1960 (including two cases of Mouton Rothschild 1945 and three cases of Latour 1938) at half a million. Paul put the lists into the office computer under *The Billion Dollar Dream*. Then he hid *The Billion Dollar Dream* in the *Robert Day* folder that he had created when the author had come to read.

Beyond what there was to buy, Paul needed a place to live. Florida did not seem compelling, partly because he could not imagine who he might be in Florida: maybe somebody out of the movies like Jon Voight in *Midnight Cowboy*, only with piles of unexplained money. Maybe California: but who can you be with a lot of money in California besides a Dot-Com Somebody or a film star?

Perhaps in Europe or in Africa and the Far East, he could use the money to make of himself someone not Paul Andrews. But who? And then there was the matter of how to get there. He would have to give up his pleasure of not traveling. Life is a trade-off. These were problems for his nights ahead.

So What If He Had to Give Them Back

After Lilly had awakened him when she came over, Paul realized that by getting up in the middle of the night and putting himself to sleep a second time (and even a third time), he could spend more money. The best way was to drink two big glasses of water just before he went to bed. It was during these double and triple Billion-dollar dream nights that he began to buy islands and ranches and gold mines and finally, after some art books the store had ordered came in, hugely expensive paintings.

Not knowing what was for sale in the art world and impatient to get on with it, Paul imagined that various museums were selling off a few pieces of their celebrated art in order to finance their operations: the *Luncheon of the Boating Party* for sale by The Phillips Collection Gallery: fifty million. And as long as he was into Renoir, there was *The Swing*. Another fifty million. For a week of nights he bought Della Francescas and small Leonardo drawings. Why not? He had an apartment building in Paris and one in Barcelona that needed furnishing. A few Elgin Marbles came on the market from a dealer in Kiev (no doubt stolen) and Paul snapped them up even if he would have to give them back. Five million dollars. Each. And there were ten. So what if he gave them back and lost the money.

Paul bought Francis Bacons, Gwen and Augustus John, Warhol's soup cans and his Marilyn Monroe (which he paired with a Joe DiMaggio), a fine southwestern painter named Fritz Scholder, a whole family of Wyeths, and some Catlins and Caleb Binghams.

Then one day, looking through *100 of the Most Beautiful Women in Painting*, there was Sargent's *Madame X*, and Paul saw that Bonita's neck was her neck. Before he fell asleep the first time (the painting might not be available later in the evening), he bought it. A hundred million.

By the end of the spree, he had purchased hundreds of millions of dollars' worth of art. The next week he bought a building in

Washington to house the American part of the collection. Twenty million. After two weeks of two and three glasses of water a night he'd finally made a big dent in the Billion dollars. It put a spring in his step at work; a sense of accomplishment. The weather was getting warmer; it would soon be May.

"She's Lovely, Isn't She?"

"You cannot leave the money to anybody when you die," says Robert Day. "Nor can you invest in houses. That is, you cannot buy them unless you plan to live in them. Nor can you be discovered living in them by your friends or family. Nor are you allowed to pay off your mortgage, nor the loan on the bookstore. If you get married, you may not let your wife know your secret wealth, although you can treat her lavishly. Buy her minks and diamonds if you like. Which brings me to this: I have learned you bought an apartment building in Paris for one of the women employees in your bookstore. And for another woman, you made a similar purchase in Barcelona. As I said at the beginning, you cannot reveal in any way to your friends, your associates at work, your relatives, or your would-be lovers that you are a wealthy man. No Paris apartment for your store employee. No flying off to Spain on the Concorde with some woman just because you think her neck is pretty. And no buying paintings that are not for sale, and never will be. Return the paintings. Sell the buildings."

Bonita comes in with her tray of coffee. She is wearing black slacks and a yellow blouse in which her breasts jiggle. As she leaves the room, she turns toward Paul and cups her hand at her waist and makes a movement not unlike someone snapping castanets. She smiles.

"She's lovely, isn't she?" says Robert Day.

"Yes."

"She's my daughter."

Once Robert Day says that, Paul could not rewrite it. No matter how many times over many nights he tried. But later that night, and night after night, he could—and did—change the rules against buying Lilly Frame an apartment building in Paris as long as she did not know who did it, and he fixed it so he could buy Bonita the Gaudí building in Barcelona—again as long as she did not know the source of the gift. And he also fixed it so the paintings (*Madame X* among them) need not be returned; but still Paul could not rewrite:

"She's lovely, isn't she?" says Robert Day.

"Yes."

"She's my daughter."

What Do You Think About Before You Go to Sleep?

"Would you really not accept a lot of money if it were left to you?" asked Paul. He and Lloyd were in the basement of Books-and-Joe-to-Go.

"How much money?"

"As much as you want."

"You mean if I won the lottery? A hundred million or so just last week. Would I turn that down?"

"Yes."

"No. But I'd be wrong not to."

"Why?"

"See this?" said Lloyd holding up a sheet of paper.

"Yes."

"It's a love poem. A single sheet of a love poem. I wrote it. I set it. I printed one copy. On paper I made myself. Then I distributed the type. It's unique. I've done twenty of them. They are dedicated to a woman I love. I don't really love her. It is just that I need somebody to love other than Janet. Let's call her Lilly. Just like Lilly upstairs. Or Arlene. Like ex-Arlene. Or Dee-Dee. Are the poems good? Not as good as the other poetry I write myself, which I think can be pretty good. But better than Rod McKuen. At least that. Our Lilly is my

Beatrice Portinari. Your ex-Arlene is my Dark Lady. Dee-Dee can be either Helen or Hera; I prefer Hera even though Helen was more beautiful. But then there is the problem of Zeus." Lloyd looked at Paul. When Paul didn't say anything, Lloyd continued:

"We all need something to imagine, and then we need something to do with what we imagine. I am not a great poet because my love for Lilly is not great, and it is not great because I do not see her circa 1290. In my mind's eye I cannot make her die young. She is not an ox-eyed beauty. She is not even the poet inside of me, which is who I think the Dark Lady was to Shakespeare. The love and woman of my poems are weak illusions. But at least they are *my* weak illusions. My inner eye is making what I want to see. A poet is a seer and a maker. Got it?"

"What's this got to do with the lottery?" said Paul.

"Money steals you blind. It is one thing to be Milton or Homer or Borges; it is another to have an eye full of getting and spending. Even as is, I have too much of it. Janet wants to dig a swimming pool because we have the money. And we're not talking by hand. I drive a stretch Volvo. I have IRAs and 401ks and Janet has a money counselor. By now on my best days I've got cataracts. If I took a hundred million dollars from the lottery what eyesight would I have left to see Lilly Frame as Beatrice? Or me as my own Dark Lady? I'd have only money. It's a rotten deal. Having enough may be too much if you want to be a poet."

Lloyd put his poem on the job case.

"You know that Robert Day who was here a couple of months ago?" Lloyd continued. "The one who read a story about a crazy populist rancher in the middle of Kansas with nothing but short-grass prairie and blizzards. Day had it right when the old rancher tells his banker son that time's not money it's 'gossamer.' Nothing is money if you have it. It not only steals you blind, it steals your time. And you need time to breed lilacs out of desire."

There was a long pause in which Paul found himself thinking in bits and pieces: old maps; the tight binding of new books; Bonita's neck; the conductor saying *You'll see, you'll see*; Lilly that night she came over; Janet, an afternoon long ago; the lovely woman who read him poetry and kept asking him what he most wanted in life; two sets of washers and dryers; and *Behind that line lie all the capitals of ancient Europe*, Paul said aloud. Or thought he did, but probably not, because Lloyd said:

"What do you do with money anyway? Buy boats. Apartments in San Francisco like Janet wants to do—and where, coincidentally, your ex-wife lives, as I happen to know but Janet does not. What else? Planes. Cars. Swimming pools. How about I buy everything that is advertised in the *New Yorker* in one of those big fat issues that comes out just before Christmas? Everything. A week's worth of 800 numbers and emails. That would start the little brown attic-stuffer truck driving up to the house three hundred and sixty-five days for a year. Then when the house is full I'd rent stuff-storage-sheds, or—here's an idea—I could buy houses all over the country: beach houses on both coasts and the Gulf of Mexico; *Lord of the Flies* islands; Peter Fonda ranch houses in Montana; *Up in Michigan* lake cottages; Santa Fe adobe houses out of Willa Cather—all so I would have someplace to put the little-brown-truck-attic-stuffer *New Yorker* stuff." Lloyd picked up his poem off the job case.

"But you said you'd accept the money," Paul said.

"Yes."

"Because of Janet?"

"No," Lloyd said. He was reading his poem to himself.

"Why?"

"Why what?"

"If you wouldn't accept the money for Janet's sake, why would you accept it?"

"I'd accept it for you," said Lloyd looking at Paul. "So you could run off with Lilly Frame, if that's what you want to do."

"That's not a straight answer."

"I'd take it because I am not gifted enough to imagine not taking it," Lloyd said looking at Paul over the edge of his poem. "And it would ruin my life and I would know it every night I go to bed and don't put myself to sleep imagining Lilly reading the poems I have written to her and don't imagine her doing what she is doing with her buttons and her body as she reads them. I may not love her, but I want to. What do you think about before you go to sleep?"

Paul's Dream Was Stuck

Paul's dream was stuck. He had bought nearly everything in the magazines that came into the store, as well as islands and ranches and boats and planes and wine cellars and Bentleys and, in fact, all there was in the recent *New Yorker*. He had run out of ideas. And where to put everything was a problem, just as Lloyd had predicted. Maybe he could buy a town.

"What kind of town?" asks Robert Day.

"Some town in Kansas."

"With people in it?"

"I would buy them out. To get their houses for everything in the *New Yorker*."

"I don't think so," says Robert Day. "But there is something else you need to know."

"What?"

"The money is earning two million a week."

"Even with what I spent?"

"Our investments in hedge funds have paid off very well. Two million a week and maybe more by the end of year. You're filthy rich. Get used to it."

Bonita arrives with coffee. She looks even more lovely and younger than on previous nights: She is wearing a dark blue dress cut just above the knees. A small, white ribbon is pinned to her hair. Paul is about to speak to her, but she seems distant. Maybe she's unhappy in Barcelona. Maybe she's taken up with someone else. Lloyd? Whatever the trouble, it takes Paul a long time to get to sleep, what with lying awake thinking about what Lilly had said to him, both the night she came over and later, when they finished off the wine. Then there was what Lloyd had said, and finally, in the background of his mind, a thought that seemed like an elevator moving up and down slowly, out of which came a voice saying: *You'll see. You'll see.*

He got up and went through the living room to the kitchen and poured himself a glass of milk. He looked in the trash can, then at the clock on the microwave: 10:12. 10:13. Then he picked up the phone and called Lilly.

"Hello."

"Lilly?"

"Is that you Paul?"

"Did I wake you?"

"I was just reading."

"I'm sorry to have bothered you."

"You haven't really." There was a moment of silence, and just as Lilly was starting to say something more, Paul said:

"Are you coming to work tomorrow?"

"Yes. Of course. Why do you ask?"

"I don't know," said Paul.

"Is something the matter?"

"I'll talk to you tomorrow," said Paul and hung up before he could hear what Lilly was saying.

Later that night Paul tries to see Robert Day but Robert Day is not in. Nor is Bonita. The building is there: tall and full of glass with marble floors and a spacious elevator that takes him to the top floor. But when Paul comes into the offices of Day, Schwartz and Whitehead, there is nobody. He goes back down to the lobby and into the street, where he meets Robert Day, but when Robert Day speaks he sounds like Lloyd.

"I want to give the money back," says Paul.

"You can't," says Robert Day, whose face is the face of Arlene.

"Then I won't spend it," says Paul.

"Fine. We don't care if you spend it or not. But each month we will still send you an accounting. When it reaches ten Billion you die. Or maybe it is five Billion. I'll have my daughter check the contract."

"Where's Bonita?" says Paul.

"She went to Paris with Lloyd."

"Aren't you Robert Day the writer?" asks Paul.

"I used to be," says Robert Day, who is now sounding like the train conductor. "Who are you?"

"I'm in love with your daughter."

"She's gone to Paris with Lloyd," says Janet, who is suddenly standing in the street holding Robert Day's hand. "She's taking off her clothes to the beat of poetry. Button by line. Her blouse is off."

"He's dead at five Billion," says Bonita, who is nowhere to be seen.

When Paul awoke, the clock read 4:23. He could not get back to sleep even though he tried by having the woman who read him poetry and poured him wine come into his head so he could tell her what he wanted most in his life, but she would drift away as if she were not, after all, interested. Then Lilly and Janet showed up, but they had become fat and old and the head of Lilly and the head of Janet had switched bodies and in that way they both talked to him in Spanish about washers and dryers. Finally, Paul got out of bed and went and sat in his car in the driveway until the sun came up.

"I do not have another woman in my life," Paul said to Lilly Frame later that morning.

She was shelving in the cookbook section.

"What happened?" she said.

"She left me."

"A house with two sets of washers and dryers," said Lilly, "is like having your pie à la mode with the ice cream on one plate and the pie on the other. Or like dividing Czechoslovakia in half, which they should have never done because who wants to buy a travel guide to the Czech Republic and then another one to Slovakia?" She smiled. But only slightly. And it seemed cautious.

"I am sorry I said you were 'provocative,'" Paul said.

"But I was," said Lilly. "I want you to be in love with me the way I am in love with you."

"No two loves are alike," said Paul, rather surprised that he had something so interesting to say. And in his mind's eye he saw Bonita.

"That's what your brother says."

"He does?"

"It's a line in one of his poems. The ones he prints downstairs. I think they are meant for me."

"I didn't know about them until the other day," said Paul.

"Some minds think alike," Lilly said. "Here." She handed him a copy of an Elizabeth David biography.

"What's this?"

"It's a new book we got in. Two copies. It doesn't mean anything that I handed it to you; it's just that I'm nervous and don't know what to say."

Neither one of them spoke for so long that both of them thought the other one would soon say something.

"How about we go downstairs and open a bottle of wine that I've got in the office and I'll read my brother's poetry to you?" said Paul. Again, he was surprised at what he had said. At its audacity.

Lilly was silent for a moment. She looked at the floor.

"I'd rather not," she said and went to the front of the store to check out a customer.

Arlene Was a Sorority Sister of Janet's

It had been while digging the elevator-shaft hole that Paul met Arlene. Arlene was a sorority sister of Janet's. Once, when Paul climbed out of the hole to get some water and to start lowering the bucket to get the dirt out after the hole got too deep to throw it out, there was Arlene. She asked him if he'd like something to eat, because she'd be glad to run to the Food Shack. Paul was the only one of the four of them who did not have a girlfriend and he learned later that Janet had arranged for Arlene to show up. After that, Paul and Arlene dated throughout college and then married.

But they almost did not get married because of a conversation between them a few weeks before the wedding: Arlene asked Paul if he had ever slept with anybody and he lied and said no. Then Arlene asked if he had ever wanted to sleep with anyone and Paul said of course. That was natural. Then he thought he better not lie to Arlene because that would be a bad way to start a marriage, and so he told her he had slept with two women: one was a prostitute the fraternity had hired for a bachelor party and one was another girl. When he wouldn't tell her about the second one, Arlene said she was going to call off the wedding. So Paul said she was his high school girlfriend and that her name was Bonita. In fact it had been Janet. Janet had asked him over to her apartment before she dated Lloyd, and when he went there she was naked to the waist, saying come on, hurry, hurry. They were lovers until she took up with Lloyd. But not after that.

It never seemed an important lie. Nor had Janet ever mentioned the matter. Nor had Lloyd, if he even knew. But just now, seeing Lilly at the front of the store, the memory of that lie blinded Paul's mind. What he wanted most in life was to tell Lilly the truth—not only about the lie he had told Arlene, but the story about Robert Day and the Billion dollars, and how he had made up Bonita for both Lilly and Arlene, and that Bonita had not left him because she was never Bonita in the first place. He might not be in love with Lilly Frame, but what was there to do with not being able to see what to do? But Paul said nothing. Later in the day Lilly asked if she might leave early that afternoon, and Paul said yes.

That night Paul tried to put himself to sleep by thinking of Lilly Frame and what it would be like for the two of them to be married, and how they would live in the house together, and what Christmas would be like with his children and Janet and Lloyd—and maybe even Arlene, if it came to that. But in his mind's eye he could see none of it. The best he could do was get a Christmas tree in the living room, but it had no lights and there seemed to be nobody in the house. Not even himself.

Next, Paul imagined the countries he had studied as a student. A flickering Albers equal-area projection came into his head, but when he tried to put in Armenia or Ethiopia or Goa, or a town in Kansas, it vanished. Next he tried a stereographic projection, and for a moment he could see Cuba and the edges of Mexico and Central America, but maybe it was the sea coast of Albania. As for the Mercator grid he finally conjured, there was nothing in its boxes: not seas, not plains, not mountains, nada. No matter what view of the earth Paul tried to imagine, it was not there. Nor were his books. No Rhys or Forster. No Mavis Gallant or Colette. Paris was gone.

Later that night, Paul went back to Robert Day's office. He was going to say he wanted out of his Billion-dollar dream so he wouldn't have to spend the money or die. But when he got to Washington, the city was gone. There was only the vast shortgrass prairie through which the train in his nightmare traveled.

He tried to see Bonita. He tried to hear her voice. He tried to have her say *I love men who take their coffee black.* He tried to smell her, to have the pearls string down between her breasts. But in so doing even the shortgrass prairie flickered and vanished, and finally there were tiny dots and now and then a reddish vertical band. He opened his eyes and turned on the light, then closed his eyes again to see what he could see. A pale nothing this time, but still nothing.

"You'll see," he said out loud. "See what?" he said to himself, again out loud. He turned off the light and with nothing to put him to sleep, lay awake for hours until morning. He stayed in bed while the phone rang and he could hear that Janet, then Lloyd, and yes, Lilly Frame all left messages wondering where on earth was he?

Sometimes It Is, Sometimes It Isn't

"Your uncle Conroy writes that he has a fellowship for you," my mother said. I was home on lunch break from lifeguarding at the local pool. "It pays wages and you get college credit. You need good grades in science."

My mother has said this without much enthusiasm. She was reading the letter a second and third time.

Uncle Conroy was my mother's older brother, a pediatric researcher of international fame. In the cultural gulf between our 1950s linoleum-floor kitchen in Merriam, Kansas, and Doctor Conroy Watkins directing a medical research lab in Berkeley, California, circa the mid-1960s, there was a pleasing pride—as if in our small house we had a first edition signed by Clarence Day.

"Let me see," my father said. He had closed his auto repair garage for lunch and was also home.

"At the University of California at Berkeley," said my mother handing him the letter.

I have an hour before I have to be on duty at the pool. After closing, I am to take Muff LaRue to Winsteads for a Frosty. My plan is to drive back to the pool for a swim.

"That's what it says," said my father. "A fellowship in Conroy's research lab that could lead to medical school. He should get there as soon as possible for training." My father left the kitchen with the letter in one hand, his meatloaf sandwich in the other, and headed for the front yard to sit in his aluminum lawn chair.

"I don't know that General Science counts," said my mother through the kitchen window.

"Two semesters of *A*s," my father said, talking straight ahead.

They were referring to my freshman grades at the state teacher's college of Emporia. I seemed to be present only in the third person.

"I'm going to be a doctor," I said to Muff LaRue as I unlocked the gates to the pool.

Muff dove in fully clothed and swam to the deep end. When she got there she pulled herself out and said if I'd turn off the lights she'd skinny dip. I flipped switches.

"I've never dated a doctor," she said. "What kind of doctor?" She walked to the end of the low board, took off her summer shorts, and tossed them on the deck. Then she pulled her t-shirt over her head and threw it in the pool.

"A surgeon. I am going to Cal-Berkeley to be a pediatric surgeon."

I was treading water beneath her.

"I'm going to Sarah Lawrence to study classics," she said as she dove in.

I had not been a good enough high school student to go "East" for college. My father had hoped for a scholarship to Yale or Harvard: an Ivy League education was to a young man from Kansas as a wealthy marriage was to a young woman. It went unsaid that the young man present in the third person was thought none-too-bright.

As for my mother, she had discovered that any college in Kansas had to take you if you had graduated from a state high school.

"I think he should stay in our *domain*," she'd say, using in context one of the *ubiquitous* words she was forever trying to teach me.

"He should go East," my father would say without—I would learn later—any sense of history or irony: "Go East," you could hear him say summer evenings in our front yard as he drank a beer in his webbed aluminum lawn chair.

"I think he should stay in our *environs*," my mother would say through the open kitchen window as she cleaned up. That spring I was accepted at Emporia State Teachers College.

"William Allen White's town," my father said.

"Teachers and government workers are never without a job," my mother said.

The summer after my high school graduation, I lifeguarded at the local pool and helped at home: I mowed the lawn, painted the basement walls, cleaned out the attic, ran errands, and hung the laundry on the backyard clothesline. Some days I fixed flats, pumped gas, and changed oil at my father's repair garage and filling station. I didn't know what I was going to do with my life, but I didn't sit around looking into a gold fish tank.

At the swimming pool that summer, I saved a boy out of the deep end bottom but never said anything about it until my father saw it as a news item in the local paper. I was the kind of kid who did not explain himself. It seemed natural.

After some discussion, my father won the argument and I accepted my uncle's invitation and went to Berkeley, even if it might have *agitators*—as my father called them, not unlike Dustin Hoffman's landlord in *The Graduate*. On the other hand, my mother feared *impertinence* among the rich students. She told me to find the word in the dictionary she had given me when I left for college with instructions to learn four words a day: *aplomb, domain, environs, impertinence.*

"He'll have to learn some table manners before he goes," said my mother. "At Conroy's they don't 'just eat.'"

It took me a week to quit my job as a lifeguard, say goodbye to Muff, and pack. My uncle met me at the airport.

"So you want to be a doctor?" he said.

"I don't know," I said.

We were driving over the Bay Bridge toward the East Bay. You have to be a young man from a small town in Kansas to understand how astonishing it is to see the San Francisco Bay for the first time. There is nonchalance about its grandeur.

When I said I didn't know if I wanted to be a doctor to one of the most famous and accomplished physicians in America, a man who had no doubt made special arrangements to get me a fellowship, it sounds, even at this distance, something Californian-sixties: Mellow. Really, man. Yeah. Wow. Far out. That's not what I meant. Perhaps I thought—as we crossed the Bay Bridge to the East Bay—that if I couldn't be a doctor like Uncle Conroy, I didn't want to be a doctor. I'd like to think that now.

"I don't mean..." I said as we drove up Grove Avenue past the lab where I would be working.

"I understand," he said. "Don't worry about your future. It is always there."

"Thank you," I said.

From Grove we drove into the Berkeley Hills behind the Claremont Hotel to my aunt and uncle's house overlooking the Bay.

My uncle's laboratory was the Hansen Pediatric Research Center. My first week at work, I had met Hazen: Hazen Edmond Floren Reynald, who was pleased to introduce himself by all or part of his name, just as it pleased him to pick one of his names (including his last) and use it for a week. Or this:

"My name is Hazen Edmond Floren Reynald, and you may pick the name you like and call me that from now on. I will remember. But sometimes I won't."

I picked "Hazen." My uncle had picked "Edmond." Aunt Lillian picked "Howard," and no one had told her that was not one of her choices.

"You may change names as I do," Hazen said. "This week I am to myself *Floren*. But you may call me *Edmond*."

Hazen grew up on Russian Hill, where he and his mother and Doctor Reed still lived. He was a large-nosed, black-haired, short stout-chested guy four or five years older than me. He had dropped out of college after his freshman year to travel in Europe: a trust provided him with funds to "poke around the world and among the girls."

"Do you have a girlfriend back in Kansas?" Hazen said.

"Muff LaRue," I said.

"*Rue* means *street* in French," Hazen said. "My mother is French. I understand we are all coming to dinner at your aunt and uncle's house. Very formal. Mother usually brings her favorite hors d'oeuvre: *pâté de canard*."

I must have looked puzzled because Hazen went on—as if to reassure me.

"Just remember, it is impolite to take the last hors d'oeuvre, which, if you think about it, means you can't take the second to last piece because you're being impolite to the poor bastard who is stuck with not being able to take the last piece. And if you think about it from here to eternity, you can't take anything off the plate. You just starve."

My mother's fear of *impertinence* had come true.

Beyond our routine duties in nutrition experiments, our "apprenticeship" included working with researchers who had grants to use my uncle's lab. A Doctor Doyle killed hamsters with women's hairspray.

The hamsters were kept in small, square plastic cages designed so you could open and close their air holes. After we sprayed the hamsters we'd close the holes. There were twenty cages, each numbered, and each with a chart that indicated how many seconds of hairspray the hamsters were to get. My job was to run the stop-watch; Hazen did the spraying.

An hour later, we opened the holes to let in fresh air. In the cages where the spraying had gone on for sixty seconds or more, we'd usually find a dead hamster or two. When that happened we'd cut out the lungs and freeze them in small glass containers that had the same numbers as the cages. Doctor Doyle would make tissue slices for study under a microscope.

"What you see is pneumonia," Doctor Doyle said.

Hazen and I took turns peering into the microscope. My uncle was with us.

"Why does it take a grant to prove hairspray is bad for you?" said Hazen. "The stuff is nasty."

"Science," said Uncle Conroy, "is, among other things, the controlled observation of nature that accounts for the variables. Medicine uses science to effect cures. It may be that hairspray is bad for hamsters, but not bad for people. Or that the hamster got pneumonia from other causes. Just because we see the effect doesn't mean we have caused the cause. Or know it."

Doctor Doyle nodded.

"Does your wife use hairspray?" Hazen asked my uncle.

"I won't let her," he said, then peered into the microscope: "Chemical pneumonitis."

"*Hang up medicine,*" said Hazen later in the day.

It was his mantra around the lab: "*Hang up medicine, unless it can prove a Juliet.*"

Living with my aunt and uncle that summer had its pleasures. Even after I moved to an apartment on Derby near the university in the fall, I was always welcome. If they were away (to a medical conference or to a retreat in Mexico in which they owned an interest), I had the run of their house with its splendid view of San Francisco Bay. I was well fed, and when necessary, could use one of their cars. For this, my uncle asked only that I drive Aunt Lillian to the store and on errands.

"Let him drive," my uncle would say. "That way he can learn his way around Berkeley."

When he had me aside he said:

"Lillian is many fine things, but while she can set an excellent table for a dinner party—as you shall see here shortly—she cannot cook a breakfast egg nor drive a car."

"Your uncle thinks I am a poor driver because I am alert," my aunt said one day as we left for errands and to drop me off at the lab. "That is why he wants you to drive. He has told me more than once I am dangerous, but ask him how many tickets I have gotten. None. Or how many accidents I have had that were my fault. None. It is just a prejudice he has about women drivers because we are cautious."

Aunt Lillian had stopped for a green light on Durant because— as she explained amid the honking of horns behind her—men sometimes run red lights.

"You must be defensive in your driving. Defensive and alert. Not alarmed. But alert to what is coming at you from all sides: front, back, right, left. I am perched high and straight in my seat and I am always alert and defensive."

She achieved her "perch" by sitting on a folded pillow so that her head was well above the steering wheel, and not all that far below the car's headliner. From there she could see as well as any present-day SUV soccer mom.

"You must be careful of rocks rolling off the mountains," Aunt Lillian said one day when she came to a full stop in the middle of West View Drive, not far from the end of their lane. I looked up the hill at a large rock protruding from underneath a few scrub trees. It had probably been deposited by an ice age.

"Would you like for me to drive?" I said.

"Not at all. You think that rock has been there a long time and will not roll down. That is what Conroy says. But because it has been there a long time means it is more likely to roll down. Hills flatten into plains because rocks roll off them and grind themselves to dust. That is what happened in Kansas. It can happen in California. We have earthquakes. There was a famous one years ago that started a fire. They still talk about it. You must be watchful wherever you are in a car. On the small roads. On the highways. In traffic. In the hills with rocks on them. Just because we are very close to the house doesn't mean an accident can't happen. Most car accidents happen close to home."

"Did she stop at the top of the hill by the rock?" asked my uncle when I told him I had not been able to drive her that day.

"Yes."

I drove Aunt Lillian very little, and I never understood why some days she was pleased to have me do so, but on most days she was insistent that she drive. Nor could I determine why she stopped at some green lights (and ran red ones), but not at others.

"Has Lillian pulled off the road when a truck is coming?" asked my uncle on another occasion.

"No," I said.

"She thinks some trucks are too big for the roads so she'll drive off the shoulder to let them go by. Once I had Triple A pull her out of a ditch, and all she would say was that it was better to be in the ditch than 'squished like a beetle.'"

A few days later Aunt Lillian veered the Cadillac onto a lawn because a cement truck was heading our way, very much on its own side of the road.

"Better up on a lawn than squished like a beetle," she said as we came to a thud of a stop in a well-tended yard. "A wreck involves the police and smashed fenders and a broken windshield and medical bills. Just because your uncle is a doctor doesn't mean we get hospital-care free."

Aunt Lillian looped back onto Stuart just ahead of a woman dashing across the lawn shaking a vacuum cleaner attachment like a fist. At the next green light we made a full stop. At the next red light we drove through.

"Doesn't he look good, Conroy?" said my Aunt Lillian. I was wearing a tuxedo borrowed from my uncle. I had seen myself in a mirror before coming out of my room and thought the same thing: not bad.

"Very good," said my uncle, who, I understood, did not put much stock in the formalities of social life but had come to a routine acceptance of it.

Just as Hazen had predicted, my aunt and uncle had invited Hazen and his parents to a formal dinner party. The reason was Hazen's father's Nobel Prize for experiments (done a number of years before) in which he had taken the amino acid "package" off proteins, then put it back on. At least that is how I understood it at the time.

Aunt Lillian was wearing what my mother would have called "a cocktail dress." Not the kind of dress you saw Harriet Nelson wearing on television in those days (and not the kind my mother owned), but the kind that Olivia de Havilland wore in the movies. It was pale green with tiny gold flecks that seemed to have been woven into the fabric. I had never seen anything like it. Later in the evening, I would notice that her dress matched in a subtle way the dinner plates, goblets, and even a small glass dinner bell that were put out by Bella, my aunt's maid.

"Now use your forks from the outside in," said Aunt Lillian, taking me to the table. "'Outside' being the fork all the way to the left. And do not use the spoon or the fork above the plate until the plate has been changed, and then use the outer one first; in this case that will be the spoon for the sorbet, then the ice-cream-cake fork for the ice cream cake that they make at the lovely bakery on Shaddock where they make so many fine things. When you are finished with your courses, put your knife and fork at four o'clock on your plate. That way Bella will know you are finished. And hold your wine glass by the stem, although Howard's mother takes hers by the bowl and puts her—I must say—rather large nose into it. And sniffs quite loudly."

By this time my uncle had escaped to stand in the driveway to wait for his friend.

"Hazen," I said. "His name is Hazen."

I had never been to a formal dinner party, much less in the presence of a Nobel Prize winner. And I had never worn a tuxedo. My brother rented one for the high school prom. My sister's boyfriend picked her up in one for the same dance. I wore a dark suit, went without a date, and stood by the record player and watched Muff LaRue dance to Dean Martin's "Memories Are Made of This."

"When Bella serves a new course," my aunt continued, "it is polite to change the direction of your conversation. You will be sitting between Doctor Reed on your left and Madame de Ferney on your right, and if you have been talking to Doctor Reed for the first course, you then talk to Madame de Ferney during the second course, then back to Doctor Reed for the next course. Madame de Ferney may not converse this way. She has a habit of talking to whomever she wants."

Aunt Lillian paused for a moment and looked at the table, first at one chair, then another, slightly nodding at each, as if more than counting.

"At home we just ate," I said. I thought I should say something by way of thanking Aunt Lillian for telling me how to behave.

"It *is* all a bit fussy," she said. "Conroy doesn't much like it. He says dinner parties are fork-fetish feasts. I suppose he's right, but we women have to keep up standards. Do you see a young lady in Kansas?"

"Muff LaRue," I said, thinking I didn't know the meaning of "fetish."

"When did you last see her?" said my aunt, now circling the table to make some adjustments in napkins and silverware.

"At the swimming pool where I work."

"How nice."

"Yes," I said.

Aunt Lillian stepped back to look the table over at some distance. "Everything is in its place," she said, more to herself than to me. Then: "One more thing. Madame de Ferney always brings the hors d'oeuvres. A duck pâté on toast points. I will put them on a large plate and we will have them in the living room with some white wine before dinner."

"I know it is not polite to take the last one," I said.

"Yes," said my aunt, and looked pleased. "Madame de Ferney has kept her curious name," Aunt Lillian continued, now looking past the table and around the dining room and into the living room, where Bella was putting out napkins and wine glasses on the coffee table, "even though she has been married all these years to Doctor Reed, who, as you know, is Howard's father, just as Madame de Ferney is Howard's mother, even though she doesn't have the same last name as Doctor Reed. Or maybe Doctor Reed is Howard's stepfather and Madame de Ferney is his mother. I think that's what Conroy once told me. She came to America when she was very young and brought Howard with her."

"That's what Hazen told me," I said.

"And for some reason I think Howard doesn't have the same last name as either of them because Madame de Ferney named him for an uncle for whom a French village is named. Or maybe she is named for the village. Howard is an only child so I suppose it is easier to do that when you are an only child. And Madame de Ferney always calls Doctor Reed, 'Doctor Reed,' not by his first name as the rest of us do. So we all call her Madame de Ferney and have for so long by now I don't remember her first name, but I think it's Mimi. You should ask Howard. Very curious."

"Hazen," I said. "Howard's name is Hazen."

"Here they are," said my uncle from the doorway.

"There is something else," Aunt Lillian continued, but in a lower voice. "Madame de Ferney keeps both her hands on the table, sometimes even her elbows. She is French. They have peculiar manners. And her English after all these years is still odd. A bit of French mixed in with English. Very odd."

"My mother said I should cut my food with my elbows down, not up. And that I should bring my food to my mouth and not my mouth to my food," I said, again trying to reassure my aunt. But this time she seemed not to hear me and said:

"I am thinking maybe I should seat you...but no I can't...that would disturb the arrangement."

"Is it the case," Madame de Ferney said as Bella was clearing the table of the second course, "that in Kansas...how shall I put it?... *comment dirais-je? Je ne sais pas...*"

She said something else in French to her husband. I saw Hazen frown. I saw Doctor Reed frown. Doctor Reed said something in French. Then Madame de Ferney said to me:

"Is it 'provincial' in Kansas? Provincial?"

She pronounced her second "provincial" with a certain prairie flatness, as if to make sure it was not the English but the American version. Not that it mattered: It was not a word I had discovered in my mother's dictionary: *Rube. Ff.*

While it was true that Madame de Ferney had used her forks according to Aunt Lillian's rules, she had not—as my aunt had predicted—abided by the formalities of conversation; also, her elbows had been on the table repeatedly, and (my mother would have been shocked) Madame de Ferney had removed her bread from the bread-and-butter-plate and put it on the tablecloth where it left crumbs. And she not only stuck her nose into the wine glass, she swirled it around before holding it to the light and said: It is the first duty of a wine to be red.

"Don't you agree?" said Madame de Ferney to my aunt.

"Yes indeed."

"And from what you call the *environs*. Is that the right word, Floren?"

"Yes," I said. Everybody looked at me for a moment and then Madame de Ferney asked me what kind of wine we drank in Kansas.

"My mother has a glass of Mogen David as she fixes dinner," I said. "My father drinks Coors. My mother is Polish. My father Irish." In the small silence that followed, everyone took a sip of wine.

"I ask about Kansas being provincial," Madame de Ferney said, "because I am told they were provincial *ici* in San Francisco before the *gros* earth cake. The *gros* earth cake and the fire did them a great good in that regard because the rebel lost their shanties."

"*Rabble*, Mother," said Hazen.

Madame de Ferney paused only to mouth the word *rabble* silently with what seemed to me impatience toward the English language.

"Mother's '*gros*' is French for 'large,'" Hazen said to me. "The Great Earthquake."

"Thank you," I said. And as if to show I was going to learn French I repeated "*gros*" out loud.

"You'll need to work on your *r*," Hazen said. I had no idea what he meant.

At this point Bella came to serve another course, while Madame de Ferney continued:

"The families whose furniture came 'around the Horn' began to *assende* and that gave the city its culture. Some people who first arrived in San Francisco brought their furniture with them over the prairie ground in wagons. It must have been very hard on chairs. Not to mention desks and tables. All of Doctor Reed's family furniture came 'around the Horn.' Our chairs are very solid. *Très solide.*"

Madame de Ferney had been speaking to the table at large, but then she again turned to me:

"They have no earth cakes in Kansas to make matters better. *C'est très mal* in that regard, don't we all think so? Maybe a dust storm or a prairie bison fire could do the same thing. Does your family have the particle?"

"'Quakes,' mother," said Hazen. This time Madame de Ferney did not mouth the word.

"They have tornadoes," said my aunt. "Tell Madame de Reed about the tornadoes. How Dorothy went to see Mr. Oz on the Yellow Brick Road. That might be just as good as earthquakes."

"'Madame de Ferney,'" my uncle said, but Aunt Lillian seemed not to notice.

I was about to ask "a particle of what?" thinking Madame de Ferney might have wondered if we owned a bit of farm ground, when Doctor Reed coughed rather loudly a number of times to my left and we all looked his way. My uncle patted him on the back and asked if he was all right.

"I was telling our nephew the other day," Aunt Lillian said when Doctor Reed's coughing spell stopped, "about that big rock at the top of the road, and how it might fall down if we had another earthquake like the one Madame de Ferney has mentioned." My aunt stopped for a moment and seemed befuddled.

"You were about to say something about the rock, Lillian," said Doctor Reed.

"Yes! Well, if it rolled down the hill it would squish that nice bakery on Shaddock where we got the dessert for tonight."

"Ah *oui!*" said Madame de Ferney. "It is a lovely bakery and

196

Doctor Reed always buys something from it whenever we are coming to the university. There is *rien* like it even in San Francisco."

"'*Rien*' means 'nothing,'" said Hazen. I nodded. "'*Rien*,'" I said, this time doing no better with my "*r*," judging by Hazen's look.

"*Nada*," in Spanish, said Doctor Reed.

"*Nada*," I said, thinking at least there wasn't an *r*. Again a moment of silence while everyone took another sip of wine and Bella bustled.

"And they probably don't have a bakery in Kansas like the one on Shaddock that we all like so much," said Aunt Lillian. "Just like they don't have hills down from which rocks might fall because they already have fallen down and that's why it is flat. And maybe that is why Madame de Ferney has asked about it being provincial. No quakes. No hills. No rocks. No bakery."

"Ah *oui*," said Madame de Ferney, at which point Aunt Lillian rang the bell for Bella, who was standing beside her.

"Maybe I should not have asked about Kansas being provincial," said Madame de Ferney. "It is of no matter, but sometimes those of us who live *la vie de château* cannot imagine remote places in the United States as being other than provincial. That is true in France as well. We have peasants in many places south of Paris. Some of them harvesting their own *poulet*."

"*Chicken*, Mother," said Hazen.

"I know it is 'chicken' in English," said Madame de Ferney. "But I prefer the French. Who can like a word like 'chicken' instead of '*poulet*'? Or 'duck' instead of '*canard*'?"

"It is what we had this evening," said Aunt Lillian. "A recipe right from France. Chicken cordon bleu. Not that we raise chickens or ducks here in Berkeley. I expect there is some kind of rule against it. I know there is one about hanging your clothes out to dry, isn't there Conroy?"

"There is indeed. It is called a 'covenant,'" my uncle said to Doctor

Reed, who smiled. "As if good taste were a religion. No rabbits in cages. No chickens. Or ducks. No horses or goats. It was quite a list they gave us when we moved here. No clothesline, as Lillian says."

"In Kansas we have a clothesline," I said. "I do the hanging out when I am home." Uncle Conroy looked at me and smiled. I was about to say the Simms down the road had both chickens and ducks as well as pigs they fed, when Madame de Ferney continued.

"It is our own limitation, I suspect, and I would be pleased to learn otherwise. How did your parents' furniture come to Kansas?"

"Here is dessert!" Aunt Lillian said, and once again rang the bell, even though Bella had returned to the table.

The arrival of dessert and the clatter of plates and forks and the general talk about the bakery on Shaddock changed the course of the conversation—or rather the monologue by Madame de Ferney—and as we ate she turned to Hazen and asked:

"Do you remember when you were an *adultlesson* and we took you to Paris?"

"*Adolescent*, Mother," said Hazen. "It is the same in French."

"Yes, I suppose it is," said Madame de Ferney. "It is just that we were showing you where I was reared—is that the word? You raise something like cows but rear children. Do I have that right?"

"Yes," said Doctor Reed. "Edmond was in fact born in Paris but they soon moved to America and he was reared here."

"Conroy and I have not reared any children," said Aunt Lillian. "This is our nephew," nodding toward me. Aunt Lillian seemed either to have forgotten my name or was continuing my family's tradition.

"Ah *oui*," said Madame de Ferney to Aunt Lillian.

"Ah *oui*," said Aunt Lillian. "But do tell us about your rearing in Paris."

"We lived in the Sixth, but below Saint-Germain. The Sixth goes all the way to Boulevard Montparnasse, but my father would not admit that. For him it only went as far as Saint-Germain. So I was reared in that domain. Is that the right word?" Madame de Ferney asked me.

"Ah *oui*," I said. I saw Hazen smile. "Or you could say 'environs,'" I said. Madame de Ferney seemed pleased at this information and this time said *environs* out loud with a peculiar guttural sound on the *r*.

"My father was *très* formal and would not even '*tu*' my mother. Of course, he did not '*tu*' me or my sister." Madame de Ferney paused for quite awhile and looked away from the table. The only sound was Bella putting out coffee cups in the living room.

While Madame de Ferney was thinking of her days growing up in Paris, for my part, between the rocks tumbling down and squishing the Shaddock bakery, the tornadoes that might be as good as earth cakes, covenants against chickens and clothes on the line, I had been thinking in bits and pieces about home: my father's webbed aluminum lawn chair and how he took my uncle's letter and his meatloaf sandwich outside and read the letter while my mother cleaned the kitchen counter where we "just ate" on summer nights, my mother having her glass of Mogen David wine while she cooked with no idea about its duty, my father with his beer in a bottle after dinner as he read the paper or, on Fridays, watched boxing on television.

And it wasn't when Aunt Lillian asked me about a girlfriend that I had thought of Muff LaRue. It was when Madame Ferney was talking about chicken *poulet* and duck and *canard*. How, after both Muff and I got dressed and, not having gone "all the way," sat in two chairs under my lifeguard stand, and talked into the night about our futures: me to California to become a doctor, she going East to Sarah Lawrence to major in classics—and I thought then that studying classics at a fancy East Coast college for girls and skinny-dipping in a Kansas municipal pool with the lifeguard somehow didn't go together. But I did not say so.

Later I drove Muff home, and we promised we'd meet again

over Christmas break—at the swimming pool, cold and snow or not. Assuming my key still worked.

My aunt fingered the spoon on the top of her plate. She picked up her wine glass by the stem and studied the color. She rang for Bella.

"Thank you," my uncle said to Bella as she began clearing the table of dessert plates, all forks now at four o'clock.

"*Maintenant* that you are *ici* in Berkeley," said Madame de Ferney, "do you think it provincial in Kansas?"

My uncle was about to speak and so were Hazen and Doctor Reed when I said to Madame de Ferney—and, with considerable *aplomb*—to the rest of the table:

"Sometimes it is, and sometimes it isn't."

"Ah *oui!*" said Aunt Lillian.

"My mother was blown away by your quip extraordinaire," Hazen said the next day in the lab. "You are quoted on Russian Hill. She thought you were serious."

"I was."

"Did you miss Kansas?" Muff says to me. We are sitting in my father's lawn chairs that I have taken to the pool and put beneath my old lifeguard stand. It is snowing. The pool has been drained, but not to the bottom. There is a skim of ice on what water remains. "I did not," says Muff before I can answer.

"I did."

"Are you going back?" she says. "To Berkeley to be a doctor?"

"Hang up medicine," I say. "Unless it can create a Juliet."

She seems not to hear me and says, "I learned that Socrates took up dancing in old age. So I've started dancing. Modern dancing." She gets out of her chair and does a small pirouette in the snow in front of me.

"I've never dated a dancer," I say.

And then there is a silence between us. I take a sideways glance at her. She is looking at the space just in front of us where she has done her pirouette. The snow is falling faster now and it is filling her footprints. I never knew her well enough to guess what she might be thinking. But I was thinking I would not see much of her ever again, and I would be right about that.

"You haven't said if you are going back."

"In Berkeley," I say, "you don't just eat, and you can't hang your laundry on the line." She gets up from her chair and does a second pirouette, this time putting her toes into the same place where they had been before, and in so doing her feet make their marks in the same place where the snow had almost filled in her previous pirouette. And in coming back to her chair she steps into the same footprints she had made before, and smiles at being able to do so.

As I drove her home, Muff asked me if it was true I had once saved a boy from the deep end.

"Yes."

And it was at the door of her house that she told me it was from Shakespeare ("Hang up Philosophy"—not medicine) that Hazen had gotten his *mantra*, and even used the word, which I did not know until I came home that night and looked it up in my mother's dictionary.

The Four-Wheel-Drive Quartet

Nor is one silence equal to another.

—Donald Justice

It is Sunday. Where I live you get the *New York Times* at a tiny filling station whose habit it is to change brands of gasoline every so often. George's Exxon a few years ago. George's Texaco last summer. At present it is George's Co-Op Gasoline. George is a portly man who wears sports coats and jeans throughout the week and adds a tie for Sundays. He is a hummer and whistler of songs, and you sense he has made some division between ones to be whistled and ones to be hummed. This morning it is "As Time Goes By." A hummed version. The Quatrain Theatre in the mall has been showing *Casablanca.*

Not one person, George tells me when I pick up the paper, not one person all morning knew the first line of verse: "This day and age we're living in gives cause for apprehension." It has meaning, he says, and taps the *Times.* "All people remember is the popular: 'It's still the same old story, a fight for love and glory!' Nobody remembers the nooks and crannies. That's where life and death is. Read it (and here he points to the paper under my arm), read it and remember we are all in this together." He rotates his arms and shoulders through an imaginary golf swing à la Johnny Carson. It is his way of moving from one customer to another—in this case to the dark blue Oldsmobile of my neighbor's wife just arrived at the gas pumps. Crossing behind her car George swings again. His shot is a slice that trails out over the pastures which circumscribe our suburb. At night, I think, it would make coyotes howl—the way shooting stars will: *Light and sound are friends. Most accidents occur after a rain, not during it. Baseball, like life, is not a timed sport. Pull the shade and light the light, we'll be home late tonight. Reynolds. Tommy. Nine Fingers. We are experience that has decided, for once, to talk.*

More and more Sundays are becoming as routine as the rest of the week. I worry about that. I would rather export Sunday's placid ambience into the preceding days than to have it slimmed down to their ilk. I think of Sunday as a large Hudson parked in the haze of an October afternoon. I am sitting in the back. Others are poking around outside. There are books, magazines, and papers on the back window shelf; the light is right for reading. Verdi is in the radio.

The news in the *Times* is messy. The Beirut fighting. It is not only the headlines, but the back pages have a day-to-day account. Four days. Four pages. Pictures. Reports. Opinion. It is far away though, and if you read the paper as I do—the front page through in total, then turning to the page where most of the stories are completed and, holding the bits and pieces of one story in your mind as you put it with the chunks of another—if you read that way, then the news is a matter of print. Nothing more.

The *Magazine*'s cover story is "Beyond Newton and Einstein." It is about physics and the universe. The *Times* is not a trifle weary of Mister Einstein's theory. There are other articles in the *Magazine*: France. The Psychic Toll of the Nuclear Age. Fenway Park. I'll save Psychic Toll and Fenway Park for the week; the article on the universe will fill the stalled Hudson before I'm through. Like some young man on the prairie who looks up at the stars one night and realizes that is where his death lives, I get frightened at having myself scattered by a physical law that rearranges me into sub-solipsist particles and scatters them across the theories of the future.

Still, I can resist neither myself nor my death. Both are stored, I have come to believe, in my head. I wonder, as Tommy once did, if the electrical soup of my brain and the cosmic weather of the universe amount to the same thing.

I read slowly. I listen to records. I take an hour out to watch *Meet the Press*: someone from the government explains war. It has taken me most of the morning to get through the first section. The following sentence arrests me, perhaps forever: "Theoretical particle physicists ponder questions that, by comparison, make *Alice in Wonderland* seem as mundane as baseball in Kansas."

One summer in the early sixties I had a job working the oil patch in Western Kansas. I was a suburban teenager and my father thought it would be good for me to thrash around with working-men instead of clipping hedges and waxing the Oldsmobiles that rested on their dark asphalt driveways up and down the curving roads of Fairway Manor. My father had interests in Western Kansas oil.

It was the summer before my university freshman year, and I remember my mother would forward the various letters, maps, and pamphlets the admissions office sent to "campus bound" students. These publications were so precise and detailed, so full of regulations and specified freedoms, that they seemed to steal away any chance of adventure. I said as much to Tommy, Tommy Duggan, who although my own age, was not going to the university, but who would read with great interest every word of the material that came my way.

"Maybe if I were going," he said, "I wouldn't want to read it either." But he was just being decent about my transparent and callow hostility for bureaucratic mail. Tommy lived to read.

"You don't get letters from the dean when you come to work on a rig," I said, imitating Nine Fingers' burly disdain.

"Reynolds doesn't write," said Tommy. "He reads but he doesn't write. Not much, in any case. Besides," Tommy said looking at a map of the university campus, "it's not like you want to picture yourself washing down a rotary table." He asked for the map if I didn't want it; I'd give him whatever came along.

He liked me, and I knew that because he felt free to be quiet around me. Or to read. Sometimes we'd be alone in the truck before the shift began, and Tommy wouldn't say much, only a few words now and then—like breathing, so you would know he was still there. But every once in a while he'd produce some stray fact his mind had stored and that, for reasons which seldom seemed evident, surfaced: Alfred Hitchcock appears in all his movies.

"There is a man," he once said while we sat on the bench outside the Pool Table Tavern in Ellis, "there is a man in England who never sleeps. Never."

There were four of us that summer. There still are; I live on the East Coast near the Chesapeake Bay in what is called (when you come to sell or buy such property) a "discreet" development. Few of us here know one another; none of us can see the sprawling ranch house of the other; there are no outbuildings with bleached skulls, no turtle barrels; we are all in Echo Hollow. A distant relative of my father's briefcase is parked in the back seat of my German car. I have interests in many things. A wife and I are separated. Children are at small private colleges that field lacrosse and soccer teams. I am self-employed in torts. Reynolds, Nine Fingers, and Tommy are where they were—living in that thick strip of land my university geography professor was to call the Great Plain—with the accent on plain. He was from New York. Manhattan in New York, as Reynolds sang it.

Reynolds was Tommy's father; Nine Fingers was his uncle and they lived together and worked the rigs. Reynolds led the singing. Like the rest of us he sang badly, but beyond that he couldn't remember the words, so neither the tune nor the lyrics gave you a clue to the song: "Manhattan in New York," Reynolds sang to the gears of his truck as we drove to work: "Telegraph cables, they zip down the highways…" It was one of the songs he would sing by himself; there were others we would all sing: "Red River Valley," "I've Been Working on the Railroad," "I Ride an Old Paint." The cowboy songs were for Nine Fingers; he wanted to own a ranch when he'd saved enough money to buy a share in an oil well that came in.

"I ride an old paint, I lead an old dam, I'm going to Montana to throw a houlianhan," Nine Fingers sang. He was a short stubby man whose voice, for all his thick chest, seemed to come from his cheeks.

"A houlianhan is a party," said Nine Fingers one day when we were driving to the rig, "and the guy is going to Montana to give himself a big bash just for getting there."

"A houlianhan is a steer," said Tommy. "They're going to a rodeo. Not a party."

"I want it to be a party," said Nine Fingers. "When I sing it I'm the guy in the song, and I'm going to a party: 'They feed in the coulees and they water in the draws. Their backs are all matted, their tails are all raw," Nine Fingers sang in his puffy voice.

"Get a sea song," Reynolds said to me. "I need a new sea song."

"Reynolds's going to buy a boat when he hits a well of his own," said Nine Fingers. "See these," and he held up copies of *Sail Magazine.* "Five years now he's been getting them on subscription. He's even got a map on the wall showing where he's going."

"A chart," said Tommy.

"He's got a timetable as well," said Nine Fingers.

"A log," said Tommy.

"A log," said Reynolds, and I could see him in the windshield, his face lit by the lights of the instrument panel of the truck.

"He's got a compass in the Hudson," said Nine Fingers.

"I'm on the Pacific Coast off Alaska," said Reynolds. "I sail south when the leaves turn. I follow the autumns down and the springs back. I sail my Octobers all the way to lower Mexico. The first couple of times I stay close to shore. But one day I'm looking off to the right heading south and I see the blue water. I head out. Blue-water sailors, that's what they call you when you get out of sight of land," he said.

Later, weeks later, as Tommy and I rode along in the truck from the motel to the Pool Table Tavern for a few beers before our shift, Tommy told me it is a tiny bone in your ear that makes you seasick; and that when you go through the water with a boat at night and hit algae, they'll light up and glow in their dying, like tiny depth charges, or like lightning bugs on the truck's windshield.

"It's the electricity being rearranged," Tommy said. "Your brain is electric soup."

Tommy worked derrick, a job high in the rig where you rack pipe. Tommy's was a punishing job; it was the job that took the most strength. Reynolds was the driller, the boss of the crew. He ran the rig, hoisting and lowering the blocks with a diesel-powered draw works. Nine Fingers threw chain, screwing the drill pipe together when you added a joint. I worked backup. I washed down the drilling table, racked pipe, helped the water hauler fill the pit, and cleaned out the Dog House—a tiny shed on the edge of the base that had lockers for your gear, benches, logs for the well, various gauges, and a stove for winter. Greenhorns like myself were called "worms."

"I was a worm once," said Nine Fingers. "Worms can grow themselves out again when they get cut in half, but fingers can't." He pointed his right index finger stub at Tommy. "Isn't that right, Tommy."

"That's right," said Tommy.

"I tell the ladies a shark bit it off," said Nine Fingers. He jabbed the stump into the air, then thumped it on his chest. "They love the missing finger," he said, "and they love the story that goes with it."

He pointed the stub at his mouth and bit the air where the finger would have been.

"He used to flinch when he'd do that," said Tommy. "That's because you can't help but think that whatever got cut off is still there."

"My little lovely," said Nine Fingers making with his hands the outline of a portly woman, "I was picking up sharks' teeth from the old days when this was an ocean. A shark was still alive after all those years, living in cold water inside a rock from the Ice Age, just like a carp will freeze up in a backwater of the Saline and come to life in the spring." Nine Fingers put his arm around the form he'd made in the air. "Let me tell you about it over a beer, you little fat girl." Then, turning to us, he said, "God, they love it." He bit the air in front of himself.

Nine Fingers did have an eye for the sharks' teeth that you'd find when they pushed around the dirt to make a drilling site. Sharks' teeth and the popping rocks that would make tiny explosions when you put them on a fish fry fire. He always seemed to have a shark's tooth in his pocket, and in the Pool Table Tavern you could watch him give them out to women at the bar. He had a taste for wildly ugly women: he could find the toothless one among a full table of close-mouthed ladies who had stopped by after the bowling league. Women with warts; fat-backed women with beer kegs for legs; women with sheets of stringy hair who, as Nine Fingers himself once said, looked like chewed toothpicks.

"He likes women with bugs on them," said Reynolds, making again the outline of Nine Fingers' woman, only this time fatter and misshapen.

"God made whiskey so even ugly women could have fun," said Nine Fingers. "I take a big drink and give them some sharks' teeth and popping rocks from the old days. I tell them a story. It warms their warts and coddles their fat. We all get to be alive," he said. He pointed the stub of his finger at each one of us: one, two, three, four, and then on to himself. I was four. After the woman. His finger's end was dark red, almost black. It was to Nine Fingers later in the summer that Reynolds would say I had about me the mark of death.

The old days turned out to be the Paleozoic Age to my Manhattan-in-New York geography professor—an age when the dusty towns of Wakeeney, Hill City, Munjor, and Palco were all on the bottom of a sea—much like the farms and ranches that had recently been flooded by irrigation projects, so you'd have to watch out for Dick Wilson's silo when you fished the west cove at Cedar Bluff, or Frank Murray's hedgerow that used to run up to his house but was now the lure trap for bass fishermen in Baylor's Bite. Sometimes, Tommy would say in his dreamy way, it seemed to him we were all in circles—not just the earth as a ball—but what the earth did with itself all seemed to be turning in circles of various sizes. When he'd say that, or when he'd talk about other matters he'd thought about for a while, he'd rotate his hand in the air beside him, as if stirring the void. Pack up all your care and woe, here we go, singing low.

My hammock is still up. There are mums coming into cool bloom, and there are leaves on the maples that twist their backs to the wind and show their shiny side so they look silver. One tree has shed its leaves early and it stands in flagrant contrast to the rest. The retired army colonel who lives across the street says it is in trouble—a gentle euphemism here in Echo Hollow for a variety of illnesses that have but one thing in common: Mrs. Thomas, down the road on the left, grey with pancreatic cancer, is in trouble. The colonel tells me that in the fifties Echo Hollow was a golf course; perhaps, he muses, the trees that line the roads once lined old fairways. It is Monday as I write these notes.

It has been dry in recent weeks and many of the leaves have fallen without turning color—only going to a thin veneer of themselves, a gaunt patina. From where I sit I can see such leaves on the hammock: a breeze rearranges them now and then, and some blow off or fall through. It seems as if only so many can gather there, although there is room for a man-sized bundle. Dust, the colonel tells his wife's cleaning lady, collects four years and then it builds up no more. Such erudition amuses him.

The hammock wants to come in. Its time is over. I leave it out nearly a month past when I'll use it. I like to see things out of season: beaches in winter; firewood stacked along the back edge of the property that I can see summer afternoons while lying in the hammock. Stopped clocks. The truth is I don't get much use out of the hammock: I could never sip a gin and tonic supine; reading there puts a crease in my neck. Once, I thought I might sleep overnight in it—like a sailor—as if by so doing I could, all at once, justify its purchase. But it remains exterior decor, a glossy catalogue arrangement of life. The view I have from my window is the picture that sold me the hammock (sans leaves) and I wonder if I should return it to its catalogue for winter or bring it into the garage. The professor who lives behind me suggests I dry onions in it.

My hi-fi is more definite about its needs: it wants to be repaired. Its left speaker is weak. It has gone out before. Old Barbara Streisand records at top volume will do it, but this time Dave Brubeck did it. I must take the speaker to the mall to be fixed—something I don't mind. I rather like the man who runs the audio store (his lady assistant is young and pretty). He used to live in Echo Hollow, but not anymore. His wife does. She is a long dogleg to the right from me. Something must be done to the speaker's base or coil or tweeter or horn. I refuse to understand.

My first semester at the university, that autumn of my working summer, I learned it was important to have a record player. My parents had had the idea that I should take piano lessons: my mother said that to be able to play would make me the center of attention at parties. My father said women liked men who could entertain them. What was left of these desires got invested in a record changer. Mine had its speaker in the lid, and you could put a whole stack of albums on it so that it would play through half an evening, the soft thud of Peter, Paul and Mary falling on the just completed Kingston Trio. You were known to women for your changer and your album collection.

The young woman assistant in the audio store smiles at the owner and says to me that it is not quite that way anymore. They are both amused at my language: record player, changer. My father had a hi-fi. It was a large low box whose top you could open and inside was a tiny cockpit of pale green and orange lights, firm turn dials, stiff push buttons, and needles that bounced with the music. Once, when it went dead in mid-Mantovani, my father lifted the lid and removed the access panel to a tangle of brightly colored wires and tiny tubes. He stared at it all, much as I did the other day when, for no reason that I knew (or now know two hundred dollars later), my German car stopped, and I was forced to play out that comic American male routine of lifting the engine hood only to look as knowingly as I could at a maze of hoses, wires, pipes, coils, pollution control, fuel injector carburetors, transistorized ignition—looking at it all with the practiced eye of a jet engine mechanic, as if I could see right off that a computer chip had gone wrong and that, plus some aberration in the fuel flow, had brought me to a halt on the side of the beltway. There I was, without a spare computer chip. My father and I look a bit dismayed. I see our faces in the windshield of the car from which no music comes. Neither of us will get the Mercedes or the Mantovani going again.

You have components, says the man who fixes my speaker. His assistant nods and touches him lightly on the sleeve. You do not have a changer, she tells me, you have a turntable. You have a tuner, not a radio, he says. A tuner wired into an amplifier. What I need next, they both agree, is an equalizer. With a few judicious purchases I will have a system compatible with the future, so that when tiny satellite discs come onto the market I can bring the world into my living room.

It is, I think, as if my house in Echo Hollow is about to be stuffed with the cords and boxes and wires of an intensive care unit. An attack of ennui can be moderated by a transfusion of "Penny Lane." Angst needs the slow dripping somnolence of liquid Mozart. Terminal isolation will be cured by the broadcasts of the BBC. Cosmic absurdity can be repaired by the divine stitching of a Bach fugue. But what is to be done about chronic memory? That summer I worked in the oil patch, Reynolds' truck did not have a radio: we sang our way to work and back home again. A darkening shadow on your brow, oh I will take you home again Kathleen.

"You got a song yet?" asked Reynolds one June night on the way to the rig. He was humming something to himself; it was difficult to say what.

"A song to sing," said Nine Fingers sitting in the front beside Reynolds. The truck was a double cab pickup with four-wheel drive so we could get in and out of the job no matter what the weather was like. The few times it rained, the oil lease roads turned to a slick ebony, and once we had to pull a tool pusher's truck out of a ditch.

"Not yet," I said.

"The kid out here last summer, he had a song," said Reynolds.

"Waltzing Matilda," said Nine Fingers. He sang the verse and then Reynolds joined him. If Nine Fingers sang from his puffed cheeks, Reynolds sang from his wide shoulders; together they were astonishingly bad. Tommy and I joined in from the back seat as a matter of self-defense, but we weren't much better.

"What's a billy-bong?" said Reynolds.

"English infantry," said Nine Fingers.

"Billabong," said Tommy. "It's 'billabong' and 'jum buck,' not 'junk buck.' A 'billabong' is a pond, and they call sheep 'jum bucks.'"

"Is that true?" said Reynolds.

"You learn something from Tommy every day," said Nine Fingers to me leaning over the bench of the truck seat and looking into the back of the cab. "You sure you don't have a song?"

"'If I Had a Hammer,'" I said.

"What's that," said Nine Fingers to Reynolds.

"What's that?" said Reynolds to Tommy via the cab mirror.

"Peter, Paul, and Mary," said Tommy.

"Protest?" said Nine Fingers.

"Not really," said Tommy.

"Sounds like protest," said Nine Fingers. "Let's you get another song." He turned back around. Reynolds started humming the remnants of "Waltzing Matilda."

"When I make that right turn off the coast," Reynolds said, "I'll sail all the way to Australia. Then I'll be a blue-water man, no doubt about it."

"'Red River Valley,'" said Nine Fingers suddenly. I could see in the mirror Reynolds' grin, wide like his shoulders. He punched the accelerator and the truck jumped forward as if it were a downbeat. "'Come and sit by my side if you love me / Do not hasten to bid me adieu / Just remember the Red River Valley / And the cowboy who loved you so true.'" In this case Tommy's efforts to get the words right had succeeded. Other attempts that summer failed.

"Why don't we stop in the music store in Ellis and get a copy of the song," Tommy said one day when there was a debate over "Bye, Bye Blackbird." Did it go "Pull the shade and light the light, I'll be home late tonight," as Nine Fingers said, or was it "Make the bed and light the light," as Reynolds sang it?

"Sing it the way you want," said Reynolds to Tommy. "It's your song."

"Song books are for piano benches," said Nine Fingers.

"I wonder what it means," said Tommy.

"What?" asked Reynolds.

"Bye, bye blackbird. Not the song, just those words."

"Same as 'Hi Lilly, Hi Lilly, Hi Low,'" said Nine Fingers. "It doesn't mean anything only it helps you remember what to sing."

"It means good-bye to winter," I said. It was the first opinion I'd offered.

"Is that true?" said Reynolds.

"It might be," said Tommy.

"Did you learn that in a book?" said Nine Fingers.

"Not really," I said.

"Nine Fingers doesn't think you learn much from books," said Tommy.

"Not about beer, weather, guns, women, trucks, rigs, or songs," said Nine Fingers. "You pick that stuff up or you don't get it at all."

"How about electricity?" said Tommy.

"You can learn about that from books," said Nine Fingers.

"Electricity is the index finger of God," said Reynolds.

"My hair stands on end when there is lightning in the air," said Nine Fingers.

"He's a rare man," said Tommy.

"Tommy read about me," said Nine Fingers.

"Nine Fingers has got to squat down on one foot when there's lightning around so he's not a big target and not grounded through the heart," said Tommy.

"That's all true," said Reynolds, more to me than just out loud.

"The song of love is a sad song," Nine Fingers sang from his cheeks, and we all joined in after the chorus. Hi Lilly, Hi Lilly, Hi Low.

There is a college near Echo Hollow. Not a great nor big school, but still it has its bucolic campus: Large elms with benches under them. Cherry trees with marble plaques testifying to the learning of an otherwise forgotten professor. A plaza in front of the library. Brick walks. Bicycle racks. A modest flock of pigeons that, I remember from "Introduction to Literature" the autumn of my freshman year, forever make an emblematic poem as they sail in unison over the trees toward the cupola of a classroom building.

It is the college where my professor neighbor teaches. He tries to get me involved. I should take an evening course. He offers "Aquatic Grasses of the Chesapeake Bay." There is also the college community band: perhaps, he wonders one summer evening while leaning on the stack of wood that divides our property, perhaps I should play an instrument. They can use a French horn (Mrs. Thomas down the road has had to retire). It is important, the professor thinks, not to become islands in this world.

I go to the college during vacations. I rather like the campus on Thanksgiving and Christmas, and I even take the trouble to find the dates of spring break and walk there then as well. There is something generous and rich about an empty campus, as if it has gone into its head to think. No classes. No lectures. No movies. No professors gossiping like figures in a Daumier drawing. The books loom in a locked library.

It is weeks until Thanksgiving. I find myself counting the days on the historical calendar I got as an advertisement for the college's concert series. I must get through the coronation of Elizabeth the First, the death of Robin Hood, the delivery of the Gettysburg Address, the births of Voltaire, André Gide, Paul Céline, and Laurence Sterne. But from Laurence Sterne through Advent the campus will be empty, save for the pigeons making a poem about the solitary prose walking along the walks: Sometimes we move in circles, sometimes in lines.

In Western Kansas that summer I lived in the Warm Blanket Motel in Ellis, Kansas. Ellis is where the trains switch their clocks to Mountain Standard Time, and even though it is not until fifty miles west that people change time, still being on the edge of a large time zone, plus Daylight Savings Time, made it so you could see a glow in the west even past nine o'clock when we would start our drive to work.

My family owned the Warm Blanket Motel. We seemed to own bits and pieces of other businesses in Ellis—and we owned various-sized shares in wildcat oil wells in the country—but we owned the Warm Blanket Motel, mice, miller moths, centipedes, scorpions and all.

It had been my father's habit to house his nephews, nieces, and associates' children (all shipped to Western Kansas for real work)—to house them in the numberless room next to the motel's office. Taken together we were known as the Drew people—for that was the name of an uncle in business with my father, although it is not my name—and each of us over the summers of the fifties and sixties were called the Drew girl or the Drew boy, with the women being called Miss Drew and the men being called Drew, as if it were a first name. I was called Drew by Reynolds and Nine Fingers and at times they would confuse me with previous Drews of previous years.

During the first few weeks of work I was a collection of young men, an anthology of eighteen-year-olds about to go to the university. It may not have been a bad way to gather an identity. Had I any sense of irony, I would have gladly accepted my montage; it is one thing to adopt fully the life of another, but it is another—as it has turned out—to become an accumulation of many.

"Hand me the hammer you busted," said Reynolds one day early in the summer. At first I was too timid to correct Reynolds and Nine Fingers about my identity. No, I didn't want to swim the English Channel by the time I was twenty-five. No, I didn't play the guitar. No, my girlfriend's name was not April, and she was not coming out to see me that weekend. No, my father was not a doctor in Denver. Tommy kept me straight. He got the hammer.

"Kevin broke the handle two years ago," Tommy said as he

flipped it into the air so that it twisted and turned like a clumsy diver off the high board of the country club swimming pool.

"When you throw a hammer," Tommy said, tossing it into the air again, this time with purpose, "in one loop the head will change sides so that when the hammer comes back down the head will be pointing the other way. Left," he said as the hammer handle smacked into his palm. "Water," he said, looking at the hammer doing another round of twists and turns in the air, "goes down a bathtub clockwise in the northern hemisphere. It's the same way tornadoes turn."

"Hammer," Reynolds yelled from the Dog House.

In a shopping mall, not far from where I live, is the Quatrain Movie Theatre. It is run by a pleasant man of my own age who has taken it upon himself in the age of quad theaters to insist upon calling his place The Quatrain, and to spell "Theatre" in the English fashion, as if mere words might bring some civility to the video-game quality of the mall. He is an Anglophile of sorts, and as such seems sadly out of place in the huge corridors and among the fake rubber tree plants. In London, he told me once, you know when a train is coming on the underground because it pushes the wind in front of it and there is a strong breeze on the platform minutes before the train arrives. In the mall, he says, it is impossible, even when it is completely empty, to know if a door is open. Everything is assimilated.

Still, he makes an effort, walking out in front of his theater among the patrons handing out tiny flyers (of his own making) that describe the evening movies. He seems to take modest pleasure in explaining the two hours of dark you are about to undertake.

His four theaters play different kinds of films. To be precise, and he would want me to be, he shows both "movies" and "films": all foreign movies are "films," while only some California movies are "films." These semantics are not judgmental: "films" may be as good as "movies"; it is just that *Casablanca* is a "movie," while *Virgin Spring* is a "film." Quatrain One plays children's movies (*E.T.* this week); Quatrain Two shows popular movies (*An Officer and a Gentleman*); to those of us who visit Quatrains Three and Four (serious movies and foreign films), the theater owner will confide that all popular movies are "white bread." He says it in a low voice, "white bread," as if it were a racial slur, not the words themselves, but the movie itself.

Breaker Morant is a serious movie. *La Cage aux Folles* a foreign film. There must be subtitles in foreign films, therefore British and Australian movies are not foreign. But since the owner rather admires Australian movies, they are almost always to him serious, as are many English movies as well. *Stevie*, for instance, is a movie that warms the cockles of his heart. It is the poetry of English house life.

This evening was the first showing of *Melvin and Howard*. It had one of our songs in it: "Bye, Bye Blackbird." The story is of a young gas station attendant who picks up Howard Hughes on a highway and talks him out of great gloominess by singing "...pack up all your cares and woe."

The movie has left its mark on me, as if there were, in its frames, a code to trigger a playback of my past: Did the light from that summer twenty years ago set itself free into the circles Tommy twirled with his hands, and then rotate its way through Hughes' Nevada, the movie's Hollywood, and into the Quatrain Three, only to loop over a largely innocent audience, save for one who found himself spooked and rearranged, as if irradiated by the past? I followed the light's beam into the pickup truck: Here we go, singing low. Outside our windows the night is full of itself. Blackbird, bye, bye. Sunday's Hudson has gone her own way. I am inside the songs we sing. We hear ourselves among the nooks and crannies. We follow the spring to Fairbanks. The sun, sad rogue, is out all night. There are reasons God makes whiskey. We vanish with the houselights.

I've come home tonight full of rings of dark and light like some petrified, yet oddly living tree. No doubt in trouble.

We worked Morning Tower. There was Morning Tower, Evening Tower, and Daylight Shift, and even though Reynolds had enough experience in the oil patch to get a Daylight Shift, he'd always sign on for Morning Tower: eleven at night to seven in the morning.

"You don't get the tool pusher coming through," he said, "or some sport coat from the office."

"The owners are the worst," said Nine Fingers. "They'll own a sixty-fourth and come out every afternoon with a thermos of martinis and sit on the tailgates of their station wagons to watch the pipe go down and yack the geologist."

Even on Morning Tower you'd get owners if the samples looked good. When we got below 2500 feet we had to call the geologist on the mobile phone in the Dog House, and he'd call around with the news. It happened one night halfway through the summer.

"Tangerine, she is all they claim, with her eyes of night and lips as bright as flame..., and I've seen toasts to Tangerine raised in every bar across the Argentine..." That was our song that evening: Reynolds' song, to be exact. He liked songs about places he thought he could sail to. I had a song by then, and it had pleased him: "I've got sixpence, jolly, jolly sixpence." After you wind your way to the chorus you sing, "Happy as a day when a sailor gets his pay, as we go rolling, rolling home."

"I think that's a fine song," Reynolds had said. He made me talk him through it, and then he sang it once himself before he led us all in a rendition.

"There are four qualities of the human voice," Tommy was fond of saying in the moment after we had sung a song. "Pitch, timbre, tone, and range. We have none of them."

"Her heart belongs to Tangerine," sang Reynolds as we drove on toward the drilling site. In the west you could still see the faint glow of the previous day banked up along the horizon's edge. Tommy was looking out the window of the truck toward the west; he seemed to be studying the arrangements of light in the night. I looked with him: The radio beacon at Wakeeney blinks like a stranded airplane among the southwestern stars. We see tower lights from distant rigs. Shifts are changing. All around us truck lights edge along the section lines; one, fast and to the west of us, goes dark at the crossroad to look for other trucks so he can run the intersections. Stationary yard lights make small blue domes above farmhouses. We see the haze of swirling moths and millers, and the pale yellow light coming through a pulled shade in the kitchen. Someone is asleep. Someone will be home late tonight.

About two hours into the shift when we reached 2500 feet we called the geologist. He came out and read the drilling time and it looked good. He went into the Dog House and made some calls, then left.

"Every lawyer in town will be here before long," said Nine Fingers. "The place will look like the country club parking lot. In the daytime I've seen them bring their wives, and they all play bridge waiting for the well to make."

Reynolds, Nine Fingers and I were sitting in the Dog House watching the indicator and reading magazines. The drilling had been hard for the previous few days: we were deep in the hole where the rock is dense so that the pipe takes two hours or more to go thirty feet. Nine Fingers was flipping through old *Playboys*. Reynolds kept his *Sail Magazines* in a cardboard box which he hauled from site to site to read when it was slow time. All books are wishbooks.

You seldom found Tommy in the Dog House when the pipe was going slow. He'd either sit in the truck or walk out to the water pit and sit on the bank. That's where he was when the owners drove up.

"Lawyers," said Nine Fingers when you could see from where we sat that the lights coming up the lease road were those of a

Mercedes. "Oil gets them their money back on those polyester suits. Tommy told us polyester is made from plastic and that plastic comes from oil. That's why lawyers got to be careful not to rub up against one another or they'll jump a spark and burst into flames." Four men got out of the Mercedes and two of them came onto the base and over to the Dog House.

"How you guys doing?" said the man who drove the car. He was wearing a yellow Ban-Lon shirt.

"Hard drilling," said Nine Fingers.

"I hear we're looking good," said the other man. He was wearing plaid pants. "We got a piece of this," said the man in the Ban-Lon shirt.

"It will make or it won't," said Reynolds from behind his *Sail Magazine.*

"That's experience talking," said the man in the plaid pants. Then he said something to the man in the Ban-Lon shirt and they talked a moment before the man in the Ban-Lon shirt asked Nine Fingers:

"You the driller?"

"He's the driller," said Nine Fingers, pointing to Reynolds.

"He wouldn't mind if we hit a few balls, would he?"

The two other men were still at the Mercedes, and one of them pushed a button inside the glove compartment, and the trunk lid popped open.

"What?" said Nine Fingers.

"Golf balls," said the man in the plaid pants.

"You all wouldn't mind," said the man in the yellow shirt, and here his glance took me in as well, "if we hit a few golf balls. With the work lights we can see them partway into the pasture—we'll come back and pick them up tomorrow."

"We all got slices to work on," said the man in the plaid pants.

From where I sat I could see that the other two men had gotten a bucket of balls and some clubs out of the trunk. Nine Fingers was about to say something, but Reynolds said from behind the magazine:

"Do what you want."

"Thanks," said both men and clattered off the table toward the Mercedes. Nine Fingers put his *Playboy* away and went out to the platform. I walked down to the pit where Tommy was lying on his back. The way the derrick lights were rigged, the pit was in the dark, but you could see the pasture to the east where they were going to hit the balls.

"Lawyers hitting golf balls," I said as I came up to the pit. And then: "What are you doing?"

"Watching stars come in from the west," Tommy said. He sat up.

"Meteors," I said.

"Yes," he said. "It gets better in August, but it is good enough now."

"Do you know the names of the constellations?" I said.

"Some of them," he said. "Why?"

"It's just that I don't," I said.

"I got a book on them," he said. "They're in different places depending upon the time of the year. They migrate."

"I get scared looking at the stars," I said. "I can't do it for long."

"It's the outside of atoms," said Tommy. "We're in the middle looking both ways. Microscopes in one direction and telescopes in the other."

"I think it's where we go when we're dead," I said.

"So do I," said Tommy.

Off to the right we could see the pasture with a belt of light going down it. Every now and then you'd see a golf ball sail out over it and bend to the right and then into the darkness. They looked for a moment like moths coming through the light on a huge summer porch, a space age bug all aglow for a brief instant as it zipped from behind us somewhere and then into the light for a brief bright moment, and then into the dark.

"He's not doing any better on his slice," I said as one curved left to right out of sight.

"I wouldn't know," said Tommy. He laid back down again and drew a circle in the air above his head before he said:

"They say you can hear after you die. I read it the other day in the barber shop; they think the reason you should be quiet in a room where someone has just died is because they can hear. Even though their heart is stopped, and they're not breathing."

There was some silence between us. A shooting star made a long line west to east.

"It will make the coyotes howl," Tommy said.

"What?" I said.

"When you get a long one like that it will make the coyotes howl. You can hear them all along the line the light makes, so that their sound seems to chase it. Light and sound are friends," he said. He paused. "I don't like the noise on the rig, though." He pointed his head toward the derrick.

"It gets to you," I said.

"I like to think about things," he said. He made another circle with his hand. "It's hard to hear what you're saying to yourself on the derrick. What I like about reading is that you can hear yourself in your mind."

One of the golf balls went over our heads along the edge of the darkness and then curled back into the light. We could see it hit the pasture and bounce a few times.

"You know," said Tommy, "how on Sundays, when you haven't worked Saturday night, it seems like you got a fat day because you're up early?"

"I can't get used to working nights," I said. "I feel loose all the time."

"Not me," he said. "What I can't get used to is only one fat day a week. It's not like you can put a piece of Sunday in every other day, although I'd like to think I could."

He was about to say something more, but he sat up and looked at the pit instead. Nine Fingers yelled for me to wash down the base before he slipped and lost another finger. Fifteen minutes until we made a connection, he said.

I got up; Tommy laid back down on the ground and looked at the sky. I walked over to the truck for the hose nozzle, and then toward the rig, coming up on the Dog House from behind. Both Reynolds and Nine Fingers were out on the table watching the golfers.

"He's not a bad kid," I heard Nine Fingers say. He pointed the stub of his dark finger toward the pit where he thought I was.

"They're all stamped on the same machine," said Reynolds. "No missing fingers. New paint forever."

"Yeah," said Nine Fingers. "His pa is rich. His ma is good looking."

"It's their mark," said Reynolds, "their future being all sure and padded. He's dead for being so safe."

From where we were you couldn't see Tommy looking for shooting stars—nor for all the noise of the rig, hear the coyotes' howl chase the streaking light. We teach ourselves to hear ourselves think. Jolly, jolly no-pence. As we go rolling, rolling home.

I wear out my Sundays. By the afternoons I am looking for islands along the shore. A glass of jug Chablis with some leftover crab quiche at two. A nap. The long local news at five: a water pipe has burst. One downtown grocer is an uncle of a Marine wounded in Beirut. A guest star on the Waltons is acting in a nearby dinner theater. The weather woman points to a storm south of us that moves in the multiple pictures of a stationary satellite. These must be the layers of reality my university philosophy professor assured us existed.

The day rotates down: A drink. A friend. Drinks. Friends. Dinner. Wine and dinner. Chopin in the speakers and among the talk. Espresso I make myself from an Italian machine that spits and steams, wheezes and coughs. Irish Cream on the side. Friends leave. The Chopin changes to Mozart; the Mozart to Beethoven; in the blue black of night the Beethoven gives way to Charlie Parker, Lead Belly and Coltrane. A friend leaves. Terry Riley in C arrives. It is the story of our lives as we know them.

We are a landmass and there are no hopes for islands. The storm to the south goes out to sea; the satellite is looking for anything that moves. We are stationary. We can't get our days to fray and fade like some old pair of jeans we used to wear and wash and hang on the line for the wind to tousle. Our days wear out like tough plastic: discarded, compacted.

We always had water pits instead of tanks, and that meant you could take a swim during slow drilling, and it meant you could wash up at the end of the shift. There was something splendid and manly about riding back home in the truck, the sun cracking the east, and you all clean from having bathed in the pit after a night of mud and oil. It is like sailing all day in a rainy chop only to attend, that evening, a Grieg concert, and to join friends for late dinner afterward: it is not the same. All similes are flawed: they try to reach outside circles of being, as if to shake hands with indifferent strangers.

"Let's take a swim," Reynolds said to me one night. Tommy was racking pipe on the catwalk and Nine Fingers was looking for sharks' teeth. We walked down to the pit, and I took my boots and socks off and sat on the edge. Reynolds stripped naked and climbed in. He did an awkward dog paddle up the pit and back; it was curious to see a big man doing a child's stroke.

The well was running deep and we were toward the end of the job. If you're on a site long enough you'll get frogs and turtles in the pit. You can see the turtles' heads poking out of the surface, tiny black dots on large black water. Nine Fingers had already caught some good-sized ones and was feeding them out in rain barrels: when they got fat I was invited to dinner. A big snapping turtle can drag down a goose and drown it.

"What's college going to be like?" said Reynolds as he paddled back to where I was sitting. He squinted his eyes to look at the rig. From where we were you could see the weight indicator and I realized Reynolds had the pit dug with that in mind: you could see the draw works and the Kelly—all the things a driller and his crew needed to watch while the rig was going.

"I don't know," I said. Reynolds looked at me.

"What do you think about all those facts Tommy's got in his head?" said Reynolds. "The other day he was saying that you can swallow food even if you're upside down. Is he right six out of seven, or is he like Nine Fingers and makes it up for fun?"

"I think he knows things," I said. "He reads."

"That he does," said Reynolds. He looked down the water pit away from me and said: "Do me a favor."

"Yes," I said.

"When you get to college check up on one thing for sure: Nine Fingers wants to know about hunkering down on his foot when there is lightning around."

"Does his hair really stand on end?" I said.

"That's true," said Reynolds. He didn't say anything for a moment. "See about it for me, will you?" he said.

"Yes," I said. Off to one side I could see Nine Fingers poking around in the dirt by the light of the rig.

"Nine Fingers and Tommy can't swim," said Reynolds. "I taught myself in case I fell off my boat. I took one lesson at the town pool to see how it worked and I practice in the pits." He hoisted himself up on the bank. We sat there in silence for a moment. I looked up and saw Tommy making a count on the pipe. For some reason I felt embarrassed talking about college to Reynolds. I pulled my shirt and jeans off and slid into the water, swimming a lap away from Reynolds and the rig. I thought it might make a difference and smooth things out.

When I got to the far end of the pit, I pushed off the bank and started back. I had swum a crawl down, but I came back with a slow heads-up breaststroke, looking into the rig with all its lights and girders. Tommy had finished racking pipe and I could see he was staring out across the pasture. I remembered what he said about the noise getting into his head, and I wondered if he was trying to concentrate on the silence of the prairie that was out beyond the site.

I thought about Tommy as I swam toward him: I thought about myself. I thought how I had been sent to work on the rig so there would be something in my past to which I could point whenever I became whatever I would become: a little something for my character; a piano playing of labor. It seemed to me (even then) as I swam in the pit toward the rig, that the future was dancing not all that lightly with the present.

No one seemed to think Tommy needed a summer at a splashy country club working as a lifeguard and scooping the previous evening's bugs from the cool blue morning pool. He wasn't getting any insurance against some future night when his stereo failed to win friends and he needed a story to tell about the twists and turns a diver makes off a high board. Maybe all he needed, I thought as I swam toward him in the rig, was a way of making sense of all the knots of facts he'd picked up like so many popping rocks around the site: Alfred Hitchcock appears in all his movies. Don't we all, I am thinking, and in so doing I see that I am slipping out of myself. At first I think that for all my steady strokes I'm only treading water. It is as if I'm swimming a line to the derrick and into Tommy. From there we watch me in the pit breaststroking toward Reynolds.

Beyond the lights on the rig we know there are lightning bugs that emit different types of glow so that attraction is a matter of light. It is the amount of carbon that determines the hardness of steel. We are having a difficult time hearing ourselves even though we are full-minded. We set ourselves sailing across the prairie in search of fat Sundays. Fragments of songs are layered in our head like staff in sheet music. Or strata in rock. We're at home, late at night. We think we must tell Nine Fingers why his stones pop on the fish fry fire, and how once in Siberia, men lost and starving, found and ate an animal frozen in the ice from a previous age. The fiery and the sniffy are raring to go. We are homeward bound in all directions. We see Reynolds getting dressed and ask ourselves if that was experience talking about the mark of death. We are, we think, the circles we make with our hands.

"Tommy can't swim," said Reynolds as I reached the bank, "and Nine Fingers told me you can't go to college unless you can swim ten laps of a pool. Tommy couldn't do that. Find out if that's true while you're at it," Reynolds said, and he began to hum something I did not know.

"Yes," I said.

There is an ongoing debate in the local evening paper today about geraniums and what to do with them now that winter is coming down in the center part of the television weather map. Recently there have been flurries of heavy clouds over what we were told is the Midwest. The television computer etches its lines into the satellite picture of North America, and boundaries of states and nations cut up through the clouds—even the Lake-of-the-Woods puzzle piece, the one you can always spot in the puddle of other pieces. My mind stirs among other maps: a current events Kansas state map of the late fifties that hung on a grade school bulletin board that showed, among other things, where President Eisenhower had lived. A recent computer-assisted demographic map that demonstrated a drift of people over sixty toward some tiny town in Alabama where, in theory, they would all gather and retire, but where in practice none had. A forty-eight state map with capital cities, Washington, D.C., and a tiny circle in a rectangular midwestern state where the geographic center of the country was located north and east of my family's interests. Memories are maps. I like their fiction. The weatherman points to some ground clutter and says that it is of course the Chesapeake Bay. Shorelines make lace work in the haze. Rivers, islands, estuaries draw themselves on the screen. I am at the end of the weatherman's finger. All will be clear by morning, he tells me.

I did not read the original article on geraniums, but I have read the letters of rebuke and defense. You can either read three or four news articles partway through and put them together in some fashion when you turn to the back pages, or if you want to be more inventive about your news, you don't read the story in the first place so you can reconstruct it from editorials, letters, and op-ed pages. The news is irrelevant—or relevant: it amounts to the same thing, just as it makes no difference if we shoot our missiles at the Russians and they shoot their missiles at us, or if we both shoot our missiles straight up in the air so they fall on ourselves. What matters is what we make of it all in our minds, and in order to give my mind more room to work, I've read the letters about the article on geraniums rather than the article. In much the same way I have a painting of geraniums in a window rather than geraniums themselves in a window itself. We must do what we can to walk into our art and vanish among its hard-edged geometric lines.

Today's letter was by my professor neighbor. Recently he brought some cuttings over, thinking, he told me, that I might want to start a few plants to brighten up the fall and to give me something to take care of through the winter months ahead. Life can be pretty grim in January—even when you know you've turned the corner. He also wanted to know if I'd like to go sailing; fall is the best time, with brisk winds and a slight chop. We might, he suggests, sail some Sunday afternoon and then we would all (his boat holds four; his wife would ask a friend of hers) go to a concert at the college and out to dinner afterward.

I have declined, but too politely I think; my guess is that he will ask again. The man who runs the Quatrain Theatre tells me that in London a polite expression of interest would be taken as no interest whatsoever. Further, he wants to recommend the dignity of privacy the English have: they are like tiny islands gathered on a larger island, and they make a great effort not to invade one another. That is not unlike Echo Hollow. We are full of questions we never ask: Why do you go to the movies alone? Do you really come from Kansas? What do you plan for your geraniums now that winter is on television? What was the matter with your car the other day when we saw you peering into the open hood on the beltway? Do you know any songs to sing?

They lived, and still do, just off the Ellis-Palco Road—a stretch of blacktop that runs thirty miles out of Ellis north, through the Arian Hills, over the Saline River and up her breaks toward Palco, Demar, and Nicodemus. We had been by their place many times that summer and I never knew it. Once, in early June, we had worked a rig three miles east of their house and passed the long treeless dirt road that was their lane every evening for two weeks. From the derrick Tommy could no doubt see the yard light, and in the morning at the end of the shift, the yard itself with its skulls on the outhouse, Nine Fingers' turtle barrels, and the old Hudson. He never mentioned it.

One Sunday in late July Tommy picked me up at the Warm Blanket Motel. Nine Fingers was making good on his promise to cook the turtles he'd caught on the early sites and had been fatting with grain and leftovers. Tommy was driving the Hudson—it was the first time I knew they had anything but the truck.

"It's our opera wagon," said Tommy as I got in. "Reynolds

bought it a few years ago. He has this idea that on his way to Seattle to pick up his boat he's going to stop in Santa Fe, Denver, and San Francisco to attend operas. We drive it only on Sundays so not to wear it out."

"It has a radio," I said.

"If you take it up on Buffalo Mound you can hear Junction City and Texaco's Metropolitan," said Tommy. "We do that sometimes. Fill it up with beer and sit out there until the sun goes down. Nine Fingers hunts sharks' teeth. Reynolds looks at *Sail*."

Tristan and Isolde travels the section roads west. Verdi is in the opera wagon. Britain spills out the windows and down the bluffs toward the river where Nine Fingers walks. We are stalled. Callas is singing "Tangerine." Reynolds has set his spinnaker; he is wing on wing and does not know the name for how he sails. We think of Sundays—even as we occupy them—as days which forever lie ahead: corpulent, and full of blue water that never sleeps.

We drove north toward the house and then down the lane: Nine Fingers and Reynolds were in the side yard tending a pit fire and cleaning the turtles.

"How come," said Nine Fingers to Tommy, "you can get fish in a pond when the state hasn't stocked it? Nobody has." He was putting a pot of water on the grate over the fire.

"Birds," said Tommy. "Fish eggs get stuck on their legs and they go from pond to pond feeding."

"Is that true?" said Reynolds.

"That's true," I said. "I learned that in biology last year." My verification of Tommy seemed to stop everybody for a moment.

I looked around. On the two outbuildings, a shed and an outhouse, they had hung a variety of skulls and turtle shells: deer, steers, what looked like a buffalo head, and a number of smaller heads that had been bleached white as if they had absorbed all the paint that over the years had been worn off the gray wood. "How come," said Nine Fingers to me, "I like ugly women?"

"You can't learn that from books," I said. We all laughed. Years later in a literature class my university professor would tell us that when the men on the *Pequod* put their hands into the tub of whale meat to squeeze out the oil, their hands touching as they worked, they became aware of their affinities.

"You're not bad," Nine Fingers said. "Here," and he bent over and picked something off the ground. "A snapper's head." He dipped it in the pan of water. "Watch," he said. With his left hand he held the head by its neck and pointed its mouth at me. It opened in a slow motion snap. Using his right middle finger Nine Fingers tapped it on the nose and put his stub up close to the mouth. It bit where the finger would have been. "Snapped my finger right off and been dead an hour," said Nine Fingers.

"He's got brain nerves all through his body," said Tommy. "Even his flesh will twitch if you touch it."

"Stirs on the plate," said Reynolds. "You'll see."

"I butchered two and saved four," said Nine Fingers. He pointed to a row of wooden rain barrels along the side of the house. I went over and looked in them. There was hog wire over each barrel and it made a checkered pattern on the inside as the overhead sun streamed into the water. At the bottom were the still, dark turtles.

"One barrel from each location so far this summer," said Reynolds.

"This one," said Nine Fingers as he tapped the turtlehead again to make it snap, "is from the first one you worked with us."

"Ceremony," said Reynolds.

"Watch," said Nine Fingers. He fished a popping rock out of his pocket and tossed it on the fire. In a moment it exploded like a small firecracker, stirring the coals. "They have water trapped in them," said Tommy.

"God's gunpowder," said Nine Fingers and smiled.

"We got some cooking yet to do," said Reynolds. "Go in and make yourself at home. Beer in the icebox."

Tommy and I went inside. The house was a shambles of tools, clothes, books and magazines. There must have been no closets: winter coats were hanging on the same line of pegs with summer shirts. There was a piano bench in the middle of the living room, but no piano. In one corner was a pile of boots: work boots, snake boots, cowboy boots, hunting boots. No one boot was near its mate. The north window behind a Riverside stove had cracked and there was a strip of appliance tape holding it together: looking at it I realized I had never asked Tommy about his mother. I didn't.

Along one wall was a long large couch, and there were magazines and books on the top edge where the back met the wall. Tommy cleared some papers away and sat down. I could tell by the way he took his place right in the middle that it was where he read; he had rigged a wall light at one end, away from the stove. Above the couch was Reynolds' coastal chart. I sat down on the piano bench.

Tommy looked out the window. "You're supposed to read by natural light when you can. And read sitting up. Less strain on the eyes. But I like to stretch out here with my head at this end so I can look over the book and out the window." He laid out on the couch, bookless, but as if to show me what he meant. "What do you think it will be like at the university?" he said.

"I don't know," I said. I toyed with the edge of the piano bench under my legs. It was a lid. I stood up and opened it, thinking there might be song music there. It was full of the admissions letters and pamphlets my mother had sent me throughout the summer.

"Do you want to go?" I said.

"Not yet," he said.

"It doesn't cost much," I said.

"Reynolds would send me," he said.

"Why not go then?" I said.

"He thinks it's because I can't swim," Tommy said.

"He told me that."

"I know," he said. "They don't care if you can swim."

"Go then," I said.

"I want to think about it," he said. "I want it in my mind: not just the streets and the buildings, but I want to make it up in my mind so that when I go there it will be some place familiar and strange at once. Like when your brain waves short circuit for a moment and you think you've been here before." He sat up and looked at me. "Even if you have, it's splendid because you're amazed you're back. That's the feeling I want."

Sometimes on the rig an air hose would pop and the whole operation shuts down. There is a moment of silence that seems to have been waiting in the ground to come up. Reynolds would send me over to the rig to fix the broken air line. Even though the noise is the same when you get going again, it is, of course, not the same.

"Baseball," said Tommy after a moment's silence between us, "is not a timed sport, and that's why it's more like life than football or basketball."

Friday. There is a chain saw growling in the neighborhood. The Colonel is clearing trees from the south part of his property: his wife, he explained to me, has subscribed to the American Express bulb collection, and every quarter, beginning this fall, there will arrive a package of bulbs shipped directly from Holland. That is why they need an open space to the south of the house. You can't let good bulbs go to waste. Besides, the trees will make fine heating wood for his new stove. It is time, he tells me, that we become more independent from foreign oil.

I know all this because he's been talking to me for the previous few weeks. He stops over around sunset, walking his dog down the black ribbon of asphalt that is his driveway and that, going the other way, disappears up a slight hill toward his house—a house hidden from the road by a blanket of trees to the north. Even in midwinter, when the branches and trunks are but India ink lines on gray drawing paper, you cannot see through the matrix to where he lives. Our golf course has become a woods. The dog—a frantic and thin Irish Setter—precedes him; my impression is that she won't venture beyond the property without her master. I have never seen his wife walk the dog; in fact, now that I think of it, I have never met his wife. She drives a dark blue Oldsmobile which descends from the driveway into the road—all washed and waxed by some Echo Hollow teenager.

The Colonel is thinking of putting in a submerged gas tank. He remembers well the lines at George's Getty station just a few years back. Did I know, he asks me one evening, that a very long time ago, George's family owned all of Echo Hollow? Even before it was a golf course it was a farm, and what is left of it is George's filling station. From shirt sleeves to shirt sleeves in three generations, says the Colonel. He shakes his head and looks after his dog, who he thinks has gotten lost in the professor's yard.

When we came to work we could see lightning in the west, and the radio reported that thunderstorms were predicted: severe weather either side of a line extending from five miles west of Brownell to ten miles east of Natoma. You have to flatten out the way you think of the world and draw a line across the map in your head. Sometimes the local weatherman will tell you if you're in for it: that means Hill City folks, better take the glass ball off the birdbath stand and get the dog food out of the back of the pickup.

"Although we're few in number," Reynolds sang by way of introduction to "McNamara's Band," "we're the finest in the land." We sang it through five times on the way out but could never get it right about General Grant or what instrument McCarthy played.

"The Basso," said Reynolds. "McCarthy plays the big basso and I the pipes do play."

"What's a 'basso'?" said Nine Fingers.

"Bassoon," said Tommy from the back seat, but nobody was paying any attention.

In the rig we could see that the storm was going north of us. We were on slow time again. Reynolds parked the truck west of the rig so that the wind would keep the noise off you if you wanted to go over there and sit. Around three in the morning the wind shifted and started coming in from the east; we could see the edge of big thunderheads against a high moon. They had gone by us, and we watched the storm hustle on toward Salina, Junction City, Topeka, Kansas City—where, sitting in the hospital two days later, we would learn that all across the state the storms had caused flooding, property damage, and perhaps one life. We made a pipe change around 3:30.

Then the indicator slid to nothing, which meant something was wrong in the hole. When that happens the blocks rattle against the pins, and if you're a worm and you hear banging on the rig, you run. I jumped from the edge of the base into a pothole of drilling mud. Reynolds looked up to see if anything was going to break free. Tommy was coming down from the bit trip. Nine Fingers had bolted off the west edge of the base and stood in the pasture until Reynolds—convinced that nothing had come loose—picked the pipe back up.

A moment later when the elevator latch spring broke and a joint of the drill pipe fell, there wasn't much noise, only a slight snap that didn't sound too ominous even when we thought about it later. Noise is a function of waves. Of layers of reality. It is a friend of light. None of us saw the latch spring break. Nor the drill pipe come loose. We all remember Reynolds yelling to get clear, get clear. And we all remember where we were when the drill pipe stopped its banging on the base: then there was some creaking in the rig above us, followed by an echoless thud when Tommy, hung up for a moment in the draw works, came free and fell out, landing on the drilling table in front of us.

At the filling station George asks me if I read last week's article on Fenway Park. Baseball, he said, is a game of many components: not just ballplayers, which is the notion we have now, but of place as well. There is a lot to learn about life if you think about baseball. As I started to leave he asked if I knew that the Quatrain Theatre was showing *On the Beach* as the first movie in a series of Sunday afternoon classics. The owner had been in that morning and said he hoped to get people away from their television football games. George whistled the movie's song.

I walked down through the roads toward home, the *Times* tucked under one arm, past trees in and out of trouble, over bunkers, toward maps of knowing, my mind beginning a slow waltz with everything around it.

It was Nine Fingers who said it would have been better had Tommy died. Reynolds didn't say anything. Not about how it happened. Not about Tommy. Not about what they were going to do. Reynolds dropped into a silence I suspect has not been broken, except for the way it was during that week: a few perfunctory remarks in order to get the days done.

We had come into the Pool Table Tavern because by then everybody knew what had happened, and it was our duty to be there and say how it had turned out, and take condolences. Reynolds would nod when someone he knew came up to speak, and then the other fellow would nod, and that would be it. Once, Reynolds looked at me, but I didn't know what the look meant. He seldom spoke.

"We should have filled in the pit and called it a day," said Nine

Fingers. "Let some professor digging through here in the future find Tommy's bones and speculate."

"He might recover," I said.

"He knows he's dead," Nine Fingers said. "He hears us just like he thought; it's like he's dying the rest of his life."

"I don't think he can hear us," I said.

"What do you know?" Reynolds said. I looked down at the table and didn't say anything else.

We can hear four of us. The speed of sound is different at different altitudes. We have come to throw a houlianhan. Like boots in a pile by the door, we intend to dance by ourselves, yet entangled with, among others, one not unlike ourselves. New fossils have been found in the *Times* that indicate we are older than we thought. Still, hammers twist like divers in the air and come down forever as if never sleeping. Storms turn. Cowboys prance over sharks' teeth. Rocks pop. Wonderful ugly women hop fast about. We glow like algae split and rearranged by a great sailboat chased by the fall. We are the components of music. We see ourselves in the maps we have made, and we draw lines with our movements. We are the paintings of flowers and windows. We are the electric soup. Nothing is mundane. We are experience talking. Time goes by. The mark of death (we see now as we swim together in circles, listening to everything, full of ourselves, arranged by theories), the mark of death is with us in our future. We join ourselves.

Speaking French in Kansas

"They got somebody down at the Bus Stop that don't speak English," said Mr. Fergerson to David's father as they came into the Palco Co-Op. "W.D. called the sheriff."

David and his father were in town to buy paint for David's first summer project: painting the fence that ran around the farm house; his father had just fixed it so the horse wouldn't get in this summer and eat the tops of the geraniums. Aunt Belinda was to help with this project even though David said he could do it all by himself.

"They deaf and dumb, Manny?" asked David's father.

"Don't think so," said Mr. Fergerson. "They talk. W.D., she says they speak up loud and clear, but it ain't English they're speaking." Mr. Fergerson ran the Co-Op, and his wife, W.D., ran the Montgomery Ward Catalog store one block west down the street where the bus stopped: one bus each way, to Denver to the west of them and Kansas City to the east.

"Bus drop them?" said David's father.

"I guess it did," said Mr. Fergerson. "But not like when they put the hippies off. These people got off by accident, or on purpose, but I guess it's going to be hard to figure out which without knowing what they're saying. So W.D., she called the sheriff."

"I saw his car down the street when we came in," said David's father.

"He was at Nip's at coffee when they found him, but he came right down."

The last time the sheriff had to come to the bus station was when the hippies came to Palco; David was in school and their teacher kept them there even after school until the hippies had been taken away. That was last spring, just a few weeks before the summer vacation. David hadn't known what hippies were, and he'd look out the window by his desk and watch the fuzzy cottonwood seeds float across the playground and wonder if the hippies were like Krauts, because his father and Aunt Belinda used to talk about the Krauts the government brought to the farm during the war and how his father and Aunt Belinda weren't allowed to go near them, and how they didn't speak English.

"Maybe they're speaking in tongues," David said. He didn't know what 'speaking in tongues' meant either, but his mother said Aunt Belinda spoke in tongues and that nobody could understand her. Mr. Fergerson and David's father looked at him and smiled.

"Not likely they'll be speaking in tongues at the bus station," David's father said to him.

"Maybe up at the Nicodemus church," said Mr. Fergerson, and both men laughed.

That was the problem with not knowing what things meant, David thought. It was the same at school: there were words (of strings of words) he'd hear and he wouldn't know what they'd mean, and he'd hope that one way or another he might find out without asking. His father had just asked if the people at the bus stop were deaf and dumb, and David knew what it was to be dumb because everybody at school knew that stupid Benny Thompson was dumb, but David didn't know about the deaf part. Aunt Belinda once said that the preacher over at Natoma got so excited he turned deaf and dumb, and maybe being deaf had something to do with going to church, as speaking in tongues did.

Nor did David know what the cook at school meant when she'd say to him that he couldn't have his cake and eat it too. That seemed to him exactly what he did. He'd take the cake (chocolate was his favorite) from the counter and then go to the table and eat it. Sometimes he'd eat it before he'd eat the sloppy joes; always he'd eat his cake first if they had liver. So he couldn't understand what the cook meant. He had his cake and ate it.

"You been down to W.D.s yet?" said David's father to Mr. Fergerson.

"Just heading that way," said Mr. Fergerson. "But I'll see to what you need first."

"Why don't you go on down?" said David's father. "That way you won't have to close up and David and I can watch the store. Besides, it will take me a while to figure out what paint I used last year. The wife, she says I got to match it and I lost the can."

"Answer the phone if she rings," said Mr. Fergerson as he went out the door.

"It was something off-white," said David's father to himself he walked over to the paint shelves that lined the east wall of the Co-Op. "Something like Sahara-White."

What David thought he would do with words that puzzled him was make a list and keep it in his room, and then when he found out what a word meant he'd cross it off. He might also put the date he learned the word beside it, and he could write out who said the word and where they were when they said it, and that way he'd remember just what it meant. It would be just a way of keeping track. He had a blank notebook left over from school and he would use that. But it might be a long time before he'd be able to scratch any words off the list; he hadn't figured out 'speaking in tongues' for more than a year now, and as long as he had been in Palco Grade School he hadn't been able to figure out what it meant that he couldn't have his cake and eat it too. In classes there would be some things he'd ask about, like where the wind comes from and why it blows the cottonwood seeds only once in the year, or he'd ask questions about Egypt because when he wrote 'Egypt' in his penmanship book he liked the way the three letters right in a row went below the line. But he wouldn't ask about words; it was as if he should know them when they came upon him.

"Flaxen Gold," said David's father as he ran his finger along the rows of fat gallon cans, calling their names off the labels. "Nimbus Blue, Georgia Peach, Winter Prairie." 'Flaxen' and 'nimbus' David would put in his book.

"We should have stuck with whitewash," said David's father. "We used to whitewash that fence once a year and there was never any of this coming into town to buy paint. Vanilla."

"Did Aunt Belinda whitewash the fence?" asked David.

"Me and your Aunt Belinda," said David's father. "Your grandfather had the Krauts build it during the war. They built the fence and they built the pole barn. And helped with two harvests. Forty-three and Forty-four. It was my job to whitewash the fence, just like it's your job." David's father ran his eye along the cans: "White Wine. Mummy White."

"Mummy White," David said. "That's what it was." He remembered because of 'Egypt,' and now that he thought of it, last year he didn't know what 'mummy' was and he'd found out this year when they talked about Egypt and the Nile. He could put 'mummy' in his book and cross it off right away. Just then Mr. Fergerson came back into the store.

"That was quick," said David's father.

"Those people are French," said Mr. Fergerson. "And so the sheriff's called the College at Hays to check if they had someone down there who could see what they are saying up here. W.D. says they said plenty right at first, but when I was up there they didn't say much. Only the man. There's a man and a woman. And when the man talks you can't understand a thing. It's amazing."

"Is it like when the hippies talked?" asked David.

"I was in Dodge that week," said his father.

"The hippies didn't say much," said Mr. Fergerson, "but it was just like now. W.D., she called the sheriff and they found him at Nip's. Just like today. But then they didn't make the call to Hays, they just drove the hippies straight there. The sheriff did. The bus driver put them off. Said he wouldn't have no more of them and their crooked cigarettes. Put them off right here in Palco." Mr. Fergerson stopped to get his breath. David's mother said Mr. Fergerson could talk the hind legs off a donkey.

"You can't leave hippies standing around the Montgomery Ward store," said Mr. Fergerson. "W.D., she can't like that. People with no socks standing by the catalogue book. No, it was the right thing the sheriff did with those hippies, taking them to Hays. They got a college down there and a bus that comes and goes from every direction twice a day. We got no place for hippies here in Palco. Now these French people, we got no place for them, but they're different." He paused again. "You find what you want?" he asked.

"I guess we did," said David's father, and held up the paint can.

"You want it shook?" said Mr. Fergerson.

"I'll just turn it upside down in the pickup," said David's father. "Amounts to the same thing."

"Mother said to have it shook," said David. "She said Aunt Belinda wants it that way. I heard her on the phone."

"Shake it then," said David's father. "The boy and I, we'll go to the Monkey Ward Store and see the sheriff."

"See you later," said Mr. Fergerson.

They went outside and walked down the street toward the blue and white Montgomery Ward sign that was overhanging the sidewalk a block down, and that was leaning toward them in the wind. There were cottonwood seeds in the air, blown in from the trees in the schoolyard farther up the street. It was kind of like a snow, David thought, this blizzard of white seeds. When it snowed around Christmas you got out of school, and then in May when it snowed with cottonwood seeds you got out again.

"I don't know if they're going to find anybody at Hays that speaks French," said David's father as they walked down the street. "It's summer for them, too, and I expect they're all gone."

When they got to the Montgomery Ward store they stopped in front of the window and looked in. David could see the sheriff leaning against a washing machine, and behind the catalogue book counter there was Mrs. Fergerson talking on the phone. In two blue and white lawn chairs that had large red 'Sale' tags on them sat the French people: a man about David's father's age and a younger woman.

"It's not polite to stare," said David's father. "Let's go in and say hello to the sheriff. You know the sheriff."

"Hey there," said the sheriff when they came in the front door. "You don't happen to speak any French do you?" The sheriff winked at David as he shook his father's hand.

"I guess I don't, Norbert," said David's father. "Me and the boy thought we'd come up and see what you got here."

"Nothing much. Not like when we had the hippies," said the sheriff. "But I'll say this: I wouldn't have gotten off the bus in Palco, Kansas, if I was French and didn't speak any English," the sheriff said and nodded toward the couple sitting in the chair.

The Frenchman stood up and came over to David's father and said something nobody understood. To David the words were strings of sound, something like music, that couldn't be separated into words. Then the Frenchman went on and said quite a lot nobody understood. David noticed that Mrs. Fergerson covered the phone with her hand when the Frenchman spoke, and that when he finished she went right back to talking, but she was talking softly so David couldn't hear what she was saying. After a while the Frenchman just shrugged his shoulders and went back to the lawn chair and sat down and said something to the woman and she said something back to the Frenchman, and they both laughed.

"I tell you I'm glad to see them laughing," said the sheriff. "They weren't laughing for awhile, and we weren't getting anywhere at all."

"Had any luck down at Hays?" David's father asked the sheriff.

"Not yet," said the sheriff and he nodded toward Mrs. Fergerson on the phone. "We called the college and they're in between sessions, but they think that maybe one of their French teachers is still in town. They're out looking for him now. My idea is to get some translation done over the long-distance phone."

David found himself staring at the couple and then suddenly the woman said something to David, and he looked away. Mrs. Fergerson stopped talking and hung up.

"The bus leave them?" asked David's father.

"I guess so," said Mrs. Fergerson from behind the counter. "There wasn't anybody here for them to pick up, and I don't really pay any attention, but then these people came in and started talking so I couldn't understand them. That's when I called the sheriff. I called Manny at the Co-Op first and then I called the sheriff."

There was a long pause among them and David felt strange; he hoped he could keep from looking at the woman again so she wouldn't start talking, but he wasn't sure he could. For some reason he thought no one ought to talk: not his father, not the sheriff, not Mrs. Fergerson; not if these people couldn't understand. It seemed like cheating somehow, or wrong like when some of the boys at school would huddle together and whisper about somebody else. He wanted to hear the French people speak again, though. David looked at the woman; she caught his eye and said something to the man, who stood up and came over to David and said something directly to him.

"David," said David. He said it before he thought.

"How'd you know what he said?" asked his father.

"I didn't," said David.

"DAVE ID," said Mrs. Fergerson from behind the counter. She spoke every inch of the word as she worked her mouth. "DAVE ID," she said again. The Frenchman looked at her, then back at David.

"We tried everything on them," said the sheriff. "We showed them the telephone, and we even took them down to the drug store and Ed showed them some aspirin. But we can't get at what they want." The sheriff paused and then said in an exaggerated fashion: "What is you name?" And then pointing to David, the sheriff said: "His name is DAVE ID."

Very slowly the Frenchman said: "Je m'appelle André," and he shook David's hand. "Je m'appelle André."

"What'd he say?" said the sheriff. "What'd he say?"

The phone rang and Mrs. Fergerson answered it. David and the Frenchman stood looking at one another for a moment. David tried to say the phrase in his mind without moving his lips. The French sounds seemed like words now, though still like music.

"It's the professor at the college," said Mrs. Fergerson." They've got a professor at the college who speaks French. They found him in the K-Mart and he's calling collect. What do you think?" The Frenchman went to the lawn chair and sat down.

"About what?" said the sheriff.

"About accepting the charges. I'm not to do that," said Mrs. Fergerson.

"Accept them," said the sheriff. "The county will pay. Let me talk to that professor." Mrs. Fergerson accepted the charges and handed the phone to the sheriff.

David was still trying to remember what the Frenchman said, but he thought he might lose it unless he went outside and said it aloud a few times. He didn't want to leave without his father though, and besides the sheriff was talking on the phone and everybody was listening, so David looked out the window onto the street and tried to make the cottonwood seeds float into patterns in the air that spelled out what he thought he'd heard. But that was too difficult, and so he'd give one floating seed one sound and the next floating seed another sound until he got to the end of 'Je m'appelle André,' and then he'd start over again.

"O.K., Professor," said the sheriff, "here they are," and he tapped the Frenchman on the shoulder and pointed to the phone. The woman said something, and the man took the phone; David turned away from the window to watch. The Frenchman seemed instantly happy when he heard the voice on the phone, and he said something to the woman in the chair who got up and stood by his side and put her arm around his waist and smiled. They both talked at once, and they both moved their hands as they talked, and David couldn't tell if the woman was trying to talk into the phone (like Aunt Belinda would do to his mother) or if she was just trying to tell the man things to say. But they talked so fast there were no words again—only those strings of sounds—and the laughter sounded different too.

The Frenchman was looking everywhere in the room as he talked: up at the ceiling with one burst of words, then at the floor when he'd laugh, then at the woman as he'd listen to the phone. Once, he winked at David.

"It's like when we had the Krauts out at the farm," said David's father to the sheriff. "First they brought one up from the Experiment Station at Hays and he stayed with us a week not saying a thing. Then Dad said they were going to bring us another one, and I remember Mother and I tried to explain that to the Kraut we had." David's father laughed. "Mother used to say, 'You will soon have a friend,'—real slow, just like W.D. That Kraut would look at Mother not saying a thing, and she'd try it again. It got to be a joke around the house and any time we could work it in Belinda and I'd say, 'You will soon have a friend.'" David's father laughed again. The Frenchman talked away on the phone.

"What'd the first Kraut do when the second one came along?" the sheriff asked David's father.

"Just like now. Talked. Talked. Talked. You'd think they were Baptists, they talked so much."

"You had quite a bunch of them before it was all over," said the sheriff.

"Toward the end they'd bring them out in the back of a grain truck. I bet Dad had a dozen of them out there that fall putting up feed and painting the barns all at eighty-three cents an hour plus noon meal. They built the fence David's going to paint." Both the sheriff and David's father looked at him. The Frenchman said something and held the phone out toward the sheriff.

"I guess I better talk to that professor," said the sheriff and took the phone. "I think we can do that, Professor. That doesn't sound like much of a problem," and the sheriff smiled and nodded his head. "Thank you, Professor," he said and hung up.

"Got it figured?" said Mrs. Fergerson to the sheriff.

"I believe I do," said the sheriff.

"According to the professor in the K-Mart these folks aren't even French. They're Algiers. Or something like that. But it's French they're speaking, and they just got off the bus 'cause the bus bathroom was full or broken or something, and all they wanted to do was take a leak here in Palco and the bus left them."

"The driver probably didn't have any better time understanding them than we did," said Mrs. Fergerson.

"I guess not," said the sheriff. "I'll take them down to Hays and they can catch the evening bus to Denver. The professor said he'd meet us at Dirty Dan's and take over from there."

"That's nice of him," said Mrs. Fergerson.

"He probably wants to practice his French," said the sheriff. "He wouldn't get much of a chance in Hays. I got to make some calls and then we'll take off."

"I think we'll be going too," said David's father. "No doubt that paint is shook up by now."

"Tell Manny how it turned out," said Mrs. Fergerson.

"That I'll do," said David's father.

The Frenchman said something to the woman, and then he pointed at David. The woman nodded and smiled, and the Frenchman smiled too. By now David had lost the phrase in his mind; it had gotten mixed up with the Krauts and Algiers and all the French sounds; he only hoped that when he got outside in the flurry of cottonwood seeds he would find it again.

"Ready, David?" said his father.

"Yes," said David. He looked at the Frenchman, and then with his father walked outside and down the street toward the Co-Op. He couldn't find the words and he felt himself giving up; it was as if his mind wouldn't tune itself, except to the nearest station, and all he could hear himself think were words he heard many times before.

"Do hippies speak in tongues?" asked David.

"I don't think so," his father said. "What made you ask that?"

"I just wondered," said David. He paused. "What's a Kraut?" David asked.

"A German," said his father. "We called the Germans in the war Krauts. I don't know why."

"They fix Sour Kraut at school," David said.

"That's different," said David's father. "That's hot dogs and cabbage." They walked on in silence.

"André," said David suddenly. "André."

"What?" said his father. They were right by their pickup truck in front of the Co-Op.

"May I go back down to the bus stop?" said David.

"If you don't stare," said his father. "I'll call your mother and say we'll be late."

David ran down the block and stood in the window of the Montgomery Ward Store and looked in. Above him the sign creaked. Inside, he could see the sheriff was on the phone; Mrs. Fergerson was standing behind the counter and the French people were standing beside the sheriff. The woman looked up and saw David and smiled. She pulled on the Frenchman's coat and said something to him. He looked up and waved and mouthed something at David, working his lips in the same exaggerated fashion Mrs. Fergerson did when she had spoken David's name to the French people. David shrugged his shoulders. The Frenchman said something to the woman and then he walked across the store and out the door into the street where David was standing.

"David," said David and put out his hand. The Frenchman shook David's hand and said a lot of music, but nowhere in what he said was David's phrase. No matter how hard David listened he could not hear what he had lost in his mind.

"David," said the Frenchman to David, and he tapped David on the chest.

"David," said David and tapped himself on his own chest, and then put out his hand again. "David," said David again, as he shook the Frenchman's hand: "DAVE ID."

The Frenchman said nothing for a moment, and then he pointed to himself and said, "André." David smiled. "Je m'appelle André," said the Frenchman, and he laughed.

"Je m'appelle André," said David, "Je m'appelle," and he shook the Frenchman's hand again and then ran back down the street where he could see his father was just getting into the pickup truck. And as he ran down the street repeating his phrase, David thought that all through the world there must be words floating—beautiful words like the cottonwood seeds that scattered across the spring sky—or even odd words like the leaves the winter wind blows out of the shelter belt at the farm—but that all these words are blowing through the world, and that among them are 'speaking in tongues,' and 'flaxen,' and 'having your cake and eating it too,' and 'hippies' and 'Krauts,' and one he just now remembered from the second grade when they'd sing Christmas carols along with the teacher, and he could never figure out 'round John Virgin' in "Silent Night." All of these, and 'Je m'appelle André' were afloat in the world, and it was just a matter of running through the cottonwood seed storm of early summer and collecting the ones he wanted and putting them down in a list or a book, and then they would be his forever.

My Father Swims His Horse at Last

Verbena

In fact Verbena was not my father's horse but my mother's horse, and by the time my father got around to swimming her across the Big Pond a few years ago, both Verbena and my father were getting old, "long in the tooth, long in the tooth," as my father was fond of saying in his repetitive way and with his life-long affection for things wizened and cranky, a kind of self-affection, now that I think of it. Given my father's spectacular case of procrastination—something he also cherished—it was remarkable that the swim took place at all.

"I'm going to swim the horse this year," my father would say in his annual autumn phone calls to me. "You come back and I'll teach you a few things about swimming horses you might need to know—even if you are a vice president of some business that makes its money off the raw, red backs of the working poor." My father was a dusty and battered High Plains Populist, probably one or two beyond the last of a dead breed, and his concern for the raw, red backs of the working poor permeated his life—as did his hostility toward business vice presidents.

"I am not a vice president," I'd say, something my father knew very well. I sell mortgage insurance. Badly, as it has turned out. Still, my father didn't approve of my job—no matter how poorly I did it, nor with what little conviction. After I graduated from college, he had wanted me to return to the ranch to raise the low-dollar steers we'd buy at auction in the spring to sell off in the fall, never making much money in the process—not that making money ever seemed the point to my father. But more than work, I think he wanted me around for talk.

"Tell me what profit is," my father once said to me in his rhetorical way over supper. Before I could answer he said, "It's time turned into money. Now what do you think of a system of human endeavor that turns time into money?" As a young boy I usually didn't know what to think of my father's opinions.

"What madness is it?" he went on, his John Brown beard jumping with a frustration it has taken me a very long time to appreciate. "What madness is it?" he said. "Tell me, son. Tell me. What madness is it?"

I could not, of course, tell my father what madness it was. But I did vaguely understand, even then, that the phrase was to be one of the several refrains of our lives: What madness is it? The use and beauty of work. Where is Sockless Jerry Simpson (a Populist, like my father) when we need him? Language is life. Time. Your poor, dead mother. Time.

"Time," my father continued after a few minutes, and with some walking about the kitchen to calm down. "Time. Contemplate it, son. Muse on it. Watch it stretch out before you like a long afternoon down by the Big Pond. Look at the Russian olives on the dam wave back and forth through it. Time: See how gossamer a thing it is." Here my father paused and drifted into a detached look, the skin below his eyes bunching up and the point of his beard dropping toward his chest. It seemed as if he was looking through me to find mother, and when he failed, his head would shiver slightly, and that would start him talking again. "Do you know what gossamer means?"

"No," I said.

"Well, it isn't something you'd want to turn into money, now is it?"

Some sons learn to agree with their fathers when they are angry; I learned to agree with my father when for a moment he grew distant. But my father was not distant the last time he called about swimming the horse; he was buoyant.

"You coming back to watch me swim the Big Pond with Verbena, or don't you think you can learn anything from your father anymore?" I sensed a grin behind the gathering hair of his winter beard, a beard he would not trim between the first of September and the first of May.

"I'll be there," I said. "I'll learn what I can about swimming a horse."

"You'll learn more about life from swimming a horse than you can from clipping coupons or figuring interest on your CDs," he said.

"I don't clip coupons," I said. "I don't have CDs."

"No, but I'll bet your bank has neon signs that advertise its money market rates," he said.

"It does," I said. "You have those in Hays as well."

"I expect we do," he said. "That's what we need: the perpetual instruction of the youth about interest rates: Six-point-three-nine percent with a yield of seven-point-two percent. Material madness."

"It's pretty harmless given today's youth," I said.

"It's not harmless to rot their minds so nothing of use or beauty can grow," he said. I could tell the grin was going and my father was about to go *around the bend in the river*—a phrase my mother apparently used to describe my father's quick turns of mood on matters political.

"Better the young should read Jack London," my father went on. "Study the *Iron Heel*. That's use and beauty in a book. Peruse the *US Farm News*. Peace, Parity and Power to the People. Let the youth memorize that."

"We live in a capitalist country," I said.

"Don't tell me about it," he said. "The least the robber barons can do is not afflict the general population with the interest rates some steak-and-potato vice president is getting on his money belt wad."

"They eat pasta salad these days," I said. "And the banks are just trying to tell the public the facts." My defense was only halfhearted; I am—to a larger extent than I've ever told him—my father's son.

"I don't want to know anything banks want me to know," my father said. "It's pollution of the eyes, and the eyes are the portals to the soul. Why cobble up a good soul with dirty money? Do you know what 'portals' means?"

"Yes," I said.

"It's about time," my father said.

The conversation reminded me once again that to my father, the mortal enemy was the Vice President—in whatever form he appeared. I have a feeling that the printed complaint forms you find on the counters of the business are a silent, although misguided, tribute to my father's forty-year war against vice presidents, and something he called "establishment fat."

"When you see the Vice President in his three-piece DuPont suit," my father said to the manager behind the counter at the Stockman's Supply a few years ago, when we had come into town to get—among other items—some feed to lure Verbena into the corral, "tell him for me they waste our money wrapping these salt licks in paper that advertises we ought to buy more salt licks. I know how many salt licks I need. Don't cut down trees in Oregon just to be absurd."

The manager, like most store managers who knew my father, stared at the counter and studied the sales slip.

"And don't quote your horse-feed prices for fifty pounds just to make me think it's a bargain when you've raised it ten cents," my father went on. "It's a hundred weight that names the price. Not fifty. Use language to cheat the public, and you'll pay a price you don't know exists. Have you read your Orwell?"

"We had an increase at the home office," the manager said as a last line of defense, forgetting it was best to remain silent in the face of my father's jumping beard.

"Well, don't pass it on to your customers," my father said. "That's madness of the second order."

"We have to," said the manager.

"No you don't," said my father. "Wear out your shoes and grow a garden. It will be good for you. Shoot rabbits in the fall. Tell the Vice President to eat soup and save soap slivers. We do. Take a bath twice a week. If you bathe every day in hot water, your skin will peel off your bones. A little frugality would be healthy for the establishment fat. In the meantime, you can keep your horse feed until the price comes down." That was only one of many times we didn't get around to swimming the pond with Verbena.

Over the years it never occurred to me that we would ever swim Verbena—nor did I understand my father's fascination for insisting we should. The swim seemed the essence of something destined never to be accomplished, a kind of ultimate I'm-a-going to. I do remember, however, when the plan got fixed in my father's mind.

"The internal combustion engine is a bad idea," he said to me one summer afternoon as I was shooting baskets at the goal in our farmyard.

"Yes," I said.

"Don't agree with your father just because he's short," he said.

"OK," I said.

"We're not going anywhere on the farm in the truck anymore," he said. "We're going to use the horse."

"OK," I said. "What about taking trash to the dump?"

"We'll use the truck for the dump," he said.

"What about fishing?" I said.

"We'll use the truck for fishing," he said. My father had a way of compromising immediately. "But we'll use the horse to check the cattle and look at the fences."

"We don't look at fences," I said.

"We're going to start looking at fences," my father said. "On horseback."

"OK," I said.

In order for my father to get onto Verbena, it was necessary for him to use the stump of a cottonwood just outside a shed we called the Electric Company. He would never let me watch him swing into the saddle; instead, he'd dream up some chore for me to do while he led Verbena out of the corral and across the yard. When I'd come back from wherever I'd been sent, there would be my father—full in the saddle—and Verbena would be twisting her head in the air against the bit. Small cyclones of dust would rise around her prancing feet.

"Did you see her buck?" my father said.

"No," I said. "I was in the tool shed. Here's your hoof pick."

"Don't need it now," my father said. "You should have seen her buck. She always bucks when you first get on her. It's what gets your heart started." Then my father would send me off to the north end of the yard to open the gate into the pasture, and out he and Verbena would ride to check fences and peer at our homely steers.

It could all have been done much more quickly in our pickup, but instead, once a week or so, from about the time I was in my early teens until I left for college, my father would ride Verbena through the pastures and back. An hour adventure at most, after which he wouldn't say much—not even during the evening radio news when it was his habit to make a running commentary on the events of the world. But on one such evening, not long before I went to college, my father said:

"Someday I think I'll swim your mother's horse across Big Pond."

"Why?"

"Think what you could learn from that," he said. "Just think."

"What?"

He looked at me over whatever he was reading and shook his head as if he had failed.

"Well," he said. "There's much to learn from swimming a horse—if you contemplate the prospect for awhile."

"What?"

"I don't know yet," he said. "I'm just beginning to think on it. You might do the same. You don't learn anything in this world unless you consider what there is to learn."

"Yes," I said. My father was given to being dismayed at his only son. In fact his only child.

"We'll swim the horse next fall," he said. "When you come back from college for a weekend. It'll fatten up your education. I'm sure it will need it by then." The very next fall my father and I began a rather long tradition of not swimming Verbena across Big Pond.

It was with the knowledge that we would fail to accomplish the swim—a friendly knowledge, now that I think of it—that even after college each fall I'd drive from Kansas City back to the ranch, taking Friday and Monday off to spend the long weekend helping with the various chores that needed doing if we were going to "button up the place" for winter. For three days we'd split and stack stove wood for the Melrose Oak; tack up plastic sheets as storm windows; lower a small evergreen cut from the shelter belt down the chimney to scrape it clean; and lay square bales of straw around the house's foundation against the chance that the great blizzard of '86—my father's favorite historical storm—would reappear. All this, and the great horse swim of Big Pond.

Saturday mornings we would pile into our sturdy Studebaker

pickup and, with our coffee mugs spilling onto our jeans and my father's bag of unshelled sunflower seeds dribbling onto the floorboards, prowl the west pastures looking for Verbena—a rather hefty roan of a mare who, as she got older, seemed to feed farther and farther from the house so that our trip to catch her usually covered most of our pastures.

I remember the look she'd give us when we'd pop over some rise and find her browsing peacefully on the late grass coming up in one of the draws that grows wet with the springs that seep out in the autumn. "You guys again," her shaggy visage seemed to say, for even by early October she had grown the remarkable winter wool coat that was her hallmark, and by which my father judged—badly it always seemed to me—the depth and length of the High Plains blizzards he imagined would come roaring down on him out of the Januarys and Februarys in the Dakotas above us.

"Two weeks of snow before the New Year," my father said, rolling down his window and looking at the mare, while his coffee mug steamed a small balloon onto his side of the windshield.

"It didn't turn out that way last year," I said.

"No two years are alike," my father said as a way of putting his past predictions behind him. "You've got to learn to read the coat. Look at that shag; look at how the halter is getting buried in the hair. That's a nasty winter right there on a horse's head."

My father never read a mild weather in Verbena's coat; indeed, some falls he'd want to encircle the house with the huge round bales of prairie hay he had cut off the pastures as winter feed for whatever stock he might be keeping through the winter.

"She always gets a good shag on her," I said. Like cattle trails to our water tank, these conversations were well worn.

"Cold after the first blizzard," my father went on. "Bitter cold. And wind. Blowing snow for a week. I won't be able to see the Electric Company."

"Maybe it won't be that bad," I said.

"Worse," my father said, as he'd point his beard defiantly toward the north. "So bad the television will rattle on about wind-chill factors and tell me not to go to the horse tank in my boxer shorts."

"They're being helpful," I said.

"Why doesn't the television tell me about Spain if they want to be helpful," he said. "The radio used to tell me about Spain. The *US Farm News* told me about Spain. But no, it took the television two days to tell me Franco was dead. Franco! What a scoundrel! Dead for two days and I didn't know to celebrate."

"Nobody in Western Kansas cares about Franco," I said.

"Well, they ought to," my father said. "You've got to learn something about life besides the price of wheat. Why would the television tell me the wind-chill factor and not tell me that Franco was dead?"

"I don't know," I said. "I don't know." It was my own all-purpose refrain that I'd use—even as a small boy—to change the direction of the conversation, not that I give the technique high marks.

"Do you know what Brendan Behan said about Franco?" my father said.

"No."

About this time Verbena would have edged her way to the truck for the grain we'd put in a bucket in the back. Somehow she knew my father's rant meant food: that, and a harmless walk back to the yard where she'd be fed again, perhaps saddled, but not ridden far, if at all. On balance it must have seemed a good bargain to the old horse. And as chance would have it, she seemed to always stop my father short of telling me what Brendan Behan had once said about The Generalissimo Franco.

"Catch that horse and put a lead on her before she bolts over the Saline Breaks," my father whooped when, in the middle of his diatribe about Franco and television, he heard Verbena rattling around in the feed bucket in the back of the truck.

"She's not going anywhere," I said.

"She'll be in Nebraska by morning if you don't jump quick." Jumping quick had been my job since boyhood.

What I'd read in the shag of Verbena's head as I snapped a lead to her halter was that the old mare had no intention of bolting through any breaks on her way to Nebraska and into the blizzards lurking in the depth of her coat. It is something a son, at least this son, doesn't tell his father.

"Now you'll learn what there is to swimming a horse," my father said as I got back in the truck. "You'll learn something more than the useful in life. You'll learn something to talk about when you're old and long in the tooth like that horse."

"I expect I will," I said.

"And talk about it at length," he said. "You're too quiet a boy for the good of the country. You've got to learn to scream bloody murder when the four-door Cadillac of capitalism is about to make roadkill of your bony hide."

"I'll speak about it at length," I said. Good, my father would say, and put the truck in gear for the ride back to the yard, Verbena trotting behind.

But no matter how easy it might be to catch Verbena, nor with what efficiency my father and I would get together the tack from various sheds and storerooms, year after year we never got around to swimming her. We'd get close though; some Octobers we'd even get as far as Big Pond itself. And five years ago my father had the idea we should celebrate our impending accomplishment by grilling steaks in a pit fire on the south point that poked itself out into the water.

"Ceremony," I remember my father saying on this occasion, "is a drama we can all write for ourselves." We were cutting cottonwood logs for the fire. Verbena was tethered to a tree, her saddle cinched tight.

"We've got plenty of wood," I said. We had enough for a high school bonfire; my father was as excessive as he was frugal.

"Cut some more," my father said. "I'll want to dry off by the blaze when I come out of that pond, and so will you."

"We've got enough for that," I said.

"Not for both a blaze and a bed of coals for the steaks, we don't," he said. "And then we'll want some fire in the hole to talk by. Don't you want to look across the flames and see your father's face when he tells you what you've learned from swimming a horse?"

"Of course," I said. We cut more wood.

Looking back, I suspect it was all part of my father's dallying dance before the swim. I guess in some dim way I knew that and I was glad for it. Perhaps I sensed we had gotten such a good start on the swim that year I had half a fear we might pull it off. In the end we spent our time in a kind of slow motion puttering: first with the pit, then with the fire; and several times with the horse (my father walked over to Verbena to say something to her and then came away still talking—but to whom I couldn't be sure).

Once, late in the afternoon, he walked around to the dam and along the double line of Russian olives that grew up on each side. I watched him as he looked back at me over the pond. I remember he didn't wave. He stood there a moment. Then he walked back around. As evening came on and the muskrats began to etch their Vs onto the flat water, my father said, "It's gotten away from us again, now hasn't it, son. We've run out of daylight."

"I guess we have," I said.

My father went over to Verbena and unsaddled her and tossed the gear into the pickup.

"I can't teach you about swimming horses in the dark," he said. "It's a lesson of life. You need to see it clearly. You should have been shown long ago." My father looked out over the pond to the other side. "Time flies when you're having fun," he said. "I've never known what to do about that."

"We'll swim her next year," I said.

"For sure," said my father.

We cooked our steaks over the cottonwood coals and talked, the flame dancing in the pit. Verbena didn't go far; as we ate, we could hear her moving through the trees, grazing. Once, I thought I heard her at the pond, taking water.

"Your mother never rode Verbena," my father said as the fire got low.

"I didn't know that," I said. It was getting difficult to see his face. I got up to get another log, but he held out his hand, palm down, to indicate he didn't want me to.

"Your mother wasn't political," he said. In the distance I thought I could hear the night flight of sandhill cranes.

"We'll get it done," my father said.

"OK," I said.

"Her world was flowers," he said.

"You've never told me that."

"We'll swim her horse," my father said.

"Agreed."

But the truth became that, in the years after that evening we cooked our steaks on the pond's bank and listened to the old horse browse among the cottonwoods, we seemed to recede from the swim. The following year we only drove to the pasture and looked at Verbena, while my father held forth on the rising cost of electricity, due, he felt (correctly, I suspect), to the new atomic power plant they had installed down the wires from the ranch. A few years later we didn't even get out of the yard, and, had not Verbena come up to the corrals on her own that weekend, I might not have heard my father's dire prediction of yet another bad winter.

"We're not talking the blizzard of '86," he said, as we stood by the horse just before I was to drive back down the highway. "But we are looking at the blizzard of 1912. Or '48. Do you remember the one in '48?"

"I was pretty young," I said.

"Couldn't get out for a month," he said. "You, me, and your mother. All buttoned up in here with rice and beans and pickles. Jerry Simpson would have been proud."

"Call me if you need help," I said.

"Maybe," he said, looking back at the house, "we should have put the round bales around me this year. At least lay them along the north side so I don't get drifted in."

"If you want to," I said. "I've got some time yet. The front-end loader is still on the tractor. It wouldn't take an hour." But he shook his head no, then said:

"You come back next year, and we'll swim that horse first off. Friday afternoon. Make your mother proud of us and teach you something at the same time."

"OK," I said.

"Keep track of what you learn," he said.

"What?"

"Keep track of what you learn from swimming that horse so you can tell me what it is in the long run."

"We haven't done it yet," I said.

"We will," he said. "You've got to get ready by thinking ahead. See the swim in your mind's eye. Watch the water part at her chest. Watch the cottonwood leaves coming down on the pond. Don't think of anything without seeing it in your mind's eye. That's the problem with you vice presidents. You don't watch what you're doing in your head. It's all dry columns and furniture-appliances."

"'Furniture-appliances?" I asked. Generally I don't ask.

"Like dish-washing machines," he said. "God help us."

"I'll try to watch what I'm doing in my head," I told him.

"Good thinking," said my father. "Don't watch television because it will rob you of the ability," he said.

"I know," I said.

As it has turned out, the following year my father swam his horse at last.

My Father, My Mother, and I

We raised each other, my father and I. After we lost Mother, that's what my father used to say when asked about it by some well-meaning relative who wanted to spirit me off to a more normal home. But my father would have none of it: We raised each other like kid goats, he'd say—and we were pleased to do so.

I know it sounds strange because I, too, have watched the television dramas where, with the death of the mother, the father gets older. Or he goes out to find another wife and in so doing becomes serious—or a fool. Sometimes he grows distant with grief and becomes gray to his children, like the back side of a cold front moving east away from you across the pastures. But that's not what happened to my father and me, and it didn't have anything to do with how my father felt about Mother.

Our ranch was small by High Plains standards, so the sign slung under our mailbox announced us as the *Half-Vast Ranch.* My father's self-proclaimed, lifelong case of I'm-going-to was occasionally relieved by fully completed projects. The making of the *Half-Vast* sign was one of them.

"Language is where life is," my father said to me as he burned the H into a cottonwood plank he'd cut from an extra-large piece of stove wood. "Get in trouble by what you say," he advised. "That's liberty."

He was a short, muscular man who seemed to be in his body something like the wild burliness of his beard. I took after my mother: thin to gaunt, and taller than my father by the time I was fifteen—as my mother was taller than my father in the pictures of them.

"Liberty," said my father as he burned the wood with a propane torch he'd adapted from a weed burner. "She's a French woman with bare breasts. They won't teach you that in the public school. Bare breasts!"

We had been recently studying "liberty" in civics class (breastless,

to be sure) and it was my father's habit to extend my lessons—
which he always thought were truncated and Milquetoast at best—
into a richer version of political meaning, sometimes illustrated
by life as the two of us led it on Half-Vast Ranch, but just as often
by wider sources of learning: *Little Blue Books* and the *US Farm
News*, both of which gathered like dust bunnies around the house,
until once or twice a year—roughly equal to fall and spring cleaning—my father would sort through his piles of "radical paper" and
stack it in a small room next to mine in the unheated upstairs of
our house. There its continued growth marked my own, but only in
height, not (given my father's political sensibilities) in substance.

"What do you know about Bolivia?" my father asked me one
winter day after school. I had been feeding Verbena, and my father
had taken the chance to browse through my geography book. He
was sitting at the kitchen table when I came back in.

"It's where we get our tin," I said.

"And what about South Africa?"

"Gold," I said.

"Madness," my father said. His beard began to twitch as he
slowly turned the pages of my textbook. "Every country you study
in this book is represented by a picture of either some mineral that
is mined by the enslaved population or a crop harvested with the
bent backs of the poor."

"I have a test tomorrow," I said.

"You have a test right now," said my father. "Do you know what
South African gold and Costa Rican coffee have in common?"

"No," I said.

"They both get shipped to America so the rich can thicken their
money belts. Is that what you learn about the countries of the
planet?"

"I have to pass the test tomorrow," I said. I had been through
this before.

"No you don't," my father said. "What kind of test is this to pass?" Here he waved my book at me. "Tell your teacher Argentina hides Nazi war criminals. Tell him the Negroes in South Africa are slaves. Tell him about the United Fruit Company. Have a hissy-fit. Get *hippa-canoris* for once in your life. With any luck you'll get in enough trouble they'll call me to school."

I knew better than to get into that much trouble. And I had never gotten *hippa-canoris*—a term my mother had apparently used to describe my father's political rages.

"I have to know what the countries of the world make," I said.

"Oh, really," my father said. His beard twitched. "And what about the countries of the world that don't make anything we use here in capitalist America? I don't see a picture of Tibet in this schoolbook. Did you study Tibet?"

"No," I said.

"How about Goa?" he said. "Did you study Goa?"

"Goa?" I said. At least I had heard of Tibet.

"Goa," he said. "Did you study Goa?"

"No," I said. Not even my world-history professor in college knew much about Goa; how my father developed his interest in it I never learned.

"I thought so," he said. "Goa doesn't sell us anything we can buy and turn into junk, so Goa doesn't exist to the Board of American Education."

By now the point of my father's beard was shaking like a fist. When he'd get angry, the skin on his brow would quiver, and his eyes would widen and narrow as if some hidden camera adjustment were being manipulated to find the light.

"I am the prince of Goa," he bellowed out just as all his facial contortions seemed to come into concert. "I am the prince of Goa, and I take my oath on this text." He rose to his feet holding my geography book in his left hand and slammed the palm of his right hand into the crease of the open pages:

"First, God made idiots," my father recited, as if he were hearing someone saying the words for him to repeat. "That was for practice." Here he paused a moment as if to hear the oath giver. "Then He made school boards." At this point my father peered over my book to see—I suppose—if I were still anywhere in the room, or if I had simply concluded he had gone so *hippa-canoris* that I had left with the horse for town to get the school nurse. When he reassured himself that his son was still in the kitchen, he said, directly to me: "I am quoting Mark Twain in case someone asks you. Pass on what Mr. Twain has said to your school principal and get in trouble for once in your life. If that doesn't do it, tell your principal you heard Mr. Twain's remarks from the Populist Prince of Goa, a short fat man who happens to be your father. At least get me in trouble. It could be a leg up for yourself."

Although I left for school the next day remembering Mr. Twain's wisdom, much to my father's disappointment I never got into my share of trouble.

*　*　*

"We're going to hang the *Half-Vast Ranch* right under the mailbox and see if the United States Post Office objects," my father said to me the day we made our sign. "See if they stop delivering mail. That's what they did when Cody put his mailbox too high after someone from Hays City blew it down with a shotgun. Oh, where is Sockless Jerry Simpson when we need him? Do you know what *Half-Vast* means?" my father continued.

He had given me the burner so I could burn Vast into the wood. We'd split chores like that: in this case my father had outlined our sign in pencil, fired up the torch and told me to watch as he burned in the first word. Next, I'd get to do my part; then my father would finish, showing me what I had done right and what I had done wrong—only what I had done wrong usually came first, and my father would end his lesson with praise of my efforts, even if that was difficult to do. Sometimes, he'd couple his praise with a small speech about the dignity of work and what a privilege it was to have a nature that enjoyed it. Coming from a man who put off most of life's chores, these talks seemed odd to me, especially as I grew older and began to learn something about the cosmic stresses between body and soul. But then—and even now—what my father had to say about labor never struck me as hypocritical; it was as if he had wanted me to like labor more than he had. Along with getting into trouble, it was his ambition for me.

"*Half-Vast* means we don't have much land," I said. My father looked at me with no little chagrin. I might have been nine or ten at the time, and even though I went to school in Hays and had heard my share of profanity, the pun didn't occur to me. My poor father must have thought me dense; or worse, bland, like "processed cheese" or "even heat"—two virtues of modern life that were being extolled on the radio in those days and against which my father raved repeatedly. It was probably his great fear that he was going to rear a son with neither a sense of outrage nor a sense of humor.

"It's a small joke," my father said grimly, looking at the smoking wood.

"What kind of joke?" I said. I was watching him burn *Ranch* into the cottonwood slab, and I noticed how his hand shook slightly, how the wood caught fire for a moment when the blue bullet of the flame was on it, and how *Ranch* came out with a ghost of a wobble to it, as if it wasn't all that sure it had been truly burned into being.

"It's a half-assed joke," my father said as he turned off the propane. "Don't you see?"

"No," I said. At least I was a frank and forthright boy.

"Do you hear me when I say something's half-assed?" my father said.

"Yes," I said. But most every idea I brought home from school in those days was "half-assed." The problem with being a child is that you don't expect your parents—your father in my case—to be more eccentric than your average American historical hero:

John Paul Jones, for example, who, from my landlocked place on the prairie, seemed pretty wonderful, at least in the placid biographies we were allowed to check out from the school library. But John Paul was never given to railing on about suburban ethics, robber-baron capitalists, the Revised Standard Edition, or "even heat." Not even the vile British got diatribes from John Paul such as my father had dealt out earlier in the week to the local electric company for tacking a surcharge onto our bill:

"See that sur in front of charge?" he had said to me. "They want a buck a letter for thinking that up, and a buck more for the hyphen. Committee English always costs the workingman. Remember that, son. When the Populists come to power, the first thing we'll do is straighten out the language. Speak plain English with a flair, and you can be The Commissioner of Language." By the time I went away to college, my father had offered me a variety of jobs in his future government.

"You think about *Half-Vast* the rest of the day," my father said, as the smoke cleared from our sign. "Use it in a sentence, such as 'a Republican has a half-vast way of thinking.' Try it out in show-and-tell. Instead of bringing a bull snake to class, tell them about some of the half-vast ideas you've found in your geography book."

I knew even then to keep quiet at show-and-tell about my father.

When we finished *Half-Vast Ranch*, we slung it below the mailbox, where it still is today, the wobble in *Ranch* growing more pronounced over the years.

It is curious, but in many ways our sign's literal meaning turned out to be just as appropriate as its irony. Our ranch was small and not very pretty. The pastures were rocky and filled with soapweed. We didn't have any canyons or breaks. We did have a spot to the northwest of the house where the limestone broke ground and a cut had formed, creating large holes in the bank; there a family of coyotes would raise its young every year. We did, as well, have a shelter belt of locust and cedar that wasn't bad to look at. But for the most part our place was hardscrabble country.

We did have one thing that was lovely, and we were famous for it: the Big Pond. My father built it himself, and I can remember him doing so—although barely, and in fragments. I remember my mother from this time as well: she seems tall and certain of herself. I recall her at the round waffle iron on Sunday mornings. I see her coming into my room at night to read to me. She is taking me to school and leading me into a room with other children. We walk together down our lane to the mailbox, and she stops coming or going to pick flowers near the end by the road. In all my memories of my mother, I never hear her voice: There are only pictures in my mind, as if in a slow motion silent film.

In the same noiseless way I remember my mother dying—or at least I see in my mind's eye the hospital where I visit her, and days later I see my aunt coming to stay with us. We all move around the house, slowly and in silence.

I see as well the night my father does not come home, and the next afternoon when he does; I see that my mother is dead, although in my memory I cannot make anyone speak to me about it, nor can I see that I understand what it means that my mother is dead.

"Do you remember the summer when I built the pond?" my father would ask me now and again when I was growing up.

"Yes," I'd say. It is not so much a memory as a sense of a memory. Like smoke from a wood stove will stir something in your mind, but you can't be sure what.

When I'd try to recall my father building the pond, it is more through a series of questions about what I see: Am I sitting on the tailgate of the Studebaker, and is my father on a tractor going down the gully that leads to where the dam is forming? Later, do I walk across the crest of that dam and look down at the film of muddy water that is beginning to gather below it? That summer do I notice frogs along the edge? Does my father show me tadpoles in the shallows? During the first winter, do I go down to the pond and see that it is only half full, ice along its edges, with a flock of small ducks huddled in the west slough?

And do I remember for sure the huge, wet snow the spring after my mother died, and how it melted quickly, so that when my father and I went to the pond we discovered it full to the banks, backed up along both sloughs, and edging over the spillway?

"Big Pond," my father claims to have said that day with me standing beside him. "We got ourselves a Big Pond here. I wish your mother could know. She'd feel good about it now."

While our pond grew to be something lovely, over the years our farmyard became a five-acre circle of rusting trucks and tractors and various cobbled equipment in various stages of decay. My father, as it turned out, was given to farm and ranch auctions where he'd buy "iron" with the idea of converting his purchases to some use he imagined we had. The parts we assembled over the years for a log splitter that never got built covered most of the south side of the stone shed: hydraulic hoses, I-beams, two rear axles, and nearly a dozen wheels. And long before energy conservation came into vogue, my father was going to build a wind charger. He even had a plan to sell the excess electricity back to the power company, which, through a regulation my father claimed to have inspired, was obliged to pay us hard cash—or at least reduce our meager bill. To that end, we bought and scavenged assorted rotors and pipes and rusted generators we stacked in a tin shed to the west of the house, the shed that came to be called the Electric Company.

"I was born with the finest case of the I'm-a-Gonnas in Ellis County," my father said to me one day while staring at the rusting iron in the Electric Company. He always seemed amused whenever he contemplated his procrastination, as if he were talking about someone else—someone he was fond of, but someone other than himself.

"I can help," I remember saying, but I remember, as well, my father didn't pay much attention to me.

"Well," he said as he picked up a generator off the pile of junk. "You won't grow old if you postpone everything you're supposed to do, now will you, son?"

"I guess not," I said.

"After I'm dead and gone," he said, "if the Populists come to power I want you to put me in charge of the Office of Not Getting Things Done. Have them dig up my bones and put them behind a desk with an oak swivel chair. I want to be Commissioner of Procrastination. Do you understand?"

"Yes," I said.

"That's the only way I'll come back from the dead."

"Yes," I said.

One project that did get done—along with the *Half-Vast* sign—was a basketball goal we made for me out of a square of old plywood bolted to a length of oil-field pipe. All through the summers and into the great, long High Plains falls K. C. Jones and Sam Jones of the Boston Celtics—whose team I imagined I was on those days—would sink their long set shots as we defeated again and again a historic all-star team composed of Clyde Lovellette, Dolph Schayes, and George Mikan. I was Bill Russell.

"Good thinking," my father had said when he learned I imagined myself to be a professional basketball player whose exploits we'd hear on the radio at nights. "No sense in staying inside yourself. Get out and pretend to be somebody else. George the Third thought he was a tree. Franco thought he was human. A little madness here and there refines the soul so that it soars above the politics of capitalism. Not that it helped in Franco's case."

"I pretend I'm Bill Russell," I said.

"Do you ever pretend you're anyone else?" he asked.

"No," I said. I was fibbing; going to sleep at night, I'd imagine I was John Paul Jones.

"Too bad," my father said. "Some days I think I'm Sockless Jerry Simpson. I put on my shoes without my socks and give campaign speeches to the mirror in your mother's room." My father's room was always called my mother's room; it was just below mine.

"I don't hear you," I said.

"You're at school," he said. "You wouldn't want to think your father's daft, would you?"

"No," I said.

"Here," he said, and tossed me my basketball. "Go be Bill Russell. How splendid that in America a short fat white man can have a tall skinny black man for a son. There's hope for the damn country yet."

So, amid the junk and the bindweed of our yard, Sam Jones would flick a pass to Bill Russell, who in turn would sink yet another hook shot to win for the Celtics yet another world championship under the dome of the yellow-blue western sky while the Commissioner of Procrastination (alias Sockless Jerry Simpson) looked on with profound approval.

Probably my father thought my imagination held the seeds for a better education than the one I was getting in school. It was not just the school; it was the town itself that bothered him. My father didn't like going to town, as if it tainted him—as if it tainted us. In those days Hays was slowly growing its suburbs into the surrounding pastures.

I remember one fall when I was in high school, the tailgate on the pickup dropped as we sat at a stoplight near Scotty Phillips Hardware. The stove wood we'd cut that morning on the Smoky Hill rolled out onto Eighth Street in front of the station wagons and among the Bel Airs and Impalas that began honking at us— some of which were occupied by the June Allyson look-alike girls who led cheers at my school. When I jumped out to gather up the wood, my father stayed in the truck, rolled down his window, and began to rant at the traffic jam we had caused:

"When the Populists come to power, my son's going to be Commissioner of Vehicles and everybody's going to drive a truck," he bellowed. "Or ride a horse."

My father was not given to yelling in general. His idea was to pick out someone in particular and tell him or even her his story of social injustice; perhaps they'd go tell someone else. It was as if he meant to convert the twentieth-century acquisitive America to nineteenth-century Populism by virtue of gossip, a kind of ripples-on-the-pond theory of political activism. In this particular case he had fixed on my math teacher, a tiny young woman who had just come to Hays from Chicago and who was so startled at the pile of stove wood in the middle of Eighth Street that she had stalled her car and couldn't seem to get it going again. All around her—and us—other cars were honking their horns, and then peeling out to the afternoon football game.

I recall it as one of those fleecy golden afternoons you sometimes get in late October on the plains: so deep with yellow warmth you think it will never grow dark or cold, and if you are a boy in your early teens you can't readily see the point of spending such days cutting wood against the blue-black blizzards of January, much less imagine yourself as the Commissioner of Vehicles.

Neither my math teacher nor I acknowledged one another in the middle of all this honking and ranting; nor did she acknowledge my father—not that it made much difference; he was used to talking to brick walls as well as mirrors. When my teacher finally got her car going again, my father was still in full bellow with a variant of his stock speech about the nature of language and beauty of usefulness.

"Carpets in cars," he yelled at her, "what madness is that? Wait till my boy comes to power. Cars named after African animals and French resorts. What madness is it?"

"That's my teacher," I whispered to my father after I'd loaded the wood and gotten back in the truck.

"What madness is it they bus all the schoolchildren to Hays?" he bellowed at the poor woman with renewed vigor. "*Unification.* What kind of word is that for education? Who wants everybody to learn the same thing? You'll turn our kids into Coke bottles. We'll have to look at their bottoms to see where they come from."

By now she had gotten her car started and was off down the road as fast as prudence would allow. My father continued his monologue for a moment or two, then started the truck and headed up Eighth Street.

"Did you hear me talking?" my father said. "Did you hear what I had to say?"

"Yes," I said.

"What did you learn from all that?" he said. We had begun to weave our way through the streets of Hays out of town toward home.

"I'm not sure," I said.

"Come on," he said. "What did you learn?"

"To check the chain on the tailgate," I said. "And to learn from my mistakes." To learn from one's mistakes had been that week's theme in civics class.

"That's not what you learned," my father said. "You can always pick up wood. Labor is never a waste. If the only learning you acquire is from your mistakes, you'll grow up to be a capitalist and live in a place like that." Here my father pointed to a two-story imitation English Tudor house that was getting built on a treeless lot near the golf course on the edge of Hays. "With matching furniture," he went on. "Carpet over good wood floors so you can't hear the creak of yourself walking. And air-conditioning to steal your summers. Do you want that for a life? Do you want never to be hot or cold, and to live in a house with no sounds of its own except little electric motors running all the time? Is that what you want?"

"I wish my clothes didn't smell like wood smoke," I said.

"What?" my father said.

"I heard some kids talking about me the other day," I said. "They made fun of me because I stink like wood smoke."

"What do they smell like?" my father asked.

"They don't smell," I said. "Maybe the girls smell of perfume sometimes," I said.

"Dried and boiled French flowers," said my father, more to himself than to me. Then he was quiet for a moment; his beard was still. I think now he must have been considering whether to have one of those heart-to-heart talks fathers and sons have—usually over sex, of course, but in this case it would have been over the differences between the poor and the rich, the country and the town, us and them. He might even have thought to go on at some sympathetic length about the virtues of our life in an effort to console his son. But to my father's credit, he resisted the temptation; he was the same man to me as he was to my mother's mirror: "If you don't smell of your own life, you're the living dead," he said. "Which would you rather be? The living dead or stink of cotton-wood smoke?"

"I'd rather stink," I said. I wasn't sure that was true, and no doubt my hesitation was reflected in my voice, but my father didn't take me up on it.

"Well," he said, "that's one thing you learned today. Now think about the rest of what you learned and tell me about it at great length sometime."

"Yes," I said.

"At great length and full of details, as if your mother were listening and needed to catch up," he said.

"I will," I said.

On the road home I remember seeing a long line of snow geese in a ragged V heading south.

"Early blizzards," said my father as he looked at them through the windshield. "We'll check Verbena's coat to see how bad it will be." He grinned through his beard. It was his deep grin: to be free from Hays was added to the thought of toughing it out through a big winter at the ranch. Round hay bales in circles against the blizzard of '86.

"Your mother loved snow at night," he said as we bolted the Studebaker over Seven Hills Road on the way to the Half-Vast Ranch. "She would get up in the dark and stand at the window and watch the yard fill up. You were born in a snow. Whenever it snowed your mother would say it was you drifting through the universe." These words of my mother's were the only ones I ever heard my father speak.

The Commissioner of Procrastination: 1904–1987

"To swim a horse across water," my father said to me, "you do not take off the saddle. Water doesn't hurt the saddle. You'll need to neatsfoot oil it of course, but water itself doesn't hurt leather." I nodded.

It was Friday afternoon; I had come home as promised, escaping—my father pointed out in the first minutes after my arrival—the impending crash of various financial markets, which, in his opinion, damn well deserved to tumble down on top of me if I insisted in living off the backs of the working poor. We were sitting at the kitchen table. Outside, it was a warm gold-and-blue day. Windless. When I was a boy, it had been my job to neatsfoot oil all the leather we had between us: boots, saddles, an old rifle scabbard my father had bought at farm auction against the day he was going to get a rifle to shoot a deer.

"OK," I said. "Let's put oil leather on the weekend list. I'll do that."

"Good thinking," said my father. He seemed dreamy, as if there was something he was trying to recall but couldn't. He fiddled with his beard; over the years it had grown two tufts to it, a kind of forked beard; and while it had gone gray, it had not turned white: My father looked in old age like some wizened satyr, modestly pleased with himself, but a little lost.

"First off," he continued rather abruptly after a moment of silence and with no prompting from me, "you ride your horse directly into the water; don't let him turn away from the swim at hand." I realized my father always called horses "he" or "him," no matter what their sex; in this case Verbena had been a mare for over thirty years.

"Yes," I said.

Usually my father took the Friday afternoon of my visit to bring me up to date on the state of politics in the country: a kind of who's who of the nation's leading rascals. After that, we'd make up a list of chores that needed doing, and often we'd get a start on them before evening. Later, at dinner, it had become our custom to lay out once more the horse-swimming plans, but until this particular weekend that had never included any real instruction on how the swim was to be made.

"When you get your horse out into the water where he can swim by himself," my father said, now more calmly, "you slide off to the left and hold onto the saddle horn with your right hand. Do you understand?"

"Yes," I said.

"Don't fight the water," said my father. "A horse will tow you along peacefully if you don't thrash about and if you let your feet come up, which they will, boots and all."

"OK," I said.

"Notice you can swim a horse without being able to swim yourself," my father said, "and cross a river or a pond in spite of your deficiency." Both my father and I could swim.

"I understand," I said.

"Now when you get to the other side of the pond," my father continued, "let your horse find his feet, and then come out beside him, walking yourself. Don't get lazy and think you'll keep your boots from getting muddy by slipping into the saddle at the last minute and riding your horse out. Let him come out by himself. Stand back and he'll shake."

"Yes," I said.

My father grew quiet: He had that distant look in his eyes. A hackberry tree had grown up over the house and its branches were beginning to touch the tin roof. When a breeze came along you could hear the tree scrape, as it did while my father and I sat at the table for a moment in silence.

"You want me to cut that tree back this weekend?" I said.

"No," he said. He seemed to have lost track of himself.

"You want to get started on the chores yet this afternoon?" I said. "We can put some square bales around the base of the house." He shook his head no, then:

"Why don't you shoot some baskets?" There hadn't been a basketball around the place in years.

"We got work to do," I said. "If you're going to make it through winter."

"We'll make it through the winter tomorrow," he said.

"OK," I said.

"You know why I'm short?" he said.

"No," I said.

"To live a long time," he said. "You don't see very many tall old men, now do you?" he said.

"No, I don't," I said. He pulled at the left fork of his beard.

"The Big Pond was the last project I saw through to the end," he said.

"There were others," I said.

"Not many," he said.

"It wasn't the point," I said.

"Shoot some baskets," he said. "Pretend you're Bill Russell. I want to read some radical paper. We'll eat turkey legs and rice at six."

"I'll cook," I said. "I've brought some things from town." I'd picked up a roast and some potatoes.

"Pizza?" he said.

"What?"

"You didn't bring pizza?" he said. "I won't have it on the place. Imagine what it does to your colon. I want turkey legs and rice. They're in the ice box."

"OK," I said.

"I'm going to read," he said. He got up and went into Mother's room.

I spent the afternoon laying square bales around the foundation of the house. Some years, when my father was convinced there would be a great snow, we'd use the John Deere to circle the whole yard with the large round bales of prairie hay he'd cut off the flat of our pastures.

Once I went out to the basketball goal and looked at it. The net was gone, and the rim was rusted. But the Boston Garden looked much the same, even though some bindweed was creeping in on the western edge of the parquet. I took an imaginary shot and made it.

Around sundown I came back to the house. I could smell the cottonwood smoke in the yard and knew that my father had fired up the Melrose Oak to boil his turkey legs. We had a fine dinner at the kitchen table and spent the evening talking about the time we'd lost the load of wood on Eighth Street. I was going to tell my father some of what I'd learned that day, but he put his finger to his lips and shook his head.

"Keep it in," he said, his finger bouncing against the shag of his beard and mustache that in winter he'd let close in over his mouth. "Keep it in until it grows wings and talons and flies out of you by itself. It will soar. It will find me. It will have good eyes."

The next morning when I got up, my father was out of the house.

I poured myself some coffee and read *The Farm News*: The editorial letters were about the Middle East and parity. The quotations at the bottoms of the columns ran from Gandhi to Reagan. I thought my father might have gone to town.

"I've got Verbena," he said as he came in a few minutes later.

"I could have helped," I said.

"It wasn't any trouble," he said. "I talked to her about Franco and she came right over."

"Do you want to swim her today?" I said.

"Was Jerry Simpson sockless?" my father said.

"Let's line out some chores first," I said.

"Let's not and say we did," said my father. The twin points of his beard were shaking with an excitement I had not seen in him before.

"OK," I said.

We went outside. Verbena was saddled and tied to the chain latch on the bed of the pickup.

"You drive ahead," said my father. "The horse and I will come along."

"You sure you don't want to wait until it warms up?" I said. "Later this afternoon." It was a bluebird day but cool. It was never clear to me who was going to swim this horse. Speaking for myself, I wanted a little warmth when I came out of the Big Pond.

"Get going," he said. "Do as your father says or I won't let you in my government when the revolution comes." He untied the horse.

I got in the truck and drove it down to the pond. As I left the yard, I checked the mirror and saw my father heading for the cottonwood stump by the Electric Company. When I got to the Big Pond, there were teal in the west slough, and they took off and circled once and then went over the hill. I drove to the dam and got out and lowered the tailgate and sat on it. Pretty soon I could see my father coming over the hill on Verbena; against the brown of buffalo grass pasture he looked like something from a poster you'd find in a western art gallery.

"How is she?" I said when they got to the truck. I noticed that in recent years Verbena had been growing a gathering of her random white hairs into a small cluster in the middle of her forehead.

"Old," my father said. "But full of piss and vinegar."

"She's as old as I am," I said. "Older than you if you count horse years."

"You should have seen her buck when I got on," my father said.

"You want me to swim her?" I said. I thought that might be best.

"What do you know about swimming a horse?" my father said.

"You just taught me," I said. "Last night up in the kitchen."

"That was talk," he said.

"You ever swim a horse?" I said.

"No," he said. He reined Verbena around in a circle. "Don't ask me questions you know the answer to. What madness is that?"

"Well," I said, "we're about even when it comes to swimming horses."

"No, we're not," my father said. On the point of land across the way a breeze came up and sent a shower of cottonwood leaves over the pond. We both watched them as they settled on the water.

"You're right," I said. "It's time you swam your horse."

* * *

It is two days later: Monday, and I am getting ready to go back to Kansas City. My father and I are standing in the front yard of the house. It is circled by the large, round hay bales he has convinced me to tractor up in advance of an impending blizzard.

"You wait and see," he says.

"For what?" I say.

"The yard will be full to the round bales with snow and the television will babble on about the frozen dead out here."

"It won't be that bad," I say.

"Worse," he says.

"I think you'll make it," I say.

"Maybe," he says. He doesn't say anything for a moment, then: "I'm not going to watch television anymore."

"OK," I say.

"You don't sell waterbeds, do you?" he says.

"Mortgage insurance," I say. "Why?"

"They're selling waterbeds on television," he says. "Chairs that vibrate. Plastic doohickeys that shoot sliced cucumbers into salads."

"What madness is it?" I say.

"It's 1886 and I am Sockless Jerry Simpson," he says, looking up through the circle of hay bales at the round blue above us. "The frozen night is coming up my legs, but I am looking for an eagle who is looking for me."

"What?" I say. I look at him to see if he is all right.

"At least I don't have to ride around this country trying to find out where I am," he says. "I get to stay put. Historical cold. You will be the snow in the universe."

I don't know what to say, and we stand together in silence.

That Saturday my father swam her here, he told me to walk around to the point on the other side of the pond and watch him from there.

"You can't learn about swimming a horse without watching me do it head on," he said.

When I got to where I could see my father, he had dismounted and was patting Verbena on her rump. A small cloud of dust came off and floated away in the slight breeze. Then he ground tied her and walked along the water's edge toward the dam. I couldn't tell what he was doing. The horse looked after him. In a moment he came back, and I wondered how he would get into the saddle without his tree stump, but he seemed to spring onto Verbena, jumping his foot into the backward-facing stirrup and swinging himself into the saddle in a sure manner like a western-movie cowboy.

Verbena was startled for a moment, then did a little crow-hop buck. My father made a circle to the left and came straight at me into the pond. Verbena kept her head up and her nostrils were flared.

*　*　*

"Answer a letter with a letter," my father finally says as we stand in the yard amid the round bales. "Not with a phone call. Don't put money in Ma Bell's pocket. Don't call me on Father's Day or New Year's or Easter. Don't send me any of those stupid greeting cards. Greeting Card. What kind of language is that? It's nothing but a gimmick so the Vice President can slip his hand into your pocket while you're under the spell of the great blue hump of sentimentality. If they don't get rich on the raw red backs of the working poor, they do it on the sentimentality of the middle class."

"I understand," I say.

"Do you read what I mail you?" he asks. "Have you read your Veblen? Have you read the *Little Blue Books*? I don't want to be sending this stuff into the void. The post office doesn't censor mail anymore. Thank God we won that battle."

"We did," I say.

"Don't eat Velveeta cheese," my father says. "Or Ann Page bread."

"I won't," I say.

"Not even rats will eat white bread," he says. "That's why they made it in the first place, so mice and rats wouldn't shit in the flour."

"I think you're right," I say.

We shake hands and stand there in the circle of huge hay bales and look at the ridge they make around the house. Toward the east, I can see the top of my basketball goal.

"Did you notice that white patch that's coming out on Verbena's head?" my father says after a moment.

"I told you I did," I say. He nods.

"Historical cold," my father says.

"It's a tough winter in the shag of the horse," I say.

"You're beginning to learn," he says.

"I guess I am," I say.

*   *   *

From where I was on the point, I could see that once Verbena started swimming my father slid off her left side. The reins were draped over her neck, and with his right hand he held onto the saddle horn. But his feet hadn't come up, and he was slipping through the water at an angle. There was a slight wake at his neck, and it was breaking into his beard. He seemed to be looking at some point just in front of himself.

"How you doing?" I shouted. He didn't answer. It was a long swim. It was the longest line you could take across Big Pond. Near the middle, Verbena turned her head south to look down the slough and then back north again toward the dam, so there was a little S to her wake at that point. By then the ripples of their swim were beginning to reach the pond's edges, and the cottonwood leaves and small branches that had been floating on the water were bobbing slightly.

"How's it going?" I yelled. Again my father didn't answer. They kept coming at me. The teal I'd jumped earlier crested the ridge to the east of the pond and circled us once then hustled back over the hill. Some wind sent another small storm of leaves adrift in the air, and they sailed out over the pond, Verbena, and my father.

"You OK?" I said again. No answer, only firm swimming straight ahead.

When my father found his feet at the pond's edge and stood up in the mud of the shallows with some wet leaves clinging to him and with water running out of the cuffs of his shirt and dripping from his beard he said:

"It didn't get away from us this time, now did it son?"

"No," I said. "It didn't." Verbena shook and the spray of water made a rainbow around her.

"Did you know your mother named this horse?" said my father, still standing with Verbena in the water and brushing off the leaves from his shirt.

"I didn't know that," I said.

"She named this horse for that batch of flowers we got at the end of the lane," my father said.

"I know those flowers," I said.

"So do I," my father said. "I'd pick some for your mother now and then to make up for my madness."

"Do you need help?" I said.

"Who knows?" he said.

In a moment, he seemed to gather himself and walked out through the mud and up onto the bank. The horse shook again, and my father stomped his boots and water shot out of the seams at the soles.

"How was it?" I said.

"Your mother would have been proud of us," he said. "That's her in the head of the horse. The white coming out. That's your mother."

"Yes," I said.

"I wonder where I'll wind up," he said. "I want to be a soaring bird. Some great soaring bird with eyes so good he can spot the wobble in *Ranch* on the *Half-Vast* sign. Did you ever notice that?"

"Yes," I said.

I tried to get my father to let me lead Verbena back to the house, but he wouldn't hear of it.

"Give me a boot lift into the saddle, son," he said. "It's about time I let you do something for me."

I followed them in the truck. The sun was to the south and warm; it was the kind of warmth that cuts through the coolness, and it warmed each one of us, and we in turn warmed the surrounding air. When we got to the house, my father gave me Verbena and went inside to change his clothes.

That afternoon we started doing the chores we usually did to get him ready for winter, and that evening I brought the saddle and other gear in by the Melrose and gave them a good coat of neatsfoot oil while we talked. My father seemed subdued.

"What did you learn from swimming a horse?" he said at last.

"That it can be done," I said. After all these years I thought I'd try a little irony on my poor father. It didn't work.

"That's not all there was to learn," he said. There wasn't any rancor in his voice; his beard did not shake itself at me.

"How about you?" I said. "What did you learn?"

"I'd rather not say," he said. Perhaps it was the flat way he spoke that made something like Verbena's shake when she came out of the pond go through my body. My father noticed it, and his eyes widened for a moment.

"You OK?" he said.

"Yes," I said. We listened to the tree scrape the roof. I felt as if I had come through some historical place and was on the other side: There the light was lively and open, bright as a High Plains summer morning. I could hear my father talking; he was speaking out of the light, and what he had to say was not in words but in the chunks and particles of our life: boots and generators and language and hoops and straw and trucks and wood and sorry cattle. And me. Standing in the stream of lovely rubble, I saw my mother.

"Do you remember your mother?" my father said.

"I don't remember the sound of her voice," I said.

"Neither do I," said my father. He looked at me as if to test his memory of who I was.

"Tell me about mortgage insurance," he said.

"You don't want to know," I said.

"You don't cheat the working poor, do you?" he said.

"No," I said.

"You don't think time's money, do you?"

"No."

"Do you know what gossamer means?" he said.

"Yes."

"There's some hope in the world yet," he said.

"I may not be it," I said.

"You might be," he said. "I was."

That was Saturday night. We worked together two more days to button up: plastic storm windows, stove black, wood, square bales, round bales.

* * *

On Monday before I leave we are standing together in the yard.

"The blizzard of 1886," says my father.

"I think you're right this time," I say.

"Keep me in mind," he says. He taps his head, then lays his hand on mine. I realize we have not touched each other much over the years. "See your father in your mind's eye," he says.

"I can't do anything else," I say.

"Good thinking," he says.

* * *

The winter was mild, but in the spring two back-to-back blizzards buried the ranch, and my father was stuck for weeks. The phones were dead. The power lines were down. I drove out.

When the neighbors and I got into the yard by using a tractor to clear the lane, we found him in the yard amid the round bales sitting on Verbena in the snowy sunshine.

"I would have made it out by myself," he said to me as I came through the drifts. "But I didn't know why I should. This horse and I have been riding in circles once a day and talking to keep in practice."

"Keep in practice for what?" I said.

"Somebody's got to stay honest," he said.

After everyone left and I was alone with him, he told me he'd heard my mother's voice during the second blizzard.

"It's a delicate voice," he said. "With small blue petals in it. She asked about you."

"Yes," I said.

The Mackinaw

The cold windy Kansas winter was about to set in again and I found myself without a warm coat. The one I wore the year before was not much good anymore, and even when it was new it wasn't too warm. In fact, I can't remember owning a warm coat—a really warm coat, if you know what I mean. I guess I just bought these cheap winter coats that looked warm but were never very warm at all—and besides they always wore out sooner than you would ever suspect they would. So when I braved the already cold wind to go downtown to get a coat, I was determined to get a really warm one—although I didn't know quite what to look for. I had a hunch that the fellows who work outdoors must get the warmest things possible, so the first place I tried was a western shop in town. I walked in and asked them if I could look at some coats.

"Sure," said a hefty old man as he started down the aisle toward the back of the store. "Follow me, son."

"O.K.," I said.

"Well, son," he said, "here they are: all kinds, all sizes, and all prices. Just depends upon how big you are and how much money you got." He said all this without even closing his fat lips over his gold teeth. But I don't mean to be hard on him, for he seemed like a nice guy.

I looked at the coats and they were all the same kind of stuff I'd seen before: car-coats (only in a western style), and cheap leather jackets with good-looking, but not warm, linings in them.

"No," I said, "I want something warmer than this. In fact, I want a warm, tough coat—one that will last a long time."

"Son," he said as he looked at his row of coats, "they just don't make things like that anymore." He said "that" with some reverence.

"How about wool coats?" I said. "Do they make wool coats anymore? What do lumberjacks wear, anyway?" I continued before he could answer the first question.

"Mackinaws, son." He said it proudly and he seemed to stand a bit straighter. "A Mackinaw, that's what you want."

I was about to ask what a Mackinaw was, but it occurred to me not to show my ignorance so I asked: "A Mackinaw, one of those big woolen coats? Is that what you call them?" I was guessing all the way—but we had been talking about wool coats.

"That's right, son—you know, they've got a big wool collar and you can pull it up around your ears and you'll never get cold." He had acquired animation as he spoke and he actually seemed to turtle down into the invisible coat. It was as if he was talking of a thing that he had once loved, but for some reason it seemed unfashionable to love it anymore. But when he talked about it in this way the love got through somehow.

Perhaps it was the love that reminded me that Granddad Warner had a coat like that: maybe a Mackinaw (I saw it only once when I was little and I convinced myself now that I could not recall it accurately so I didn't dwell on it, but turned to listen to the clerk).

"Well, son, that Mackinaw was some coat—I don't think that the buttons ever came off it was put together so well. They'd make them out of blankets—my dad had one—I guess we had one in the family for years, but I don't know what happened to it."

While he was talking you could tell his mind was full of good stories about the old days and stories about the Mackinaw, and his dad, and maybe if he was in front of a fire with a brew in his hand he might have told them—even if there was love in them, or sentiment. But now he only glared at me and sort of snapped as though he knew I had caught him daydreaming.

"No, son, we ain't got anything like that and I'll tell you one thing: you can look in this town or most any other town that I know of and you won't find one."

"Thanks," I said, "but I'll try a few places anyway."

I walked out of the store and started down the street toward another clothing store and asked if they had any Mackinaws. There were two fellows my age in there acting as clerks and they both shook their heads—no, they didn't know what a Mackinaw was but they were sure that they didn't have any "Mackins" or whatever they were called. In fact they seemed a bit insulted that I should ask for one since they didn't have it. On my way out one of them suggested I might try Nelson's Hardware store, in the middle of the block.

"Hardware store?" I asked.

"Yes," said one of them. "They used to handle work coats. I don't know if they still do or not but they carry about everything else."

I thanked them and went back outside and up the street toward Nelson's Hardware. It was getting colder and my jacket wasn't helping to keep me warm. My mind was alive with ideas about this Mackinaw. I had all sorts of pictures in my head.

I finally found Nelson's Hardware. It was a curious shop. It had a big sign facing the street which said Nelson's Hardware and two big windows on either side of the solid wooden door. In the windows the passer-by could see simple saddles mounted on sawhorses. I went inside and noticed that the place was dimly lighted. The only light seemed to come from the two windows and sort of a glow from somewhere in the back of the long store. The light from these two sources didn't seem to reach each other so that I got the impression that the middle of the store was almost dark. The store was scattered with long tables loaded with odds and ends, the usual junk, unless you looked closer. Then you noticed that there was an unusual amount of outdoor gear—such as axes—not just hatchets like an ordinary store might have, but big double-bitted axeheads, without handles, and you bought the handle separately. On the walls were skillets, big black ones, and leather goods and ropes, not nylon cords, but real ropes. At the back of the room there sat an old man in a plaid wool jacket. He was sitting on a rocker and he hadn't moved since I entered, but rather he just rocked. To one side of him was an old pot-bellied stove—grey black with use. As I walked toward him I noticed the old wooden floor creaked.

"Howdy, son," he said—still rocking. "What can I do for you?"

"Do you know what a Mackinaw is?"

"Sure," he said, and he stopped rocking. "Sure," he said again. "I know what a Mackinaw is. I used to have one myself. Warmest coat I've ever owned."

"Do you have a Mackinaw?" I said.

He turned toward the rack of coats opposite the old stove and for the first time I noticed two old men, both sitting in rockers in front of the clothing rack. I could see now that before the old man (the one with the plaid jacket) had turned to greet me, he and the other men were sitting in a circle. One of the men wore a pair of bib overalls and an old work shirt and the other smoked a corncob pipe. The two guys stopped rocking when the guy in the plaid coat turned to look at the rack.

"No, son," he said. "That rack hasn't had a Mackinaw on there since—since 1936, I guess." He paused for a moment, then looked at the old guy with the pipe. "When was the last time we had a Mackinaw in here, Ed?"

"1936 or '37," Ed said with finality. "Leroy Gibson bought it—he nearly died of pneumonia the year before when he got caught out in a blizzard trying to get the stock in. He was the only guy around these parts that didn't have one then. He learned his lesson though." He paused and looked at me as though he had just discovered I was alive. "You don't want a Mackinaw, do you, son?"

"Bet he does," said the guy in the plaid coat.

I nodded in agreement and was about to ask something when the guy in bib overalls spoke out: "I remember a story about a Mackinaw. I used to have one myself you know," and he hooked his thumbs inside the straps that held up his overalls, but did not push them out but just sort of flexed them.

At this point the man with the pipe interrupted, "Is that the one about Sam? Sam Porter?"

"No, no, it isn't Ed, and let me finish before you start telling lies," said the bib overall man.

"This ain't no lie," the man with the pipe continued. "It's the honest-to-God truth, son," and he looked at me. "Old Sam Porter was out chopping wood one morning on his south acreage and it was kind of cold so he took along his Mackinaw. Well, it wasn't cold enough to snow, I guess, 'cause it started raining. I remember that well because it was the first good rain after the long drought. Well, old Sam was out cutting wood and when it began to rain, a cold, almost freezing rain, he was real happy because we all wanted rain. Well, the spirit got in him, I guess, because he just kept chopping wood and singing away, and when it started to rain a bit harder he went and put on his Mackinaw. He was so happy that he just stayed out there all day long—in that freezing rain, just chopping wood. And it was raining hard, you understand."

The old man now rocked back on his chair farther than usual. He had a smug look and he puffed his pipe and gave the impression that he was going to let us in on a great religious secret.

"And you know what?" he said finally. "When he got home he was bone dry! That's right, he was bone dry. That Mackinaw protected him all day long; it was woven so tight that not a bit of rain got through. Now, I tell you that's some protection—there isn't much that will take care of a man like that. Well, when Sam noticed how the coat kept him dry, so the story goes, he sat down and right then and there he wrote it into his will that he be buried in his Mackinaw. I went to Sam's funeral in '46 and sure enough there he was in that four-point Mackinaw of his. And I expect that his soul and that Mackinaw are all that's left of old Sam now."

He said these last words with a reverence that one might expect only from preachers on the holiest of holy days. Indeed he seemed proud of the story, and even prouder that it was about a Mackinaw. No sooner had he stopped than the fellow with the bib overalls started in.

"Like I was saying, son, back in the '30s I was hired on as a pick and shovel man at a gold mine in a place called St. George, Utah. Well, that was the first place I heard about Mackinaws. It seemed one day along about the first of November the Devil got into the wind and he darn near blew St. George off the map with the coldest blow I've ever seen. Well, this old-timer told me what I needed was a Hudson's Bay Mackinaw and 'course I made a fool out of myself and said, 'What the heck's a Hudson's Bay Mackinaw?' Well, he took me by the ear, sort of, and showed me his that was hanging up on a peg in the cabin I was in. It was a big double-breasted thing, all red, with a big black stripe around the bottom. Right then and there I figured I had to have one—set me back 30 bucks in those days but I got one." At this point the man in the plaid coat pointed out a chair to me. I sat down, and if anyone had come to the store at that time he would have seen four people, in the back of the room, warming themselves by a pot-bellied stove, listening to a story. The old man continued in a grave, but reverent tone.

"Well, one day me and Warner, Jake Warner, were on our way to the mine."

"Stop," I said rather sharply. "I mean, well...uh, did you say Warner? Jake Warner?"

"Yes, son. That's right. What about it, son?"

"Well, I know a Jake Warner..."

"Way before your time, son."

"But, he was my grandfather on my dad's side. My name's Warner, Jack Warner. Did this Warner come from Minnesota?"

"Yes, yes, he did, son. Yes, I'm sure he did—he owned part of the mine out there, used to come down every other year till he died."

"That's him. That's my granddad." I was about to explode with questions about Granddad—but I wanted to hear the story so badly that I said only, "Go on with the story, sir."

"Well, Jake Warner and I were riding out to the mine, like I said, and he always carried this Winchester 94 in his saddle scabbard, not the new kind with the buckhorn sights and all, but the old model that held 10 shots and had that six-sided barrel, you know." And the guy in the plaid coat and the guy with the pipe nodded. And I nodded, too, because I had seen the gun up at the family cabin near Wilmer, Minnesota. "Well, Jake forgot his Mackinaw and it was a cold day. And he was pretty upset to be without it on a day like that. No sooner had we crossed the first ridge—not five miles out of town—when we saw a big buck running parallel to us down the other side toward the wooded canyon. Jake was a crack shot and always got those bucks when they ran like that. Well, he reached for his Winchester and started shooting. He was cold without the Mackinaw, you understand, and didn't feel right—and maybe the gun didn't fall the same on his shoulder or maybe a fellow needs something he knows is good and strong next to him when he has to do a good job. Whatever—Jake missed that buck the first two times and then it turned toward us and was running right at us, and old Jake got buck fever (I promised him later I'd never tell a soul but since he's dead and gone, I guess it don't matter). Anyway, he got the fever and threw out eight good shells without firing one of them. Not pulling the trigger but just throwing that lever down, and out would fly a 30-30 shell into dust. Then that buck broke to the right and was gone in a moment. Jake didn't say anything for a long time, and I don't think he ever forgot that till the day he died. You understand I've seen him kill deer with the Mackinaw on and with it off. But I only saw him once when he wished he'd had it on and didn't and that time Jake Warner wasn't much good. I guess, in a way, he loved that coat, like we all did if we had one." And the other two nodded.

Perhaps I'm foolish but I didn't ask any more questions, not about Jake, nor about the Mackinaw. I somehow felt those fellows in there would feel awkward seeing me in a Mackinaw. I still want one, but I can wait.

Pan-Kansas Swimming Champion

Swim Date, Ten Laps

I am sitting in the locker room remembering that the television doctor told me to stop thinking about my body as a bag into which my organs and bones have been stuffed. Nor should I imagine it as the biology book overlays of my fifties high school general science class: the static electricity slapping the thin plastic pages of Veins and Arteries onto Bones and Cartilage in such a way that a fatal crease runs from the superior mesenteric to the subclavian. Such transparent geography is wrong these days. Old maps. Old bags of bones. Wrong mindset.

I was assured by my morning colleague in the glass that we should now see our body as a plethora of waters: creeks and streams and oxbows. Lakes and ponds and marshes. With banks and beds, and now and then small dams—wanted or unwanted. "We are," he said, leaning toward me as if in a consultation, "an ecosystem of fluids through which run ridges of minerals and rills of electricity. Drink water, be water: how we conceive ourselves matters."

To reconceive myself, I have started a lunchtime swim as a way to skip the country club's diabetic buffet. No doubt my television doctor would approve, just as I would approve such a regime for my own patients. However, I want more than health for my laps. I want to swim myself backward through time. I want to see myself slimmer, younger, stronger as the water washes past. In a previous age, I was Bobby Brown playing third base for the New York Yankees. I was as well the Pan-Kansas swimming champion. Wouldn't it be pretty to think so.

In a moment of exertion after the exhaustion of my first swim, I am trying for a watery conception. The best I can do is to conjure the thunderhead of my heart beating over the newly washed prairie of my smokeless lungs. The panorama of my mind fills with base paths and line drives; instead of the plethora of waters there is a field of 1950s New York Yankees: Mantle, Maris, Berra. Some part of my body that I do not recognize becomes an eternal Italian centerfield. The thunder of my heart turns to applause. It is early October and a towering drive to left becomes larger the farther it sails. From an unlocatable bleacher I watch my game being played out: The baseball—now as bright as a summer midnight moon—clears the fence, and I vanish, only to find myself looking with the redness of my eyes at the puddle below my bench. I try to recover a vision of myself—my body, my ball field—by going back to it through my ears. Instead of applause, I hear the faint ring of a tiny mechanical insect: tinnitus. It is the sound of ear nerves dying. A part of hearing lost in its own death cry: the essence of irony.

There are more kinds of irony than there are names for it. Or nerves dying so, while the dream of my new self has been hit over the fence, and yet another insect is cranking up to die in my other ear; I feel pretty good. Not like clear bays or brisk running creeks. Not like a crisp double play. But not bad. I drain my newly bought "water caddy." Life is good.

Swim Date, Twelve Laps

That's a third of a mile in the pool where I swim. A college pool. Up to the College, we say in town. The man with the locker next to mine, a Mr. Taylor (it is he who uses the Mister for himself), explains the nomenclature of our swimming.

"A length is up," he says. "A lap is up and back. It takes thirty-six laps to make a mile. Mr. Taylor is up to a mile. Even though we are newly retired. And we know what that means. Agewise."

We wonder what business Mr. Taylor practiced that robbed him of his first person. Or if he shed it like some skin along the way only to grow another against new visions of mortality. We have seen him now and then around town and at large parties, but we do not circle in the same smaller circles.

Mr. Taylor tells me that I need a pair of goggles. In my youth I swam the municipal pools of Kansas with my eyes awash and open. The world then wasn't red and blurry when I got done. Nor was my skin dry. It was probably all that iodine and baby oil. Either that, or—as we learned in medical school—I am drying from the inside out. ("The skin is an organ," the professor of dermatology made us repeat out loud three times the day he visited one of our classes.) A body that was once a vibrant sea has given way to a swamp that is turning into a marsh that will turn into an alluvial plain with tiny flowers going to seed. (I must remember not to talk to my patients in extended metaphors.) But Mr. Taylor is right: I need goggles. I need skin balm (some sample sizes of an ammonium lactate I have at the office). I need earplugs.

"And time on your side," Mr. Taylor says. You need time on your side as well. Something we don't have. "How did we do today?" he inquires.

Like a truculent patient who won't confess to the number of cigarettes he smokes a day, I won't tell him exactly how we did: "Not bad," I say.

In truth there *was* some flaccidity in the legs, as if our kick *were* not connected to our stroke. At eight laps we wanted to quit, but we threatened ourselves with the horror of a long-gliding airplane crash if we didn't swim on. It is an old device of ours. We dream up a superstition to suit the moment: Don't make the morning rounds and get lymphoma. Don't see the hypochondriac wife of the mayor, and the television hurricane will bend up the bay and sink the sailboat. Such mental violence is what is left of our Puritan Ethic. Tomorrow we fly to Kansas City. Medical School Reunion. As we turned into lap nine, we saw our plane climb back to altitude.

"We tried jogging and this is better," says Mr. Taylor. "Too much jarring of the bones in jogging," he says, as he goes through the door to the pool so that his voice echoes. Jarring bones. Bones. Bones. It is as if he takes up our laps where we have left off.

We all agree, even though we are beginning to feel uncomfortable in Mr. Taylor's persona and that of our morning medical man. Tense and person. Bays and bones. Water, water everywhere. Balls and strikes. Mainly strikes today: fastballs belt high that reduce our reflexes to a flinch. We pack our cell phone and drive to the clinic.

Swim Date, Eight Laps

Yogi Berra's number.

Kansas City was cold. But bright and windless. I took an afternoon off and went down to McGee where the old ballpark had been. I once saw Berra play third base there. The Kansas City Blues were a farm team for the Yankees, and every summer they would come to town and play out of their positions: Phil Rizzuto at first base. Jerry Coleman in right field. Ralph Houk in left. Mickey Mantle at shortstop.

As I did lap seven, I thought about some X rays of Mantle's badly torn anterior cruciate ligament I'd once seen in a journal and how now it could be repaired, but then it could not, so the "fastest man to first" played for years in bandaged pain. I thought about how he played shortstop in Joplin where I first set up practice. I thought about his father teaching him to hit left-handed, and about how I kept a Louisville Slugger 32/34 in my office in those days so I could practice my swing between patients, standing in front of a mirror

I had on the back of my door and hitting mostly from the left side.

As I come into the turn halfway through lap seven, I watch Mantle make his drag bunt to the right side of the diamond and race toward first. I pick up my pace; I hustle the ninety feet. My hand touches the side of the pool. Safe. Mantle turns toward the stands, his number rippling on his back, his effort to stop etched in his face. The crowd is ablaze with applause in the late July sun. We are all applause.

Coming back down seven, I lay my body out in the water in front of me and notice someone coming up beside me. A girl. A young woman. Black tank suit. The flutter of her kick drives her past me.

I swim up Berra's number toward Maris and Rizzuto—and an obscure infielder named Jerry Lumpe—none of whom I reach. I finish awash in bad ball hitting and only modest satisfaction. The girl has passed me coming and going.

Mr. Taylor is heading for two miles. "We are pleased with our one-mile accomplishment, so we are going to make our advance toward two miles beginning tomorrow. We are going to add a lap a day for a week, then level off for a week. A plateau at forty-two. Then forward again."

Inside Mr. Taylor's locker, there is a strip of white adhesive tape running lengthwise, on which he has some kind of marking system. He peels off an old tape full of cross-hatched lines and lays in a new one. There is a small wrinkle in it, which he notices and fixes by popping the tape off and laying it back on again, smoothly.

"Mrs. Taylor is no longer with us," he says. She has gone to Florida. He closes the locker and leaves.

Swim Date, Twelve Laps

The goggles make it all clear. I especially like the patch of sunshine in the deep end that comes through the window of the pool to the west and lays itself down along the bottom like a slab of white chocolate. Then there are the bubbles from the turns: how buoyant they are. A trail of my previous self through which for a moment I swim. The bubbles thin out by the time I've coasted to the end of my push-off, and then I am into the clear water of the new me. "All of three," I say to myself in order to keep track of what lap I am on. All of three. Even as I am thinking all of four. "All of three."

When I was younger, I did the tumble turn at the end of the lengths, where you duck your head just before you touch the edge of the pool and then twist so your feet wind up flat against the side. The trick is to turn and push all in the same motion. It isn't difficult to do, but to do it now would mean I'd lose a breath—and the sense of rhythm I need to get to all of twelve. Everything in its time. The tumble turn of yesteryear. Clichés are thrilling when you feel good.

Just as I am about halfway through five, I sense a swimmer in the next lane. The girl. She passes me and I follow her in and out of the turn midway through five—but she is fast. And steady. And she comes off the wall before I do. I watch the beat of her feet as they plunge air into the water ahead of me. Then her lane grows calm, her trace engulfed. I thrash on in some kind of silence I hadn't before known, and watch for her to come back up the pool. Which she does.

I see her face as it turns toward me, mouth agape, eyes strangely hollow in their goggles. In my mind's eye I mark the spot where we have crossed to see at what rate she is gaining on me. The next lap we meet nearer the middle, and the lap after that I see her coming into turn seven just as I am going out. It is taking something out of me, but I push myself to stay ahead of her into lap eight.

Going into nine I hear a thud at the surface that tells me she has flipped the turn; I am lapped. I feel taken, and I am surprised at the sensation: lightness and calm, and something blue in my mind for a moment. I watch the trail of bubbles she lays down in front of me. They are becoming smaller, then a froth.

When the water clears, I no longer think of keeping any kind of pace with her. I swim along toward ten through twelve, not marking where we pass but knowing she is lapping me at some rate immeasurable, each lap bringing with it a swell of anxiety and then something like a small nap. All of twelve. All of King Kong Keller and Gil McDougald. All of black tank suit.

"We are going to use the training crawl to get to two miles," says Mr. Taylor. "Do we know the training crawl?"

I say we do, although I have not been using it.

"For the long run you need it," he says. We wish we'd used it from the beginning. There is a pause while we both putter with the gear in our lockers.

"We were watching you just now," Mr. Taylor continues, "and you need to bring your kick up higher." He makes his hands my feet, and beats them in the air above his forehead.

Mr. Taylor is right about my kick, just as I will be right this afternoon when I tell my first patient that he must bring down his weight and cut out salt or he'll explode from the blood-pressure numbers I have threatened to write backward across his forehead so he can see who he is when he looks in the morning mirror: We are how we see ourselves, I will tell him. Drink water. Take no salt before its time.

"You'll do better," Mr. Taylor says, "with your feet up. Up." His hands rise on the beat of them as my feet. Lest he swim backward out the door I assure him we'll do better tomorrow.

My patients are never so quick to assess or value my opinion. They take their advice, I suspect, from someone else—perhaps from the same television doctor I watch in the mornings; or if not from him, then from the business correspondent on the evening news. It amounts to the same thing: Advice is news, and it too shall pass.

Maybe my patients are right in resisting cures that are not pills or shots or surgery. Who am I to tell them about their lives? Some days (today, for one) I think I should keep to my place: Name their malady. Note its history. Describe the length and number of its lap. Tell them it is either self-limiting or fatal.

Then say: "There, there."

Maybe I should try it this afternoon when I read again the chart of my second patient: "There, there." Diabetes: Glucose 200 up from 150. Then all of 250 by this time next year if he doesn't stop drinking his "Industrial Strength Martinis." Think smoke stack, Doc, think "Industrial Strength." ISM for short. Blood pressure all of 170. All of PSA, all of Prostate: all zip. He lost it four years ago to my right index finger and to one of my partner's scalpels. Think moderation, I'll say to ISM.

As for myself, tomorrow I'm going to raise my kick and move my laps to fifteen. When I get to half a mile, I'll make the tumble turn of my youth and sprint for home, Zeus's sperm flying.

I leave the locker room and go into the lobby and look through the glass doors at the pool. The girl in the black tank suit is still swimming, lapping Mr. Taylor at some fantastic rate. Her head is high as she bites the air for breath. Her feet boil the water with the precision of even heat. She seems younger at her age than I was at her age. Beautiful and carnivorous, she swims as if she's after something.

I do not wait to see Mr. Taylor lapped again but walk outside and across the campus. It is early October. Warm as World Series weather.

Swim Date, Zero Laps

To put myself to sleep at night I think of swimming: The placement of my head. The angle of my hands as they break the surface. The trail of bubbles my hand makes before my eyes as I pull it through. The boil of my feet. The glide of the final stroke before the wall. The integrity of laps. Laps. All of dreams. When I was a boy, I'd put myself to sleep by playing third base for the Yankees: Furillo is at bat. I have crept up along the line for the bunt. I nod to Rizzuto at short and to Joe Collins at first. We understand. Reese takes a lead at second. Lopat is on the mound. McDougald is hedging his bets toward Collins. Should the bunt go toward first, I'll break back to cover third. We have done this before; it only takes the slightest gestures among us to make the play.

When Furillo hits the ball down the line, I switch my dream to the radio announcer's play-by-play: Like the drive itself, my dive to catch it is an instantaneous tight rope to the ground. Furillo takes a step toward first then stops dead, head down, in his tracks.

Some nights I am suspended above the third-base line, the white ball smack in my glove. Other nights—after I have hit the dust with the catch—I bolt off the ground and hold the ball up for all to see. Sometimes, it is the end of the inning and my body thumps into the dirt for a moment while the crowd gasps that I might be hurt; then I spring to my feet and walk to the dugout, where Casey Stengel ignores me. On nights when there is only one out, I pop to my knees and fire the ball to McDougald, who has come over to second, and we double up Reese in a play that has him stopped in the same state of amazement as is Furillo. The crowd roars. The radio announcer describes it over and over again until the stadium glows with the words.

However, these nights in bed my goggles are fogged and the slab of light at the deep end has a melted quality. My shoulders ache, but my feet have come up (Mr. Taylor approves), and I can see they are driving me. Turning my head, I study the way my arms rise out of the water. I watch the spray of my stroke and imagine I am a camera in charge of perfection. Doc Counsilman is reviewing the films and waiting for my body-density charts. I am doing the training crawl: two strokes on one side, one stroke to change over, and two strokes on the other side. Breath, breath, stroke, death, breath. All of looking to sleep on, some second self.

To keep track of my laps I roll over my IRAs one lap at a time.

I give the IRA a name: Apollo, Bacchus, and I fill the lap's length by trying to compound the interest until my retirement. It is all further away than my college classics class or my weak math skills can take me. Still (I can hear Mr. Taylor whispering), we must begin somewhere. Besides, there is something gaining on me as I name and number my yields: something slimmer, stronger, younger. It laps me, and I struggle for a moment to the surface of my dreams but do not come awake.

My night's swimming has left me exhausted. I lay off a day. None of today. All of none today.

Swim Date, Fifteen Laps

The other evening I met Edward Albee at a party. The College had invited him to campus. I have not read Albee's famous play, but I've seen the movie. I've seen Martha make fun of George Segal. I heard her call him "Pan-Kansas Swimming Champion."

George Segal and I look alike. I know when he has been on television because the next day my patients will comment on our similarity. It also happens that one of my favorite actresses is Sandy Dennis, Sandy Dennis of *Sweet November*. Mine is bad taste, I know. But there it is.

"Were you satisfied with Taylor and Burton?" asks a professor standing in our small circle by a sideboard of drinks.

"They promised me Brando and Bette Davis," Albee says. He tilts his head and runs his hand along his ear. There is some chatter about this response, but Albee seems distracted. He notices me watching him. He runs his finger around his ear's helix and down into the concha where he makes a small drilling motion.

"A tiny ringing inside the ear," he says. The sign that one of the nerves that collects sounds is dying. He looks at me.

"How did you happen to create George and Martha?" asks the professor. Albee still has my eye; it is as if he has seen me somewhere before. Behind our group, Mr. Taylor, in an Orvis tweed sports coat, is talking to the college president, who is talking to Mr. ISM, who is drinking one.

"Were you satisfied with George Segal and Sandy Dennis?" Albee says to me.

I say very much so. Albee nods. We don't continue because he is swept along in some conversation about theater of the absurd and talk of Shakespeare and George and Martha.

They promised me DiMaggio and Monroe, I say to myself on lap five—or is it six? Outside an early winter storm has made a mess of the bar of deep-end light. The slate-gray color of the sky is the color of the water. I have lost track of my lengths, and my way of keeping myself honest is to swim another lap for each lap I've forgotten. If I'm on five, but I'm not sure of that, I assume I'm on four—and I'll do five again. In this way I stretch myself.

Into lap six I begin to make divisions. I am halfway to the one-third mark. I swim up seven as a lucky number, and turn all of eight as some numerical cousin to thirty-six. Nine is Maris. Poor dead Roger Maris. Ten will be even. The decimal system. The Bill of Rights. Kilometers. Five-eighths of a mile. The Ten Commandments. I lose track again and go back down the lineup. Poor dead Roger Maris. All of Roger Maris Berra. I punch a low-and-away fastball down the left field line for a double. All of "Industrial Martinis." Cholesterol at 200, all bad. All of fifteen.

And then some.

"We were in kitchens," says Mr. Taylor, as I sit on the bench. "We built kitchens from New York to Newport. Our Silver Line Division put kitchens in tract houses, but our Sterling Division did theme kitchens: Italian modern kitchens in black and white with built-in pasta cupboards. French provincial kitchens. Early American kitchens with Flemish Bond brick fireplaces. Oriental kitchens. One guy wanted a Wizard of Oz kitchen. Judy Garland wallpaper. Yellow brick floor. We did it."

Against his locker I see the strip of white tape and a number of black marks. He adds another one and then lays the marking pen on the top shelf from which he fetches something else.

"Lisbon," he says, holding a small plastic bottle for me to see. When I shower today I'll use shampoo we got at the Ritz in Lisbon. My wife in Florida, she packs her bags with all the free soap you can get in hotels. Madrid. Paris. Rome. London. I got it all here." He points to the top shelf of his locker as he puts back Lisbon, then walks into the shower.

As if he is somehow aware of me, my television doctor has recently recommended our swimming. It uses all our muscles. It returns us to the water. It suspends us. It does not pound us. It helps our fluids circulate. Our blood must run to our capillaries—a corner of the universe where it seldom goes. We must open up small creeks and wash out the litter of the dry beds. The secret to health and long life, he tells the camera that I am beginning to think is located just behind my head, is in both our waters and in the channels in which those waters flow. No wonder I feel better.

Swim Date, One Lap

Water streams into my goggles going up; coming back, I tell myself unless I finish the first lap the price of IBM will drop twenty points by the closing bell. I thrash on to the end and stop. I empty my goggles and press them onto my head with the palm of my hands. I push off for the second lap; the goggles fill again. I stop. Standing in the shallow water about five yards from the pool's edge I tighten the straps. I can't decide if I should go back and push off again or go ahead from where I am. There is no one else in the pool. Only the lifeguard who has run the wires of his iPod up inside of his sweatshirt and who is listening to a different drummer than I am.

I lose track of everything; I can't seem to count backward far enough to make up for the laps I've lost. I wade to the pool's edge, pull myself out and go inside to take a shower. As I leave, I notice the girl in the black tank suit has begun her laps. Alone, she seems bent on besting herself.

Swim Date, All of Twenty

A quantum leap. A point in time. The whole nine yards. Beyond Whitey Ford and Vic Raschi. Out into deep water. The modest achievement of my precious bodily fluids. All done in her presence, all done with her by my side. Many times by my side.

"How did we do today?" asks Mr. Taylor. I notice the tone of his body: papier-mâché white, an old fork break in the left forearm—and that I also have become we. We did all right, we say; we have learned the value of understatement.

At all of eleven, she goes by me going into the far turn. I follow her bubbles out and catch sight of her arches. Her legs and thighs disappear into the agitation of blue-and-white water. I lay back, looking for what kind of pace she has in for me. I am heading for half a mile, while playing a night game in Flatbush.

In Kansas City we do not know what Flatbush means, any more than in our Methodist Youth Fellowship we know the location of the Holy Land that we imagine is east of Florida. Nor do we know why the New York Yankees are called the Bronx Bombers. We tend to believe that "the Bronx" is some kind of secret plane that our *Life Magazine* book about World War II does not show us. With the handles of our bats, we draw the Bronx in the dust of our infield: It has fat wings, a tall tail, four motors, and streams of bombs that drop all around home plate.

Later that night the Yankees play a game in Flatbush. I am

Bobby Brown at third base. I go two for four against Chicago: a pair of sharp singles, both up the middle. Not screamers like Bill Skowron will hit, but hard liners hit off good pitches that other batters might curse themselves for watching into strikes.

I have developed this theory that Bobby Brown never hits a bad ball. That he's the hitter who watches for a good pitch and slaps it—that's the word I want—slaps it into right center. Berra can hit all the bad balls he wants; I wait for the waist-high fastball over the fat of the plate in Flatbush, Kansas, as I swim myself down the pool's lane in pursuit of the black tank suit. All of four for four.

I have our pace. She crosses my path three strokes closer to me each time we meet. At fourteen we go into the turn together and I follow her heels halfway until I lose sight of them. The slab of sunlight is set rippling, and I know where she is ahead of me. We cross at two strokes before I come into the turn. Out of the turn I slip back into Flatbush, where I am stationed at my sack, steady and methodical.

I am watching my hand come into the water. Bubbles trail from it; it wavers through its pull. I watch it, my hand, come out, full of spray and droplets as if in a photograph. Beside me, she goes by in the arch of my arm. I feel on cruise control. I turn and head into water I had not intended entering. All of sixteen. The rivers and lakes and bayous of my body hustle to catch up. All of Whitey Ford. All of Bob Cerv. All of Don Larson.

At nineteen, I lose track of what I am doing. I put myself in the on-deck circle, my number six flapping on my back in the desert wind. Studying the pitches, I collect myself. Coming into the far turn at twenty, I remember that I wanted to do my tumble turn; I tuck my head for a moment but think better of it. Something to save for a mile.

When I am playing at Yankee Stadium I am flamboyant. A crowd pleaser. A diver to the left. A diver to the right. But when I am Bobby Brown in Flatbush, I am methodical. I check my spikes for dirt, and I check my leggings to see that the arch of white along the side is what it should be. I touch the bill of my cap. Robinson is up. I see that Berra has called for a curve from Lopat. Of course. This one is down and away, but still Robinson pulls it toward me. A chop that has hit the ground before the pitcher's mound and which is destined to clatter on into left over Rizzuto's outstretched glove until I cut it off and—fielding the half-hop so it doesn't have the chance of a bad bounce—fire it over to Mize at first. All of which I do while keeping myself inside myself. No flip turn. End of the inning. Start of the final lap.

I push off hard. I feel my kick rise in the water. I see it driving me. I stretch my arms. I raise my brow so that the water breaks across my forehead. Doc Counsilman, here I come. I am swimming down the lens of the underwater camera. My body-density chart shows that I am lithe in the pools of my dreams. I touch myself out. I am the Pan-Kansas Champion. I take off my goggles and look around. She is all of gone.

Swim Date, The Pool at Night

After the Edward Albee party I walked through the campus to my condo. A fog hung over the lawns; the sidewalk lamplights were confined to lighting themselves. Ahead, I could make out the figures of a faculty couple as they turned down the lane to their campus house. By the intermittent growl of their talking, I concluded they were in a post-party row.

I stopped by the pool. It has large glass sliding doors along two sides, and the front and back doors are glass as well. You can see clear through.

The building was lit in that obligatory nocturnal way: a few lights in various corners and one coming from someplace you could not see. It looked like an Equity lit stage, something an actor might come back to at night just to see one more time before he left the show for good. I went up to the side door and looked in. The water was level, but there were tiny swirls and miniature eddies coming from its circulation. There was nothing to be seen beneath the surface.

Swim Date, 12-32-10

I can't get into my locker. Some set of numbers out of my past has come forward into my head, and I can't unlock my brain to get my present combination. Where must I go in my youth to unlock the lock with the combination I keep dialing? I sit on the bench and probe.

I think of brain scans I saw the other day in a journal. It showed that very smart people solve problems only with the part of the brain that is designed for such functions, but that those less gifted must have their brains search everywhere among the lobes and hemispheres for the solution. I see lights on deep in my fornix. I see that I am aglow along all twelve of my cranial nerves. All of brain. All of memory. A television on from top to bottom and side to side. All of twenty-four inches on the diagonal. We are how we conceive ourselves.

"We're closing in on two miles today," says Mr. Taylor, as he comes into the locker room and notices I am still dressed. We have our rhythm. He pauses. "What's the matter? Forget the combination?" Yes, we say.

"It happens to me," he says. He goes over to a fire extinguisher housed in a crèche in the tile wall and opens the glass door. He tilts the extinguisher away; under it is a small piece of yellow notepaper:

"Twenty-four, eleven, twenty-two. Most of the time I've got the combination right up front" (and here he taps his forehead), "but sometimes not. Today not. When I was younger I could use the twitch system. Do you know the twitch system?"

"No," we say. Mr. Taylor seems to have forgotten it himself as he opens his locker. Oddly, I wonder who his doctor is.

"You can get your combination from the pool staff," he says as he pulls off his clothes. "You don't want to miss your exercise. A day off is a day backward."

Something in me wants to go backward today, so I spin the dial on my lock in the knowledge that the combination is in my desk at the office but that in between patients instead of hitting left-handed into a mirror (something I've taken up again of late), I'll devise a way to remember my numbers. Maybe I'm young enough to use the twitch system, whatever that is. In the end, I'll probably have to open the desk drawer.

Leaving, I notice someone young and lithe and lovely and not yet a black tank suit go into the women's locker room. The sky is gray. Winter is north and west of us.

Swim Date, A Mile

I guess I've done a mile. Early on I lost count, thinking about something I don't recall now and so went back to the last number I remembered. I got through five laps just keeping track of the numbers, and then she slid in beside me and I followed her for a few laps before I had to go back to a number I remembered. From eleven through twenty, I had my rhythm. I counted my strokes and calculated the interest on my IRAs and played baseball and swam up and down the long flat roads of Kansas.

Beyond twenty, I swam Yankee numbers when I knew them; and when I didn't, I put the number on myself and played third base the whole lap, the announcer saying that "old what's-his-number has done it again, diving to the right to rob Reese of a sure double." It wasn't the same.

Around lap twenty, I began to wonder if I would remember to do my tumble turn on thirty-six. Then I drifted off somewhere and began thinking of the waters inside me and about the ironies involved. I lost track of losing track. I was treading water while keeping pace and heading for all-of-some-number I could not figure. I found myself thinking of a patient who this afternoon will learn from me the nature of his death. Not ISM, as it has turned out.

A splash of feet in front of me going into a far turn snaps me out of it. I remember lap twenty-seven, but I think I'll add a number because surely I must have gone on past my memory. All of twenty-seven, I say to myself as I make the turn. It feels like twenty-seven, gritty and sure of itself. Twenty-seven. I watch my hands hit the water and watch them pause for just a moment, floating almost, before I pull them through again. "How many laps to go?" my patient asks me. "Less than all of nine," I say. Poor Roger Maris.

I start counting down the lineup, while the girl is no doubt counting up; the snap and spray of her youth seems vicious in its vigor. I am diminishing, like some old center fielder trying to catch one last fly ball before he mysteriously pops into the outfield bullpen of middle age. With nothing else to do, I go back down the roster toward the wall: All of Berra. All of Mantle. All of me. All of DiMaggio.

She laps me at Gehrig. I lose track. I do the Iron Man twice. All of ALS. I swim through Ruth, wondering where at my back she is hurrying near. All of Frank Crosetti in the coaches' box. I tumble the turn at the far end of the final lap, and my nose fills and my ears pop. For a moment I am lost. Tiny insects fly out of my head. I see the bubbles of my previous self gathering in front of me and push off through them into the bright fresh water of Billy Martin. All of Billy Martin.

I see myself watching a World Series pop-up. I remember to raise my kick so that it propels me forward. I stretch myself for the length that remains. Blood goes up dry creeks. Oxbows swell with new pride. The infield is clear. No one but me to make the catch. She is closing with precision. Racing forward, my hat flying, my glove at arm's length, I touch her out at the wall to win at home. The radio announcer describes my feat to my teammates in Kansas City. She flips her turn beside me and prowls back up the lane.

"Did we do well today?" asks Mr. Taylor. "We look like we did well. As for ourselves, we are closing in on two miles today and washing with a small hotel soap my wife found for us in Venice. Well, not Venice exactly, but some island off Venice."

We did well, we say.

"Good," says Mr. Taylor. "We talked to Mrs. Taylor last night and told her we were close to two miles. We are not divorced. We are not even separated. She just lives at our place in Florida during the winter. Never go to Florida in the winter," says Mr. Taylor. He has that look on his face as if an aphorism is…is…somewhere, somehow connected to his advice—but in the end he cannot think of it. We ask if he notices the girl in the black tank suit.

"We do not," he says, and makes another mark on his adhesive tape.

Swim Date, Third Person

It was Mr. Taylor at the end of the rescue squad siren this morning during the television doctor's segment. It was not my call. Nor his.

Ours is a small town, so we share duty at the emergency room. Some nights I sleep over in the Spartan cubicle on the second floor. I rather like it—at least for the few days once or twice a month that the obligation is mine. The room reminds me of my university days, institutional: yellow cinder block, a brown plastic sitting chair, a black-and-white television mounted on the wall (on which I never tune in my colleague.) I can't fully say—beyond my association with my previous undergraduate living—why I find such a meager place pleasing. What I do not like is the medical duty it predicts: farm boy and college fraternity men, drunks with beer-bottle gnashes, indigestion mistaken for a coronary infarction, poison ivy. Nothing my "There, there" is good at curing.

It wasn't until later in the afternoon—after my swim, but with no particular concern that Mr. Taylor and I had not crossed paths—that I learned for whom the siren sounded. All of DOA.

Swim Date, There, There

I am sitting in the locker room. I have remembered my combination. I get up and go over to the fire extinguisher and get Mr. Taylor's numbers. I open his locker. The white tape with its marks is there. There is room for another row. I take down his bowl of soaps: Lisbon. London. Mexico City. I imagine myself in the third person doing theme kitchens: Toto is in the wallpaper. I am a morning television doctor who comes on with the coffee maker. I am talking but I can't quite make out what I am saying.

The camera backs up and reveals a girl in a black tank suit sitting beside me. She is taking phone calls from the viewing audience. My ISM wants to know what to take for the pain of moderation. Someone who sounds very much like myself asks about the effects of old athletic injuries on the life of the mind, and what are the best prophylactics for the loss of memories. *Water*, says a voice from somewhere. All of water everywhere. Mr. Taylor calls to say that we have lived a long and useful life by not going to Florida in the winter. The girl beside me makes no comment as she goes from caller to caller, clicking them on and off with the twist of a tiny button on the voice speaker. *All of water*, I hear myself saying through the buzz of yet another nerve dying.

I put back the bowl of soaps and place Mr. Taylor's combination inside his locker and shut the door and snap the lock. I go over to my own locker, open it, and stand there for a moment trying to see the near past. Nothing. No vision of laps done. I am not at any base. No Flatbush Holy Land Bronx Kansas. No irony. The lineup card is empty. There is nothing in my locker but my tank suit, my goggles, a towel.

I walk into the lobby. I have patients this afternoon: stomach discomfort that will need Reglan; we are beginning to see some flu; young men from the College come in with condyloma. *There, there*, I will say to them all. *Have you thought about creeks and oxbows? Would you like an irony? Take two with a bay of water and don't call me.*

There, there, we say to ourselves.

A lithe and lovely girl in a skirt and sweater carrying a bathing bag says hello as we pass each other on the sidewalk outside the pool.

Where I Am Now

We Are a Country of Stories

The sheep have been through the hay meadows in recent weeks. Dominique and his herders drive them in a round robin route of about twenty kilometers, staying two or three days in each meadow. My guess is there are three hundred, including goats. They were below me for two days, the ewes giving birth so that the lambs are growing the flock as it moves. Now they are west of me, past the village of Saint-Philippe; I see them on my way to the Monday market in Castillon.

I live in a small stone house perched high in a vineyard. From my bedroom window, at a distance I see the castle of Montaigne. It is more than sufficiently large for royalty. Close by, and out the same window, is the wreck of Château Montagne, lived in by a *très difficile* countess who had her fingers broken (one at a time, according to the story going up and down the *côte*) last year by robbers until she produced the keys to her safe. Montaigne would not have believed it had he seen it himself. We are a country of stories. And skeptics.

* * *

I type in the mornings unless it is a market day, when I do my shopping. Food is dear, but wine is inexpensive—at least for the *vin en vrac* I buy from Monsieur R., stopping by his *chais* to fill my four-liter straw-covered bottle and gossip in my weak French.

Afternoons I cut logs, clear brush, and help with the sheep at a small farm down the road. In exchange, I am offered meals and wood for my stove. I walk to work, as it is only five kilometers. I move my feet to move my words.

I may become a father: the farm had six of its sheep killed by a mad dog. One of the ewes had just given birth, and we saved the lamb (now named Molly). Because I carried her into the house and laid her by the fire bright, she thinks I am her mother and follows me everywhere, bleating, bleating for her bottle. I don't have a place for her, but I might rig one. We'll see.

The hunters are busy these days, shooting from early in the morning until sunset: pheasants, *colombes* (a dove-like bird that migrates through on its way to Africa), wild pigs, and small deer with a high-pitched bark. I see these men by the sides of the small roads that wind through the hills, sometimes with dogs. The other day one of them blew a brass horn as I passed. I do not know if he was calling something, or calling to other hunters that something (*pas moi!* I had hoped) was heading their way. The cheese rinds, eggshells, wilted lettuce, apple and pear cores, bits of old pâté that I have been trying to compost in the woods between my house and Château Montagne seem, instead, to be feeding Boris—my *nom de cochon* for a wild boar with an indiscriminate palate. Not that I have seen Boris, only that there are never any leavings from what I put out. Called to the hunter's horn or routed by their dogs, he would be good game—and no doubt a hearty ragout. Now that I have named him, I hope not. And he might be Borita.

A few days ago, a hunter brought a hindquarter of deer to the family that has Molly. The *femme de la fermière* used her butcher knife to carve the evening meal—and then some. Two sheepdogs shared the bones. I was invited to stay. My host opened bottles from his best years.

"There was a saying on the Kansas frontier," I said by way of a toast, "that the men were so hungry when they came in from the roundups, that the women fed the dogs first." Having once worked on a small ranch in Kansas, I am known by the French as "Cueboy," and in that guise I am expected to offer *bon mots* from the American West. We raise our glasses.

A great storm of wind and rain has come and gone, and now it is clear—although I have learned by the French radio (I do not have television—or the Internet) that it will get *très froid*. So be it: I have wood, wool sweaters, and maybe Molly to keep me warm.

In the meantime, off to lunch today at the home of a painter friend where we will be joined by the widow of another painter friend. The afternoon will be a buzz of Bernard and Johns and Cassatt; as I know something about art, the talk among us will be a pleasure for me to recall—not unlike laying down bottles of good wine for a future of meals with friends. The most fruitful and natural play of the mind is conversation. I'll hold forth and dispute, but only for my own pleasure. *Tant pis* about death and all that.

I Have Not

Madame F., an eighty-year-old American ex-pat from California who lives beyond a line of poplars down the hill from me, fell leaving my house after dinner the other night and hurt herself badly: a nasty twisting of bones and cartilage in her left foot and lower leg. I got help from neighbors, and we took her to the hospital in Libourne. The French medical system is excellent; true, it is in a high fever of fiscal misery these days, but I sense the French think it is better to be in debt to themselves for their own care than to China for television sets, or to the Middle East for oil and war. After a few days, Madame was taken (not sent) home in a hospital van where medical attention continues: visits by a nurse a few times a week, and a doctor less often, but routinely—or as needed. Of course, there are her friends. Me among them.

In the mornings I start her woodstove, a long arrangement of cook ovens, griddle plates, burner tops, and water reservoirs that not only heats her old mill of a house but cooks the meals she makes for those of us who have been her guests. Evenings I walk her dog, Ginger, a tall Rhodesian Ridgeback who sits partway into the large fireplace in the evenings because, out of her country, she is cold.

My neighbor and I talk books: Russian stories we read together in the early fall, and now de Maupassant: "Boule de Suif," which made him famous; "The Story of a Farm Girl"; and "Madame Tellier's Establishment." (We have agreed not to reread "The Necklace"...in protest...but of what we are not sure.)

In between the Russians and the French, we confess our literary prejudices and affections: how much better Carlyle is as a writer on the French Revolution (even if wrong) than Dickens. The splendor of Chekhov. The recent death of Alain Robbe-Grillet and the novels of Duras (and while we are there, the wine by the same name). How neither of us have read Radiguet. All this and whatever comes from our mutual reading of *The Guardian* or *The New York Review of Books* (she subscribes to both), and *The New Yorker* (my subscription)—along with other literary journals and belles-lettres magazines we share with one another, and with others in our circle.

The other evening she asked if I had met the *jeune fille américaine* who this past summer moved into a farmhouse at L'Étang on the Montagne estate; she is a painter. *Très belle.* I have not. Madame confesses that she has asked her to do the Monday morning market shopping. I am thanked for bringing in wood from the sheds below the house and building and stoking the fire, for walking Ginger—but the market needs a woman's touch. And no doubt better French, not confusing *rougette* (a small reddish lettuce) with *rouget* (a large reddish fish). Then there was the matter of *aiguilles*, which I understood to be sewing needles but were, in the market patois, *aiguillettes*, thin strips of meat; sewing needles cannot, as it turns out, be sautéed with garlic in olive oil. Nor can lettuce be poached with lemon and Herbes de Provence.

Perhaps, Madame suggests, the three of us can read Radiguet (in French) and talk about it over dinner one night. In French.

I Am to Be a Godfather

It has been decided I am to be a godfather to Molly with visiting rights. It seems best she stay with the flock as she has made friends with the other young lambs—three sets of twins among them. That is fine by her, and by me. In the evenings, I prepare her bottle, and when she hears me come out of the house into which I first carried her, she bounds up the rows of vines to bleat me a greeting. I know it is not love, but the bottle I carry, that is love. French folk and flocks are not confused—or conflicted—about such matters. We understand I will not take her home but might, if the weather turns foul, carry her to the fireplace where we first were father and daughter.

Tomorrow to the Saturday morning market in Sainte-Foy for myself, and to get a wedge of old *brebis* (I can't make a mistake about that) for my broken-footed friend. Cold tonight, but good wood in my stove. Sans Molly, extra blankets. Maybe a nip of Armagnac. Maybe more than a nip.

Some Wines Are at Home in a Pichet

My house sits at the *carrefour* of four wine districts. West is Saint-Émilion, one of the great regions of France. I have a few celebrated bottles that my friends gossip I am saving for my *lit de mort*. The younger French—mainly from the cities—think it is better to drink the good wines now, my prized Saint-Émilions included. I'll split the difference one winter night over a good cut of veal. And Saint Agur. Or maybe a meal with Madame when she is well enough to return to my table. That's it. The future is a promise you keep to yourself.

Across the Dordogne River (about ten kilometers south) is Entre-Deux-Mers—a light, white wine that I am told does not travel but is splendid here in summer. Or with *truite de mer* anytime. Crisp. Dry.

To the north a kilometer or two is Côtes de Francs. I can see the vines from my second-floor windows. It is good wine and a good value. There is something tough and lean about it. In winter, it gets better if you open it and put the bottle by the woodstove thirty minutes before dinner. I drink half a bottle one night, then the other half the following night. Sometimes I fail at this arrangement.

The vines that surround my house are Côtes de Castillon. It is those vines that produce Château Perreau Bel-Air, a wine I save for the few visitors from America I have these days. By looking out the French doors in my dining room cum office, they can see what they are drinking. Our toast is to tip our glasses to the grapes.

East five kilometers is Bergerac, a sturdy, dependable red wine. Monsieur R. resents the upscale vintners who are making Bergerac a Bordeaux-styled wine, so that it might be exported. "Some wines are at home in a *pichet*," he says. "That way, 'if it gets broken at the table, desire shall not fail.' Confucius."

Monsieur is a *chais* of aphorisms. Roughly the age of Madame F., they are *chers amis*. He, too, is helping with her these days.

I don't catch Monsieur's meaning, but he seems pleased with himself for his saying, which he repeats while he fills my jug. The wine—a *mélange* from his scattered small vineyards of various appellations—is strictly illegal, and that pleases him as well. One of his vineyards is not far from where *la nouvelle américaine*"—as Monsieur calls her—lives. Between Madame F. and Monsieur R. her full name will become Mademoiselle Nouvelle Américaine.

"*Très nouvelle*," says Monsieur. "A young *tête sur les jeunes* shoulders,' to quote Catullus."

From time to time I have seen Mademoiselle Américaine driving the roads in a *très ancien* blue Dyane truck with potted flowers painted—by her?—on the doors. She zips by with such speed and apparent determination to get where she is going that I cannot get a good look at her. I doubt she sees me at all. Because I drive a maroon Deux Chevaux made by the same company and of about the same vintage, I thought one day to flash my lights as we passed: one *voiturette* to another. I got a quick flash in return. Next time I'll honk.

I say to Monsieur that all I remember from Catullus is, "What a woman says, you can write on the wind, write on the rushing waves."

"*Ah oui*," says Monsieur, "but wind and waves are lovely, and it is better to have a *faux récit* than *rien*. Far better, as Cicero says. And a man has well lived his life if he drinks the last bottle from his cellar on his last day," he continues as he corks my jug. Walking me to my Deux Chevaux he quotes Shakespeare that a young man should be whipped who plays at being a connoisseur of wine and sauces.

"It was Montaigne who said that about young men and wine," Madame told me when we were talking of Duras and Radiguet, "not Shakespeare. He gets many things wrong, and I think it is on purpose. Either that, or he is finally addled."

I ask her about the "broken pitcher at the table," and she believes it might be the Old Testament but is badly quoted and has nothing to do with wine. She'll look one day. I decide not to mention Cicero.

Many Shades of Gray

Gray is the color of the Dordogne sky this time of year. Many shades of gray. Sometimes with streaks of red or pink as the sun tries to burn its way through. The other day nothing got through because of a deep fog that came in the night. When I walked down to start Madame's fire the spider webs from summer were wisps of tendrils, white with the frozen frost. As I passed, they moved as if shivering. There was both the shade as well as the substance of things.

The grapevines and the wires on which they are strung were a dark brown, speckled with the white of the frozen fog. The grass in the pasture and the few large, round hay bales left from the fall mowing looked a pale yellow covered by a thin white shawl. Ten meters from my friend's house, I could only make out its shape: no doors, no windows. It will be the same for my house when I walk up the hill: only wizened webs in the icy air, and lines of brown vines making a perspective into the mist.

"Do you get fogs in Kansas?" Madame asks me as I load her stove.

I tell her not many, at least in the west where I lived. She is also curious about horizons. She understands that in Kansas you can see the edge of the earth in every direction. I tell her this is true.

"In California," she says, "you could see the edge of the earth in the sea. Here it is as if we do not have a horizon. At least I never think of it with all the trees and the hills."

She seems to study something in her mind, and I wonder if it is a recovered vision of the sea, or she is imagining the vast sweep of High Plains pastures with its circle of horizons that is, for a moment, my own recovered vision.

When the fog cleared (two days' worth) it was such a lifting of gray that I saw the landscape as if for the first time. There were other, albeit muted, colors: dark evergreens among the brown and gray trees; trunks of the oaks and chestnuts with pale green-gray molds, and lichens up and down their barks; in the winter's pale light, moss is everywhere on the rocks and trees—not just on the north side as it is in Kansas. With evening, the tree trunks and the tree limbs grow a Manet black before all else.

Large dark green balls with dots of white (like Christmas decorations) appear in the trees after the leaves have fallen: mistletoe.

It is not prized by the French but is by the English who live in the area. High in the tall trees, it is difficult to get. When I was a college student I saw similar balls of mistletoe, also out of reach high in the trees. I made Christmas money one year by shooting into them with a .22 rifle so that they splintered and I could collect the stems and berries when they fell. It is not a trick I am going to teach the French hunters.

I had a friend in those days who made wreaths of the mistletoe by adding greens and holly berries that she gathered from the woods. We sold the wreaths to the professors' wives and spent the money on books not required for our classes. And for a case of wine we shared, my first, and hers as well: Château Lafleur. I still have a bottle, empty to be sure. And a small volume of Montaigne, still full.

Charlie Brown's Snoopy Fighting the Red Baron

I am a father again: Noel, a ram this time, lost his mother a few days after she gave birth. Sometimes the ewes in this country die mysteriously, perhaps of a calcium deficiency, and we think that is what happened. Noel, like Molly, is now bottle fed three times a day. Two orphans together. We wonder if they will become friends, as they run to the farmhouse side by side to get their meals. Molly seems to bleat more; Noel is the serious one. As a parent, I should not have favorites. Molly is my favorite.

Cold and damp in recent days. Cold is cold. Damp is damp. In the Dordogne, they add up to more than Cold and Damp. Because the bottom half of my house is built into a hillside it does not get warm in winter. My woodstove is in the fireplace upstairs, as is (thankfully) the bathtub. Only the kitchen and the dining room are downstairs. It is where I type, in my red stocking hat and white scarf—a vision of Charlie Brown's Snoopy fighting the Red Baron, should a blue *voiturette* stop by now that we have flashed one another.
I might go to Paris for a few days to see friends. Paris is what makes

me an American writer, and I need to visit it now and then to make sure it is still there. And I am still there as well.

I Am a Man of a Certain Age

Madame asks what I will be writing. She is discreet enough not to ask what I am writing. Verb tenses matter in matters of literary decorum.

For lunch we are having *soupe éternelle*. At the Monday market I had bought a sturdy, wood-fired dark bread. If kept in a box in a cold room, it will last the week. In addition to the bread and soup there is the *vieux brebis* from Sainte-Foy and a *pichet* of *vin rouge* from Monsieur R. Ginger is partway in the fireplace. Anna, Madame's cat, is curled on a wicker chair. I am at the stove.

"You don't need to say about your writing," she says. "If you are *superstitieux*."

My friend is trying to improve my French, and she does this not only by using words I do not know, but cognates as well. In this way she is an excellent teacher; there are days when I walk home with a new word in my head, repeating it as I go, until I get back to my *Mansion's French/English Dictionary* from my student days.

Pinceau, pinceau, pinceau, I said to the vines the other day after Madame and I had had a long talk about Piero della Francesca: *Pinceau, pinceau.* Up the hill I talked and walked and talked until, settled by my woodstove, I found on page 471 it had been a "paintbrush" that the *vignobles* had heard on my way past them—and that a phrase I had misplaced along the way was waiting on the same page: *coup de pinceau,* the stroke of the paint brush. Piero della Francesca, we had observed the hour before, has lovely ones.

I tell Madame I am not *superstitieux,* and that in answer to her question, one day I am going to write a story—maybe a long story *à la* de Maupassant—that is *méditatif.* A *récit méditatif.*

"Will it have dialogue?" she asks.

Not much, I say. It will be composed like a Montaigne essay, but it will be fiction. I will use his aphorisms, but not put them in italics. There would be no plot.

"*Pas d'intrigue!*" Madame says in mock alarm. "Will anyone in America read such a story? *Pas du tout!*" She smiles as I bring the soup to the table and pour the wine. I decide not to tell her I am indeed *superstitieux*—but not about what she has asked, or how she has asked. I touch wood as I put down the soup.

"*Soupe éternelle, c'est moi,*" says Madame. "*Et toi.*" It is her traditional toast over her traditional soup. We tip our glasses toward one another. She seems amused that I could write a story bereft of readers. Delicious pleasures when enjoyed by themselves don't need the world's touch.

"The soup," she says as we start our meal, "has a *supplément* by Mademoiselle Américaine. She was here yesterday."

It is a rich soup: beans and rice, mixed with bits of both rabbit and chicken. It is pleasing enough, Madame and I think, to warrant a second glass of wine. And more bread to mop the plates clean.

"You should put French words into your *récit méditatif,*" Madame says. "Add a phrase or two: *et peu à peu,* you will get the language. And in this way your book will make you."

I walk off lunch on my way to Molly's, sensing snow in the air. When I get there, I rack the stove wood cut from the previous day, then cut long logs and stack them like tepee poles around straight trees. That done, Molly and Noel are to be fed (they remind me in not-so-subtle ways) before all is dusk, then dark. I am invited to stay for dinner but decline. I have a dish of my own making at home: a casserole of potatoes, carrots, onions, and *saucisse de canard* into which I stir (a secret) my unique *moutarde douce* sauce. There is also a glass of *eau de vie de prune* I have promised myself for some reason I will fabricate along the way: Better a *fausse raison* than none.

As I walk along, the scent of snow becomes snow itself. I am to stop at Madame's to stoke her stove for the night. Getting there I see the blue Dyane in her driveway, and I see Mademoiselle walking toward the house: tall, a holly berry scarf around her neck. Black peacoat, its collar turned up. Jeans. Long legs. Yellow stocking cap. As she goes in the door, the light from inside shines on her face. She is young. Half my years. I am a man of a certain age.

A puff of smoke comes from Madame's chimney, and I know all inside is well and warm. Before I head up the hill home, I study in the dim light the potted flowers painted on the side of Mademoiselle's truck: a mixture of geraniums, deep purple petunias, bright-eyed pansies, and a tiny orange flower I do not know. Cold as it is, there is a sturdy glow to them. "Audacious," I think, both the flowers to be out in the winter night, and to paint them on the side of the old truck. Audacious: I'll look it up.

Monsieur R.

Monsieur R. is French, but lived a number of years in California where he worked in the movie business, and so speaks excellent English. However, we have agreed to speak French in order that mine might improve.

But Monsieur's French occasionally slips into a stream of French and English, unbroken, as if he is speaking an integrated language, a patois that is richer and more fluent than mere Franglais. He seems not to notice this. Madame tells me he speaks that way to her as well, and the times he has joined us for a meal, I observe this is true.

Monsieur is also given to asserting the truth of matters that are not, strictly speaking, true. The other day, as he was drawing my four liters of his *vin rouge* plus another five liters for Madame, he announced (apropos of nothing I could fathom) that "Jesus said *casseroles* should *pas* call kettles *noir.*" And later, in the same conversation, he quoted Montaigne that a man needs six hours sleep, a woman seven, while a fool takes eight.

"You should hear what he does in the name of Cervantes and Brillat-Saverin," Madame says when I stop by with her wine. "'A meal that does not end with cheese is like a pretty woman with a mustache.' It is not a mustache but with one eye, and it was not Sancho who said it, but Brillat-Saverin who wrote it. Oh well," she says with a laugh. "And the way he quotes you!"

"Me?" I ask.

"Yes," she says. "And me as well. We are all personas in his *oeuvre.*"

"Me?" I ask again.

"*Ah oui!*" she says. "You have *une histoire à la* Monsieur. Complete with intrigue and dialogue. And aphorisms. The other day he had you saying there is no royal road to learning, which I think comes from Dickens or Trollope."

I said I remembered saying no such thing, but that I was pleased to be credited.

"He quotes me as saying 'far-fetched and dear bought is not good for women,' which comes from where I don't know, but not from me," says Madame. "And he quoted Mademoiselle Américaine saying art is long but life is short, which she might have said because it is an old saying; at least I have heard it before. Still it is not what someone young would say. And I don't think they have even met. But soon she, too, will have *une histoire.* No doubt entangled with yours. He is trying to decide if he will have you returning to what he calls black-and-white Kansas when spring comes, or if you are staying here in Technicolor France. It is some reference from his movie days. You are in more than a *récit méditatif,* I assure you."

I am at Madame's sink bottling her wine when I notice something new over the fireplace: her portrait. Acrylic, I think. A pale gold background that sets off her white hair and against which her face is luminous. Her head is tilted right to left against the traditional line. Her eyes are rendered large and dark brown, but not enough to be piercing. The painting is beautifully composed and rich with underpainting. Madame is lovely in it, although likeness was probably not the object of the artist.

"I have no wrinkles," Madame says, when she finds me looking at it. "She put Botox on her palette. Her *coups de pinceau* are unique—*Seul en son genre.* The same as in the potted flowers on the side of her truck. I like especially the orange million bells because they are from pots of mine. Have you seen the flowers on her truck?"

I say I have: *Intrépide.*

"*Ah oui,*" says Madame and smiles at my new word.

Vin Included

If I go to Paris, it will be from the train station in Castillon, the small market town where on Mondays I buy my fish and *fromage* and, from the tall Madagascar woman, the wood-fired bread that lasts a week.

After shopping, I take a *grand crème* at the Commerce Cafe with friends, also there for the Monday market. We gossip—mostly in English to accommodate my poor French—about the usual: weather, grapes, the price of gas, and the good lunches to be had next door at the Hôtel des Voyageurs, the home of Yu-Yu, a small parrot that does not like anybody very much, and me, it seems, in particular: always squawking with grating intensity when I come in.

"Before Yu-Yu there was Mal-Mal," says Monsieur R. "He had excellent French profanity. Some very good words."

The Hôtel des Voyageurs is a "ticket restaurant." In Castillon there are no Michelin stars, no Rotand Walking Men stickers. A "ticket" sign on the door means it is for those who work in town and do not want to go home for lunch. In that case, their employer has made an arrangement for a meal: If you come back over and over again—a kind of *habitué*—I think you earn a discount on a future meal, or maybe the meal itself. I am not all that sure how it works. I should ask. Now that I think of it, I have seen such restaurants in Paris. At the Hôtel des Voyageurs you can get a three-course meal for eight euros. *Vin* included.

The restaurant has two rooms, divided by the kitchen in which there is a fireplace, used as a grill. The old vine stumps (*pieds de vignes*) that are pulled each winter from the vineyard below my house (and others all along the *côtes*) are bundled and sold for firewood. There are mathematical odds *à la* Diderot that the *côte de porc* I ate for lunch at the Hôtel des Voyageurs the other day had been cooked over the *pieds* that made the wine that was included in the meal.

As for the room behind the kitchen: I am not allowed. Once when I looked, it was packed with men eating *ensemble* at a long broad wooden table. They were pouring the dregs of their wine into the dregs of their soup and drinking it out of the bowls; crusts of bread were scattered about, the men's spoons and forks making a *porte couteau* of them. From the front room we heard the swarthy laughter of these men. I am not sure women are allowed. I am pretty sure they are not.

I have decided: In a few days I will ride my two-horse, maroon Deux Chevaux to the train station in Castillon, park it, and go to Paris.

What Rat?

"Does she ask you to pee in her compost?" says Monsieur R. We have arrived by chance at the same time to do chores for Madame and are walking her lane toward the house. Before I can answer, Monsieur says: "Every cock will crow upon his own dunghill."

For a moment in my mind's eye I see him taking a pee on Madame's compost while crowing away. The vision passes and I say no, she has not made such a request, although she has asked me to continue her compost while she is unable—a small square plot fenced off against Boris, should he get tired of my fare.

"Nor me," says Monsieur. "But Burton in his *Melancholy* writes that peeing into the compost makes it richer."

Monsieur is a tall man with large hands and long arms. He is older than I am, but the bounce in his stride is younger than mine. There is a movie-actor visage about him, something beyond handsome or distinguished. No doubt he has broken many hearts.

"And what shall we do with the rat?" he asks. We are at the door, and, without knocking, Monsieur walks in—not waiting for an answer from me, which would have been: *Quel rat?*

Monsieur has come this day to make croutons out of the bits of Madame's bread left over from last week, including the forked ends of the *baguettes serpentines* she has me buy. He takes great care in making his croutons, using sea salt, good garlic, and Spanish olive oil he gets from a friend near Seville who, Madame confides, may or may not be a woman. *Un peu d'intrigue.*

"And we do not know for sure if he is married as he claims to be," Madame has said. "I have never seen a wife. First, she was in California; then she is in Greece with her dying mother; recently she has come and gone from London. She is in Paris. She is in Belgrade. She is with a friend in Addis Ababa. I think Monsieur R. only says he is married so he won't be pressed to marry. This has been going on for years—even before he returned from California. I would not marry him if he asked, so he has nothing to fear from me. And Countess P. will not have him in her house, so he need not worry about her."

It is Countess P. who lives in Montagne with—or without—broken fingers. I have never seen her, although it is said she drives out now and again.

I had wondered why there always seemed to be a large bowl of croutons on the kitchen counter. And when I thought of it, I should have wondered about other dishes that seemed to appear: Who had made the *potage Crécy* or the *saucisson* with horseradish sauce? Or the *potage bonne femme* (which became the base of my own *soupe éternelle*, now in weak competition with the Mademoiselle Américaine's version). And who was leaving lovely apple tarts with thin, delicate crusts?

"What is to be done with the rat?" says Monsieur from the counter, where he is mixing the stale bread chunks in the iron skillet with its hot Spanish olive oil, garlic, sea salt, and a concoction of spices.

"I think it best to take him to the Dordogne," says Madame. "Is he caught?" They are talking about a Ragondin rat for whom Madame had set a trap by her pond before she fell.

"He is not," says Monsieur. "But when he is, let me drown him in the trap. I take him to the Dordogne and he returns and you catch him again; then, I take him to the Dordogne and he comes back. Voltaire writes that 'man is born free but that everywhere he is like a rat in a trap.'"

"You have it wrong," says Madame from her wheelchair. "It is 'that everywhere he is in chains': *dans les fers*. And it was Rousseau, not Voltaire."

"I take it," says Monsieur (and here he uses Madame's pet name at which she blushes so that he smiles with the youth that is in his walk), "you would rather not have us say: 'How now! A rat? Dead, for a farthing.' And yes, he is caught."

"It's Shakespeare," she says, "and I doubt it's a farthing. But I thought you said the rat has not been caught."

"What difference does verb tense make?" says Monsieur. "'Will be caught,' 'has been caught,' 'is caught,' 'shall be caught.' Since the war and Camus, we are all *'aujourd'hui c'est moi qui suis mort'. Et le rat*, also!"

"No," says Madame (and here she uses a pet name for Monsieur

R. at which he smiles toward me), "I do not want him dead. To the Dordogne. Swim, swim, vile rat, swim. And you don't know for sure the same rat returns."

"I'll paint him," Monsieur retorts. "Polka dots of orange water-resistant paint from a spray can I have in my truck. If Monsieur Ragondin comes back, we will know. Then, Madame," and here he turns off his frying pan and scatters his croutons on a paper towel, "will you let me drown him? He would make excellent fertilizer for your tomato plants. I will cut him into pieces and put one piece per plant: a hindquarter here, the *tête* there, the butt end here. The innards there. A big Ragondin will be food for a dozen tomato plants that will produce sixty round, red, *grosses* tomatoes with ease."

"The tomatoes will smell like rat."

"No more than your onions smell like pee."

"A dead rat stinks more than a live man's pee," she says.

"That's Ovid. Ovid says that."

"He did not," she says. "I said that."

"Well, then," Monsieur says, bringing his croutons to the table so we can taste-test them, "let us talk about Countess P's. tongue."

"What about her tongue?" says Madame.

"How the tip of it was cut off to get the keys to her safe and now she talks gibberish."

I Never Fail to Touch It

From the Castillon *gare*, the local train goes first to Libourne—a large wine center of a city—where I catch the TGV to Paris. Three and a half hours later I am at Gare Montparnasse. I stay at a small hotel not that far from where Gertrude Stein had her salon.

I have friends in Paris, among them Jane and her husband, Jean Louis, who join me for lunch at Balzar near the Sorbonne. Years ago we saw Barbra Streisand and her husband, James Brolin, eating at a table against the wall. Jane noticed the husband, who, I was told, is a "hunk" (no French translation possible, unless Mr.

Brolin is a hunk of cheese: In that case he is a *gros morceau*, which he is probably not).

After lunch I walked past the nearby bronze statue of Montaigne, his legs crossed with his right shoe sticking out tempting the students to touch it for good luck. Over the years it has lost its patina and is now a very shiny shoe indeed. I never fail to touch it.

I am also friends with a short-story writer of *New Yorker* fame, Madame G. We met years ago at Reclaimer, the restaurant where she had fed one of her characters. I ordered the meal of her story. Madame G. smiled.

These days I have been walking through cemeteries. I made my way to Père Lachaise and, for a populist friend in Kansas, stood against the wall where the members of the Paris Commune were shot. Nearby, I put my hand on the stone of Oscar Wilde because we share a birthday, and because I like the remark attributed to him as he lay dying in a Paris hotel: Either the wallpaper goes or I do.

Other days I walk as I always do: in no particular direction except along the *rues* I have walked before. The bloom of novelty has given way to the autumn of the familiar. I like to see where I have been, and where I have lived: Place Dauphine, rue Xavier-Privas (where I once rented an apartment above a couscous restaurant, but not so far above that Boris-sized cockroaches were put off by the climb). I use the Pont des Arts whenever I cross the Seine.

One sunny summer day a few years ago I came upon two students—a young man and a young woman—standing by the railing of the bridge in raincoats; a third student (I supposed they were all students; they had that look about them of going for pleasure to get their profit) collected money in a hat—all the while checking for the police. When the hat was full (I put in a euro not knowing to what I was contributing), the young man and woman began laughing, then stripped off their raincoats and, to a "standing" ovation, dove naked into the Seine. Their business associate ran down along the *quai* with the raincoats and the money as they swam ashore. No gendarmes out of Truffaut arrived, whistles blowing.

Before my train departed for the return trip to Libourne, I spent an hour walking through Cimetière Montparnasse. Just inside the gate are Sartre and Simone de Beauvoir; some way in, and with the help of a small map you get at the entrance, I found Man Ray. I have always admired his photograph of Gertrude and Alice with the paintings as a backdrop. I found the stone of Samuel Beckett and sat there for a moment, waiting.

After three days—and a meal at Closerie des Lilas as a guest of prosperous friends—I returned. It was Sunday and the oyster market was open in Castillon; I bought a dozen number two Arcachons. In my refrigerator was a split of Gremillet: cold and crisp. I steamed the oysters in *vin blanc* and water until they opened. Some cheese and red wine and bread in front of my woodstove, and then, as Pepys says: So to bed.

The next afternoon when I go to the farm, I learn that Molly does not exactly remember me (how quickly they forget), but Noel does. And there is Sylvester. Sylvester? Yes. He was born (perhaps while I was waiting on Samuel Beckett) and his mother will have nothing to do with him: So now there are three. Bleats all around. And well, yes, Molly does remember me. Or something about me.

"Hello," says a tall young woman as I return to the kitchen carrying three empty milk bottles.

My Cork Basket Is Half Empty

I am more than halfway through winter. I know because the basket where I keep old corks is much depleted. There are many clocks that mark the seasons in the Dordogne. These days you can see the vineyard owners planting new vines. The shooting from hunters has stopped. Primrose is blooming. Paperwhites are for sale in the markets. The daffodils that were planted up against the stone walls of the old houses and barns where the ground is warmer are coming up. V's of cranes are heading north. The wild plum trees between me and Montagne are starting into bloom. And my cork basket is half empty.

I use the corks to start my woodstove. When I open a new bottle I try not to pierce the cork so that I can turn it around for the wine I bottle from my jug. There is a curious pleasure in pulling a cork from a fine Saint-Émilion (only a few of these) from an appellation de R, illegal, and bare of label. Twice pierced, the corks can no longer be used for bottling but have other jobs: "double tasking," I have learned it is now called in America.

"Triple tasking," now that I think of it. And *tant pis* for the prohibition against new wine in old bottles.

I save the spring-through-fall corks for winter fires. They are splendid starters (candle stubs are good as well) if you stuff a few in crumpled newspaper: I use the *International Herald Tribune* or, if I am feeling pretentiously French, *Le Monde*. Once the corks catch, they burn with great brilliance and flame. And kindle the wood into warmth.

The French Make Terrible Fences

The farmer with Molly, Noel, and Sylvester has asked me to cut fence posts out of his woods. He, too, knows that spring is coming and his demand for firewood is not as great, but he will need fence posts for a new corral I am to build around the sheep shed. The French make terrible fences. Not even the most hardscrabble Kansas ranch has such awful fences as most of the farms in France have. Both the posts (twisted and tilted) and the fence itself (drooping wires) are badly done. The gates are a wobbly wreck. They don't know how to make a brace post or set a dead man. They don't see the need to make the gate posts bigger than fence posts.

If there are not more pressing chores, I will show the owner how to build a proper fence. But it won't be easy. There are no fence stretchers to be bought or borrowed; the French fence wire is thin and of poor quality. They use bent nails for staples. But we'll see. In the meantime I am cutting the posts, plus extra wood for the fireplace should spring be false. For sure, I am going to build a sturdy and straight-lined corral, stout enough to hold a High Plains gomer bull.

Yesterday from the woods where I was working, I watched Mademoiselle drive up to the farmhouse and go in. She was wearing a bulky white sweater and the same stocking cap and maroon scarf as when I first saw her.

I turned off the chainsaw and thought to join her now that we have met, if briefly ("I'm sorry, I must be going," she had said. "An errand to run for Madame." And out the door she went.)

I am not shy. I talk a good game. But something—not being covered with wood chips, or that I no doubt reeked of work—stopped me.

No Denouement

"And will there be a gun over the fireplace to go off before the end?"

Madame is again curious about what I will be writing. I tell her there will be fireplaces, large enough for cold dogs to sit by on winter days, but no guns over them.

We have been reading Chekhov: Yalta is warmer than the Dordogne this time of year. The pleasure in reading Chekhov is in rereading him. There is no story we plan to boycott. Monsieur R. wants us to read *King Lear*, but Madame has resisted.

"He thinks the play is funny," she said. "However, what he quotes from it is accurate—at least by my memory. The other day he was here saying that 'age is unnecessary,' and sure enough, after he left, I found it. I suppose that is amusing in a way, but I am not in a good enough mood to be amused by *King Lear*."

It occurs to me that Monsieur R. has never asked what I do or why I am living here. When first we met, he seemed to assume I had been in my small house on the hill for as long as he had been in his assortment of stone barns and buildings and *chais*. Or as long as Madame in her converted mill. And further, it was as if we had all been in California together, whenever that was. Not that I know that Monsieur and Madame knew one another in California, but there was that remark she made about Monsieur's *fausse épouse* in California. I am shy to ask.

It is also true that Madame has never asked what brought me here, or why I have stayed. Or why I am alone. She may be shy to ask. I think this is true.

"Will there be a curtain that bangs?" asks Madame.

I say there will not be a curtain. A scrim only. Through which the *intrépide* reader can see.

"But *dénouement*? There must be a *dénouement*."

We are waiting for Monsieur to join us for dinner, and—perhaps—Mademoiselle, although that invitation by Madame has not been unconditionally accepted, something about getting to Bordeaux and back in search of art supplies.

From the stove where I am fixing the meal, I say to Madame that since there will be no raveling, there will be no unraveling. *Pas de dénouement.* However, "age will be necessary." She cannot help herself now and smiles. We hear someone has arrived. "And some things will be left not said, or explained," she says as Ginger goes to the door to see who has come.

"*Ah oui*," I say.

Francis Bacon

Monsieur has asked if I am married. I tell him I am not. He has finished filling my jug and Madame's as well. Outside it is raining: drip, drip, drip, as Dickens would write to earn his penny a word. It has been too warm in recent days to start the woodstoves for the few evenings that it is damp and cold. I do, however, keep Madame's fireplace going. It cheers her, I think, to sit by it with Anna in her lap and Ginger toasting herself first on one side then the other.

"All was not merry as a marriage bell?" Monsieur says, his voice half a question. I am trying to guess if it is one of his quotations. But before I can ask, he says, "Madame used to be married and now she is not: 'Hush, hark, a deep sound strikes like a rising knell.'" He is quiet for a moment. "Byron," he says.

"And you?" I find myself having the nerve to ask. "Are you married?"

"There is a story I am," he says. He smiles the way he did when he used Madame's pet name. Then putting his arm around the side of the vat out of which he has just drawn the wine he says: "Which wife is this? The one I adored first and so took a second, or the other the other way around?"

"Oscar Wilde," I say.

Monsieur looks at me for a moment as if to drop a mask. Then he says:

"When I was a boy, I worked in the Montaigne vineyards. One day the owner gave me a book of quotations in English that a guest had given him. He knew I wanted to learn the language. Before that, I had no English. Each night when I came home, I would study the book. I set myself a goal to learn three quotations a day and say them out loud as I was working in the vineyards. It was only later that I would get the meanings. After I understood what I was saying, I would only learn the quotations I liked. Nobody knew what I was saying, so I was talking to myself, and after awhile I would have one of me say a quotation to the other of me, and the second me would answer in a quotation. For two years I did this."

I realize Monsieur has answered a question I did not ask, and not answered the one I did. I am charmed by this evasion, if that is what it is—and it is probably not.

From a bin behind the vat he fetches a bottle, checks its cork and its punt, which I can see is deep. It has no label.

"Here," he says. "There is a story in this wine. It is yours for the drinking and telling."

I thank him. Looking at the bottle, I say that we are of an age when old wood is best to burn, old authors best to read, and old wine best to drink.

"I don't know it," he says. "But now I do. I assign it to Bacon."

Today I Told a White Lie That Helped

Madame is getting restless. Over the years she has been the epitome of independence, and it vexes her not to be so now. The doctor says she will be walking on her own in a few weeks (it has been two months since she fell), but she doesn't quite believe it. Monsieur tells her Virgil says we do the most damage to ourselves by impatience.

"It comes from Montaigne," she says to me. "I don't think he ever gets any of them right, and I wonder if once upon a time he knew better and just set about to test and tease me, but by now he has forgotten that was his purpose, and has it in his head as fact that it was Virgil. And that you said 'Never trust the writer; trust the tale.'"

I smile and she knows I said no such thing.

"He is Google itself," she says.

I ask how she knows about Google—as I don't know much about it, only that it exists. She says the same, then adds:

"I understand you can find what you want to know in an instant, and that seems to me a bad way to go about the life of the mind, as if knowing something in an instant will lead to knowledge, much less to wisdom. Where is the pleasure of serendipity? And of friends who read as we do. I don't drink instant coffee. I don't make instant tea. Or minute rice. I make *soupe éternelle*. There is more than a difference."

She seems gloomy at the thought of Google. I have been teasing her about one thing or another in the past few days to bring her cheer, but that is wearing thin. She knows her flowers are starting up and the garden needs tending. We all help as we can, but not much will lift her spirits until she can get around pretty much by herself.

Today I tell a white lie that helped. I say the fishmonger at the Monday market had asked after her; she likes the fishmonger, a broad-faced, large-shouldered man who juggles lemons at his stand in between customers. In fact, it had been the flat-nosed egg woman (whom she doesn't like). Anyway, what's a fib good for, if not to bring on a smile? At the ranch where I worked in Kansas, they were called "right lies," some mishearing passed down through the generations.

"Tell the fishmonger," says Madame, "that I will return when I can walk on my own through the market, and that we shall have champagne and snails for lunch at the Hôtel des Voyageurs to celebrate. He will be charmed to know we can turn *boudin noir* and *vin de table* into escargot and champagne."

"As will Monsieur R." I say.

"It is where I got the menu," she says. "Only he claims such a menu is there, and after we have not had it, we will have had it. I know this to be true in advance of it being so." Now, I am the one who smiles.

Someone is at Madame's door.

A Recovered Vision in Place of a Denouement

If I stay in this country, will I stir fact into fiction? Have others say for me what I cannot say so well for myself? Will *soupe éternelle* be the life of my mind, and intrigue find me—but not in an instant? Will I learn my *histoire*? And will it have neither raveling nor unraveling? Will I be as *intrépide* as flowers on the side of an old truck? Will blood sausage and table wine become snails and champagne one Monday in a ticket restaurant with a parrot that does not like me?

Or is the story for the telling in Monsieur's wine bottle that I return to a recovered vision of black-and-white Kansas where moss is only on the north side of the trees and rocks. Where we build fences with good wire, and stout corrals with strong gates. Where we feed the dogs first and know why we set dead men.

Looking at the great sweep of pastures and horizons that stretch to the edge of the earth in all directions, do I believe it myself?

Someone is at my door.

By the Light of the Silvery Moon

I cook at the Corner Pocket evenings when they need me. Burgers. Fries. Catfish. Chicken-fried steaks. Frozen hash browns I toss on the grill. Ribeyes. After closing, I dig graves. We're on the edge of a big time zone so in summer there's light in the west when I start. I watch the sun rise when I'm done. It's a pleasure.

My day job is what I pick up in repairs. Roofs after a hailstorm. Cement work. I've got my own mixer. Sidewalks. Plumbing. Most of us out here are dead or dying so I've got widows who need a leak stopped. While I'm there, could I fix the third step on the way to the basement? Sure. And the screen door needs to be rehung since the grandkids went back to Denver. Sure. But best I like my graves. I dig them by hand. Not like Harper. Harper uses a backhoe.

Clara waitresses at the Corner Pocket. Not always when I do, but sometimes. She's younger than me by more than I told her. She's tall. I'm taller a bit. She's one of the tallest women we got in and around Blaze, Bly, and Cottonwood. Mostly in her legs. But being tall is not what I like about her. It's her shoulders. The way they connect to her neck. And her face. Open like a charm. Black hair with long curls that hang down her cheeks and spring-bounce when she walks. Also tattooed words on her hands and arms and legs. She says she's part Cheyenne. Could be. Dull Knife's tribe went through Whitewoman County and left their breed in the settlers' wives. I've got the blood, tall as I am.

I'm good at everything I do but living by myself. My lane's junk.

Iceboxes from remodeling jobs that I was supposed to haul to the dump. Stoves. Washing machines. Tires. ACs I took the copper out of when the price was high. Trash bags of beer cans the time I started to pick myself up. OSB board that's got wet. Five Roper motel gas ranges from when they did over Pleasant Valley Manor. Maple cutting boards from the same job. Tubs. A couple of couches. A fold-out to sleep on nights by the edge of my garden summers. Or sit on with a Dos Equis afternoons. There's a story to the fold-out. Two oak pews. My front porch has a pile of plaster that fell off the ceiling that blocks the door. Tilly and I go around back. Tilly's my dog.

Harper says I'm scum. He should talk. His pickup's still in my yard. He ran over a tree stump halfway to drunk one night and put a hole in his oil pan. That was three years ago. There's a vitamin-M plant growing in the bed for all the dirt that's been blowing in. More than one. Beer cans. A work coat. Two coolers. Tools turned to rust by now. Other shit. Harper and I go back. But something changed. He won't come down. Not even to tow his truck for parts. Bought himself a new one. Turbo diesel.

I've got six pence, jolly, jolly, jolly six pence. It's a song Clara sings. There are others. I don't have a memory for songs, but she does. Something about having *six pence to last me all my life.* She wants us to sing it *ensemble.* That's one of her words. She says she'll sing some parts and I'll sing others, and some we'll sing together. I can't sing for shit.

I mark my graves with a chalk roller I got from the high school when they dropped the baseball team. Plus two bags of dust the coach said I might as well take. They're in the house. When it gets cold and the woodstove in the basement goes out, Tilly sleeps on them. Talk about your ugly dog. Homemade sin ugly. Bares her teeth like she'll bite your balls off for standing still. But she won't. Bark. She'll bark. And kick the shit out of other dogs. She can turn around in her skin she's so quick. When she's happy she chews tires. Wheelbarrow tires. Rotor tiller tires. The tires on Harper's pickup. They're all flat by now. When I come home she starts chewing my tires before I stop rolling...*rolling, rolling, rolling home.* There's a bit more of it.

At the Corner Pocket we get our catfish from a dealer. They're farmed and frozen. I catch mine out of the Whitewoman and keep them in a stock tank to get the mud out of them. A fish is the water it's been living in. Sometimes I clean one and take it to work for after we close. That's how I start with Clara. I'm cooking my fish on the grill with butter and onions and sliced new potatoes from my garden. It's summer.

What's that? she says. My own catfish, I said. Out of the White-woman? she says. Yes, I said. I know some places, she says. So do I, I said. There's enough to share, I go on. I got McCormick's in my truck, she says. Vodka. We got a plan, I said.

*I got two pence to spend, two pence to lend...*I can't remember it all, but maybe I will. Sometimes it takes time to remember every-thing. Clara also sings about a skylark. *Skylark, have you anything to say?* She sings it more to herself than me. You go someplace to find the skylark. Or maybe it goes someplace for you and then flies back with a story about where it's been. She sings it some, then stops. Then starts up again. It's a pleasure to hear her.

The last person in my house was Harper the night he runs over the tree stump. We drink a case of Dos Equis and he crashes on the couch. There are two weeks of dishes in the sink with hundred-legs living in them. Clothes on the floor. Dishes on the floor. Beer bot-tles. Cigarettes in the ones Harper uses as ashtrays. Coffee cups where I've left them. You don't notice your shit when you're going through a case of Dos Equis.

You're scum, Harper says when he wakes up. *Scum* is Spanish for fucked up. You'll get brown recluses if you leave your clothes on the floor. A hole to the bone in your foot is a sure sign of scum.

Get fucked, I said. I'm working on it, he says. For sure you won't. What woman's going to like this? Get your shit together and take it to the dump.

That's what he says to me these days. You got your shit together? Or are you still living in it? He thinks I'm trash. I think he's trash for thinking so. But he's right about the brown recluse. Only it isn't my foot but the palm of my left hand with a hole all the way to a bone before I go to the clinic.

I'm married, Clara says, the night we're eating my catfish and drinking her vodka. I didn't know that, I said. He's not around, she says. Where? I said. Minnesota, she says. We just never split the sheets for the judge. Tall? I asked. Like you, she says. I'm not married, I said. I know, she says. More? she says, tapping the McCormick's. Sure, I said.

We drink it iced at the table by the front door like we are customers, only it's just us and the pool tables, and the glow of the Corner Pocket sign in neon outside coming through the curtains.

I made these, Clara says, pulling the curtain to look into Blaze where there's nobody. Sewing's my day job. Digging graves is mine, I said. I heard that, she says. Only I do it nights, I said. I heard that, she says. *Star light, star bright*, she goes. *First star I see tonight*, I answered. She smiles. I could mend that shirt for you, she says. Thanks, I said. We go quiet. Do you know you've got real green eyes? I said. Yes, she says. She smiles again, and this time it's as deep as it is wide. I'm thinking she likes me.

I dig my graves four by eight. I got a plywood frame for the chalk lines. I have a metal one for winter so I can cook the ground before I dig. I do my marking in the afternoons. When I'm done, I cut off the sod and stack it in strips to one side. Then I sit on my tailgate and have Dos Equis Amber. That's not much work to take a break, but I like to look at the other graves to see if I've got mine lined up. It's like wanting things straight when you work carpentry. Even a widow woman who's going to get parked in Pleasant Valley Manor by her Denver kids gets to have her closet square to the rest of the house. And her grave square to her husband's.

When my Dos Equis Amber is a dead soldier, I go home and feed Tilly. Then up to the Corner Pocket if they need me. If not, I work my garden. Sometimes I'll go down to the Whitewoman and pull a flathead or two. That's what I do the time I share with Clara, only I get a fresh one from the stock tank. Lucky it's big. There's only skin and bones when we finish. No potatoes. For a girl she eats like a horse.

I'm not much with women. I had one once. Maggie. She'd come over and keep the place picked up. She started inside and worked her way into the yard. It was spring and she planted a garden. It was how I got to gardening. She's the one who gave me Tilly. Also the fold-out. I liked it. I'll admit that. I liked coming home knowing that Maggie was going to have supper for me and a six-pack of cold Dos Equis Amber while we sat on the fold-out by the garden. And later we'd unfurl the couch and sleep on it. That was her word. *Unfurl.* I liked it.

You think we should get married? she said one night. It was summer and she'd been waiting on the fold-out for me to come back from a grave. I don't think so, I said. Why not? Why? I said. I want to be married, she said. Then find somebody who wants to marry you, I said. How come you won't let me dig graves with you? she said. I could help. Don't you love me? I don't think so, I said.

She pulled on her jeans and left. Came back once to check the garden. Say goodbye to Tilly. Pick up things. I'd see her around Blaze, then gone. Maybe a year ago in Cottonwood I saw her. We didn't talk. Maybe she didn't see me. I think she did. I saw her once or twice with Clara. Harper told me they're related.

If I know whose grave I'm digging, I talk to them. Back and forth.

Too bad your liver gave out, I say to Al Johnson. I had fun while it lasted, he says. At least you know I'm digging your hole and not Harper with his backhoe, I say. Make it square to Bella's, Al says. But don't let her fall out on me. I want some peace and quiet as long as I'm dead. Not to worry, I say. Thanks.

Until I met Clara, I worked alone. Then I liked digging graves with her while Willie Nelson's on the tape deck in my truck and her singing along. *If you've got the money, honey, I've got the time.* Or her singing by herself and trying to teach me how to remember the words and carry the tune. I like how we share her McCormick's and not get so drunk we don't talk. You got to like a woman who likes to talk. And not about the grocery-store magazines. Or Jesus. Or television. I got a lot of shit in my house but I don't have a television. I did. Harper threw a Dos Equis through it. When I turned it on it exploded. Glass and wires and white dust everywhere. Not really, but that's what I tell people. Mainly it just smoked and blew a fuse. Better it exploded for the telling of it.

I've been thinking about Harper calling me scum. How you getting home? I said. Lend me your Harley, he says. Sure, I said. After he leaves, I go back to bed. When I get up, I wash my sheets and the clothes off the floor. Five loads. I wash the dishes. Kill the hundred-legs with a spatula. Take down the plastic from winter on the windows. With the new light coming in, I clean up. Toss the beer bottles in boxes. Wash more dishes. Look for brown recluses until I find one. Sweep the floor into a scoop shovel. Then I pick up beer cans in the lane and put them in plastic trash bags. Change the sheets on the fold-out. It's coming summer, so I start sleeping out at night. Only I don't *unfurl* it. Just sleep on it like a couch.

Two weeks I clean off and on. Weed the garden. Pull onions and radishes and take them to the Corner Pocket to give away. Put cages around my tomatoes and plastic around the bottoms against the wind we get out here just like Maggie did. Then one day I stop.

Maybe if I'd taken the beer cans to the metal man in Cottonwood

I'd keep going. But one night I'm sleeping by my garden and I wake up because Tilly's running a fox and I test myself by starlight to see if I feel any different from when my house was full of shit, and I don't. Then I ask myself if I feel like scum, and I don't. So the house fills up with shit again and I still don't feel like scum. I don't feel one way or another about living in shit. If you don't like who you are, call Doctors Smith and Wesson. Who wants to live with someone they don't like?

That first night at the Corner Pocket Clara talks about words. The words tattooed on her body. On the back of her left hand has Cynic. It's not some guy who doesn't want to vote because politics are shit, she says when she sees I'm looking at it. Or a woman who's had it with men. It's old philosophers who thought you've got to raise your own food. Don't have both a truck for your day job and a car for town like they do in the Rest of America. Don't own anything you don't need, she says.

I didn't know that, I said. Catch your own catfish, she says and taps her fork on the plate. The potatoes and the rest of it are from my garden, I said. She smiles. I read about Cynics at this house where I did their slipcovers, she says. I read, do you? Not much, I said. But I'll give it a try. I have this book, she says. *Cowboys Are My Weakness*. I'll read it, I said. You know any good words? she says. *Unfurl*, I said. Like a flag, she says. Or a fold-out couch, I said. She smiles. I love words, she says. The best ones never leave you. Know what these are called? she says as she pulls one of the curls that hang down along her cheek. *Tendrils*, she says before I can take a guess. Don't you like it? she says. *Tendrils*. It's why I grew them. For the word.

Somebody outside goes by and their headlights come through Clara's curtains. You want to dig a grave with me sometime? I said. Sure, she says. You'll see the sun come up, I said. Fine by me, she says. Yet tonight? I said. Sure, she says.

We finish my catfish and not all her McCormick's to take in my truck. That's when she starts singing *I've got six pence, jolly, jolly six pence, I've got six pence to last me all my life. Two pence to spend, two pence to lend, and no pence to send home to my wife, poor wife.* Thinking about her, I remember more of it. Funny what will crank up memory. For me it's what's in my mind already.

Harper's the one who gets me started with graves. Baker Johnson's casket busts out from the grave next to the one Harper is digging and breaks his great toe. That's what he calls it. His *great toe.*

I'm yelling What-the-Fuck for my Great Toe, Harper says, and the casket lid pops open and there's Baker, nothing but bones and dust and rags and teeth. No thank you, I say. No fucking thank you. I'll dig graves with a backhoe or not at all. That's when he comes up to Corner Pocket and asks me to finish the job. Sure, I said. You got to do it tonight, he says. Sure, I said.

I dig the grave another three feet deep, close Baker Johnson's lid and slide him on down, fill and patch the hole on the side, then tamp everything firm. The next day they plant Doug Johnson on top of Baker Johnson and nobody knows the difference. I think they're cousins anyway. Along with Al Johnson who I bury two doors down. After that I'm on my own. Hand-dug graves for half the price of Harper's backhoe.

Cynic was my first tattoo, Clara says. She's up above the hole sitting on my tailgate. I'm in pretty deep by now. The ground is soft because I haul water to it the first part of the week. Duluth, 1997, she says. I picked it because I liked the way it looked. With the "C" at the start and then the "y" and then just before the "c" at the end there was this "i." It was later I found out what it means. Hand me my level, I said. Sure, she says. The square, too. Here, she says.

It's good work. Even after the McCormick's it's good work. I look up but she's gone to the truck. I hear the tailgate creak. I think she'll be beautiful when I climb out. *Skylark, have you anything to say*, she sings. Help me up, I said, not needing a hand but wanting hers. Here, she says coming back to the edge of the grave with her hand and a smile I can see in the light of sunrise coming.

And sometimes "y," I said as we sit on the tailgate and she offers me the last pull of her McCormick's.

What? she says. And sometimes "y," I said. Like we learned in school. That "y" can be a vowel if it wants to be. In your *cynic*.

I wish I'd thought of that, she says. Then I'd have *c y n y c* that would spell itself in reverse like *kayak* and *radar*. I'd like to have *Egypt* because of those tails that go below the line but I've used my "E" for *Ensemble*. What about *Radar*? I said. I'm saving my "R," she says. I want to say something, but I don't.

Harper keeps telling me I must be depressed to live in shit. It's something he learned from television. Harper watches television. And listens to talk radio. That's where he gets his shit. His shit is in his head. At least mine is on the floor. And in the yard. You got to know what kind of shit you want in your life because everybody's got it someplace. I like mine where it is.

When I'm frying catfish at the Corner Pocket or working my garden or digging graves with Clara, I'm happy. How not to be happy with a tall girl younger than yourself who likes spending the night drinking McCormick's in a graveyard and talking about the words on her body? And who can't like an ugly dog that's so happy to see you she chews tires?

No cares have I to grieve me, no pretty little girls to deceive me, I'm as happy as a lark, believe me, as I go rolling, rolling home. There you go. That's more of it. How not to be happy when you can remember a song even if you can't sing for shit?

The graveyard at Rose Hill has the best view. It's the township cemetery. If you're a Christian, you don't want to be buried there because you'll be in the ground with Seculars. That's what Pastor Black calls them. Seculars. I've dug graves for his dead as well as Father Wilcox's dead. Dead's dead, I think, no matter whose graveyard you're in. But Rose Hill's the only place I take Clara. It's where we watch the sun come up that first night. And the moon go down. *By the light of the silvery moon.*

From Rose Hill you can look down the road that curves into Bly and the grain train tracks that run by the Co-Op where The Committee to Save the World meets. We don't really save the world, but some days we talk like we can. Ranchers. Wheat farmers. We trade jokes. The same ones more than once. Ones you can't tell in the Rest of America. You'd think in a free country you'd be free to tell jokes. Maybe that's their shit, not telling jokes.

Some of the men know I'll bury them. If it's late in the day and there's Black Jack being passed around because Mencken Cody or The Broke Rancher sold low-dollar steers for a high-dollar price nobody minds. We're running out of sunsets in Whitewoman County. Most of our cattle drives are in the graveyards. We drink and joke about what I do. Baker Johnson falling out onto Harper's great toe. Al and his rotgut liver wanting some quiet from Bella.

All summer they put it to me about Clara. How tall she is for her breed. How she's got the same black hair as Maggie. I think they know. Sure they know. But since she's been gone, they don't say much. It's been awhile by now.

We talk about getting through winter until spring against the wind that blows the wheat out of the ground when it's been frozen for thirty days. And stock tanks that ice partway to the bottom overnight. Nothing but hand-pump wells working in Bly. Goddamn.

On the palm of her left hand, Clara had something I couldn't read because of the wrinkles and how she wouldn't open it all the way. I wanted to ask her about it, but I didn't. Sometimes at the Corner

Pocket in summer she'd wear clothes so that I could see the edge of a word along her shoulder. And a word on her front where her tits start to begin. Or on her legs when she'd wear a skirt instead of jeans. But I didn't ask about those either. You want to go slow with women if you like them. It's the way you learn to like them. Not that I knew this before. Being with Clara helped. Or maybe it's just becoming who you are when you like what you're doing. *I wish I may, I wish I might.*

You think a lot digging a grave and sitting on the tailgate nights with a Dos Equis Amber. Thinking isn't all bad. Some men won't have it. I like it. It's like coming into good-looking country with your own country still in your head. I do that. Get in my Pick-Me-Up-Truck with Tilly and drive into the Breaks or Sand Hills or the Front Range off the paved roads.

I park in the graveyard of some town more gone than Bly or Blaze, and Tilly sleeps under the truck and I sleep in the back on a bedroll. Every graveyard is different. They all have the same dead, but not the same view. The one in St. Francis has a sign saying watch for rattlesnakes.

I want twenty-six words, Clara tells me one night. We are pushing September into October. I am working at Rose Hill after two days of rain. We don't get much rain in the fall. I'm not digging for somebody just dead, but with Pretty Wilson breathing her last at Pleasant Valley and her relations having asked me to dig the grave when the time comes, I think I'll get it done. I'll put my frame over the hole until I come back to trim it out the day they plant her. Plan ahead to get ahead.

One for each letter of the alphabet, she says. I don't have "A" yet. I got others. I'm up to ten. Maybe I don't have enough body for twenty-six.

What are the others? I said. She says she isn't telling. A girl's got to have some privacies. You got "B"? I asked. She doesn't say anything. I think maybe I don't want to know about "B."

What's that? she says. I've had her help me out of the grave and she's touching the palm of my hand where the brown recluse bit me. It's ragged and rough because I didn't take care of it. A privacy, I said. Fair enough, she says. But make a story for me. Something not true. Sure, I said. Let me think it out so it's good. I'll wait, she says. Why you saving "R"? I asked. She looks away. I want "R" to be for me, but I don't say so.

One day at the Corner Pocket she isn't there. The next night either. Then a whole week of nights not being there. I know where she lives and go by. Her truck isn't there. The house is shut up and nobody answers the door. Not a note. The postman is walking the street and says she's had them hold her mail. Harper comes along in his turbo diesel with his migrant and a backhoe for a grave.

She's not here, he says. I figured as much, I said. You been here before? he says. I tell him she wouldn't let me come over. Not that I asked. You? I said. I guess he doesn't hear me and says he's got to dig the hole for Otto Bond. Then he's off down 4th heading toward Pastor Black's cemetery.

I wish it was better for me and Harper. Maybe it will be when he gets his truck out of my lane. He brought my Harley back, but it was a month. I've put it on the porch so Tilly won't chew the tires. When summer comes again I'm thinking to give Clara a ride. We'll do figure eights through the graves, her tendrils blowing in the wind. Maybe she'll help me plant my garden and we'll go fishing together. It will be what we do together days and save nights for digging graves. Work the Corner Pocket like we used to.

When I see her again, I'm going to tell her I going to be buried in Rose Hill. I'll ask Harper to dig my grave but by hand. I'll show her the plots I bought up in the corner. Two plots side by side. Five dollars each. I'll tell her one could be hers if she doesn't have a place of her own. Even if it doesn't work out between us, she could still have my extra plot. That way she'd have a grave to come back to. She wouldn't have to plan ahead.

Maybe it's not what you tell a woman when you're only getting started. Maybe I ought to clean up my place first so she can come over. More than just the garden. The yard. The porch. Get Harper to tow his truck. Make it all handsome like Mr. Badger does in the spring, when he sits on his mound and hoots for the women badgers to take a look-see. Maybe. Mostly I don't know a lot about what I ought to do for myself.

But sometimes I do. I know the catfish I cook for me and Clara are better than the frozen farm fish we get at the Corner Pocket. I know tomatoes out of my garden are better than what you get in the store. I know I cut my graves cleaner than Harper with his backhoe. I know to set the sod aside so when the funeral is done I can lay it out just like it was, and so you don't have to scatter Pasture Number 8 and wait for it to come up. I know to sit on my tailgate in Rose Hill on an August night and watch the lights of Bly blink on, but not so much that you can't see the tracer stars. That's what Clara and I do that first night. There's one, she says. Another over by Levi Johnson's place, I said.

No cares have I to grieve me, no pretty little girls to deceive me,
I'm as happy as a lark believe me, as I go rolling, rolling, home.
Happy as the day when a sailor gets his pay, as I go rolling,
rolling home.

I tell myself I'll have it all in my head when she gets back. She says it should be my song. I think her song must be "Skylark." But I can't get that in my head. Maybe I should. I'll tell her she could have the words on her gravestone if she wants. And I'd have something from her song for me on mine. "By the Light of the Silvery Moon" would be mine. Something to remember her.

I don't live so well, I said to Clara one night. I hear that, she says. I've finished my grave. Maybe she's been with me half a dozen times by now. Leaving from work at the Corner Pocket like that first time. The days are shorter so we got no light to the east just yet. It's not winter in the air, but it's something. Neither do I, she says.

Harper says I'm living in shit, I said. For me as well, she says. She leans back into the bed of the truck and because she's long-legged tall her feet are on the ground and she is tapping out something with one of them. Sing me a song, she says. I'm bad at it, I said. I don't care, she says. I don't know so many, I said. Mostly Willie. Then I think of one from grade school in Blaze.

> *I was born in Kansas, I was bred in Kansas,*
> *and when I get married, I'll be wed in Kansas.*

Clara sings the rest of it with me to the night sky from on her back from where she's at. *She's a sunflower...*

It's the last time I saw her before she left for I don't know where.

Winter works for digging graves. You wouldn't think so. But it does. Blowing snow. Frozen dirt. I build a fire over where I'm going to dig. Cottonwood is good, but elm and ash are better. Hackberry if it's old. Stack it like a brush pile then splash it with diesel fuel mixed with gasoline. Torch it with my weed burner. Sparks fly. After awhile it settles down.

When I've got a good bed of coals I spread them out and ease my metal frame down over them as a cover. I do this in the afternoon so that when I come back the top is glowing low red and the ground is cooked. All you got to do is get through a foot or so. Even with the grass burned I cut the sod off and make a stack. I stand up the frame and start digging.

I don't need much light. You get used to the dark. When I'm at the bottom, I lie down and look up. The stars from there are brighter and blink harder. Harper says if you dig a hole deep enough you can see the stars in the middle of the day. *Star holes* he calls them. A relative of his on the Whitewoman used to dig them and let the kids come down and look up. Maybe.

Nights I don't have a good moon, I prop my plywood frame against a nearby tombstone. I paint it white so it will catch starlight or the moon's sliver. I could turn on the parking lights of my truck, but I don't. If you like digging graves at night, you like the dark. Or by the light of the silvery moon, now that I think of it.

You dig winter as well? Clara says the night before she goes away. Yes, I said. How so? she says. I'll show you when the time comes, I said. Tell me, she says. A man's got to have some privacies, I said.

By now I'm out of the hole and I can see she's smiling at what I've said. But I'll know in the end, she says. Trade you, I said. "B" for how I dig in winter. Or why you're saving "R." Maybe, she says and looks away as if to find a shooting star. There, she says. About where you live near Bly. But it isn't there because I'm looking that way as well.

After I find her gone, I start cleaning up. We have some warm days left to us and it's easy. My late tomatoes are still coming in. They're green but you can fry those. Peppers too. Then we have a bad frost, and not much later a blizzard with a foot of wet snow comes through for three days and it's all done for the garden. Good thing I put a tarp over the fold-out. Sometimes when I come home, Tilly's sleeping on it if I haven't put her in the house.

Then the snow melts and it turns warm again. Winter warm, not real warm. I go back to cleaning and I think about what kind of story to tell Clara about my brown recluse scar. But it won't come. I think about Clara when I'm digging graves or at the Corner Pocket cooking chicken-fried steaks and catfish. I think about her privacies. About where she's gone. About the songs she sings. I think maybe her story should start and end with my scar, but she'll be everything that's in-between. Songs. Talk. Words. Only my scar won't be a brown-recluse scar. It'll be a scar that has something to do with her. A woman's got to like you if you put her in a story as if it's a home with words you've made for her.

Two times I dig winter graves without her. Once I cook chicken-fried steak and hash browns on my metal lid. The other time I grill buffalo burgers. I fix more than my share. I cook early to do the digging early. That way I can go to the Corner Pocket and help out. They usually don't need me much in winter. But I go anyway. Once I sit by the window by the door after they close and down a pint of McCormick's.

It's cold that first grave, but it hasn't been cold enough so that I can't get through the sod once it takes the heat of my fire. Then going down isn't much trouble. It's in January when we've had thirty days of below zero that you have to let your fire cook the ground long enough to roast a hog. In winter, I trade the Dos Equis for pulls of Knob Creek. I like the bottle. It's like a tombstone.

The second grave is about the same kind of thin cold, only with my buffalo burgers instead of chicken-fried steak. Then between Christmas and New Year's, I get two graves. Car wreck. Kids. Brothers. It's deep cold that night. A blizzard coming.

Hello, she says. I'm in the hole of the first grave and it's snowing and blowing up above. I've got my lid on the other one cooking the ground. Maybe I can get both dug the same night. I've been at it since sundown. Hello, she says again.

I heard her come up. Even in the hole with the wind blowing, I hear somebody drive up. It might have been Harper. But I'm making in my mind that it's Clara.

Yo! I said. That's my way of saying hello.

I had thought about it, and what I thought was if she comes

back I won't ask her where she's been. Maybe she'll tell me, maybe not.

You need a hand up? she says. Sure, I said. Here, she says. I see she's got on those white cotton work gloves you wear under leather work gloves when winter comes. Just as I'm about to take her hand she takes off the glove, so I take off mine and she pulls me up. Her hand is warm. How'd you know I was here? I said. Just thought you might be, she says.

It's been at nights in bed that I try out stories about my scar. Some nights my story is when the squeeze chute breaks the time I'm helping Walter Wilcox brand cattle and he catches a piece of iron in his leg. I take a hit of iron myself through my hand and we both go to the hospital in Cottonwood. But Clara might know about Walter Wilcox so I drop it. I want a story that isn't true but could be.

So I start thinking, I'll get the scar doing something to keep her safe. We're in Denver coming out of a motel going for a nice dinner and some punk tries to rob us. He grabs Clara, pulls his Colt, and shoots me through my hand. But quick as Tilly, I've got him on his back with his pistol cocked into his eyeball. I'm asleep before I get to where Clara takes me to the hospital. Or maybe it's back to Blaze, because you've got to call the police in Denver if you go to the hospital with a bullet hole in you.

Some nights we go to her house, but since she doesn't want me to see it, maybe not. Then I make the story in summer so she can take care of me on the fold-out. That would be good. Summer it is. We head to my place. Even with my bullet hole I drive us back from Denver. She helps turning corners with her left hand on the steering wheel.

Coming out of the grave, I am looking at her and she looks at me, but then she doesn't. I don't much notice how women dress. But this time I do. She's wearing jeans as always, but she's wearing a red plaid coat like a lumber jacket. You don't see those around here. Under that there is a long, yellow scarf wrapped around her neck and then over her shoulder. She's got a white stocking cap pulled down over her ears.

You been back long? I said. Just drove in, she says. Haven't got to the house. You want something to eat? I said looking at the lid over the fire on the next-door grave. I got ribeyes and a bottle of Knob Creek in the truck. Hash browns. Sure, she says. She goes to her truck. Maybe she's cold and wants to get warm. Maybe I should get in with her, but I don't. I go to my truck and turn on my tape deck and listen to Willie: "Help Me Make It Through the Night." Then I get my ribeyes and packets of hash browns. I open my Knob Creek.

Can I come in? she says as she opens the door. Sure, I said. You want a pull? Yes, she says and takes the Knob Creek by the fat of the bottle. How's Tilly? she says. Chews tires, I said. You? she says. I'm working on your song, I said. *No cares have I…*We are quiet between us. She takes off her stocking cap and shakes her head so her tendrils fall down.

Have you got my story? she says. Yes, I said. Outside the snow blows in gusts. A foot by morning, I said. So I hear, she says. I think to say something but I've lost it. So I go, What's "B"? Harper, she says. Bud. She opens the palm of her left hand and there he is.

That's not what we call him. We call him by his last name. Sometimes Rabbit because of what rabbits do. Not that he brags about it. I'll give him that. But never by his first name. The same for me. Which is why I hope she might save "R" for me because of my last name. The wind gusts so hard we feel the truck rock. We go quiet again. Then:

Would you want to get married? she says, looking at me as she passes the Knob Creek. Me? Yes, she says. To me, she says and laughs and takes the bottle back out of my hand. I'm not married anymore, she says. Where would we live? I said. Maybe buy a place in between us, she says. But both keep our own.

We don't talk. Only breathing. The windows are fogging. I am thinking about her with me on the fold-out by the garden in spring. I'm thinking how we've never much touched unless you count her helping me out of the graves or me taking her arm when we cross the street out of the Corner Pocket at night going to my truck. Or how I walk her back to her truck after the sun's come up and open the door and help her in, and how she seems surprised the first time I do that, and I'm surprised at it myself. That kind of touching. Hands mostly. Or once I put my fingers along her cheek under her hair and she closes her eyes. Usually I'm all over them right away to nail them.

I'd be good to you, she says. I know about Maggie. She's my second cousin. I know she gave you the fold-out and Tilly and how you wouldn't marry her. She'd have been good to you, but I'll be better. You can live like you want. Or I could help you clean up, if that's what you want. Then we wouldn't have to rent a place in-between. You could be my "R."

I hold out my hand with the scar on it. My story's about us, I said, and how I got shot in Denver protecting you and this is a bullet hole. Then you take care of me on the fold-out. Yes, she says. I never had us married, I said.

Skylark, have you anything to say, she sings, taking my hand and looking at it and then out the shotgun window where you can't see anything for the blowing snow. Not even the metal frame which for sure is glowing red and spitting as the snow hits it.

I get out of the truck with my ribeyes to toss them on the grill. It's cold. It's not just the wind. It's cold. I go around back and get my spatula to move dinner around. I look at my truck, but I can't see her. I walk over to my first grave and drop in. Not to think. Just to get out of the wind while supper's cooking. But I think anyway. It's not about what I should do with Clara in the truck wanting to get married. It's all kinds of thinking coming at me like snow in gusts. Tilly. *Unfurl.* Bud. I know some places. So do I. Star holes. The Committee to Save the World. My old Harley. Rattlesnakes in the St. Francis Graveyard. And how, when I put new wood in the stove on nights like this, I go outside with Tilly to watch the smoke come out of the chimney and what a pleasure that is, and that I never told Clara that in all the time we talked. And maybe if we were married, she'd go outside with me even when it's blue cold to look at the smoke coming up from the woodstove inside, and then we'd go back and it would be warm.

I hear a door open and shut. Then another. I hear her truck start. I don't move. I hear her turning around. She's by the grave going along though the snow. Then I don't hear her anymore because of the wind.

I say to myself, well, that's that. What? I say to myself. She's gone, I say. You should have said something, I say. I didn't say no, I say. You can't leave it at that, I say. Maggie left and what difference did it make? I say. Maggie never dug a grave with me, I say.

I stop talking and listen to the wind. Nothing but the wind. I think I'll climb out and take a pull of Knob Creek and go home to my shit. Finish the other grave tomorrow.

You want a hand out? she says. This time I don't hear her before what she says. I see her white work glove and she's taken off her cap so her tendrils are flapping around her face. She's next to where the lid is cooking our supper so she's got a glow to her cheek on that side. Sure, I say. She takes off her glove and I take off my glove. Sure, I say.

At least that's what I have myself say for both of us with the wind being the only other sound I hear in the bottom of the grave.

Stealing

First, I check your dishwasher. Widow women don't use dishwashers. They hide money in them. That's what I did when Mrs. Walters died. Priscilla Walters.

I work at Running Meade Court. Old Folks' Burg. Jack Dogle, the estate buyer, calls you the Nearly Deads. Jack's my brother-in-law. We get on. Sort of.

Lorraine in the front office is always saying *Old age doesn't have to be a wreck. Running Meade's here to make your Golden Years Twenty-Four Carat.* Lorraine's got a big smile. She's tall and young. She's the one who phones me when you're dead. In the Green Shed. It's where I work.

When I get the call your cottage has five days to be cleaned out. That includes the day you're dead. I'm through your door 8 a.m. if 911 hauled you the night before. By then you've got four days. It's in the contract.

If the Bereaved are nearby they can clean you out. Sometimes I work with them. Sort things. Haul trash to the dumpster. Box the Deductibles for Jane Moore at Second Hand Rose. Call Jack to make a Quick Price on whatever's for sale. I get my hourly on Running Meade's clock and maybe a tip from the son. The daughter usually won't tip. Daughters-in-law won't tip for sure. They're all the time sticking things in their purses. Rings. Pearls. Watches. They look for the money, but they don't know the places I know.

The best deal for me is when the Bereaved are in Hong Kong or Texas or Bermuda, and they tell Lorraine to clean Aunt Alice out. They'll get there when they get there. *Be careful. Be careful,* I've heard them say over the speaker phone. *She had Wedgewood from England. And the wine goblets have been in the family since Great Grandfather Baxter ate dinner with General Custer.* You can tell they're having second thoughts. But they don't come back if it's not convenient. Convenience is big these days.

For your "arrangements," Lorraine recommends Eternal Peace. They do Cremations and Full Body Burials. Or they'll store you in a cooler until *the Whole Famm Damnly* gets back. That's what Lorraine says when she's off the phone. *We're to clean out the cottage but Eternal Peace is to put Betty Beulah Land on ice until the Whole Famm Damnly gets back.*

However it works out, somebody's got to go to Eternal Peace and say that's you that's dead. It's the law. Usually Lorraine goes. I just went. For Mrs. Walters. Mostly I don't go. There's a reason.

The Green Shed's got bays with shelves so you can store what won't fit in your cottage. Along the sides of the bays are racks for clothes. Everybody gets a bay whether you use it or not. It's where I put your stuff from your cottage when you're dead. Clocks and mugs of pens and pencils. Flower vases. Candlesticks. Dishes. Silverware. I wash your last dishes. Housekeeping is supposed to do that, but I call the shots when I get the call.

What won't fit on the hangers or shelves I put in boxes. You get charged for the boxes. I magic marker them: *Kitchen. Bath. Bedroom.* I put your name and cottage number on the box, and the date I moved you. I'm organized. I have to be in case I get two calls. *Piggybacked.* That's what Lorraine says. *We got a Piggyback,* she'll say for the second one.

We don't store Consumables. We'll get a tax slip from Jane at Second Hand Rose for what she puts in her Poor Box. We'll do that. But Jane doesn't take frozen food or booze. I take beer. Jack takes your hard stuff. I take your soups. It's my lunch most days. I heat it on a burner in the Green Shed.

Running Meade charges for me. For the dumpster, too. We're both under *Surcharge. Two boxes of Waste @ $10.00 per box surcharge. Labor, surcharge.* I'm labor. There's mileage on their truck to Second Hand Rose or the dump. If you put a pencil to it, the Bereaved would be better off paying another month's rent on the cottage. That way I don't go through it.

Not that I think one way or the other from what I find of yours. Letters. Pictures. Books. Sometimes I get a laugh. But I don't think one way or other about you. Except for Mrs. Walters. I think about her.

By the time you're boxed, I've got the money. And the Consumables. I like it when you have tuna fish. Chicken of the Sea is my favorite. The frozen food I take home pronto. My freezer is sorted so the oldest stuff is to the top. Ice Cream always goes on top. The Nearly Deads buy the best ice cream. They figure if they eat Lean Cuisine, they can eat real ice cream. Starbucks Coffee Almond Fudge is my favorite.

I get your Brasso. Baking soda. Salt. Flour for the wife's baking. Onions or potatoes if you've just been to Whole Foods. Rice. Noodles. Coffee. When I've packed a load, I head for home with a stop at Jane's to drop off the cans. Evaporated milk. I don't even know what it is. Beets. I hate beets. Olives. Those tiny onions Jack says you put in martinis. Jane checks the seals on the jars and the date for the cans. You'd be surprised how long a widow woman will keep a can of food. Ten years once for salmon. That's the record. Jane pitched it. What she keeps she puts in the Poor Box by the back door. We've got migrants. By closing time it's empty. Evaporated milk. Martini onions. Gone. Beets. Gone.

Jane knows I take my cut. We go back. High school. We kept at it afterward, even though we both got married. But we've stopped. Jane's husband works for Eternal Peace. He runs the backhoe that digs the graves. He's the reason I don't go there to see if it's you that's dead. He's the reason Lorraine usually goes.

The wife and me, we live out of town, so sometimes when I'm hauling your stuff I'll call her where she works and we meet at home for lunch. We take potluck on the soup. The same for T.V. dinners. I like Swiss steak but the Nearly Deads don't eat much meat. They go for Chinese chicken dishes. They're O.K. But Swiss steak is better.

We have our soup. Then I unload into the basement. My wife doesn't help. She's gotten jumpy about it. Even about the ReGiftables. That's her department. The ReGiftables. She does the dishes and won't look at what I'm bringing in.

I've got shelves in the basement where everything's arranged. Food on one shelf. Products on another. Money I put in glasses and jars with your cottage number on it. Even a shelf for the cat. Pebbles. He's a cut cat. Always sniffing his bowl to see what's in it this time. Picky cut cat if you ask me.

After I get back from lunch, I move what's left of you to your bay. Usually I can get it all in if you've *peeled your onion down.* That's what Jack says when he's buying off you when you first move in and you realize you've got too much stuff for the cottage. *You peeling the onion down?* Sometimes they don't understand.

Jack buys furniture. Plates and silver. Crystal. Tablecloths. Whatever he thinks he can sell in his store. *Old Time Times* it's called. I think he should call it *The Peeled Onion.* But Jack's all business.

"I put it all on the AME," he says. The American Money Escalator. "If they sell Irish Belleek for less than what they paid for it, the AME goes up for me and down for them. But the AME doesn't go anywhere if you don't put something on it. That's America. Running Meade's America. Dead or Nearly Dead."

What Jack won't buy, I take to Second Hand Rose and bring

back a tax receipt for the Bereaved. Sometimes I get a tip, even though I'm on Running Meade's clock. If you ask me to take it to Jane, I don't take it to my basement. Usually it's clothes that go to Jane. But even if it's ReGiftables or Consumables, I take them straight to her. Soups too. I put them in the Poor Box myself. Jane gets her lunch from what I bring.

To live at Running Meade you have to have *Deposit Ks*. And you don't get your Ks back if you move out the next day. Not a dime. Your Bereaved don't get it either. Not the money and not the cottage. Or anything you added to the cottage like a deck, or one of those pullout umbrellas over the deck. It's all no longer yours once I've gotten the call. After the *Deposit Ks*, there's the monthly. If you die November 2nd, you owe all of November. They take it right out of your checking account. It's in the Contract.

Most of your Bereaved don't understand and so they're in the office howling at Lorraine. When the lawyers get entangled that makes matters worse. Go back to playing golf in Bermuda, is what I'd tell a Bereaved. The Contract is what you get for not having your mother die in your guest room. Leave the Ks on the AME and forget it.

I don't fool with books except to flip through them for money. That's how I found the note from Mrs. Walters. The note to me. Not really to me. Well, maybe. It's to me. For sure, it's to me. It was in a big dictionary that had its own stand. It's the reason I went to see Mrs. Walters at Eternal Peace. I'll get to that. And about the mink coat.

I hold the books by their spines and give them a shake. *The Whole Famm Damnly* will look through the books for money, but they haven't got a system. I shake the books and sometimes money comes out. It's not like finding a dime on the sidewalk or how once when I was in the Whole Foods parking lot I found a trail of twenty-dollar bills. Finding money in books doesn't have so much luck in it. Maybe it does. It's the shaking them up and down until you find it that's fun. All kinds of stuff comes out. It's like panning for gold.

The woman who lost the twenties didn't know she was losing them until I followed the trail across the parking lot. By then two hundred dollars' worth of twenties. She told me to keep one, but I wouldn't do it. You don't want to be paid for kindness. That way you lose the pleasure when you think about it later.

Sometimes letters will drop out of the books. I don't read them. There'll be matchbook covers or reading glass tissues, and once a thin silver bookmark. I find slips of paper with lists of things to do. I'll read those. *Call Oliver. Clean sink. Walk. Bank. Library.* I see where they've crossed out what they've done. If it didn't get crossed out, I guess you didn't do it. You can't do everything.

Sometimes I find clippings about the books you've put them in. Mrs. Walters did that. She was the one who had the silver bookmark. Sometimes a book's been autographed. Jane asks me to sort those for her cut.

I find notes like *Make it $30,000 and it's a deal.* Then there was scratching like this guy was trying to get his pen to start. It was on a paper napkin from a bar in New York. Once I found a note that said *Next time don't be in such a rush.* And on the other side it said *O.K.* I make myself a story that the *O.K.* was a note that was supposed to be sent back.

I find pictures. Kids at beaches. On horses during a vacation. Pets. People standing around Old Faithful with it going off behind them. Men in uniform next to airplanes. One picture of this man's wife when she was young and not wearing her bathing suit top and on the other side it said *Southwest Coast of France, 1954.* I put it back in the book. I put everything I find in your books back. Except the money.

One man had money from all over the world. Jane said I should have kept it in case my wife and I ever went overseas, but I gave it to Lorraine. I give Lorraine half the money I find in the purses and billfolds. *Here Lorraine. Mrs. Jackson's wallet. I found it on the kitchen table. Thank you Randy. Did you find her purse? That too. In the bedroom. Here it is. Thank you Randy. We'll put them in the safe.*

The Bereaved get fifty cents on the dollar from the purses and billfolds. I get a dollar on the dollar from what's in the dishwashers. Or under the tray in the microwave oven. Not under mattresses. Jars they've put way up high behind the cans of soup. In between placemats is good. Under ironing-board covers. You look for flat spots. Finders keepers. I'm the Finder. A dollar on the dollar for what I find. Plus ReGiftables and Consumables.

Toilet paper. Clorox. Dishwashing powder. Vitamins. All kinds of pills. I toss those. Kleenex. You'd be surprised how much Kleenex old women have. They're always tucking it up their sleeves. You see it sticking out of them by their wrists, or high on their arms if it's summer. I have a theory that the more Kleenex they put in their sleeves the closer they are to death. When it's sticking out all over them like big white flaky warts, you know you'll be 911 by spring.

I take keys. Master Keys. Yale Keys. Car Keys. House keys. Skeleton keys. Tiny keys that go to suitcases. Keys that go to riding lawn mowers. I sort them into jars. Big Keys. Little Keys. Sometimes nights in my basement I put the keys on my workbench and make up a story about them. How the husband died with his John Deere riding-lawn-mower key in his jean pocket, and when the hospital returned his clothes his widow washed the jeans and the key came out in the laundry. Then she put the key in a jar, and when her kids moved her into Running Meade, they moved the jar as well. That kind of story.

My wife says it's stealing what I do. I say maybe taking the money is stealing. But not the Scrub-So-Soft and Lubriderm. Not the keys. Not what we give our daughters for coming to see us. Or what's in the ReGift Drawer. Like dish towels if they're in a set with fancy potholders and a kitchen apron. My wife thinks giving that to her sister for a birthday isn't stealing. Maybe the money is stealing.

But if the money's stealing, then it's all stealing. Not just the money. The money and the Lubriderm. The soup. The keys. The Starbucks ice cream. It's all stealing.

Jane takes your laundry soap for the Poor Box. The Pine Sol. The soups. She sells your scarves and purses you never took out of the boxes. But not to the poor. There'd be too high a price on them for the poor. But I'm poor if you pencil me against the Nearly Deads. My wife works a job at the county and I cut grass weekends in the summer. I plow snow in winter. We got medical bills. I put one daughter through state college and the other one halfway through before she got knocked up. The house is mortgaged once to the bank, and again to Jack. Not that the bank knows about Jack. I'm not poor like the Migrants. I know that. It's just I'm getting first pick. Is that stealing? If somebody else gets second pick, is that stealing? What about Jack's AME? Think about it.

Fifty cents on the dollar out of the purses might be stealing. It might be. But a dollar on the dollar out of the dishwasher might not be. For sure I can't tell my wife a thing about what's stealing and what's not. We stopped talking about it. Until I brought home the mink coat.

It was in Mrs. Walters' attic. I knew her because she'd call me at the Green Shed and say that Nike was on the loose. *I'll find Nike, Mrs. Walters. I'll find Nike.* He never went far. He was a pug. A low-to-the-ground dog. Always running away.

After Mrs. Walters died, I took him to the pound. You get charged for that too. The *Puff of Smoke Pound*, Lorraine calls it. Mainly your Nearly Deads have cats. I'm to take those to the pound but I don't. I put them out by the county lake. Only once I kept Pebbles.

By the time I find Nike, Mrs. Walters is walking over. I have these two aluminum folding chairs from one of the bays years ago. She pats Nike and rests herself. We don't talk much except about the headline news or the weather. Every once in awhile she looks at the bays filled with stuff Jack hasn't put on the AME and says, *Getting and Spending, Getting and Spending*, like it was something she'd read in a book or the newspaper.

Mrs. Walters died during the night the last time she came over to get Nike. The light was blinking on the phone when I opened the Green Shed. I knew what it meant. I just didn't know who.

Right after 911 hauled her, Lorraine called me and said Sales had some Nearly Deads who wanted to move in *Pronto*.

Get her out so Housekeeping and Painting can get in. Don't store it. There's no Whole Famm Damnly. Call Jack and get a Quick Cash Price right out of the cottage. Take the rest to Second Hand Rose or toss it. Keep track of the dumpster loads for the Surcharges.

Mrs. Walters had no Bereaved and no will, which means the county gets it all. When that happens, Running Meade's lawyers figure how to bill the B-Jesus out of your estate for all kinds of things. Like me taking Nike to the pound.

I opened Mrs. Walters' cottage and looked for the money. There was twenty dollars in her purse, and maybe it was because of Nike and how we used to sit together that I gave it all to Lorraine even though it was two tens. *Thank you, Randy.* No other money in the usual places.

I called Jack. I took Nike to the pound and went back to Running Meade. When Jack showed up, he made a Quick Cash Price for what he wanted and went to the office to pay Lorraine. I spent the afternoon hauling for Jack on Running Meade's clock. Then I hauled two loads to the dumpster.

At quitting time I locked the cottage. I took my cut of Consumables. It wasn't much. Toilet paper. Janitor in a Drum that still had a sticker on it from when Mrs. Walters moved into Running Meade. Glass Plus. Brillo. A packet of fancy soaps from France I figured my wife could ReGift. Band-Aids and Rolaids and rubbing alcohol from her medicine cabinet. But not her prescriptions. They were on the kitchen table in a row by her Days-of-the-Week pill-box. I tossed those.

The next morning I made a run to Jane with two boxes of auto-graphed books, all of them to *Priscilla Walters*. Some of the writers wrote notes as if they were friends.

After Jane's, I went back to the cottage and remembered I hadn't checked the attic. Usually we don't bother with attics unless they're finished. You have to go up this ladder in the utility room, and be careful to walk across the floor joists or you'll go through the ceiling. One guy did that with a birthday present he'd hidden for his wife and fell through and died. Lorraine said it was a bud vase. *A crystal bud vase*, she kept saying. *With a single rose in it. The vase didn't even break.* It happened before I started at Running Meade.

I go up the ladder and through the lift panel and pull the chain on the light. Nothing. Only planking. I walk across the floor joists to have a look-see under the eaves. Nothing. I'm about to go back down when I think, what's that over by the gas vent? And it's a mink coat. Only I don't know it's a mink coat because it's in a box, so I don't know what it is until I get it down the ladder into the utility room. Then it's a mink coat.

I go to the Green Shed and call the wife and say we'll have lunch. Then I sit on one of my folding chairs and put the coat on the other. I am trying to make a story that goes with the coat being in the attic. But nothing comes into my head. I think it's not Mrs. Walters' coat because all the time I knew her she was too old to be going up and down the utility ladder.

What's this? my wife says. *A Mink Coat* I say. *It's from…Don't tell me*, she says. *I don't want to know. Try it on*, I say. *No*, she says. *Take it back or Lorraine will be out here and find all the stuff you've got in the basement. The money and everything. Put it back! Put it back! We'll go to jail unless you put it back.* My wife won't even let me eat lunch she's so hot about it. *Put it back!*

I take the coat and think maybe I should just drive to the cottage and go up the utility ladder and leave it where I found it. Or maybe give it to Lorraine. But I don't. What good's a mink coat in an attic where nobody knows it's there? And Lorraine would just take it for herself. Jack would put a Quick Cash Price on it and wait for winter and up it ten times. Everybody gets a cut but me unless my wife will have it. And she won't.

On the way to town I drive the road to the county lake. I'm stalling. I don't know what to do, but I think if I drive slowly, I'll figure it out. I stop where I let out the cats. Nobody's around. Just me and picnic tables and trash cans. Ducks on the lake.

I sit in the truck. Then I get out and put on the coat. I'm not big, so I can get into it. I don't know why I'm doing this, only once I saw an advertisement in a magazine with Joe Namath wearing a mink coat. I like Joe Namath. Anyway, I put the coat on. That's when I find the note. In the pocket. It's the second note I've found from Mrs. Walters since she died. The one I find in the pocket of the mink says: *This is not my coat. I do not know how to give it back.* It was signed *Priscilla Walters*, just like the note from her I found in the dictionary. I'll get to that. Same handwriting.

Now I got a mink coat my wife doesn't want, and I got a note out of the pocket from Priscilla Walters. Plus the first note from the dictionary before I found the mink coat.

Jack drives up. Maybe he's been to a farmhouse to buy collectibles. Or maybe he's got some Strange out this way. I think he does. I think I know her. Then I remember there's an auction in Wells on Wednesdays, and he's taking the back road to town. He stops. I'm standing there in Mrs. Walters' mink.

"What's up?" he points at the coat.

"I found it," I say.

"At Running Meade?" he says.

"Yes."

"The cottage you just emptied?" he says.

"Yes."

"You taking it?" he says. "For Laura?" Just then somebody we both don't know goes by in a pickup. Migrant man.

"Laura doesn't want it," I say.

"Why not?"

"Just doesn't."

"You need a price?" he says. He gives the sleeve a feel. "It looks nice on you." He winks. I should tell him to get fucked, but he's not all bad.

"You think so?" I wink back.

"A quarter," he says. "No one has to know."

He pulls out his wad and peels off two-fifty. I look at the money. Something is happening to me. Just looking at the money, something is happening.

"I don't think so," I say.

"Three?" he says.

"It's not the money," I say.

"What's not the money?" Jack says. "Laura doesn't want it. Lorraine doesn't know about it. It's a clean deal."

"Maybe it's not right to sell it."

"What are you saying?"

"It's not mine," I say.

"Everything out of Running Meade's not yours," Jack says.

"It's stealing," I say. Jack looks at me like I'm not who I am.

I'm standing there talking to Jack and thinking about Mrs. Walters' note in the dictionary when I was looking for money and found a slip of paper. *I know what you do when we die.* It was signed *Priscilla Walters.* Underneath her name she had written: *ISTMP.* I put the note in my wallet. I am thinking all this standing by the picnic table with Mrs. Walters' mink on. I get out my wallet and Jack figures I'm going to take his money, but I'm not.

"What's this?" he says. I hand him the note from the dictionary.

"It's to us," I say. "I found it in her cottage."

He gives it a glance. Then hands it back.

"So what if she knows," he says. "She's bye-bye."

"Maybe not," I say. I don't know what I'm saying.

"You think she's not bye-bye," says Jack, and I can see he's inching away like me wearing the coat in the middle of nowhere by myself was something he shouldn't have joked about. "She's dead, right? 911 dead. On the slab in the cooler at Eternal Peace."

"She's dead," I say. "But what she says isn't."

"She's talking to you," Jack says. "I got a license for what I do. I pay taxes. I took a course in being an estate broker. I got my certificate on the wall. You're the one she's talking to here. It's your cut she's talking about. You want to sell the coat or what?"

I don't say anything. Then I say *O.K.* It seemed like what I should say with Jack standing there holding out three hundred dollars and me wearing Mrs. Walters' mink. At least I get my cut.

I take the coat off and give it to Jack and take the money. Then I hand the other note to him. The one about the coat not being Mrs. Walters' that was in the pocket.

"What's this?" he says.

He reads it, then tears it to pieces and pitches it on the ground.

"Maybe the coat was stolen," I say.

"You're getting..." and I can't hear what he says because another truck goes by.

"Maybe," I say, but I don't know what I've agreed to.

"I got to get going," Jack says as he climbs in his truck with the mink. We drive to town. I'm behind.

I don't feel good. I'm trying to think it through. I got my basement full of keys and Scrub-So-Soft and water glasses of money and paper towels. Upstairs in the guest room there's French soaps and potholders and perfume for ReGifting. Then there's this mink coat I just sold to Jack even though it wasn't mine.

Jack pulls into Second Hand Rose and I know he's going to put the coat on consignment instead of waiting for winter. *I'll buy it back*, I say out loud to myself in the truck. I'm behind him in the parking lot. I honk. He sees it's me.

"I'll buy it back," I yell as I get out. He's walking toward Jane's with the coat.

"Five hundred Quick Cash Price," he says without stopping.

"Here's your three hundred," I say catching up with him. "Follow me to the house and I'll get the rest." He stops.

He's looking at me like I'm fucking nuts. He's looking at me like he'll never think I'm anything but fucking nuts no matter how long we both live. Like maybe I was going to pull down my pants and beat my meat out there by the county lake with Mrs. Walters' coat on when he drove up.

"Jesus," he says.

We get in our trucks and drive to the house. He stays in the kitchen while I go into the basement and get the money out of the water glasses. I take a ten from one glass, a twenty from another, and so on, until I get the two hundred. When I come up I hand him the money and he hands me the coat.

"I think you're losing it," he says.

I know that's not what he said when the truck went by at the lake, and I wonder if he'll tell Laura about all this or if he'll just let it go.

"I'm quitting Running Meade," I say.

"I can't talk to you," he says and walks out the door. The phone is ringing but I don't answer it.

I go into my basement with the coat. I put it on the bench where I sort stuff. I look at my Consumables. I open the freezer and look at the T.V. dinners and the ice cream and all. I put Mrs. Walters' note to me in her coat pocket.

Then I hear the door open upstairs. My wife calls, *Randy.* I say

I'm in the basement. She comes down. Partway. She sits on the stairs. She says Lorraine has called her to see what's up.

"You sick? I talked to Jack and he said..."

"I'm not going back to work," I say.

"What's with the coat?" she says. "I told you..."

"I bought it."

"You bought it?"

"It's yours," I say.

"I don't want it," she says. But she's looking at it.

"I didn't steal it," I say. "I bought it."

"What do you mean you're not going back?" she says. "Lorraine's looking for you. She wants you to go to Eternal Peace and tell them it's the woman who died the other night that's there. She says you knew her."

"I'm not going back."

"You sick?" she says. "Jane says you stopped there with Jack then drove off. Then Jack said..."

She comes the rest of the way down the stairs. It's the first time she's been all the way down for a year. Maybe more. She takes the coat off my bench and holds it out, then puts it on. She looks good in it. I think my wife looks very good in it.

"It's never been worn," she says. "What's this?" She's found Mrs. Walters' note in the pocket. "What's it mean, she knows what you do?" My wife's taking off the coat. "I don't want it," she says. "Not even if you paid for it." But she's holding it.

Then she looks around the basement at my shelves and how neatly I've got it all organized. Maybe she's going to say we should take the money to Lorraine so we can keep the rest and not call it stealing. Maybe she's waiting for me to say it.

"I'm not going back never," I say. "I'll take the money to Lorraine, if that's what you're thinking."

"What about the rest of it?" she says. She's got the coat over her arm and looking around.

"I don't know," I say.

"I had some of the ReGifts planned for Christmas," she says.

She puts the coat back on and looks at the note from the pocket and reads it again.

"What do you think it means below where she signed?" I say. "*ISTMP.*"

"'I Stopped Taking My Pills,'" my wife says as she moves so the coat settles over her. She looks at herself over her shoulder down the back.

"How'd you figure that so quickly?" I say.

"It just came to me," she says.

I walk up the stairs and out the door to my truck. I drive to Eternal Peace to tell them it's Mrs. Priscilla Walters they got. She was on a cart behind a curtain. I found her on my own because nobody was around. I wanted to talk to her, but I was afraid somebody would come along and it would be like wearing her mink when Jack drove up.

I didn't know what I'd say, but I knew once I got started I'd say that I knew her note in the dictionary was for me. And how I gave all twenty dollars from her purse to Lorraine. That I was going to get Nike out of the pound before they puffed him. That Nike and Pebbles would just have to get along. How I missed her sitting with me in the Green Shed. Was it true about *ISTMP*? How did she get the coat up in the attic? Whose coat is it anyway? How does she know what I do when you're dead? Didn't she ever take a cut? Why were all those books signed to her? What should I do with what I've stolen? The money. The Consumables we have for lunch and supper. The ReGiftables my wife has planned for Christmas. The mink coat that's not hers. What should I do?

But I don't say anything. Pretty soon along comes this woman who wants to know if I am Randy and can I identify The Deceased. I tell her The Deceased is Mrs. Priscilla Walters of Running Meade

Court. She writes it down on a clipboard and I have to sign where she's put an X. Then because I don't leave, she asks if there is anything else. I can't talk to Mrs. Walters like I want to, so I say no.

I've quit Running Meade. I mow lawns. Plow snow in the winter. I'm spending down the money out of the glasses. Gas. Groceries. We pay Jack on the second mortgage. The cash won't last the year. But we got our Consumables. ReGifts. Nike is with us. He and Pebbles don't get along. My wife still works for the county. She won't talk to me about anything. Some days in my basement I think I should give it all back, but everybody's dead. And like Mrs. Walters said about the mink, I don't know how. Only I can't think she stole it. I've made stories about whose coat it is and how she got it in the attic, and why she couldn't give it back, and nowhere in my stories does Mrs. Walters steal it.

Not like me. When the girls open a present from the bays, I know it's stolen goods we've made a gift of. When the wife and me have T.V. Swiss steak for dinner, I know we're eating stolen food. And the dish soap she uses to wash up. The mink coat she won't wear except to take it out now and then to look at herself in the mirror. Beer, when I have one with a ball game on the television I've got in my basement. A house full of stealing. Not that it gets it off my mind to say so to myself.

Notes on the Cold War in Kansas

Russian Radiation

There were three of us who were friends in those days when I was a young boy and lived in a small town in Kansas: Benny and Than (short, I suppose, for Nathan). We were all members—the only members—of The Society of the Secret Shed.

It was the 1950s, and one winter, Grandmother White caught me putting snowballs in the basement freezer to use the following year for a summer snowball war. I say Grandmother White "caught me" because she was sure that the snows in Kansas—and all across America—were laced with "Russian radiation." Grandmother White was my father's mother.

"We'll have to throw it all out," said Grandmother White. She meant the food in the freezer: half a steer bought from—and butchered by—a local rancher. Some sausage from a farm pig. Bacon as well. Two catfish from Wagnall's pond I had caught that fall and was proud to have done so. Vegetables and strawberries from our garden that we had picked and frozen the previous summer. Whole chickens we bought live from the Simms' down the road. It was Grandmother White who had slaughtered the chickens, chopping off their heads with my father's hatchet and then hanging them by one foot from the clothesline, using her collection of string. It was my job to catch the chickens as they flopped and ran—however briefly—headless around our backyard.

"I don't know," my mother said, looking into the freezer. "It seems such a waste." When my father got home from work, he made the decision: the food stayed.

"Your son will glow in the dark and parts of him will not be useful," said Grandmother White. "The rest of us will get tumors before our time. And warts too thick for a found penny to rub away. I know about the Russians." Grandmother White's real name, I later learned, was Grandmother Wakowski.

The snowballs could go, said my father. But the food stayed. He winked at me to say we'll find someplace else for the snowballs. Which we did.

"Parts of him will not be useful," said Grandmother White, glancing at me. I thought she meant my throwing arm and that I would lose at summer snowball war—or worse, that I would be unable to play baseball in the local Three-Two League. I held my right arm with my left hand. My father patted me on the back. We stored the snowballs in Uncle Bert's freezer. "Don't tell your grandmother," my father had said.

The Girl Next Door

Sharon Fulton (for some reason I always thought of her by her full name, never just Sharon, or even Sherry—which is what her mother, and mine, called her) went to the Catholic school (Bishop Something or Other), while I attended Hickory Grove, the public school. I did this over the protests of Grandmother White, who might have changed her name but not her religion. Hickory Grove was a brief bike ride away from where we lived; Sharon Fulton's school was on the far north side of town.

Sharon Fulton's bus picked her up fifteen minutes before I had to leave for Hickory Grove, so as I got ready in the mornings, I could see her standing at the end of her driveway. Yellow became my favorite color because it seemed to be her favorite color: yellow blouses when school started and then again in late spring; yellow sweaters in fall; a yellow and black winter coat; yellow dresses that blossomed with the fifties foliage of petticoats and in which Sharon Fulton would, while waiting for her bus, twist her hips this way and that, as if to get them to settle. It was because of Sharon Fulton that I was always on time for school. It is also true that until the day I dug the atomic bomb fallout shelter, Sharon Fulton and I never spoke. And after that we never spoke.

Binoculars

Than's father had a pair of binoculars. Navy beer bottles, he called them. From Than's house I could read our name on our mailbox. I could see to the bottom of the lot and the line of small trees that hid The Secret Shed. If you stood on a chair, you could spot the flagpole on our school, even if the flag wasn't up.

"Let me see. My turn," is what the three of us would say as we passed around the binoculars. Once, I saw Sharon Fulton standing in her front yard. "That's enough," Than's father said just at that moment. He had been in the war (as had my father), and I suppose he wanted to be careful about his souvenirs from those days. "That's enough," and Sharon Fulton vanished.

Civil Defense

Than and Benny and I were Boy Scouts. For a merit badge, we needed to perform some kind of public service.

"I think we should clean up Turkey Creek," said Than one day at the shed. "It's full of bottles, and cans, and trash. We could use my uncle's pickup." Than was always trying to figure out how to make use of, or ride in (front or back—but the back was preferred), his uncle's pickup. "It's got a winch on it," said Than, as if that were the clincher. He cranked an imaginary handle.

For Benny's part, he was always plotting ways to use his .22—a bolt-action single-shot rifle that had been provisionally given to him the previous Christmas, and which could only be used with his grandfather present, and then only for target practice on tin cans. Benny's father had been killed in Germany.

"I think we should shoot the pigeons at the Co-Op," said Benny. "My mother says they're a menace." Benny aimed a long stick and fired off a few shots at some starlings on the power line that ran above the shed. "Dead menace. Bang. Dead menace. Bang." "Menace" was a new word for Benny.

"I think we should join the Civil Defense," I said. "That way we could get binoculars to look for Russian bombers." I held up two rounded fists to my eyes and turned my head this way and that, scanning the Kansas sky for enemy planes. The dream of binoculars to look for Russian atomic bombers beat out the pickup truck and the pigeon menace.

The Secret Shed

It was an old chicken house located on a bank above a small nameless (and mostly dry) creek that ran into Wagnall's pond. Overgrown with morning glory vines and ringed with a barricade of sunflowers and thistle, it was hidden (so we thought) from everyone but the three of us. The Shed had board floors, under which the three of us stashed various odds and ends (totems, Than called them) that we would get out when we gathered for the meetings of The Society of the Secret Shed.

It was at these meetings that we decided what we would do for the rest of the day: snake hunting was always on the list; tree climbing usually; skating if Wagnall's pond was frozen, stone skipping if it was not; snowball war, winter or summer. Just as important, we planned what we would do the following week, month, and year.

This list included floating down the Smoky Hill River to the Kansas River on a raft, and then to New Orleans by way of Chicago. As the only fisherman among us, I would be responsible for catching fish. Benny would shoot squirrels and rabbits and birds with his .22; and because he liked to build fires—he built the one that finally burned down the Secret Shed—Than said he would cook.

Our plans also included taking turns walking and riding double on Dan (an Appaloosa that Benny's grandfather owned) to Montana to see Niagara Falls, then taking the A Train to New York City. However, our best trip was hitchhiking to Kansas City and 12th and Vine to see a "burr-lee-q" show. (This latter adventure was something Benny's brother, Leroy, had already done—hitchhiking and all.) But, whatever our agenda, we never began a meeting of The Society of the Secret Shed without putting our totems on the two-by-fours that ran along the walls of the shed, each of us claiming a wall that was not used by the door.

Than had a bird's head skeleton, a horseshoe (that I coveted), plus a pretty nasty-looking rabbit skin that had been pried off the asphalt road that we took to Hickory Grove. He also had a collection of various animal bones—part of a jaw, some vertebrae, what might have been a leg bone, ribs—that he was trying to assemble into a composite animal on the floor of The Shed, and over which we would have to step as we moved around.

As for Benny, he had a flattened quarter that had been crushed by the local grain train after we put it on the tracks; a spent CO2 cartridge he said we could use to make a bomb by filling it with gunpowder and attaching a firecracker fuse; and two live .50 caliber machine-gun rounds that his uncle had brought back from the war. Benny also claimed he was going to bring down some "Mexican" playing cards of his brother's with pictures of naked women on them—but he never did.

My totems were a greenish stone I found in a large catfish I had caught and cleaned. I would also put out a Lazy Ike lure, whose treble hooks I had straightened with a pair of pliers so I could claim—which I did—that a huge bass named Godzilla had struck the bait with such force he flattened the hooks.

But my prize totem—prized by all of us—was a page I had

ripped out of a paperback book that had been in the rack of the local drugstore. The page (page 126) had the words brassiere and breasts toward the bottom. The complete sentence ran: "When Tricia turned around, George saw that she had unbuttoned her blouse so that he could see her black brassiere and the tops of her white breasts." The following sentence was the fragment: "Then Tricia took off her blouse and reached behind her and un-" which broke off at the gully between page 126 and 127 (a page none of us had the nerve to return to the drugstore to steal).

At more than one meeting of The Society of the Secret Shed, we decided to find Tricia—or a Tricia—and invite her to join us on our trip to New Orleans. We were also inspired to name the raft for her: *The Tricia*. Our hope was that a real Tricia could go from page 126 to page 127 as we drifted toward Chicago by way of 12th and Vine Streets in Kansas City. In the meantime, we had memorized her sentence-and-a half with the same fidelity we had memorized the Pledge of Allegiance we recited each morning at Hickory Grove Grade School.

Beyond our totems, it was required by The Society of the Secret Shed that each of us have a secret, secret, secret (being three, we thought of three as a sacred number) totem that was stored somewhere deep in The Shed. Neither the location of this Triple Secret Totem nor the object itself was to be revealed to anyone—thus Benny had something somewhere, and so did Than, and I did not know what or where.

For my part (and I have kept my secret all these years), I had hidden in a crevice in a beam above the door a letter I was in the process of writing to Sharon Fulton, its opening sentence being: "I like yellow to [*sic*]." Even then I needed an editor.

Physicals

"Yes," I am saying over the phone. "There are three of us, and we all want to join the Civil Defense. For our Boy Scout merit badge."

"Good for you," says the man at the other end. I cannot now recall by what means I tracked down whomever I am talking to, but somehow I had found my way to a pleasant and, as it will soon turn out, patient man. "What would you and your friends like to do for the Civil Defense?"

"We want to be spotters," I say.

"Spotters?"

"Yes," I say. "We want to look for Russian atomic bombers."

There are moments in everybody's youth when they know they are being fools. You don't know exactly why—or even for sure what it is to be a fool—but by some means you leap into your future, and you know that when you look back you will see yourself as very silly. In spite of this awareness, I go on.

"We want to look for Russian atomic bombers with binoculars. We would take turns during the school week. But in summer and on weekends we would all look. We each want our own pair."

"With binoculars?" says the man.

"Yes," I say.

"I see."

"We can climb trees," I say. "And we have a tree that gets us up to the roof of The Shed, so we have a good view from there." There is a pause.

"Do you know about physicals?" he says.

In point of fact, he had asked me if I knew about "physics"—not "physicals." Probably he was about to explain that whatever Russian atomic bomb was going to be dropped on The Shed (not to mention the Hickory Grove Grade School) would have been cut loose from the Russian atomic bomber somewhere around Denver, so that no matter how high a tree we climbed, no matter how powerful were our binoculars, or how diligent our looking through them from the roof of The Shed, we would not be able to see the Russian atomic bomb until it became its mushroom cloud.

However, for me, in hot pursuit of three pairs of binoculars and all the fame that would come with them, it made perfect sense that you would need physicals in order to be in the Civil Defense and issued Civil Defense binoculars. You had to have a physical to play in the Three-Two League, didn't you? There might even be a training program to get into the Civil Defense. If we had to take Civil Defense physicals, that might mean a day off from school, complete with the kind of excuse young boys dream of: I won't be in class on Friday, Miss Anderson, because I have to take a Civil Defense physical.

I saw myself returning to school with my binoculars hanging around my neck. "Navy beer bottles we call them," I would say to anyone who asked. I might even be required to stand at the classroom window—instead of taking my regular seat—all the better to scan the sky. At recess, the three of us would be "posted" around the playground looking Westward. (We always assumed the Russians would come from Colorado or California.) And finally in this movie I am making in my mind, I am sure no one at Hickory Grove Grade School (not even Miss Anderson) would be allowed to talk to us when we were on duty.

Then there was Sharon Fulton. Someone would be assigned to look out for the Catholic girls at Bishop Whatever It Was. Someone would have to patrol the outer fence of the playground with binoculars scanning the sky. Someone would have to yell: Russian atomic bombers! Take cover! Under your desks! Russian atomic bombers! Sharon Fulton would faint. Someone would have to carry Sharon Fulton off the playground in her yellow dress. That someone would be me.

"We'll take physicals," I say.

Pubic Hair

It was Leroy, Benny's older brother, who first grew pubic hair. We even knew to call it "pubic hair" because you learned about it in Boys' Health, taught by the high school basketball coach, a Mr.

Allen, who Leroy said was "doing the do" with Miss Anderson. Leroy was a hood.

Not that Leroy showed us his pubic hair; it was just that Benny reported on it from time to time. Benny's brother also shaved, had a switchblade knife, and kept a rubber in his wallet. (He did show us the rubber one day when Than and I stopped by.) Later Leroy would get Roberta Taylor "hot"—whatever that meant. (What it finally meant was that Roberta Taylor got pregnant and was shipped off to Sharon Springs to her grandmother's farm.)

Leroy's pubic hair made us wonder about girls, and what, in Than's terminology, was "down there." We couldn't really imagine what was "down there," this being well before *Playboy* showed us anything but breasts and buttocks—and in those days young boys in rural Kansas did not often get ahold of *Playboy*, so even breasts and buttocks were scarce items.

"I wonder if girls have pubic hair," Benny said one day at The Shed. Nobody said anything for a moment. For my part, I was hoping our meeting would be short, as in my mind I had composed two more sentences of my serial letter to Sharon Fulton, a letter I would only take out when Than and Benny had left.

"Girls do not have pubic hair," I pronounced.

"How do you know?" said both Than and Benny.

"Because only boys have pubic hair," I said. "That is why it's in Boys' Health."

"Stern says his sister will take down her pants for a dollar," said Than. Stern was Leroy's age. He, too, was a hood, and Stern was his last name, not his first, which made him even more of a hood than Leroy. Stern's sister was our age. We had heard this before about her. But a dollar was a lot of money for us, as we got a quarter a week allowance (Benny probably got less) and could only put together another dollar or so by doing extra chores. Then there was the question of who would ask Stern's sister.

"I think girls do have pubic hair," said Benny.

"They can't have pubic hair," I said, "because they don't have beards."

"Why wouldn't they have pubic hair in Girls' Health just like we have pubic hair in Boys' Health?" said Benny.

"They have breasts instead," I said. "We don't have breasts in Boys' Health. We have pubic hair. So it's even-steven." To this day I love reasoning from limited available evidence.

"Do you think girls have pubic hair?" Benny asked Than. Than thought a moment. It seemed a long time. I was beginning to lose track of the two sentences I was going to write to Sharon Fulton.

"I think," said Than finally, "that girls have pubic hair, but that they shed it in the summer." It seemed right.

"I agree with Than," said Benny.

"So do I," I said. Meeting over.

After we left, I doubled back and got out my letter to Sharon Fulton and wrote my two sentences and then went home, happy in the knowledge that someday, somehow, she would find it—maybe in the rubble of nuclear destruction.

It would be later that summer that the three of us would get a dollar together and draw straws to see who would ask Stern's sister to take down her pants (Benny lost). When she finally did it, standing in a small clearing uphill from The Shed while the three of us sat on the peak of the roof, we were not really able to see what we saw—or tell anyone what we had seen. However, we all agreed she did not have pubic hair.

"I told you," I said.

"It's still summer," said Than. "They don't grow it back until Thanksgiving."

Grandmother White, Television, Warts, and the Reading of Codes

We didn't have a television and neither did Benny or Than. Than's uncle in Kansas City had a television, and he told Than that you could see *The Lone Ranger* on it. This did not seem possible to us.

"He comes right into the living room. Tonto, too," said Than.

"What about Silver?" asked Benny.

"Silver, too," said Than. "You just turn on the television and the Lone Ranger and Tonto and Silver all ride around. And talk. Just like on radio, only they're in your living room."

"I don't believe it," I said. But I did. I imagined Silver and Tonto and the Lone Ranger all projected into our house, riding along while canyons and rivers and bandits and hostile Indians appeared in front of the divan or by the kitchen door or in the hallway that led to my bedroom—all as the plot required. How this happened, I wasn't sure, but I was sure I wanted it to happen in our house.

"Who's going to clean up the mess?" said Grandmother White. We were at supper, and I had asked if I might have a television for my "big" Christmas present, even though Christmas was months away.

"I don't think we can get television out here," my father said. "You have to be near a city."

"What mess?" said my mother. She was as alert to household untidiness as Grandmother White was.

"From all those cowboys and Indians traipsing through the house," said Grandmother White. "You heard the boy. That whole Ranger gang he listens to on the radio comes out of the television and into the living room. We don't need that."

"I don't think that's the way it works," said my father. "I think they are all on a screen like at a movie theater."

I was greatly disappointed to hear this, as my father was usually right about such things. But maybe not always.

"I'll clean up the mess," I said. "It can be one of my chores."

"We can talk about it later," said my mother. That meant that we would not talk about it later. If she had said, "I'll talk to your father," that meant, "I'll fix it with your father," just as my father's wink meant he'd fix it with my mother by hiding my snowballs in Uncle Bert's freezer. In such ways do children learn to read codes.

All of this talk in code may have diverted my grandmother's attention from *The Lone Ranger*, but it did not divert her attention from a wart that had recently come up on my index finger, and which she saw as irrefutable evidence of the spread of Russian radiation.

"I have a found penny," she said, "and we have a dish rag."

"Mother," said my father. That meant stop with this superstitious nonsense.

"Not that it will do much good," said my grandmother. "Parts of him may already not be useful."

"Grandmother White!" said my mother in some alarm.

Grandmother White was quiet for a moment, and then under the table I could feel her foot tap mine. That meant if I'd let her rub my wart with her found penny so she could wrap the penny in the dish rag and bury it, she'd give me a quarter; it would turn out to be the quarter I'd contribute to have Stern's sister take down her pants.

Benny

Sometime during high school, Benny went to the Army. He was sent there by the local judge who said it was either the Army or jail. Or reform school. Benny had begun blowing up mailboxes with cherry bombs; then he blew up a toilet in the high school with a CO_2 cartridge filled with gunpowder; then he stuffed a potato into the exhaust pipe of the local patrol car; then he ripped a rubber machine off the men's room of the Texaco station; finally, he started shoplifting. (He was caught stealing boxes of Russell Stover candy from the drugstore where I had stolen Tricia's page 126.) In the Army, he was first stationed in Korea; then he went to Vietnam. While I was taking graduate courses at the university, and Than was finishing his degree to be the veterinarian he is today, Benny was fighting in the Tet Offensive. Where he was killed: a fact I have only recently learned.

The Bomb Shelter and Sharon Fulton

Not long after Stern's sister had taken down her pants, I was digging a hole near The Shed to bury a bird I killed with my slingshot, and Sharon Fulton came up. I am to become a man who will never know what to do or say when first in the presence of women I find attractive. I once told a woman who had put on a stylish pea coat over her rather ample upper body, "My, what big buttons you have." What I said to Sharon Fulton was: "I'm digging a fallout shelter." It seemed like the thing to say to a girl whom I had saved a number of times by spotting Russian atomic bombers with my binoculars—not to mention carrying her to safety from the playground after she had fainted.

I suppose Sharon Fulton stood there for a moment and watched me. I hoped she hadn't noticed the dead bird. I did not look up.

"Why?" she said. It would turn out to be the only word Sharon Fulton ever said to me. I looked up. She was wearing yellow. I went back to digging.

"Because there are Russian atomic bombers coming," I said.

"Why?" she said. I stopped digging. I stood by the pile of dirt I had made. I put my foot on the dead bird. I remember thinking I had not imagined Sharon Fulton's voice.

"They are slow bombers," I said. I struck a pose by leaning on my shovel. Again, she asked why.

"Because they are very heavy," I said. "They have all this steel plate, and our fighters can't shoot them down because the bullets bounce off. We've been shooting at them for a week now, and nothing happens. They are over Hawaii and pretty soon they'll be over Guam." I made the rat-tat-tat sound of the .50 caliber machine-gun fire I supposed would come from the front end of an F-86 fighter.

I did this with a series of finger jabs meant to convey the bullets themselves, but which caused me to drop my shovel and shift my foot off the dead bird.

Sharon Fulton looked at the sky. She looked east, toward her school and mine. There was nothing but clear Kansas sky all the way to Kansas City.

"They are coming from the west," I said, and, after picking up my shovel, pointed toward our houses up the hill. "When they get here, they will black out the entire horizon. That's why you need an atomic bomb shelter. Otherwise when the radiation spreads, parts of us will become useless."

Sharon Fulton was crying. I am about to become a man who does not know what to do when women cry.

"You can't come into my atomic bomb shelter if you cry," I said. Sharon Fulton turned her back on me and walked away.

"Stern's sister took her pants down," I said. "For a dollar."

Sharon Fulton began running up the hill toward home, all yellow and lovely in my mind to this day.

At supper, my mother wanted to know if something was the matter. Grandmother White said she hoped I hadn't tried to dig up the washcloth with the found penny in it, because I'd get covered with warts just from touching it.

"Mother!" said my father. Here, he winked at me. As I didn't wink back, he said, "What's the matter, son?" I didn't know what to say.

And still don't.

Unless it is something to Sharon Fulton after all these years, and across what miles that separate us, I do not know: Yellow is still my favorite color. Even today, I don't know what to say to women who are to me now what you were to me then. I hear the sound of your voice. And the sound of your crying. If only you had fainted, I would have known what to do. My mother could never understand why I started being late for school. When Than burned down The Shed that winter, my letter to you went up in flames, but I remember every word of it—including the final sentence I added after you left me alone with my bomb shelter. It is code for all that I have written above, which I am now tapping out to you. Wherever you are. Whoever we have become.

It Puts Matters in Doubt
Here in Two Sleeps

"As I was saying," goes Bly Williams when some others come into the Side Room, "the only charge was for breaking up Bill Cody's statue. They didn't get Coda on assault. Or for wrecking the Fat-Girl's sports car. They didn't get the Fat-Girl for reckless driving. Or for nude driving, either. And they didn't get Holman for anything of what he did at the Big Chief Motel." Bly stops and takes a pull on his Coors. "That was mostly moral stuff at the motel and they can't get you on morals unless they got pictures."

Bly is holding forth in the Side Room at Rats, which is the gas station–grocery store here in Two Sleeps. It's called Rats because Bly—who owns the place—sells muskrats, skinned and cleaned, for only a dollar. We're called Two Sleeps because it's that many days' walk for the Indians at the Reservation. Bly and his wife live upstairs.

It is afternoon and there are a dozen of us sitting on the benches that line the walls of the Side Room. There are no tables, but at the west end of the room is a beer cooler—a long low chest where Bly sits to toss you a beer when you're dry. At the other end is the only chair, its back to the window that looks out onto the dirt street. Nobody's sitting there.

We are drinking beer and eating peanuts in the shell, tossing the shells on the floor. Some of us are eating sandwiches made by Bly's wife; she runs the grocery business in the room next door. In the case next to the blood red tray of muskrats are loaves of lunch meat and yellow squares of cheese. Mrs. Williams will make the sandwich you want—even put a garden onion on it in summer. A tomato, too.

Although now, late in the year as it is, the tomatoes are tight little pale green balls sitting in the sun on the shelves in the front window next to the shotgun shells. The onions are braided up behind the post office window and don't have the hots to them like when they come out of the garden the same day. You get your peanuts in a large paper cup from Mrs. Williams; you get your beer from Bly when you walk into where we are.

"Holman told me he knew it was Coda at the door by the point of the Queen Steel," says Bly. "He said he heard something rattling around outside and then whap/whap, Coda put the knife through the door twice. The second time she left it there and Holman knew that was his Queen Steel with the tip snapped off from prying at some traps the day before. Odd how you notice little things when your back is to the wall," says Bly.

He gets off the beer cooler and tosses Galvin Barlow a Coors in a can. Galvin has given Bly the high sign: you shake the empty in the air before you throw it in the oil drum trash can by the Riverside stove. The thing about Bly is that he knows the kind of beer you drink, right down to a long-neck or a short-coupled one in bottles, or a stubby-boat over a long-rod in cans. He keeps track of how many you drink and you pay him when you leave. Or whenever.

"I say thank you, thank you," says Galvin, whose way of talking is to say everything a couple of times. "I say thank you," he says once again as he pops the top and sucks off the foam you always get when a beer is tossed.

We all know the story Bly is telling, and we know the man he's telling it on. We know the man, and we know his wife. Some of us even know the other woman. Or claim we do. It's hard to tell the truth around here. Holman Kavanagh's the man. Coda's his wife;

she works at Fowler's in Charlton selling work clothes, but she and Holman live west of here six miles on three sections of pasture that's full of ponds. It's where the water-haulers for the oil wells go, and it's where some of us trap the muskrat Bly has in his case. In fact, Holman's ponds are the best we've got in this country. Bass. Perch. Channel Cat. Ducks in winter. Quail around the edges, and pheasants in the draws below the dams. Swimming in summer.

The Fat-Girl (who isn't really fat—that's only a term we use here when a woman is pretty and we'd like to make spoons with her) is a teacher at Dictionary Elementary 10 miles straight south of Charlton. Two Sleeps is nothing but Bly's place, broken down corrals, and a loading chute by the tracks where the train doesn't come through anymore. We're not on the map.

The Fat-Girl's name is Double Beth Johnson. She's from Arkansas where they give two names to everybody: Beth Lu, Beth Anne. But Double Beth didn't have two names to go with her southern accent, so for a while (the story has it) she was called Beth-Beth. It turned into Double Beth somewhere along the way. She's one of the firmest Fat-Girls we've got.

"They don't make doors the way they used to," says Bly. "In the old days a knife wouldn't have had a chance in a woman's hand against a door. I doubt myself I could get a Queen Steel through that door." He points his head toward the door we use to go out back and water the wind. "Holman said that as well. When Coda stabbed the door through twice he said it sure was too bad they didn't make them as stout as they used to. The door was hollow. Nothing but veneer over air. That'll put your privacy in doubt," says Bly.

"The lock wasn't much better, for that matter," says Bly. "It gives way the first time Coda puts her body to it. Double Beth grabs the motel's blanket with the chief's head right in the middle and runs for the bathroom. That was just prior to her jumping out the window of said bathroom." He gets a laugh from us here because he's poking a stick at the lawyer Gregg. We don't like Gregg much by himself, and we've come not to like lawyers at all.

"Which was just before said woman drove said car down said street through said town of Charlton in the said all together nothing," says Galvin Barlow. "The all together said nothing." We laugh more, and some of us give the sign that we want another beer. Shaking the empties is like a small applause for ourselves.

We get up to go to the cooler, stretch, look out the window. Some of us go into the other room to get another cup of peanuts. A Tool Pusher leaves: he has a long drive home before dark, and he can come back to Rats any day and pick up the rest of the story— although no doubt, like most of us, he's heard it through (in different versions) not a few times before. He might even return to a story about himself: we all know Bly tells them on us when we're not here. We don't mind. In fact, there is some pleasure in the thought. You get to be in two places at the same time. It's more than that, of course, but it's difficult to say what it is.

Bly resettles himself on the cooler and the rest of us take our seats along the walls.

"I think it's a sign of life," says Galvin Barlow, "a sign of life to do something worth Bly sitting here talking about it. I do."

"Look at it the other way around," says Bly. "Bill Cody's dead. All we got is that statue and those stories about Bill and my grandfather getting lost west out here for a week. Another thing: we'll all know it's over between us and Fat-Girls when there are more stories to tell than spoons to make. I'd rather have been Holman in the Big Chief than me here talking about it," says Bly. Some of the men say they would have liked to have been Holman knowing the looks of Double Beth, and how it turned out Holman didn't get cut or shot. "That's not the point," says Bly. But he doesn't go on about it. We can see that he is thinking. Presently he starts up again.

"When Coda hears Double Beth break out the bathroom window, she leaves off skinning Holman to run down the Fat-Girl.

But Coda doesn't use her car; she jumps into Holman's big four by four pickup just as Double Beth is tearing up the driveway onto Hickock Avenue. Coda makes a hard right through the ditch and catches Double Beth at the 15th Street intersection. That's when the bumper tag game begins: Whap. Whap. The canvas top pops open at the windshield. When Double Beth gets going again, she's a convertible and her Big Chief blanket is streaming out behind her and her considerable knockers are bouncing against the steering wheel. We know she turned the heads of the shoe clerks going downtown to the Toastmaster's Banquet." Bly stops so we can laugh. We have laughed here before. We know Bly's pauses. There is something friendly about the well-worn roads of a repeated story.

The wind rattles the window by the chair and somebody wonders out loud if we might be in for early bad weather. We have all noticed it is getting darker sooner these days—although there is still enough light to have a few more beers and hear the story to its end before it's dark.

"My guess is," Bly says, "that Coda bumps that sports car all the way down Hickock. About 10 bumps to a block, caving in the trunk with every bash until Double Beth takes a hard left into Library Park and loses it against Bill Cody and his horse."

We hear somebody come in the other room; there is some talk with Mrs. Williams that Bly waits to end. "As I was saying," goes Bly when a man (who turns out to be an Indian we know) comes into the Side Room, "the judge asks Coda in court how come she doesn't just ram the Fat-Girl's sports car head on? How come she backs into it by her own count 22 times? Backs into it." Bly stops here so we can see it in our mind's eye how Coda has run Double Beth's car into the base of Bill Cody's statue and then turns Holman's pickup around to crunch the sports car repeatedly against the huge block of marble that has Bill Cody's name and history carved on the side, and that holds Cody and his horse on top. We see Double Beth scramble on top of the driver's seat and pull herself onto the statue by grabbing one of the horse's legs. She takes her blanket with her, although we can see plenty of breast, thigh, and electric fuzz as she swings up behind Bill Cody on his horse.

"Coda tells the judge," Bly goes on, "that she'd been watching Demolition Derby on Channel Two that afternoon and they don't smash a car by running it frontways because that will break in the radiator of the rammer, and the rammee doesn't get the shaft as hard. So Coda puts Holman's truck into four-wheel drive and backs over the curb and pops the clutch 22 times. Double Beth's sports car comes to look like an Interstate toad it's so flat against the base of Bill Cody.

"Double Beth tells the judge the same number," says Galvin. "The same number. 22."

"She had the view," says Bly. "Sitting with Bill Cody on the back of his horse like they were riding double, that Big Chief blanket blowing in the wind. There weren't many times you could get a picture of her as decent as the one they printed in the paper."

Bly stops to give the Indian his beer. Others of us want another round. Somebody else goes out the back door for natural duty, and a pumper who works the Reservation says he's got to be heading home. We hear him pause for a moment in the outer room to ask Mrs. Williams if he's got any mail.

"Maybe I'm not young enough to have been Holman in the Big Chief," says Bly, looking past us out the window where the wind rattles it when the man returns through the back door. If we do get an early snow this year, Bly will be caught with his storms down—only the Side Room window doesn't have a storm anymore, and in recent years Bly's taken to putting up clear plastic which makes the winter light different from what you see in the windows in the other room. And different from the light you see outside through the open door.

We know this pause of Bly's well: somewhere in his stories

he'll debate whether he'd rather be its character or its teller. Not that he doesn't include himself at times. He's got a fine one about trying to tie down Buster Reynolds' balloon when he saw it coming along Buckeye Road. But that's another story. And even there, he'll stop just before he grabs the rope Buster's got hanging from the balloon basket and ask himself which end he'd rather be on. It's a question he's never settled, and we don't expect him to settle it this time.

"I asked Holman once," says Bly, "what he said when Coda came through the door and Double Beth was in the bathroom. What can a man tell his wife when he's caught full in the saddle at the Big Chief Motel with a Fat-Girl?"

"Not much to say," says Galvin. "Make something up, maybe. Maybe."

"Holman said he wasn't there," says Bly. "He said, 'I just disappeared.' He put the emphasis on 'dis.' Dis-appeared." Bly has our attention. He holds us with his look. We haven't heard this part of the story before.

"I don't think I know what he meant by that," says Bly, more to himself than to us. We hear someone come into the store, but whoever it is doesn't say much so we don't know who it is.

"I said to Holman," says Bly, "that I didn't see lying—if that's what he meant—would do much good. There you are getting it on with a Fat-Girl; said woman's car is parked out back where it blends in like a cock pheasant on a fence post; your truck is nosed right up to the motel room's door; and all in all you're about as subtle as two dogs on a playground. What's to lie about when Coda's standing in the doorway with your Queen Steel in her hand?"

"Not in her hand," says Holman from the store. We all jump a bit because we hadn't noticed him drive up. He walks into the Side Room with a big liverwurst sandwich in his right hand, a paper cup of peanuts balanced on top. He's holding his left hand open for a beer. "Not in her hand," Holman says again.

Holman is a big man: tall where Bly is short; lanky where Bly is husky. Both are men who seem to us not to have changed. Grown older, yes. But we can see from years ago their builds, their walks (Bly's two steps for Holman's one), and the shadows they throw in the morning light, and it all looks the same to us: only it is as if they both have walked all day to get here, and some grit in the wind has etched their faces and hands, thinned their hair—and gotten in their eyes and done something to them we cannot name.

Holman stands by the door while Bly gets off the cooler and holds a long-necked Coors by its top so Holman can take it on the move—like in the movies the marshal takes a rifle from the deputy holding it by the barrel.

"She'd left the knife in the door with the second whap," says Holman as he sits in the chair in front of the window. "And I didn't lie; I dis appeared by talk." He opens his eyes wide to let us think about that one. He takes a bite of his sandwich and then a pull from his beer. We are all looking at him.

"I said, 'Coda, this's not what you think it is.'"

That breaks the spell and we laugh. We've heard that one before. If that's what there is to dis appearing then we're all as good as government work at it. But Holman holds up his beer at us.

"I said," says Holman, "'I'm not here, Coda. You're not here. It's not what it looks like.' She starts to yell and goes to the door for the Queen Steel but I stop her by saying: 'Coda, I'm telling you again: I'm not here and you're not here. Nothing's here. Nothing.'" Holman takes his beer down from in front of his chin where he's been using it like a finger to hold our attention. He drinks off the neck to the label then goes on:

"Coda looks at me," says Holman, "and she says something I'd have to make up because I don't remember it. I do remember she's got the Queen Steel by now. But butter won't melt in my mouth and I say: 'I'm not going to tell you the Fat-Girl doesn't mean a thing to me. I'm not going to say me and the Fat-Girl are just friends.

414

Or that I wanted a quiet place to watch Demolition Derby and the Fat-Girl fell in bed by accident. That'd be lying, Coda. But I am telling you that we're not here in the Big Chief Motel. It isn't even a dream we're in, Coda. It's not like we're going to wake up after a nap after a nooner. I'm here to tell you I'm not here and neither are you. Nobody's here.'"

"What'd she say?" says Galvin.

"The Fat-Girl wrecked it for me or I think I'd have gotten the job done right there," says Holman. "But Double Beth hears me say 'nobody's here' and breaks the bathroom window jumping out to make it true. The noise disturbed the spell. That's when Coda fires the Queen Steel in my direction. No harm, though. I still have it." He pats his pocket.

"It didn't work then," says Bly. "Coda didn't believe you?"

"It worked like most things," says Holman. "After a fashion. It put matters in doubt. It would have been better had Double Beth not jumped through the window. Breaking glass sets women on edge." Holman drinks his beer. We all drink our beers.

"When I got Coda out of jail," Holman says, "I told her none of what happened at the Big Chief happened. I couldn't vouch for the rest of it because I wasn't there. But what started it didn't happen."

"What about the trial?" says Bly. "What about the story in the paper? What about the picture they printed of Double Beth on Bill Cody's horse with the Big Chief blanket over her knockers? What about it between you and Coda since then?"

"That's what nights are for," says Holman, and he points his thumb over his shoulder out the window. "You go to sleep and get up the next morning and you start over. Besides, pictures aren't real. Nor stories," says Holman looking straight at Bly. "You change things sitting on that cooler. I've heard you do it. First thing you know, we're not only not on the map, it's that we're not here at all. We flat ass dis appear in some story of yours." We are quiet for a moment. Around us the light is changing; it now seems to be slipping out the window behind Holman. "Do you tell Coda every day it didn't happen?" asks Bly.

"No," says Holman. "And I didn't tell her the judge wasn't there. I didn't tell her we didn't have a $500 repair bill down at Larkin's for what she did to the truck, and I didn't tell her how I settled up with Double Beth. Most things you let go by. Like treading water on one of my ponds."

"I can't swim," says Bly. We laugh at that; our laughter sputters and thins out. We are silent for a moment. It is a long, comfortable silence.

"We're getting old," says Holman to Bly, talking to him as if they are the only ones in the room. "If you push up daisies before me I'll claim you died trying to tread water in my big muskrat pond. Drowned and nobody's found you. The undertaker used a bum from Kansas City for the casket. Mrs. Williams weeps over the wrong grave. But the truth will be that the snapping turtles got you. The snapping turtles and the muskrats. You'll be in your muskrats, Bly, and we'll know because of the slight Coors taste to them for years afterward." Holman drains his beer. We are all pent-up grins.

"You want another one?" says Bly to Holman. They are smiling at one another like brothers who know something the rest of us don't.

"Does a hobby-horse have a hickory dick?" says Holman. But before Bly can get off the cooler Holman goes on:

"Bly," he says, "this is a trade we're in. That's the story I'm going to tell on you if you buy the farm first, but if I'm the first one to take the long nap, I want you to sit on that cooler and tell these men this: That I was caught with a Fat-Fat-Girl in Big Chief Motel just as I was before. I jump out of bed and say to Coda: 'Coda, it's not what you think. You got it all wrong. Let me explain: I'm not here.' And that," says Holman, "is the last time anyone ever saw me. I flat-assed dis appeared. Gone."

Bly gets off the cooler, shaking his head and smiling. Holman gets up and walks the length of the room while Bly fishes in the ice for a long-necked Coors.

"I believe I'll answer a call of nature," says Holman as he takes the beer from Bly the same way he did coming into the Side Room—as if he is going to get an outlaw with it.

When Holman pushes the door open, we can see that outside in the west there are heavy clouds, dark and down low. It will be evening before we thought it would be. The snap of the cold air that comes in as Holman goes out means that Bly might have to light the Riverside in the night.

"I've heard that story plenty of times," says Galvin, "but never with Holman telling it." Nobody has.

We drink our beers and get new ones while waiting for Holman to come back so we can hear more about Coda, Double Beth— or even some other Fat-Girl they say Holman's got now. But then maybe it's like he said; it isn't true what we tell on one another. Nor what we tell on ourselves.

Bly says he's been thinking about it lately: about men and women and the stories that come out of it all. About how, if you're a man, you'll never know when it is the last time between you and a woman, that from then on there will only be stories about it, like what's left of Bill Cody is the statue in Library Park with Double Beth riding behind him. But Holman's got it figured, says Bly. He'll know it's the last time if he's ever again in the Big Chief and he sees the point of his Queen Steel come through the door.

Too long goes by for Holman to be just watering the wind. Somebody says he must have drunk one of his ponds in beer to take so much time. But somebody else says it's a sign of age in a man when he can't piss when he feels he must, that in Kansas City in the bus station bathroom there will be a row of old men lined up waiting for their gadgets to work.

The Indian gets up and goes out the back door. When he returns he says no Holman's out there. Nobody's out there. God, it seems funny to us, and we laugh all around, although it's difficult to say why.

In My Stead

A farm back of a great plain tugs an end of the line.
—William Stafford

...old artificer, stand me now in good stead.
—James Joyce

It was Mother on the phone. She has called three times today, once waking me out of a sound sleep. "It is six in the morning, Mother. Do you know it is six in the morning where I live?" She might not. They live in Wolf, Kansas, a tiny town with the distinction of being on the Central/Mountain Standard Time line. Once, years ago, a man from the government stopped in Wolf to explain we could have whatever time we wanted: Mountain or Central. It was up to us. Well, it was up to the adults; I didn't have much to do with it. In any case, Mother took the government man to mean she could have any time she wanted on any given day—any given minute, really. She knows better, of course, but in a way she doesn't.

"I only fool around with an hour a day. One way or another," she says. That is true; it is also true that she is pretty good about honoring other people's time—the grade school's, for instance, where she teaches.

"You work for somebody, you work on their time," she says, sounding a bit like her brother Freckles, who always had an aphorism handy: "If you don't have time, you don't have talent." Uncle Freckles had more talent for alliteration than for sense.

"I can't talk about it at six in the morning, Mother," I had said earlier. "I don't care what time you thought it was, it is six in the morning in California. And I'm not going to talk about it while I'm half asleep." She wants me to come home. Aunt Hattie thinks we are related to the Pope and wants Mother and Aunt Rita to go with her to Krakow to find out. Then, of course, to Rome for an audience. We are Catholic—sort of. But that is only part of the story.

"Yes, Mother, I looked at the pictures in *Time* magazine, and I don't think Uncle Freckles looks like the Pope," I said. "I don't care what Aunt Hattie thinks. I doubt we are related." This assertion does not stop Mother—it wouldn't even slow down Aunt Hattie, who is the family genealogist. The truth is that while Uncle Freckles doesn't look like the Pope, I do: a round athletic look, like a soccer ball, or a pair of rolled-up wool hiking socks. I have the same open face. I just looked at it in the mirror. I even held up the Pope's picture next to my face, and mirrored brothers we were. He's older, of course. About the same age as my father, but if generations ago our Polish ancestors started us down separate futures, we (the Pope and I) have turned up alike—five thousand miles in between, twenty years apart, Polish and Irish/Polish, but pretty much family. Like related livestock.

"You'll see Buster all over the West," Uncle Freckles used to say about a great quarter-horse stallion he had at the ranch. "I've seen him in places where he hasn't been and where we've never bred him. I've seen him in Texas, that's how far away I've seen him. Same twitch in the nostrils like he has out here. Good horseflesh hops fast about." Dad wouldn't talk about the Pope as he is irritated that we are Catholic.

"No, I won't send the pictures to Sally," I told Mother this morning. Mother has been cutting out pictures of the Pope all week—cutting up the ten or so copies of *Time* or *Newsweek* that she can find there in western Kansas and sending them through the mails to our relations, now scattered across the state. "And don't send me any more," I said. "I have my own *Time* magazine. I have tons of *Time* magazines—a whole room full of them, Mother."

I don't have a whole room filled with *Time* magazines, but I do put them into the storage room in my garage. My ex-wife (Sally) gave me *Time* magazine a few years ago, and its subscription runs on after we've cancelled one another. Its Wednesday arrival reminds me of her, so I won't read it. I store it. I have my own subscription to *Time* magazine which, oddly, arrives on Thursdays. Mother thinks if I send Sally pictures of the Pope we will get back together. Mother doesn't understand. Mothers as a collective intelligence understand, but individual mothers never seem to know anything.

"I sent them to Rita," said Mother. Rita lives in South Bend— Mother's sister who married Uncle Charlie. Our family (if we are to believe Hattie about who is family) have scattered themselves like so many steers on the large pastures that stretch for miles behind Uncle Freckles' ranch house. I thought of this as I talked to Mother—of that huge open space that stretched out behind the ranch house, that reached in my mind's eye all the way to town where we lived, and made the small town tiny—even as we lived there—made it smaller as I grew bigger. And at the end of the phone wire as I talked to Mother, it seemed as if Wolf, Kansas, was as tiny as her voice. I am not convinced by the phone advertisements that tell us we can bring ourselves happiness (or our mothers happiness) by such calls. I don't keep in touch by long distance. Every time I talk to someone in a distant city, I think how right is the phrase "long distance," and how wrong the new phrase "keep in touch." I am out of touch with Mother, with Uncle Freckles, with Aunt Hattie, with Father, with Uncle Charlie, with Aunt Rita in South Bend, with the Pope in Rome. Sally's *Time* magazines pile up in the garage storeroom, and somewhere coded on the address slip is the date when it all will expire.

"Mother," I said in a firmer voice. "Mother, I've had enough of this nonsense. Let's say we are related to the Pope. Let us say that is true. O.K. That Aunt Hattie is right. As always. Right as the

Pope is Catholic. We are related to John Paul the Second. Strongly related." I paused as she slipped in something on me. "Yes, and that the men in the family look like him. Yes, stocky. Outdoorsmen. Let us say that is all true, Mother. So what?"

"I want you to come home," Mother said.

I live in La Jolla. La Jolla, California. I have lived here for twenty years now, and I rather like it. Not that I like everything about it, but there is plenty I do like: I don't know anybody—especially since Sally left. I don't have any grass to cut, much less a pasture to mow. The mad strangers who jog down the road in front of my house, and the quick gays who run the beach in back, remind me of the freeways I drive to El Toro and my job. I don't like my job (I rather like that). I have to drive five miles if I want a pack of cigarettes—which I never want because I don't smoke. I can't tell the time of year, and so like Mother, I move time around. Right now I'm thinking it is spring, although I know by the Saturday television listing that it is fall football weather in my remote-controlled Sony.

I even like my condominium; I am fond of its redwood and stone facade that is nearly indistinguishable from the seventeen other condominiums that line the curved streets of our tiny compound. It is hard to know where I live unless I'm at home. Once, the first day after I'd moved in, I drove down to San Diego and back again—just for the ride. When I came back, it occurred to me I didn't really know which place was mine—not really. One "sculptured roadway" led into another. One "sea view bungalow" looked like them all; all "gems of gentle living" looked alike. My automatic garage door opener might distinguish, I reasoned. I drove around the "sculptured roadways," my finger on the remote control button clipped to my sun visor, looking for an opening door, a garage agape. It worked; I advise it. If you don't know where you live, let your garage door opener lead you in—just like radar. I eased my BMW down a fifty-yard straight-away, over a speed bump, into a curve, and out of a curve, just in time to spot a distant garage door gliding open. Home. Of sorts.

Mother's point is that over the years—the previous twenty—I've not gone home, not left California, not left La Jolla unless you count my drives to work (or my weekend drive to San Diego). Not for Christmas, not for Thanksgiving, not for birthdays, not for deaths. Not for nothing.

"Is it Saturday there in Kansas?" I asked her when she called for the third time this morning.

"Of course," she said. "Why would you ask?"

"Because on Saturdays here in California there are football games on television. And I am going to watch one, and I don't want you to call me.

"The Notre Dame game?" she asked. Notre Dame is the only team she knows.

"Yes, the Notre Dame game. I'm going to watch it if I don't spend from now until the final gun talking to you."

"I just want to make sure you understand about coming home when Hattie, Rita, and I go to Rome," she said.

"I don't understand about it," I said. "I haven't thought about it. I'm not going to think about it until after the Notre Dame game."

The truth is I don't watch football. Not anymore. I used to watch it a lot when I was married, but once, when I saw the same play happen over again, I quit watching. I don't mean a play like an "end around," or a "down and out." I mean I saw the same kind of accidental violence: the very same flight of the ball, the same popping of people, the burst of dust as they tumbled into what had been an infield during the summer baseball days, the same referee dash into the left side of the screen only to get the ball tossed out of the pile at him a bit harder than he'd expected—the whole scene was played out again as if it had been an instant replay, only it wasn't that—it was two plays five years apart. I don't know if I quit watching because it was getting dull, or because I was spooked. I don't like to think that one past is a replay of a previous past, much less think the present is. I quit watching. Even Notre Dame. Even though I look like the Pope. Instead, I watch the gays run up and down my beach. The gays and the metal detector army with their sand scoops hanging over their shoulders like grenades. Maybe I should call South Bend and see if Notre Dame is playing. Either that or drive five miles to get a paper.

"Hattie says she won't go and leave Dad and Freckles alone," Mother said. "They're getting old, you know. You better come home. Rita wants Charlie to come here to Wolf. All you men could be alone together again."

"I don't think we've ever been all alone together, Mother. No 'again' about it."

"Hattie would know," Mother said. "She'd have it in her log." That's true. The family log. Hattie has everything in the family log. If Hattie insists we are related to the Pope, chances are pretty good we are.

It is summer: August, Kansas. I am riding in Aunt Hattie's Studebaker Commander as we drive east out of Wolf toward Jetmore. At Lowe we could turn south and go down through Holcomb and then on to Garden City and catch Highway 156, but Hattie travels the roads of Kansas with an eye toward family history, and not toward speed. We will turn left at Lowe and drive the dirt road north through Tennis, Friend, and Shallow Water until we reach Scott City and Highway 96 that will take us east toward Topeka.

"Tennis was named for one of your Scottish ancestors," Aunt Hattie is saying as we drive along. In a few miles she will say that Shallow Water was named by a "shoestring ancestor," but before that she'll say something about tennis being the sport of kings.

"Not that your ancestor was a king," she says, "although they say tennis is the king's sport. I'm surprised he didn't name the place

Golf, knowing what I know now of him." We drive on toward Friend and Shallow Water.

"A shoestring ancestor is one we don't feel certain about. The lines are blurry. Certain claims can be made, but we are not positive," she says as we drive through Shallow Water. I have heard it all before, and I am only fourteen. By definition, all "ancestors" are dead. "Relations" and "relatives" are alive, but ancestors, shoestring or bootstrap, are dead. At Scott City we turn east.

I am going with Aunt Hattie because it will be good for me, and because some of the cowboys at Uncle Freckles' ranch invited me to go to Santa Fe where they will get drunk and buy whores. It has been judged that I am too young to go to Santa Fe. I am in trouble because I was even asked, and that kind of trouble can be cured by a good dose of Aunt Hattie and one of her trips to the Kansas Historical Society in Topeka. Some cowboys talk too much.

Aunt Hattie is a methodical driver: slow, alert, always checking in the rear-view mirror, slowing down at unmarked intersections, stopping at yield signs and railroad crossings. She is dangerous.

In those days she drove a standard shift, but the car she has now, and has had for some time, is an automatic. Her driving technique in the automatic is legendary: she puts her left foot on the power brake and puts her right foot on the accelerator, halfway to the floor. The poor car shudders to go, but the brakes are too strong, and so it sits trembling with power. When Hattie wants to go, she releases the brake. Uncle Freckles calls it constant-speed driving.

"The rpm's are always the same," he will say. "About four thousand. Some people pop clutches; Hattie, she pops that brake." Hattie's car leaps along like a jack rabbit. In Garden City you better watch out as the stop lights and yield signs only aggravate the problem. Young men there thought Hattie wanted to drag race, her car would be roaring so at the stoplight. By sight (a maroon Studebaker leaping along the streets) and sound (the throttled roar of a V-8 engine) Garden City knows when Hattie is in town.

But back when I rode with her that August her Studebaker was a standard shift, and all she would do by way of damage was grind the gears as she'd miss second every time, hitting a piece of reverse on the way up. Then she'd panic a bit and wait before she'd shift into third. Maybe twenty miles would go by in second: Scott City to Amy (named after an ancestor on my father's side).

"You better shift," I say as we drive along. Aunt Hattie won't respond if she is being criticized.

We are going to Topeka this Friday so that Aunt Hattie might spend Saturday in the Kansas Historical Society. There she will look through bound newspapers for more evidence that our family existed: married, gave birth, got rowdy, bought farms, sold businesses, got jailed, had birthdays, died. It is all in the newspapers of the tiny towns that have somehow been trapped in the Historical Museum—not unlike, I think, the towns themselves are trapped on the great sweep of prairie that we are now crossing: Dighton, Ness City, Rush Center, Albert (a great uncle), Great Bend.

"Highway 156 is the Santa Fe Trail," Hattie says. We join it at Great Bend, the same highway we did not take out of Garden City, and when we meet up with it again, I feel as if we are getting somewhere.

"Your ancestors traveled the Santa Fe Trail, and they stayed right here in Kansas," Hattie says. I know all this from school.

In Topeka we will stay with "relations." Relations are different from "relatives," although both will be "ancestors" when they die. Relations have been discovered by Aunt Hattie in her endless search in the Kansas Historical Society. Relatives are those people we knew in the first place: Rita, Mother, Uncle Charlie in South Bend, me in a car with Hattie, or in my condominium in La Jolla. Relatives are not "family," however. Family is only Mother's side of the family, for Hattie and Rita and Mother are sisters. Freckles is a brother, and so while other kids at the school had aunts and uncles who were married to each other, I had an aunt and uncle who were not. Aunt Rita in South Bend is family, but Uncle Charlie and Dad are not. I am family: the only child on my mother's side, the only one at all on my father's side, save for Dad himself. I am the end of the road.

The "relations" we will stay with in Topeka have been stayed with before. They have a third-floor room for us. There is a brown davenport for me, a brass bed for Aunt Hattie. The house is on Gage Street, and their name is Browning: Linda and Hazen Browning, and they had been living peacefully on Gage Street for ten years before they were discovered by Aunt Hattie one rainy spring afternoon in the Kansas Historical Society. She traced them through the Eskridge papers right to Gage Street. That was fifteen years ago, and by the time I am fourteen and making this August trip with Hattie I have stayed with the Brownings a number of times. They always seem like strangers to me, and it always seems as if Aunt Hattie is a stranger to them. Relations, I conclude, can never become relatives. We have relations all over Kansas—a kind of network of family rooms where Aunt Hattie stays when she is on the family's trail. She has made herself at home in Burr Oak (a barber related to us through the Irish branch) and in Esbon (the local feed merchant found Hattie poking through the company's back room looking for records in hopes of nailing down our exact relationship to the great railroad families of Nebraska that, Mother claims, were models for a Willa Cather novel).

"You can stay in any county in Kansas," says Aunt Hattie to me as we drive along toward Topeka. "A hundred and five counties in Kansas and we have a relation in every one." I keep quiet. "Don't ever think you're not at home. If you're in Kansas, you're at home, just like Freckles says." It is true that Uncle Freckles says that. It is also true that when Aunt Hattie took me to Topeka that August he went off to Santa Fe with his cowboys.

"I've pretty much finished finding us in Kansas," says Aunt

Hattie. She has down-shifted from overdrive. On those old Studebakers there was a handle you could pull that put it in overdrive, and after she'd take a long time in second gear to get to third, she would take even longer to get into overdrive. If you were a young man living in America in the 1950s, you were aware of all these things, as cars were as important as ancestors. Just now, on the road between Keene and Dover, late in the August afternoon, and forty-some miles out of Topeka, Aunt Hattie has taken the Studebaker out of overdrive. It is like letting down the flaps. She should have been a pilot.

"Mark this day," she says to me. "Tomorrow we start tracing us back east. I've kept notes and I know where to look," she says. "Everybody came from the East, and tomorrow we start going back." She checks the rear-view mirror. Behind her is an empty road, as empty as the one that stretches out in front of us. For on all the roads there are few cars, and all day long the only thing to see moving in the rear-view mirror is the heat from the asphalt. You can see that looking straight ahead.

"Do you think the Brownings like us?" I ask. Silence for twenty miles, and then a down-shift into second as we get within ten miles of Topeka. The landing gear.

"I even have a job for you," Aunt Hattie says. "You can make lists of the foreign countries. Put a country at the top and list names below." She pauses, checks again the mirror. The car whines along in second, its flaps and landing gear down. "Tomorrow marks a new beginning," she says, looking in the mirror down the road. It took her more than twenty-five years, but Aunt Hattie found us a relation in Rome.

"Mother," I said this morning, "let me tell you that Aunt Hattie has nothing to do but look for a Pope in the family. She has had nothing to do for forty years. For sixty years. For however-old she is years. She has had nothing to do. Ask Uncle Freckles. She never cooked a meal for him. She lived out on that ranch and ate his food and used his gasoline and drove his Studebakers and never did anything but get us a relation per county." I could tell Mother wasn't listening.

My guess was that she had laid down the phone on the kitchen table, just below where the phone hung on the wall. Not that Mother won't listen when she puts the phone on the table—it is just that she will listen to the phone as it talks from there. She will sit at the kitchen table, sip coffee, and listen to the phone talk. I've seen her do it a hundred times. What it takes, she will tell you, is a knowledge of human nature. And good ears. Mother prides herself on her hearing: "She can hear better than a buzzard," Uncle Freckles says of her, his alliteration clicking along, but with no special insight on the hearing of buzzards.

Mother claims she can tell when someone is likely to go into a long telephone speech, and then, she insists, there is no need to hold the phone to your ear. Not when you can drink your coffee. Besides, there is something more friendly about it this way. How can you talk to a person if you hold them to your ear? Mother's hearing is better than her logic.

"Mother," I said to her from the kitchen table, "Mother, what does it matter if we are related to the Pope? How can it be so important that you've called me once already this morning, and sent me a whole packet of *Time* magazine pictures?"

"We are going to Rome," she said from the kitchen table. "Hattie and Rita and I are going to Rome to see the Pope. I think you ought to come home and stay with the men."

I can see her in my mind's eye not looking at the phone as she delivers that declaration. Mother could look you in the eye any time she wanted to: she could tell you John Kennedy was dead and look you in the eye doing it—or tell you she knew you'd been sleeping with Tom Harris' wife, and look you in the eye, but when she made such declarations as this one over the phone, she wouldn't look at it. She'd look at the print of Albert Bierstadt's *The Wolf River, Kansas*, that we have hanging on the same wall with the phone. Mother made the art journals one year when, on a trip to Topeka with Hattie, she found a photograph in the Historical Society that Bierstadt had used to make the painting. Someone at the university in Lawrence sent her a print of the Bierstadt, and it has been hanging in the kitchen longer than the phone. It is the source of great pride, and great debate.

"Wolf River is up by Concordia," insists Dad, who came from that part of the state. "Up in Cloud County. You can check it on the map." Not all maps, but true enough, find a good one and you'll find Wolf River in Cloud County.

"You're wrong, wrong, wrong," claims Mother, whose family comes from Finney County. "It's the creek that flows through Freckles' place and into McKinny bottoms."

"That's Tessem Creek," says Dad.

"It's not on the map," says Mother. She has him there. No map has Tessem Creek—or even the creek on their minds. I know it, though, and once during a rainy summer built a small dam across it, flooding out some badger holes upstream.

"It isn't 'Tessem' we're living in," Mother says. "It's Wolf. It's Wolf, Kansas," she says. "And that creek is Wolf River."

When she gets mad like that she'll go around the house and change all the clocks back or forward an hour, depending upon her mood.

"It's not on the map," says Dad.

"Neither are we," says Mother.

"Some maps, no," says Dad. "Rand McNally has us. Always has."

"No population, though. It says Wolf, Kansas, 'no pop.'"

"Show me a good map, and I'll show you a meandering life," Uncle Freckles will say if he is there. For years that Bierstadt has been the source of squabbles and time changes around the house.

"The only reason you are going to Rome is to get me to come

home," I said to Mother earlier this morning. "And besides, it's not Rome; it's the Vatican where the Pope lives. That's a different place. You have to go to Rome and take a taxi to the Vatican. Check your map." I paused. "I'm not coming home."

One reason I won't leave is because of my routine. I'm settled in, and I don't much want to get unsettled. I come home from work in the evenings, and over the years I've gotten accustomed to seeing some of the same cars on the freeway going south out of Los Angeles. It is a long drive from El Toro to La Jolla, sixty miles, right on the nose, from the end parking spot in the company lot to the lock washers I have hanging from my garage ceiling to clank against my windshield as a signal that I've got my BMW in just far enough to close the door, and yet get around it back and front.

I take S-18 west from work less than a mile, then catch I-5 south toward San Clemente. If I am on time (and I usually am), I see two other BMW's making the turn onto 5. One is blue, the other a light gold—both are the same stubby model as mine, and both have sunroofs. We have never acknowledged one another, but many nights we have reached the on-ramp there at El Toro together: one, two, three BMW's going points south. The blue one gets off at Capistrano Beach, but the pale gold one stays with me until Cardiff-by-the-Sea. A mile a minute, we all want to make on 5 going south. A mile a minute, and the washer on the string from the ceiling of my garage clanks against the windshield at 6:05. Twenty-five minutes to read the paper, make a drink (Creme de Cassis and white vermouth), and settle down with Walter Cronkite.

But before I get to Walter Cronkite, I have plenty of check points to pass from El Toro to La Jolla. I time myself with my cassette tape deck. If I am not at Oceanside by the time Barbara Streisand is singing "The Way We Were," then I am running late. I have made a tape; it is a kind of musical history of my life. But not in chronological order. I mix it up so that I scatter my years along the road.

It is better that way because a line of a life is too straight to seem real. So my tape may play a song I knew in my early college days and follow it by one I heard when I first came out here: "Happy Days Are Here Again" and then "Alfie" (at the San Onofre Beach exit). "What's it all about, Alfie?"

I leave the parking lot with "The Seine" (the Kingston Trio) going, and by the time I meet the other BMW's, Peter, Paul, and Mary are singing "Lemon Tree." And so it goes as I go south each night; nearly every year of my life recorded in popular songs. I think it is important to keep memory alive. And routine. Routine is the fastener of memory, like nails in a board fence that runs back all the length of your life. I believe this. I think to myself as I drive home with Michel Legrand's version of "The Last Time I Saw Paris" playing (it marks the Leucadia turnoff), I think to myself that I can't go back to Kansas and disturb my routine, and disturb my sense of what to remember. It would be like tampering with life. And as I come into my compound and push the button on my sun visor that will raise my garage door and nobody else's garage door, I think that these nails of memory must be hammered in every day or else there will be nothing in the future to recall. As I sit in my garage, and as the door drops down behind me and makes me feel snug, I let the tape play out, and if I have run my course true and on time, I will be listening to John Denver singing "Leaving on a Jet Plane"—something I won't have to do as long as I can hear the song—and see in my mind's eye those big Boeings leaving for Denver, Kansas City, Rome.

"If you won't come home for me, then come home for Aunt Rita," Mother said. "You like Aunt Rita, and she feels it is very important that someone stay with Charlie. She won't leave him in South Bend. Come and stay with him here. Do that for Aunt Rita," Mother said.

It is true I like Aunt Rita. She tells stories. She has a story about how I became Catholic. She tells it all over South Bend. She has another story about how she attacked Knute Rockne and G. K. Chesterton with her front porch broom.

Aunt Rita is the only one of the family to leave Kansas. Me, of course. Rita left in the twenties with a traveling shears salesman (Uncle Charlie). We always call "scissors" "shears" in my family, and my first memory of being embarrassed came in school when I asked my art teacher—a woman, who now that I think of it looked something like Greta Garbo—asked her for shears. Where did you get that word, she wanted to know, and repeated it to the class. It was almost as embarrassing as the Studebakers my family drove (still drive). Everybody else drove Fords, or Chevrolets, or International Harvester trucks. But not my family. Studebakers. It is tough to be a rugged individualist when you are ten and have an art teacher who looks like Greta Garbo.

All this was after Rita had left with the traveling shears salesman and made her way to South Bend, where she lived on North Studebaker Street, and where the salesman stopped selling shears and started assembling Studebakers. That's how we started driving Studebakers: through Uncle Charlie we got a good deal. We'd get one every two years, a truck for the ranch on the even-numbered years, and a car for in town on the odd. Father and Freckles would drive to South Bend every fall and trade in the truck or car, and come back with a new one. They couldn't trade them in Garden City or Great Bend as nobody would have them. Besides, the men loved the trip. It wasn't like going to Santa Fe, but it was like going someplace.

All these Studebakers caused me problems. When Studebaker decided to build cars that looked pretty much the same from the front and the back, I came in for some pretty stiff ridicule in Garden City. They were the cars that didn't know which way they were going, and from then on it was a great joke around my high school that our family didn't know which way it was going. That pretty much kept up through the years, and the only thing that calmed it down was Aunt Hattie's leap-along driving technique that came in with automatic transmissions. I think my classmates figured if they quit teasing me, maybe the great god of the Kansas prairie would spare them the ugly death of being run over by a lurching Studebaker Commander.

Nonetheless, throughout my youth there was this stream of Studebakers, and what always bothered me was that I knew that more were coming, one a year: a truck, then a car, then a truck—the only variation was that in the late fifties Mother claimed one of the used cars at the end of two years, and so when Dad and Freckles drove it back to South Bend that fall, they brought it back again. I remember thinking that the extra Studebaker made Finney County seem out of balance in some way I didn't understand. It remains so to this day, because when Studebaker quit making cars and trucks some time ago, there was a family decision to keep the last set we had: a car, a truck, and that used one that Mother had claimed. I remember there was a great buying of spare parts in those days, and one last trip to South Bend for one last truck, and a bed load of parts.

"I didn't care who they were," says Aunt Rita when she tells her Knute Rockne story. "They were drunk, all five of them drunk, and I didn't want those drunks in my house." So she beat them about the head and shoulders with her ubiquitous broom.

Rita is not only the storyteller in the family, she is the tidy one—the one with an indoor broom, a basement broom, and a porch broom.

"Those brooms got us through the Depression," she will say, meaning that cleanliness and frugality are pretty much the same thing in her eyes. It is that way with the rest of the family, also. Slivers of soap are stored in a wooden box in the basement in Wolf.

Mother still waters down the ketchup and the shampoo. Christmas wrapping paper gets used over and over again, and woe to the one who tears a hole in it.

"I pour the goddamn ketchup all over the table," I've heard Dad yell plenty of times as he's dumped half a bottle of water and ketchup onto his noontime hamburger. "We made thirty thousand dollars on steers last year and I can't find a thick ketchup bottle in the house. Goddamn, goddamn, goddamn." That goes head-to-head with Mother's "You're wrong, wrong, wrong."

"The house was clean top to bottom," Rita says in her story. "I had a new roll on the player piano, and a rabbit cut up for frying. And down the street come Charlie and your dad and Freckles, plus these two others, just awful drunk. All drunk. I can tell when Charlie is drunk by the way he throws his coat over his shoulder. Sober, it's right hand over right shoulder; drunk, it's left hand over right shoulder." The truth is that nobody need be that observant to see when Uncle Charlie is drunk; I've seen him drunk a few times, and the give-away signs are that he slobbers a bit when he talks, and he is apt to break into his version of "Galway Bay" (which tends to sound like Richard Crooks' version of "Jerusalem"), and that he can't walk straight at all, bumping into—in this case—the men on either side of him so, as they came down North Studebaker Street, Uncle Charlie was no doubt singing, slobbering, and staggering. Where he had tossed his coat is more a matter of Aunt Rita's fiction than Uncle Charlie's fact.

"I knew where they had been," says Rita. "Charlie was singing "Galway Bay."

Where they had been was Uncle Charlie's speakeasy—a fake butcher shop with a moldy pork chop in the meat case that you passed by in order to get through the back door and into the bar. It is Prohibition. It is the Depression—1930 to be exact. Uncle Charlie has been laid off at Studebaker and has taken to shooting rabbits in the morning and running the bar in the afternoon. Aunt

Rita taking in laundry with Mrs. Tuti—the next door neighbor. Mrs. Tuti supplies the wash machine, the basement, and the soap. Aunt Rita supplies the transportation and two strong arms for the work. Mrs. Tuti has only one strong arm. The other has been caught by the electric wringer of the wash machine, and because of Mrs. Tuti's conversion to Christian Science the year before, the arm has been left in God's hands (to wither), so that by the time Uncle Charlie and his crew are coming down North Studebaker Street this October afternoon in 1930, Mrs. Tuti's arm is more or less like a piece of beef jerky, the kind Uncle Freckles likes so much—in fact cures for himself, out of his own steers.

"A man's teeth ought to be good enough to jerk the jerky," he'll say as he bites down halfway up a strip, and then with his right hand gives it a good hard pull—the half in the hand popping free.

"Don't you come up here, you drunks," says Aunt Rita from the front porch. With Uncle Charlie is Dad and Freckles, plus Rockne and Chesterton. All very drunk.

"I won't have it," says Rita from the porch, getting more shrill. "I won't have a mess of drunks in my house when you haven't even cleaned the rabbits you shot this morning. Charlie, you take that bunch back where you came from." Probably the thought of those uncleaned rabbits going to waste because Charlie didn't clean them provoked Aunt Rita as much as all those drunks approaching her porch.

"They just kept right on coming. Right up the sidewalk, with Charlie leading them in singing 'Galway Bay.' I said he better stop right there and not come up the stairs to the porch or I'd be sure and bust him over the head with the broom."

It is more than the rabbits and more than Charlie being drunk. In part it is the singing, which is no doubt pretty bad. Aunt Rita has the player piano going in the living room, and out through the screen door are coming the notes of some song she likes. Dad and

Uncle Freckles have driven up that week to get a Studebaker—
Charlie can still get a deal on them, even though he has been laid
off for a spell. Rita has the house clean, dinner going, and some
music (a Rudy Vallee tune) keeping her company as she sweeps the
front porch and looks forward to having the men come home for
dinner. I know Aunt Rita. She likes to make plans, and she likes to
see them work out just her way. She won't let you change a thing
in one of her stories, even if you know better.

"Well, Charlie just kept coming on up the sidewalk, singing
away," says Aunt Rita. "Your dad and Freckles started to hang back
a bit, and Rockne and Chesterton, they stopped on the city sidewalk and didn't make the turn into the yard. Knute Rockne wasn't
a great football coach because he was dumb," says Aunt Rita. "He
knew a good offensive when he saw one."

"You didn't know he was Rockne," says Freckles. "Not then."

"That's true," she says. "Not that I hadn't heard enough about
him from Charlie. Maybe I wouldn't have busted him had I known
who he was," she says.

"Is it true you once threw lemons at Rudy Vallee?" I say to Aunt
Rita, knowing it is, and that she likes to brag about it.

"Me and girls from St. Mary's," she says. "He wouldn't sign our
autograph books. One of the girls' fathers ran the paper, and he
put lemons all around Rudy Vallee's picture in the next day's front
page. That's where all that started about Rudy Vallee's being a
sourpuss. Right there in South Bend," Rita says. "One of my lemons hit, too."

Charlie is still coming up the sidewalk, singing "Galway Bay,"
and he doesn't know that Dad and Freckles are not coming up the
steps with him.

"I banged Charlie good and hard. A whop right on his head, and
then he stopped singing and tried to grab for the broom." Dad says
Charlie staggered back into their arms.

"One of those men on the city sidewalk started laughing, so I went after them as well." Rockne and Chesterton freeze in front of a parked truck.

"Your dad says I poked him in the stomach with the broom handle," says Aunt Rita. "But that isn't true. I went straight for those two big dudes on the city sidewalk that were laughing at me. Something in me said these guys were pretty smug, and it wouldn't do the world no harm for them to have a few broom lumps growing on their scalp." If giving up the high ground of her porch is a piece of poor strategy, the swiftness and surprise of the attack on Rockne and Chesterton is good strategy. Caught by the audacity of the act, they can't get away, and in a moment Aunt Rita has them pinned against a brand new Studebaker pickup truck that is pointed down the street toward Kansas.

"I backed them into that truck, and they covered up, and I let them have it. Then they quit laughing." But the attack costs Aunt Rita her broom. Chesterton and Rockne are covered with straw, the broom is bald, and with one final blow that either lands square on the coach's head, or square on the truck bed, or square on the writer's head, the broom breaks.

"I missed them both and hit the truck," says Rita.

"She hit Knute Rockne right smack in the forehead," says Dad. "It broke the broom in half. Not that there was much left of it."

"That writer whose book we got around here," Uncle Freckles say, "got whacked right smart in the side of the head with that broom of Rita's. That's why she tells so many stories to this day. Hit a writer, be a writer," Uncle Freckles will say.

Uncle Charlie is down and out and doesn't see a thing. "Too much straw in my face, but I heard the broom crack, and I knew we had her then." Uncle Charlie has had some experience with Aunt Rita and her brooms.

"Five drunks against one woman, that's about a fair fight, and if my broom hadn't broke, I would have won," says Rita. By now Mrs. Tuti from next door is outside, as are most of the people up and down North Studebaker Street—all standing in their front lawns looking over at 521 and scattered straw and splintered wood, not to mention five men pretty much scattered and splintered themselves.

"Before they got me, I chased off Rockne and Chesterton," says Rita. "No sense in letting strangers see a family fight."

"She went after them with her bare hands," says Dad.

Uncle Charlie won't say much on the subject, only that over the years he and Rockne had shared plenty to drink down at the butcher shop, and that Rockne was showing around Chesterton that fall day in 1930 and just naturally stopped by Charlie's for a drink. One thing led to another, and Charlie got to thinking what a fine mess of rabbits he had at home for them all to eat.

"The writer gave Charlie one of his books," says Rita as a way of dealing with Charlie's silence on the subject. "I sent it back with the boys one trip," she says. That is true, and an autographed copy of *The Secret of Father Brown* is the only coffee table book we own. "Rockne, he sent me two tickets to the 1930 football season up at Notre Dame," says Rita. "I think it was his way of saying he was sorry he was drunk. Charlie wasn't sorry, were you, Charlie," says Aunt Rita. Uncle Charlie will only say that he never again saw Rockne, that the man never came back into the bar—although Chesterton once did, to give him the book.

"I went and saw all those games without Charlie," says Rita. "He wouldn't go. He'd just go down to the butcher shop and drink. After every football game I had to come home to a drunk. I took Mrs. Tuti," Rita says.

"That book was a bunch of detective stories," Uncle Freckles will say. "About a priest who is a detective. Sort of like Sherlock Holmes." Uncle Freckles has never read Sherlock Holmes, and in fact the total scope of his culture might be *The Secret of Father Brown* on the literary side, and Albert Bierstadt's *Wolf River* on the graphic arts side.

By all accounts Dad, Charlie, and Freckles dragged Aunt Rita kicking and screaming into the house, while Knute Rockne and G. K. Chesterton ran on down the street, broom straw in their hair and maybe even a lump or two beginning to sprout.

"It took us a while to calm her down," says Dad.

"Mrs. Tuti came over and beat on them with some wet towels we were doing for the Monsignor, but she'd have needed both arms to do much good."

"She didn't calm down until we cleaned the rabbits," Uncle Freckles says. "Not until we started eating, really."

"That's our fame," says Rita. "That book we got, that lemon I hit Rudy Vallee with, and those tickets Knute Rockne sent me. She pauses here. "That was a good thing Rockne did. I think about it now, and I wish I hadn't spent those tickets. I just handed over a little history at the gate there every Saturday that fall. Never even kept the stubs." She pauses again. "He died that spring," she says. That, and the story of how I became Catholic are well known in the family, and in fact, after my sophomore year at the university, Rita will tell her Knute Rockne story by prefacing it with my Catholic conversion story.

I have two phones in my condominium. One in my bedroom on a table by the bed. The other on a wall between the kitchen and the living room. The living room has sliding glass doors which open onto a small patio that has a low wall over which I can see to the beach below. In the other direction, out of my rather large kitchen window, I can see the road that passes my compound and parallels the beach. In a very real sense these are my windows on the world, and nearly every day I see out of them some pantomime of life, as when, for the fun of it, I switch on my remote-controlled television but do not turn on the sound, and then to amuse myself talk aloud the parts of the characters on the screen. What news Walter Cronkite has reported when such a mood strikes me after my hour ride home; what jokes Johnny Carson has told in his monologue late at night from my rosewood and leather Danish swivel chair. What madness this all would be declared if there were a window on my world through which my mother could look and see and hear. But there is not. In a sense I live behind one-way windows, as we all do here in California. My condominium is at the very point of the compound, the only one surrounded on three sides by the public; for that reason it was cheaper, and I have paid less over the years for something I rather like: a view of the world. I have grown accustomed to the people who pass by my window. I grow old with them, especially the old ones, the ones who walk up and down the beach with metal detectors. The geriatric beach bums: rear admirals taking double retirement checks from the government, plus Social Security, plus stock checks from an aerodynamics company of which they became vice president when they retired. Plus a pension from that company, all the pluses adding up to fifty thousand dollars a year, enough to afford the finest metal detectors on the market. Up and down the beach they go in search of gold watches and silver dollars, and all they find are roach clips used by the California joggers who sprint past them, up and down the beach.

Through my window I see the scenes of conflict played out between these groups, each having in a sense landed on this stretch of beach, each having brought into the battle equipment and reinforcements. I've played out a few of the scenes on weekends when all there was to watch on the silent Sony were golf tournaments or football games. Not much there for a dialogue man like myself.

"The beach isn't big enough for both of us," one Navy wife says to herself as she sits on my compound wall, her metal detector leaning against the steps that lead up to the road. "I almost got run down twice this morning."

She looks out over the beach; her husband, his shoulders slumped against the weight of his double-yoked heavy duty metal detector, is trying to cut across traffic to join his wife.

"John is too old for this," she mutters. "It's madness out there." John approaches, his twin scoops, one small, one large, hanging from his collector's pouch, bumping his legs. Speedy twin gays race past him, one breaking to the ocean side, the other splitting off in front of him.

"Punks," says the admiral as he stalks across the sand toward his wife. "Punks everywhere you look. When we were stationed here during the war, it was quiet and respectable," he says.

"The biggest excitement," says the wife, "was the day the little boy found a Navy mine that had washed ashore, and you went down to the beach and disarmed it." She smiles with pride.

"Well, I called somebody to disarm it," the retired admiral says. He pauses and shakes his head at the traffic up and down the beach. "Did you hear what those punks did to Eddie Cooper?" he says to his wife.

"What happened to Eddie Cooper?" says the admiral's wife.

"His legs are bad," says the admiral. "You know that." She does. "Full of shrapnel from Iwo Jima. He can't stand any change of season." The admiral and his wife both look at the sea. "Marines," says the admiral.

"What happened?" says his wife.

"Queers got him," says the admiral. "Ran him down. Just ran right into him, and Eddie couldn't get up. Busted his walker. His wife was out of sight. She had gone down to meet him at the old hotel. Eddie's rolling around in the sand all crippled up and he can't right himself. Those punks." The admiral waves his hand at a convoy of joggers roaring south down the beach. "Those punks ran right by him. Never stopped to help." The admiral is having a difficult time getting out of his gear he is so mad.

"I found him," says the admiral. "I was coming up the beach, and I saw Eddie there in the sand. A hero at Iwo Jima. Marine Corps. First landing. And not a queer on the beach would give him a hand." The admiral is out of his gear; he has unbuckled himself from it like I have seen in the movies men get themselves out of parachutes. Scoops and the metal detector are leaning against the stairs. The admiral's wife readjusts the metal detector so that it won't fall down. The admiral looks out across the sand to the ocean.

"I didn't fight in the war to save the country for this." He pauses. "No, I didn't." His wife is silent.

They gather up their gear and go up the stairs past the point on my compound where I lose sight of them until they come back into view out my kitchen window as they head south down the road toward the old hotel.

A few weekends later I was watching the runners and diggers again, and I was watching just as one of the runners took a bad spill. He tumbled over in the sand and rolled around and around in pain, grabbing for his ankle. Other runners swept around him. From my window I could see the hurt man look toward my steps, judging the distance. He started to crawl. After a while he made it to the steps.

"Those pot-holers," he yells at the beach as he holds his ankle; he is barefooted, and now he grips his foot with great firmness, as if by squeezing it he can prevent the swelling.

"Goddamn pot-holer," he says. His ankle seemed to be swelling between his fingers. I feel vicarious pain much more deeply than my own real pain. I think vicarious pain is real; the other pain, like this man felt in his ankle, is something different, and something less painful than what I felt as I watched his ankle start to puff and then, in my mind's eye, turn black and blue. The pain in his foot was now in my mind—it never hurts in me where it does in someone else: John Wayne can get shot in the arm; I get it in the head.

The runner rolls on his back in the sand and stretches his foot up in the air. He twists and turns. There isn't much I can say; I am immobilized by pain.

"Sons of bitches," he shouts as he rolls over on one side and shakes his fist at an elderly woman on the beach fifty yards away. She has stopped and is scooping up sand in her scooper. She gives the scooper an expert shake—to speed the process, much like an experienced department store shopper will always walk up escalators. She shakes, and gravity pulls, and the sand tumbles, and the fellow on the ground shakes his fist and swears. No doubt the woman is hard of hearing, but it is the earphones on her head that keep her deaf to the man in pain on the beach side.

"There should be a law against pot-holers," the man moans from the sand.

None of the joggers stops to help him. They are too busy dodging the tiny craters caused by the sand scoops. Soon, in silence, the jogger crawls up the stairs and sits out of my sight until dark. Either that, or he gets a ride past my window. I do not see him again.

I've had to put in the dialogue because I don't go outside. I was not, as it turned out, tempted to help the man crawling toward my patio, and the two scenes were acted out in front of me in silence like my silent television. I think of all this because during one of Mother's calls today Eddie Cooper played out a scene of his own, this time the dialogue being that of my mother and I in conversation, as if the sound from one television station had inadvertently jumped into the picture of another.

"I must point out to you," Mother said in her schoolteacher voice. "I must point out to you that you are our only son and that we'd like to see you once in a while."

"But you're going to Rome," I said.

"Your father would like to see you," she said. "Besides, we'll wait around a few days before we leave."

"Mother," I said, "I asked you not call me during the football game."

"I wish you were still married," she said as a response. I wondered why my reference to a football game made Mother think of my marriage. What Mother wanted, still wants, are grandchildren. If I could only have grandchildren for her, without having children for me, then I'd have grandchildren. I told her so once.

"Don't tease your mother," she had said. My mild irony no doubt caused the resetting of clocks there in Wolf. Our marriage lasted a year; there was something about me my wife didn't like. Maybe it was the football games I used to watch on television until I saw the same play twice. It had taken ten years of watching football to have that happen, and when it did, I quit watching. But it took less than a year of marriage for my wife and I to get into exactly the same domestic argument: the same flight of adjectives, the same popping of verbs, the same burst of irony, the same dash of reason to the rescue—the same accidental violence of married life. I quit watching. I turned off the football game on my Sony, and my marriage vanished, the picture of it slamming into a straight line of light, then into a pinpoint, then off.

"I'm not going to get remarried. I'm not coming home. I'm not going to have grandchildren," I said from my white kitchen phone, looking out my kitchen window. A golf cart with an elderly woman drove by. It was one of those golf carts that has a sun fringe on it, like the one I once saw President Nixon driving. There was a large whip antenna on it, and the woman driving it was talking into what I took to be a CB microphone. I could see her drive and talk all the way up the hill. She drove slowly, and when she got to the hill's top, from where she could see over our compound and onto the beach, she stopped, got out of the golf cart, and walked over to the stone wall that there bordered the ridge above the beach.

"Are you listening to me?" my mother said on the phone.

"I've put the phone on the table, and I'm turning all the clocks back, Mother," I said.

"Don't tease your mother," she said. "I think this whole thing is foolish. You'd think you never wanted to see us again. You come home. You come home right this minute," she said.

Something out my patio window caught my eye, and I turned my back on my kitchen and, stringing out the cord to the wall phone, walked its full length toward the beach. There was Eddie Cooper. Marine. Iwo Jima. Shuffling down the beach. He had his walker, one of those aluminum cages that infirm people scoot along as they scoot along. Eddie Cooper's walker was fitted with skis on its legs so he didn't sink into the sand. They left twin trails down the beach. In front of him was his metal detector, which he moved from side to side in search of watches and gold. A single-piece headset let him hear the metal detector's buzz in his left ear, for into his right ear he had plugged one of those tiny ear pieces, the kind that came with my television and which in Eddie Cooper's case was no doubt connected to the portable CB that he had strapped over his chest. Sand scoops were attached to the sides of the walker, as was a canvas bag—L. L. Bean variety. He stopped, said something into the CB, which must have had a built-in microphone. I went back to the kitchen window and looked up the street to see Mrs. Eddie Cooper at the top of the hill saying something into the mike in the golf cart, its coiled line stretched like my phone cord as she stood beside the wall so she could see her husband. Back out the patio window I looked. Eddie was starting down the beach again, his metal detector sweeping in front of him like the snout of an animal.

My mother was talking. Joggers were cutting in and out of traffic to miss the ancient Marine scooting down the beach.

"The football game is on," I said to Mother. "I'll talk to you later."

How can I tell my mother that I can't leave my glassed-out world of windows and television screens for some other world back along a road that seems not real, not as real, at least, as this account of it. When I think of travel, I think only of Monday morning, when I'll point my BMW north and play the reversed version of my songs, Nancy Wilson's "When the World Was Young" being smack in the trip's middle at the Vista turn-off, coming and going.

"Notre Dame," the man said over the phone.

"The library, please," I said.

"The main number?"

"I don't know," I said. "Do you have an archives?" There was a moment of silence, then a shuffling of papers. Then an electronic click.

"Yes?" said a voice.

"Is this the library?" I said.

"A certain part of the library," the man said.

"Perhaps you could help me?"

"Yes."

"Is this the archives?"

"This is the assistant archivist, if that is what you mean."

"Yes. Well, do you have any information on when Knute Rockne was coach? What was his last year as coach there," I said.

"Is this the Sport Office?" he said.

"No. I'm calling long distance. I'm in California."

"Just a minute." Now I could hear some papers shuffling, and a book drop. I wondered if it was *The Secret of Father Brown*. I believe in coincidence. "You're not from the press, are you?" he said quickly when he returned.

"No. Why?"

"Never mind. Knute Rockne was at Notre Dame from 1918 until 1931. March 31st, 1931." He paused. "That's when he died," said the man. "In a plane crash."

"I know," I said.

"What?" he said.

"What about G. K. Chesterton?" I said. "Can you tell me when G. K. Chesterton was at Notre Dame?"

"Where are you from?" he said.

"California. I'm calling long distance from California," I said. "Is it early there?" My confusion about time suddenly hit me; I thought I might have made my mother's mistake, and it might have been six in the morning, or six at night, or noon. Just because I knew what time it was here in California didn't mean I knew what time it was in South Bend, or Wolf, or Rome.

"It's 4:00 p.m., sir," the man said. And then I sensed he left the phone; I might have even heard something that let me know that, but in the same way I know when Mother has put down the phone, I knew this fellow had left it.

"Mr. Chesterton was at Notre Dame from October 6 until November 15, 1930," he said when he returned.

"Thank you," I said.

"You're welcome," he said.

"Just a moment," I said.

"Yes?"

"I wonder if you would tell me one more thing."

"If I can," he said.

"Is Notre Dame playing this afternoon? Are they playing there in South Bend?"

"What, sir?" he said.

"Is the football team playing today? It's Saturday, and I wanted to know if they are playing football, and if they are, where, and while I'm thinking about it, with whom are they playing?" I had a feeling this was a man who was particular about his "whos" and "whoms" and if I got that "with whom" in there, as Mother would have wanted me to, I might get the answer.

"I'm sure I don't know," he said. He paused. "I'm in the library."

"Look outside," I said, "and see if there are people walking by wearing large coats, beanies, and carrying pom-poms. And if there are crowds of people all going in the same direction. Or if the campus seems strangely empty, as if in a science fiction movie—that one with Harry Belafonte in it where he comes out of the mine and nobody's around. Do you hear any band music? Can you see a parking lot from where you are? Is it full? Are there buses parked here and there?"

He hung up.

"I wouldn't be so nasty about the Popes, if I were you," says my mother in response to a crack I've made during the Christmas vacation of my sophomore year at the university. Everybody is home, even Rita and Charlie from South Bend, and we are taking our turns sitting at the kitchen table and helping Mother with the cooking. I am taking a course in world religions, and that plus a severe case of being a sophomore has made me an international authority—and towering cynic—about religions. In fact, it isn't just a crack I've made about the line of Popes—it is more like a monologue.

"Come on, Mother," I say. "You can't justify what amounts to medieval behavior. Even if it was in the Dark Ages," I say. I'm also taking a course in western civilization. "I'd rather be a Upanishad than a Catholic," I say.

"No choice in the matter," says Rita as she putters through the kitchen. "You're a Catholic."

"A catholic with a small c," I say from under the Bierstadt, my high school copy of *Thirty Days to a More Powerful Vocabulary* flashing yellow and black in my mind.

"Don't spoil Christmas by talking about that," says Dad as he cuts through the kitchen on his way outside. What we are not to talk about is how Aunt Rita got me baptized by the Monsignor whose washing she and Mrs. Tuti had been doing when she got entangled with an English writer and a football coach.

One autumn in the late thirties the Monsignor made a trek to Victoria, Kansas, to visit the Cathedral of the Plains and to celebrate mass at the German Catholic church there, and at other churches in the tiny German settlements around Victoria: Catharine, Schoenchen, Liebenthal, Munjor, Pfeifer—none of them named for relatives, relations, or family, as far as Aunt Hattie can tell.

"What?" I say.

"We were coming out anyway," says Rita. "For Thanksgiving. So we rode on the train with the Monsignor and met your mother in Victoria."

"I don't want you talking about it," says Dad on his way back through the kitchen. Something is wrong with the propane tank, and the house is getting cold.

"The Monsignor says to your mother, what a fine baby you have there, and you smiled," Aunt Rita says to me. Apparently I was swaddled in various blankets.

"I told the Monsignor that you weren't baptized," Aunt Rita says. "That your father wouldn't have it."

"That's what she said," says Mother. Dad is out back of the house, and I can hear him banging on the propane tank. I hear by the voices that Uncle Freckles has joined him. Aunt Rita goes on.

"Well, the Monsignor says we can't have that, now can we," says Rita. "And your mother says, no we can't. And the Monsignor says that one way to look at it is that God is the father, and that He would approve. Besides," says Aunt Rita in a voice a bit louder than her narrative voice, "the family is Catholic." I am remembering Aunt Hattie's definition of family.

"Did he baptize me?" I say from my end of the kitchen table.

"Oh yes, he did," says Aunt Rita.

"Are you still talking about that," says Dad as he comes through again.

"Has anyone seen Hattie?" says Freckles from the porch.

"You mean I've been baptized a Catholic?" I say with a tenseness in my voice that I don't recognize. I am upset, and I don't know why. Rita, Hattie, and Uncle Charlie are practicing Catholics; Mother is not, and Dad is "vaguely Protestant." Taken together, it means I have no religious training, a fact that allows me to be at perfect ease with my end of the century, with my edge of the continent, with my end of the road.

"I don't like this," I say in a voice that jumps from its sophomore shrillness to something like the flat alto I am to grow into when I come out to California, and that I now still have. "I don't like this."

"What difference can it make?" my mother says.

"Why didn't you tell me?" I say to my dad, who is rattling around in the other room.

"What?" he says.

"Did Hattie go to the ranch?" says Freckles.

"Why didn't you tell me I was a Catholic?" I say to Dad.

"For a long time they didn't tell me," he says, standing in the doorway and sweeping his arm across the two women. Freckles is at the porch door.

"She went with Charlie to Garden City," says Mother to Freckles.

"What difference does it make?" my father says to me. "It's just a little water, and a crazy scheme by the women. You didn't know about it, and that was fine. Now you know about it, and so there you are. What difference does it make?"

"You wouldn't know," I say. "You're not Catholic. I am." There is a moment of silence at this clang of logic. Nobody sees that it is funny, not even me.

The phone on the wall rings and brings us the news that Aunt Hattie has lurched the Studebaker into a barbershop in downtown

Garden City. No one is hurt, she says over the phone, but the car is damaged and we should come to town to get her. In the midst of the bustle of deciding who will drive which Studebaker and who will stay, and who will go to Garden City to get Uncle Charlie and Aunt Hattie, Rita says to me that she hopes Charlie isn't drunk, because she won't let him in the house when he is drunk.

"I didn't care who they were," says Aunt Rita as she starts her Knute Rockne story.

It is either in a file kept by Aunt Hattie, or it is folded in *The Secret of Father Brown*, or it is tucked behind the reprint of Bierstadt's *Wolf River*—I think in all three places during my boyhood have I seen the wrinkled and folded and yellowed *Time* magazine story of Knute Rockne's death in a plane crash near Bazaar, Kansas. I have seen it lying on the kitchen table from time to time, as if resting en route from Aunt Hattie's Family Log to the back of the Bierstadt. I remember something about Rockne's traveling to California. He had accepted, the article reported, a position in sales promotion with the Studebaker Corporation. Nobody has ever talked about it in our family. Once, when I came in late at night after a high school football game, I looked behind the painting and found the clipping tucked in the frame's edge. I took it out and read it, while drinking a glass of milk and checking the clock to see what time zone we were in that day. My mother came down into the kitchen, saw me reading the clipping, and asked me who had won the game, and had the Studebaker given me any trouble.

"Do you remember the time you were reading the clipping about Knute Rockne's death?" said my mother when she called just now.

"Yes," I said.

"You know we think we saw that plane," she said.

"I didn't know that," I said.

"Yes," she said. "We were driving from Emporia home one

morning, and we think we saw it flying along, and your dad said it looked like it was in trouble."

"It was," I said. There was silence.

"I want you to come home," said my mother, her voice firm, but with an edge of fear in it. We both know this talking over telephones can get to you, and that in the end, long distance knifes something out of your emotions. You can't send out over the wires what my mother is feeling. She tries through silence. Then:

"Where is your wife?" she said. "Whatever happened to her?"

"I don't know," I said.

"What are you going to do?" she said.

"Nothing," I said.

There was Mother's silence.

I looked out the patio window. Eddie Cooper was out of sight, only the twin trails of his skied walker as evidence that he had passed by and even those are now pock-marked with joggers' prints. Out the kitchen window I can no longer see his wife; her golf cart has gone over the hill to make the next check point.

I see my mother sitting at the phone's end of the table. The Bierstadt is silent in its looming Hudson-River-Valley fashion. My father is not there, nor is Aunt Hattie nor Uncle Freckles, but in my mother's mind I can see that she has arranged us all in the house there in Wolf, Kansas, and that we are helping pack for the trip to Rome. Freckles is talking about good horse flesh hopping fast about, and Father is saying that nobody better say hello to the Pope for him. I am there. My wife comes in. Twin boys, one in each arm, smile, in a round, robust, athletic way, and wait to be baptized.

"Notre Dame won," I said to Mother's silence. On the kitchen counter was the remote control device for my Sony. I toyed with it. A football game was on three out of five channels. Two westerns on the other two. I did not turn on the sound, but instead kept flicking the TV channels silently through their paces as I listened to the buzz of the phone miles.

"You're all we have," Mother said. "Come home." She said it once, but if I am to write it down to get the effect of its sound, I must write it, come home / come home / come home, as if it is echoing through a bad connection from Wolf to La Jolla, from Rome to South Bend, and through all the towns and time zones and stories of the family, of which this, I guess, is the last and (like I am to my mother) all that I have, all that I can send home in my stead.

Barrel Heat

"That's a fine old trap gun you've got there. Nobody shoots those anymore, do they, Al?"

"They don't," I say.

"Not that you shoot anything new."

"I don't."

The man holding the gun—a trap-grade Winchester Model 12 with detailed engraving on the receiver, a ventilated rib running along the barrel, and a hand-checkered stock and forearm—is new to our club. In fact, this is his first time. I have been a member for twenty years. I am called The Champ. Ted, who has been doing the talking, is the President.

"My mother gave it to me when I was eighteen," the man says. "'A gift from your father long gone,' she'd say."

"There's a story for you, Al," says Ted.

"I thought so as well," says the man. "But my mother wouldn't tell me. 'Never mind,' was all I could get out of her."

The new man is sitting on a bench that faces the trap house and the five lanes that mark where the shooters stand. I am sitting beside him. Ted is standing in front of us. We have an hour or so of daylight for the shoot. It is my habit to shoot in the first squad, then go home. But I am late and so in the second squad. As it is summer and pleasant, the shoot might go into the evening with the lights on and the bright-white targets flying out into the dark of night if they don't get shot—"dropped," is the word for a missed target.

When I arrived I saw by the sign-up sheet that the man sitting next to me had put his name on position number three; that's where I usually start, and because I have been around so long, everybody lets me have it. Not that it makes much difference; I shoot well no matter where I begin. This evening I am number four.

But there is something more about the man sitting next to me other than he has taken my place: The trap gun he has, the Winchester Model 12 with hand-checkered stock and forearm and the engravings on the receiver, that gun is my gun. I know the story. I know about the engravings. I knew his mother. I recognized his last name: Kincade.

When I was a university student I worked for a sporting goods store that had an engine repair and gunsmith shop in back. The gunsmith took a liking to me, and between my work on lawn mowers, taught me about guns and trap. His name was Bob Kincade and he had once been a champion shooter. But at some point he started to flinch just before he shot, and in this way dropped the target. Even a release trigger didn't help. After that he was no longer competitive, and you could see him at various trap clubs in the area sitting in his truck, not even getting out to say hello to the men against whom he had once shot. Sometime during the shoot he'd drive away. It was in those days that I knew him.

One Friday he asked if I might like to shoot a round of trap at the local club.

"I don't have a gun," I said.

"Use one of mine," he said. "Tomorrow evening. Seven. Before the sun goes down. I bring shells. You bring dollar for shoot."

"Where?" I said. He told me how to get to the club.

No one knew much about Bob Kincade: where he lived, how he became a champion trap shooter, where he came from. Only that he lived alone with a daughter about my age—or so Mr. Wilson, the store's owner, told me. To look at Bob Kincade people guessed he had tribal blood: Sioux. Cherokee. Navajo. Shoshone. It was in his face and the way he talked. Nobody asked. He was a tall man with large, rough hands. My guess is he might have been sixty.

What everyone did know about Bob Kincade was that he was an excellent gunsmith who took great care, not only in repairing the guns brought to him, but in refinishing them with finely tooled checkering on the forearms and stocks. And with delicate engravings on the receivers, not of flying ducks or pheasants or pointing dogs as you might expect, but from drawings that he'd bring to work—drawings on a single sheet of heavy paper with a ruled line down the middle and a small *R* at the top of one side, and a small *L* on the top of the other: faces, flowers, tree branches, horse heads, moons, letters—all repeated with variations on each side of the receiver so that the repetition formed a design of its own, the letters becoming a word or a name if you looked carefully enough, or through the large mounted magnifying glass on Bob Kincade's bench that he used to make the engravings. And the designs were in a hand not his because I knew his coarse script from the receipts he'd write for the guns he was to repair. Before the summer was over, I'd learn whose hand it was.

"Don't wear ball cap. Don't sight down barrel. Keep both eyes open," he said to me when I got to the trap club. He was sitting in his truck, a sagging short bed of an old Dodge. The window was down. I saw that some of the men were looking our way. I learned later this was Kincade's home trap club and so they knew him, and knew what had happened that he didn't shoot anymore. None of them came up.

"Here," he said, and through the open window passed me a shotgun and a box of shells. "You shoot second squad. Sign for number three. Shoot quick. Choose your call. Stay with it. You got dollar?" I said I did. And then, even though it was summer and the cool of the evening was not yet coming on, he rolled up the window and stared straight ahead. I wondered what he meant by choosing my call.

Looking back on it, I don't know what made Bob Kincade think I might be a good shot. True, I was on the university baseball team and its best hitter, so I had something of an eye. Once in a while, I'd take a gun from the rack near his bench and put it to my shoulder, but that was about it. I didn't come from a hunting family, much less a trap-shooting one. Maybe he saw in me something he wanted to see and that I didn't. That happens.

"Use 'yo' for your call," said the man who kept score. "It was his, and he'll be pleased."

Most of the men said "pull" when they wanted the target, although one man grunted. Two or three of them shot quickly and the target was "smoked"—as the men called it when there were no chunks flying off. Two others dropped five or six targets. The man who grunted for his call shot twenty-five of twenty-five, all of them quickly, all of them smoked.

I missed the first target out, then broke three in a row, but not quickly or smoked. Then I missed the last one. From position four, I missed the first two, broke the last three, the final one quickly and smoked. Then I broke every target after that, some of them quickly and smoked, but not all of them until the final five, which I broke quickly—and all them were smoked. The man who told me to choose "yo" shook my hand as we came away from the line. When I looked, Bob Kincade was driving away.

Monday he was not at work. Nor the rest of the week. I had brought his gun to the shop and cleaned it. It was a Winchester Model 12 trap grade with a plain receiver and factory checkering on the forearm and stock. Ventilated rib running the length of the barrel. Sometimes I would put it to my shoulder and take aim at the pigeons flying up and down the alley that you could see out the back of the shop when the large work door was open. Once I said yo! and Mr. Wilson smiled. When I asked him where Bob Kincade had gone, he said out of town on a bus to watch a few shoots. His truck was too old for long trips down memory lane.

The following Saturday, I bought a box of shells and went back to the gun club with Bob Kincade's gun and a dollar. He was there, but did not look at me, nor roll down his window. I thought to go over and ask him if it was all right to use his gun again, but his straight-ahead stare stopped me. I shot in the first squad, broke twenty-five, all quickly, and all smoked. When I came off the line I could see his truck leaving. The following Monday, he was back at work.

You shoot trap from sixteen yards up to twenty-seven yards, each yard numbered on the five lanes running at angles toward the trap house so that, seen from above, the arrangement looks like a fan with the trap-house square sixteen yards from the fan's base. At the trap club where I first shot, that fan was called "the infield." Where the targets sailed was called "the outfield." That is also true where I now shoot.

When there is a "registered" shoot, the kind of competition where men like Bob Kincade participate, the better shot must shoot from greater distances. That first and second night at Bob Kincade's club we all shot from sixteen yards. In competition Bob Kincade always shot from twenty-seven yards, and still he beat men who shot from shorter distances. If you have no "registered" targets, you shoot from sixteen yards until you get your "number." By my memory in those days you had to shoot a thousand such targets, usually at rounds of fifty to a hundred—that is, two to four squads' worth.

The reason I was good at it was because it was like hitting a baseball, only in reverse: the ball going away from home plate of the trap house instead of toward it, but still there it was: high and fast off the corner of the plate one time, down the middle another time, then on the other corner. You never knew where the pitcher might throw the ball or the trap might throw the target. My gun was my bat; I kept both eyes open and on the ball.

"Not for twenty years," says the man sitting next to me. Ted had asked him when he last shot trap.

"My mother drove me around to the local trap clubs where my father shot and I shot a round at each for the memory of who he was. I was pretty good at it. Some of the men he shot against were still alive and they talked about him."

"Your father was a trap shooter?" Ted asks.

"Among the best. There were trophies around the house. And a rack of guns he had used. But I didn't take to it, and when my mother died, I sold the guns—all except this one because it has one of her drawings for the engravings."

He turns the Model 12 over so we see both sides of the receiver. The design is one of repeated letters and lips and hands, eyes—not that you could tell that. It seemed more like scrollwork: delicate and mysterious. My name is portioned out like code. And another's as well.

"You don't see that on most guns," Ted says. "Do you, Al?"

"You don't," I say.

"One gun and one drawing were missing," the man says. "I know because my father engraved his receivers from designs by my mother. Then he would make frames for the drawings. They were hanging on the walls when I was growing up. The drawing for this gun was missing. And there was a drawing for a gun we didn't have. A missing drawing, a missing gun. My mother wouldn't tell me about either. Only, 'never mind.'"

"Do you have the other drawings?" I ask.

"Yes. I took them when I cleaned out the house."

"Show him your gun," Ted says. "His has engravings as well. Sort of like yours."

"Later," I say. My gun is in the clubhouse.

When Bob Kincade came into the shop the Monday morning after I had borrowed his gun he did not talk to me and I sensed he did not want me to talk to him. I had again cleaned the gun and laid it out on the bench. He opened the action and looked down the barrel to see if I had cleaned that as well: I had. Then he put it aside. We worked together in silence, me cleaning carburetors, he hand-checkering stocks.

For lunch he usually brought a brown bag; I took mine across the street at the Tee-Pee Tavern because of a waitress who had been a student with me in my writing class.

"I have extra from home," he said as I was about to leave. "Pop for you."

I joined him at his bench by pulling up a stool. The sandwiches were made of thick, dark-brown bread and filled with sliced tomatoes, lettuce, onions and cheese. I drank the pop. Bob Kincade drank tea from a large Mason jar.

"Lisa," he said, as he unwrapped the sandwiches from the wax paper. "From her baking and the garden she tends," referring, I supposed, to his daughter and to the bread as well as the tomatoes and onions and lettuce. "Sun tea," he said, as he drank his tea from the jar, not pouring it into a cup or glass. "Lisa."

At the end of lunch he folded the wax paper into the brown paper bag, swept off the crumbs from his workbench, took a final drink of tea, and said:

"When we close today, I want to talk to you." Yes, I said.

Betting on trap shooters is called a Calcutta and is illegal. The shooter is "The Mark"—or was where I shot. Bob Kincade had once been a Mark, but when he began gambling on me he would become The Man. Sometimes two Marks are being bet against one another, like a two-man horse race. Not that either one would know it. This is what Bob Kincade wanted to talk about.

"And don't bring girlfriends," he said. "No women in trap clubs. Sometimes in the trucks watching." He gave me directions to the trap club where I was to shoot and handed me the gun I had used the week before. "Don't come to me afterward." Yes, I said. "Don't break all. Don't smoke all you break." Yes, I said.

In this way I began shooting The Calcutta at the trap clubs of small towns in the area: Eudora, Vinland, Overbrook, Perry, Lecompton, Pleasant Grove, Berryton, and once as far south as Centropolis. All of them clubs where Bob Kincade was known as a great trap shooter and afterward could be seen sitting in his truck watching what he could no longer do—in this case, on that first Saturday at the trap club just outside of Lone Star, me shooting from the middle position at sixteen yards and calling yo! when I wanted the target, dropping three, with only a dozen or so smoked. If he had bet, The Man would have lost money on his Mark.

"Al used to be a champion," Ted says to the man sitting next to me. "Isn't that right, Al."

The first squad is at the line. Something is not right with the trap and so the men stand there, the muzzles of their guns resting on small pads at each position.

"You were?" By my guess he is forty-plus to my sixty-plus.

"It might have been true once, but it didn't work out."

"He still smokes them," says Ted. "Not always twenty-five, but sometimes." There is a pause among us while we listen to the men fixing the trap. Ted asks if he is needed. He is not.

"You from around here?" Ted says to Kincade.

"Visiting," he says. "My son just took a job at the college. This is his gun now but he doesn't have any interest. He's the one who told me how to get here." We are quiet for a moment. More than a pause.

"Tell us the story about your old gun," Ted says to me; he is prodding. My "old gun" is a Parker single-barrel trap gun, engraved and hand-checkered. It is even older than Kincade's Winchester Model 12. And it is not my gun. Nor have I told anyone its story.

"I pay you half what you win, plus gun when it's over," Bob Kincade said to me the Monday after the Lone Star shoot. I asked him why it would be over.

"Something get you," he said. "Maybe they figure it out. I won't be there every time. Lisa, she come. Don't talk to her either. Don't smoke them unless you see my hand or hers on the top of steering wheel. Otherwise, drop two or three. When you see we leave, quit." Yes, I said.

He told me we'd keep the gun on the rack near his bench and that I should clean it each time I used it. He said he would get new wood for the stock and forearm from some town in Missouri. He said nothing about the receiver. I wondered if the "something that would get me" would be flinching. But it was not.

It took two more Saturdays before I saw Kincade's hand at the top of the steering wheel, and then I smoked them all, hitting twenty-five in the first squad, and then twenty-five in the second. As I was walking off the line I saw him collect his bets and then start the truck. I said no when asked if I wanted to sign up for the third squad, as there was a slot left.

At clubs when Kincade's hand was not at the top of the steering wheel, the next Monday when I'd clean the gun there was no money. But when I smoked them all on a Saturday or Sunday, the following Monday there was money on his workbench, stacked but not divided until we had lunch together, and then Bob Kincade would sort the bills into two equal piles as he shared his sandwiches. When he saw I was not finishing my pop, he brought an extra Mason jar of tea. "Lisa," he said. "Sun tea."

One Saturday at Pleasant Grove, he was not there but Lisa was, sitting in the truck as men came up to her at the open window. After a moment she'd put out her palm for a pat of a handshake. She was about my age: black hair, thin lipped, large deep green eyes, delicate hands—one of which was on the top of the steering wheel. Around her neck, which was long and pale, she wore a red kerchief. If there was tribal blood in her it did not show. Going back and forth between the club's bench and my car, I'd pass the truck and look. Once she smiled. There was nothing about her beauty that would make you think she was Bob Kincade's daughter.

I shot twenty-five, but did not smoke them all. When I turned around, she was still there, her hand on the steering wheel. I broke the next twenty-five, smoking them all. When I came off the line, she was driving away. I saw her eyes looking at me in the rearview mirror.

I lived in a small apartment across the street from the sporting goods store and above the Tee-Pee Tavern, and sometimes, after closing, the waitress that was in my writing class would come up the stairs from the parking lot behind the tavern with a six-pack of Coors and spend the night. She had a boyfriend who had gone home to St. Louis for the summer and once in a while she'd meet him there.

We knew we were not in love, but we were something to one another and that felt good as well. Later, she wrote a fine erotic story about us that got published. The story was called "Barrel Heat," and its title came from what finally "got me" at trap shooting. However, her story was not about trap shooting, but about being my lover that summer while not being in love with me and discovering that she was not in love with her St. Louis boyfriend either—but not in love in a different way. *No two ways of not being in love with your lover are the same*, was the first sentence of the story. It was a sentence I wish I had written, as was the story that followed.

Monday evening after the shoot at Pleasant Grove, I was having a beer at the Tee-Pee Tavern and my waitress girlfriend was not there. But Lisa was. Bob Kincade had not been at work that day and Mr. Wilson said he had taken the bus to Missouri to get stocks and forearms.

Lisa was sitting by herself on a barstool. I had come in the back door from the parking lot after having made myself dinner. Lisa was wearing the same red kerchief around her neck, blue jeans, and a yellow summer blouse with pearl-like buttons and a red collar. Her legs were long. She turned when I came in, smiled, and patted the empty stool beside her. I sat down and ordered a draw.

"You are a very fine shot," she said. This was after a moment of silence between us because I did not know what to say other than "hello" and found myself looking at her reflection in the mirror behind the bar. "Bob has told me this, and it is true."

"And you make very good sun tea," I said as I turned to look at her. "And grow a garden, I understand."

"Yes," she said. There was a moment of silence. More than a pause. I looked at her in the mirror.

"I understand your father has gone to buy gun stocks and forearms," I said.

"What?" she said.

"I understand that..." but I did not finish the sentence because she pushed her half-finished beer away, turned on her stool, got off, and walked out of the mirror behind the bar and through the front door.

The trap has been fixed and Mr. Kincade and I are now sitting by ourselves because Ted has gone to push the button that throws the targets. He also has a clipboard on which he'll mark the hits and dropped; under normal circumstances I would have gotten a folding chair from the clubhouse and done that chore for him.

"Was your father Bob Kincade?" I ask.

"Why, yes."

"I went to school in Lawrence," I say before he can ask how I knew. "I worked at Wilson Sporting Goods store when he did."

"Did you shoot with my father?"

"I did not."

The first squad is starting. There is no one among them smoking targets; no one will break twenty-five. The reason I am called the Champ is because I am graded on the curve. I give my writing students the same consideration.

The next Monday morning Bob Kincade was at work. He had stocks and forearms on his bench. From a sink he'd wet a shop rag and wipe down a stock, then run his hand over it, then wet it again. When he'd do that the grain would show, and in this way—as he told me at lunch—he knew the quality of the wood and how to checker it. For the gun I was using, he had picked a burled walnut. That afternoon he began to checker the stock. By the following Saturday, both the stock and the forearm were done. The engraving, he said, would come later. "Lisa," he said.

It was Mr. Wilson who one day showed me the gun Bob Kincade had used to shoot trap: a single-barrel Parker. Hand-checkered stock and forearm. Engravings on the receiver and up along the lower part of the barrel where the chamber was. A matted rib. He had used others over the years, Mr. Wilson told me, but this one was special: he had won many championships with it, including a national one in Ohio.

Bob Kincade kept the Parker in the store's safe where other rare and expensive guns for sale were kept: Purdeys, Pigeon Grade

Model 12s, Winchester Model 21s. Over and Under Broadway Ribbed Brownings. And Bob Kincade's trap-grade single-barrel Parker, into which he had put a release trigger (you don't "pull" it, you pull it back before you shoot, then "release" it, and that fires the gun) in order to fool his reflexes. Mr. Wilson told me that when that did not work, Kincade took out the trigger, reinstalled the original, cleaned the gun, then put it in the safe and never used it again. Not to be able to shoot well had smoked something inside Bob Kincade. And even with no son to pass it to, Mr. Wilson told me, the Parker was not for sale.

"Great invention, ventilated ribs," said the man who grunted his call that first time I shot. We were walking out to the line at Eudora.

"I guess," I said.

He had shot with me a few times since then. His number was twenty-four, and from there he breaks that number more often than not. Sometimes more. A few times less. He was Bob Kincade's age. Like me, I suspected he was a Mark, but to whom I did not know.

"When we only had matted ribs or plain barrels you saw the heat waves coming off," he said. "Now you only see them if you look for them."

Lisa was there. Her hand was on the steering wheel. She had raised it once as if to say hello. Or at least that was what I liked to think.

"What about heat waves?" I said.

"They distort the target if you look through them," the man said. "Like water will distort a catfish if you shoot him in a creek. You shoot catfish?"

"No," I said.

"You got to aim above them in water," the man said as I walked to the sixteen-yard line while he stayed at twenty-four. "'Barrel heat' is what we used to call it," he said. "It's not what got Bob Kincade; that was the flinch. Not even a release trigger helped. I think you know about Bob Kincade?"

"Yes," I said.

I dropped one in the first squad and two in the second. Coming off the second round, I saw Lisa pay out in bills from a roll. The following Monday Bob Kincade was at work but did not talk to me and did not bring me lunch. I went over to the Tee-Pee and then again that night for a meal and more than a few beers. Later, my girlfriend not in love with me came into the apartment and spent the night. The next morning she left for St. Louis. Bob Kincade was not at work again until Friday, just before I was to shoot at Vinland. Wednesday, Lisa was at the Tee-Pee in a booth by the back door.

"Where has your father gone?"

"You did not shoot so well at Eudora," she said instead of answering my question. "We bet on you at twenty-five each time. Twenty-four and bets are off. Less than twenty-four, we pay. I don't want you to be long gone as a Mark." Her eyes were fixed on me.

"Is that why your father is not at work?"

"He has taken a bus to Norton to watch the state championship." She seemed about to say something more, but did not. With no mirror we looked directly at one another. Her face that night even now I cannot forget.

One day I stayed late at the store. There were lawn-mower blades to sharpen before the next morning. I had a key to lock up. Going through the store to the front door I noticed that Mr. Wilson had not locked the gun safe and I went over to do so. Inside was the Parker and I took it out.

On the receiver was the same kind of design I had seen on other guns Bob Kincade had engraved, only more elaborate and more difficult to decipher: feathers, letters, hands, eyes, and what appeared to be fragments of the gun itself. Moving from the receiver onto the chamber of the barrel the design seemed to tell a story, the ending of which was a ceremony of some sort that could be read only by turning the gun over, so that what began on the top of the barrel was continued in a circle to the sides and bottom: multiple hands, eyes, lips, Ls and Bs and Ks scattered about—all in delicate etching. It must be true, I thought, looking at Bob Kincade's gun, that he was indeed tribal, and what Lisa had depicted was a ceremony of that fact.

I put the gun in the safe and locked it. Halfway across the street I understood the story on the gun. And what it meant to have something inside you smoked. In the booth by the back door was Lisa.

The second squad is getting up to shoot. Mr. Kincade turns to me.

"Would you like to shoot my gun?" he says. "In memory of my father since you knew him. I don't mind watching. One champ shooting another champ's gun. Someone can take my place."

"How about we shoot together?"

"O.K.," he says and seems pleased I have asked. He stuffs his pockets with shells and walks toward the line. I go into the clubhouse to get his father's Parker and my shell pouch. I am shooting number four, next to him. We are all at sixteen yards. His call is yo! And he breaks the first target out—not smoking it—but solid. I smoke mine and he smiles, for both my yo! I think, and the quick-smoked target. In this way we begin.

One Monday after I shot poorly, Bob Kincade tied a small piece of red cloth to the end of the Model 12.

"It will keep you from looking at barrel heat," he said.

In recent shoots I had been breaking twenty-five as before, but sometimes not quickly and not always smoked. Apparently he knew the trouble. "Lisa's," he said about the cloth. "From old kerchief like she wears." Then after a moment he said: "He is good, not as good as I was. He knows you are my Mark."

The next week, with Lisa in the truck, I broke twenty-five three times, all of them smoked. Still, there was the barrel heat. It was like looking for a curve ball that doesn't come and then the fastball gets you.

The following Monday, Bob Kincade was not at work. That night in bed I heard the back door to my apartment open and thought it was my waitress lover, but remembered she was to be in St. Louis. It was Lisa. Her step was soft, as she did not know where to find me. Then she did.

The next Friday the drawing for the Model 12 was on Bob Kincade's bench.

"For the gun," he said. "Lisa." Yes, I said.

From then on I shot better and worse, and there were times when I lost money for them and times I won money. And whenever Bob Kincade was away to get wood, or at other trap shoots out of town where he would watch old friends shoot, Lisa would be with me, coming up the back stairs, and only once did she meet my waitress lover—Lisa coming down the stairs as the waitress was going up—and it was the waitress who told me about it, and how she did not continue up the stairs that night and wanted me to know she was not angry, but only sad. Some of this she included in her own story and I have wondered all these years if Lisa ever read that story, because the magazine that published it put copies around town and at the university. It was my waitress lover who asked me if I knew that Lisa was Bob Kincade's wife.

By September, barrel heat was getting to me. I could see it coming off the rib as I shot. While others were shooting, I would look down the barrel and there it was. Not even Lisa's kerchief helped. There were days when I shot twenty-two, and there were still days when I shot twenty-five, but not all of them smoked. Nights with Lisa we would not talk about it. The beauty of her eyes in the dark seemed lit from behind; her hands and neck were the beauty of her entire body, and the memory of her from the night before repeated itself the next day as if it were multiple engravings. The more we were together, the more difficult it was for me to shoot—or to be at work with Bob Kincade. No love for Lisa is like any other love.

"We will stop after next Saturday," Bob Kincade said to me one Monday. There was money on the workbench, as well as the gun. Lunch, too. For both of us. Sun tea. And at the end of the bench a small drawing. I went over to look at it.

"I will make an engraving this week," he said. "Then the gun is yours. Wilson says you are quitting to go back to school." Yes, I said. I looked at the drawing: delicate, intricate, and, like the others, with a line down the middle for right and left on the receiver. There was no obvious story, but not all stories are obvious. There was more than a pause between us.

"I know about you and Lisa," he said. I said nothing. "Lisa," he said as he put our lunch on the workbench. "Lisa," he said as he gave me my Mason jar of sun tea. *Lisa*, I said myself, saying nothing else to Bob Kincade the rest of the day—or, as it turned out, the rest of his life. "And you being a boy to me," were the last words Bob Kincade ever said to me.

Mr. Kincade and I are shooting well. He is breaking targets, sometimes even smoking them. I am smoking mine. There is barrel heat coming off the Parker but I am shooting through it with both eyes wide open and the memory of a bit of red handkerchief at the muzzle's end. The targets are fastballs on one corner of the plate or the other—or down the middle. As I have started at number four,

I am now finishing where I usually begin. The end of the game is now five targets away.

"Ready?" I say.

"Yo!" he says, and he smokes number twenty-one, as do I.

It is September. My gun was, as promised, engraved the week after my final shoot. There is money. Bob Kincade is not there; Mr. Wilson got the gun and the money from the safe. He thanked me for my summer's work and hoped I'd return next summer.

Walking across the street, I go into the Tee-Pee and sit in the booth at the back near the door and lay the gun on the table. I order a draw and study the engravings. My lover waitress comes in for her shift, but before it starts, she pulls herself a beer and joins me. It is from her that I get the drawing of the engravings on my gun. "Lisa," is what she says when she hands it to me, saying as well that they knew each other in high school. There is a pause between us as I study the drawing. Then my waitress lover makes a motion with her hand to turn it over. On the other side there is this: *I can never see you again. You must not try to find me or ask for me or ask why. One day I might want your gun. It will be a trade.* All written in a script like the ones for her designs, and like those designs, there seemed something to be deciphered. My waitress lover says she does not understand what any of this means. Nor do I.

Fall contracts into winter. Bob Kincade dies. Lisa is not to be found. That spring, playing shortstop for the university team, I don't hit very well. In the summer I go back to work at Wilson's. Bob Kincade's bench is as he left it. Mr. Wilson tells me that Lisa took the Parker. Then one day walking across the street to the Tee-Pee, I see an old Dodge truck heading out of town. When I get to my apartment, the Model 12 is gone, but the Parker is there with a one-word note: *Lisa.* Written in the script of the engravings, this time with a drawing around her name that tells a story I cannot read.

Twenty-two, smoked by two yo!s. Twenty-three. Twenty-four. Pause. Yo! Twenty-five. Yo! Twenty-five. We are two champs at sixteen yards and all smiles and handshakes.

"Take it," Mr. Kincade says as he hands me my Model 12. "My son has no interest."

"Then take the Parker," I say. We are back at the bench. "That's your mother and father getting married in the engraving. It's the missing gun." He is looking at the Parker, turning it over on his lap. There is more than a moment's silence.

"I thought they were never married," he says. The third squad is going to the line.

"What?" I say.

"I thought he died just before they were to be married. And just before I was born. That's what I thought my mother meant when she'd say 'he's long gone.'"

He is looking at the Parker as if trying to find the truth of the past. In the infield the third shoot is starting. It occurs to me I have not asked how his mother died. Or if she died. *Lisa*, I say to myself—or think I do, but he looks up and, as if he has he heard me, says:

"She died this year. She was to come with me to see my son take up his job. She..." But before he can go on I ask:

"What's your son's job at the college?"

"Baseball coach. He's the new baseball coach."

Free Writing

Since this is free writing I am not going to use commas. I don't like commas. I like periods but commas are like yield signs they don't really do all that much. Zu Zu blows them off when she drives. Zu Zu has a Tude.

I'm going to write my free writing about my father and how he quit his job and how that was such a pain to my mother and my sister who was back from college for the summer. We have some goldfish and a cat who is fixed called Mindy. And my grandmother lives above the garage. You probably know some of this. I hope I get an Excellent like I always get in writing. I know I am supposed to learn five things from free writing and keep track of them. I am also going to write some about Bernie and Joel and about my pond. But mainly about my father.

Maybe I shouldn't say my father quit his job because when I said that he freaked out and said he'd been planning this a long time. He calls it LMOL which stands for living his own life for a change. He doesn't include for a change in the initials. My mother calls his being home all the time dropping out only when she talks to my grandmother about it she calls it dropping on like my father is some kind of bomber pilot you see in all the Vietnam programs on television and his being home all the time is like dropping stuff on my mother and her kitchen. I am not going to tell you what my father did before he quit his job that way you can figure it out yourself by reading between the lines which is what you're always telling us to do.

My grandmother asked me the other day if I liked my father and I said yes. Then she asked me if I had anything more to say and I said no. She said that wasn't good. But then she didn't say anything more which I guess means she doesn't much like my father and wants someone to agree with her about it without coming right out and saying so. My father quit his job just about the same time school was over last year so we've had the whole summer together. Most of it anyway. Some kids when they say they like their father are lying but other kids are telling the truth and some kids just don't know what else to say. I don't know why anyone would ask you if you liked your father but it's not the first time I've been asked and I know some other kids are asked as well usually by some relative. I don't know anybody whose mother ever asked them that.

When my father quit his job he said he wanted to be free to pursue other interests. POI he called it. He didn't say quit but he did say other interests and POI. I am also not going to use quotation marks which I know you're supposed to use around words people say. I have this idea I want to claim three free things for free writing and I have just claimed two but it won't be for awhile that I'll know what the third one is. Not telling you what my father did before he quit his job is not one of them. Or some other things about the summer I'm not going to tell about. That's something else.

The first week my father was home I was still in school. The bus drops me up by the Methodist Church in town and I walk home from there. Bernie goes with me part of the way. Joel goes with me the other part of the way and he always has a smoke. That's what he calls them because that's what his father calls them. A smoke. I don't take it. I don't want to smoke. Joel's two grades older. After Bernie leaves and Joel goes up his lane to where his farm is I walk home down a hill in the road and then cut across a field past this pond.

Sometimes I sit by the pond and study the water. I am good at studying the water. Sometimes I talk to the water. I never said anything about this to my mother but once when I was studying the water I must have stayed too long and I saw my mother's car head up the road to town and I knew she was looking for me so I went home and was there when she got back. Where were you she said. I walked by the pond on the way home I said but I didn't say anything about studying the water or about talking to it. I don't know why I'm saying anything about it now except maybe I think in free writing you ought to say something you've never said before. Maybe that's the third free thing I've been looking for. Maybe not. I don't think it is. I'll tell you when I know.

After my father quit his job he said we couldn't spend any money for ten days. He said we had to use up what we had in the house or the planet would go broke. He said there were four things we all had to learn. Zu Zu was home from college and that made four of us if you counted my father but not my grandmother. One thing apiece to learn for each of us Zu Zu said but not to my father because when my father gets this way he doesn't like a joke. Sometimes he likes a joke but not when he doesn't.

My father said the four things were Use It Up. Make Do. Do Without. I can't remember the fourth but you get the picture. He also began planting a vegetable garden and he had a big argument with my mother about it because she wanted to plant flowers there. Zu Zu wanted to plant marijuana. You have to know Zu Zu. She was just kidding. But it freaked out my mother because Zu Zu also once said she was going to get a tattoo of an iguana on her butt which she did not and also that she was going to get an earring in her lip which she did not. Zu Zu calls this mind strafing. My sister's name is Mary but everybody calls her Zu Zu except her teachers who don't know the story about why she's called Zu Zu. My father says Zu Zu has a chronic 'tude which is true because she's always at my father by saying God Dad to dumb things he says. Like when he thought Hip Hop was Hop Hip. God Dad goes

Zu Zu only she doesn't say it like God but some other way you'd have to spell it. You have to hear it to spell it.

We are not poor I guess. We don't have to use it up or do without or whatever else it was of the four things. I don't know about money but Zu Zu does and she says we are not poor because she can't get a scholarship to the college where she goes because she didn't get good enough grades in high school and because we're not poor enough. You didn't teach her. We weren't here then.

Anyway we have lots of things and we live in this woods that we bought from Bernie's father off his farm because I guess Bernie's father needed the money. In this woods we built a big house and we came here and I started school even though for a while my father stayed behind to work and only came over on weekends. That was when he had an apartment plus the house where we live now. Sometimes we'd stay at the apartment and drive past our old house just to look at it. My mother didn't want to move and neither did my grandmother. But my grandmother didn't live with us then. She just didn't want us to leave where we lived before because it was close to her. Which is why she came with us.

Nobody around us has a house like we do because ours was designed and built just the way my mother wanted it in order to get her to move. The garage and the man cave which is the basement were built just the way my father wanted them and some parts were built just the way the man who designed the house wanted them. Where my grandmother lives above the garage she got the way she wanted. Something like that. Our house means we're not poor just as much as Zu Zu says we're not poor. We're not rich I don't think. Maybe I should not write about money. Only you said what we wrote had to be true and we couldn't make it up. What if we leave things out. Is it still true if what we put in is true even if I don't put everything in. I should have asked in class.

It was just after I got out of school that my father had a tooth pulled and saved it. He put his tooth in this glass jar with a screw lid on it. He was saving jars and plastic containers for soup and he bought a freezer and moved it into the man cave. This was before he bought a pig and had it cut up and the lamb we called Edna. We just got her skin back before school started. My mother freaked out about the skin and said my father could have it where he is now which is not with us anymore because my mother didn't want it around the house. I am to take it to him when I go there. Also the tooth. But that is my idea. I haven't told my mother about the tooth.

Anyway my father put his tooth in this jar and kept it on his workbench in his man cave because mother said he couldn't have it upstairs even in his office where he makes all these calculations about how much money we can save. He's got a motto above his desk that reads *I'd rather save a buck than earn a buck.* I think he made it up himself. It doesn't sound like the kind of motto you're supposed to learn in Civics from Mr. Schwartz. Or in Sunday school when my mother takes me. Zu Zu won't go. God Mom she says.

When I asked my father about his tooth he told me he was going to save all his body parts from now on. He said he wished he'd saved his appendix when he was a boy and the doctor showed it to him in a jar but he didn't. From now on if he loses something like a tooth or a gall bladder or an intestine he's going to save it in a jar and keep it on his workbench. I thought maybe I should ask him why but I guess I didn't want to know in case my mother asked me. When I asked Zu Zu about it she said it was because my father didn't want to die. Zu Zu's rough.

I asked my father if he was going to save fingernail clippings and when I think about it now it seems like maybe I shouldn't go there but I didn't mean it that way and my father didn't take it that way. He didn't say anything for a moment and then he said when he was a boy his father and grandfather always saved the lead pellets they'd find when they were eating the rabbits they'd shot. That would be my grandfather and my great grandfather. They are both dead and I only remember my grandfather because my father told me a few years ago I was to get his shotgun. I haven't though.

I'm not sure why my father told me about the lead pellets but I didn't say anything although one day when my father was in town I went to the workbench and looked at the jar with the tooth in it and there were no fingernail clippings. There weren't any pellets either. Maybe I thought my father had saved the pellets from when he was a boy and was going to put everything together with his tooth and other body parts that he said he was going to save. When my father came back from town is when he had the freezer.

I don't have a girlfriend. I used to but she didn't know it. I left her a note about how she was my girlfriend under a rock by the pond. The rock is on the bank where the tree fell in. The tree gets turtles on it. The turtles plop into the water when I come along but if I sit there long enough and don't talk they will start to come out. I can only sit there long enough when summer comes because if I did that after school my mother would all the time be going up to the Methodist Church to see if I had been run over and crushed by the school bus. My mother has this imagination about me getting killed. Once I had been dragged by my book bag all the way to the next bus stop which my mother thought was like in Afghanistan. Another time a weirdo picked me up on a motorcycle and took me to a den of iniquity. Zu Zu says Mother wasn't like that with her but that times have changed. Zu Zu says Mother has only two speeds forward: Freaked Out and Totally Freaked Out. FO and TFO Zu Zu calls them. It's from Zu Zu that my father gets his letters for things.

Once I saw a snapping turtle on the bank of the pond that was big as a tire but I didn't tell my mother about it because she would just FO over how it was going to grab me by the pants and haul me out into the middle of the pond and pull me under and I would be dead and my eyeballs would rot out of my head after awhile and float to the surface and my mother would see them looking at her and then she'd FOFG. That's my own for Freak Out For Good. I never told my mother about my girlfriend either. You know her but I'm not going to say who she is. She's still in school but not in our class.

My father has this book. *The Foxfire Book*. He's had it a long time because I remember it was around the house where we lived before. If I say where we lived before you might be able to figure out what my father did without reading between the lines so I'm not going to say only it wasn't like where we live now. It was in a city but not really. You could get to the city by metro which I did but only with my mother. Zu Zu could go by herself and she still has some tickets that she thinks are good but we don't go back there anymore although Zu Zu might because she's got a boyfriend from college who wants her to. I'm old enough to go on the Metro by myself only my mother wouldn't let me because she'd be afraid I'd get accosted which means like being kidnapped by Moonies or homosexuals. She's big on thinking about me being accosted.

My father's *Foxfire* book has this brown ring where he says he once put a coffee cup. My mother says an old girlfriend gave it to him that's why he still has it. They had this plan about going out west to Kansas someplace and living like Hippies and building a log cabin for the winter but living in a tepee for summer. That's what my mother says. My father just looks off up in the air when my mother says stuff like that. Or when my grandmother says stuff like that. Or when Zu Zu says God Dad. My father doesn't say anything back like Zu Zu will when my mother rags her about something. My father just looks up in the air at like a high spot on the wall but not really. It's like he's trying to look outside the house someplace. If my mother goes on about the *Foxfire* Woman he'll just puff out his cheeks and blow some air out. But he doesn't get mad or yell or anything. Bernie says his father's a big yeller and that he beats his mother. Maybe I shouldn't have said that. I've never been in Bernie's house. My mother won't let me go. Not that I've been invited.

When my father put the freezer in his man cave he turned it on just to see if it was going to work and then he turned it off. He said you can't just let it run because that was a waste of money. This was after the ten days we couldn't spend any money but even after that my father kept saying those four things about how we should live which I still can't remember the fourth. Maybe if I write them out it will come back. Do without. Use it up. Make do. That's only three. If my father were here I could ask him about the fourth. I don't want to ask my mother and Zu Zu is back at college. Zu Zu told my mother she has a new boyfriend who is black with green hair and a ring in his nose and that she is going to bring him home next weekend.

Anyway you don't turn on the freezer until only about a day before you have plenty to put in it because that way it doesn't waste money just staying cold by itself. My father says to me that we are going to have to wait until we get the pig and Edna and even some turkeys he bought from Bernie's dad and some chickens as well and a whole bunch of stuff he's going to get at Sam's one day soon which all happened about a week later. The day before we turned on the freezer and I watched it hum.

The next day Zu Zu and I helped my father fill up the freezer with the pig and Edna and he even froze cheese. I didn't know you could freeze cheese. After it was full my father closed the lid and sat on it like he was happy swinging his legs a little and whistling. My mother and my grandmother had gone to town now that they could spend money. Zu Zu split for the mall. I stayed.

My father whistled pretty good and Zu Zu once told me he had won some state championship whistling contest when he was in like high school. Anyway my father is sitting on his freezer swinging his legs and whistling and that's when he talked to me about what he's doing with his life. LMOL. Not that I asked. I was going to go to the pond to watch the turtles come back on the log after I ran them off. I also wanted to read my note to my girlfriend again. I know what it says I just like to read what I write.

But my father said wait a minute I want to tell you some things about life. He said waste was evil. He said my mother thought evil was something that was inside you and that's why she went to church and prayed. He said my grandmother said that evil was everywhere in everything we did but that was only part of the story and the other part of the story was the good that was everywhere in everything we did but that we needed to ask Jesus to tell us what was good because the Devil would tell us what was evil even if we didn't ask. But my father said he had been thinking about it a long time and that evil was waste because it led to greed and that led to war. He said the Gulf War was because we wasted gasoline and the Vietnam War was because we wanted rubber for our tires which we wasted because we always drove our cars everywhere.

My father had a waste for every war only he skipped some of the wars we studied in school. World War I for example. And the Civil War. He had a waste for World War II but I can't remember what it was. He also said there were religious wars and when he said that he looked up and away like he does when Mother starts in on him. But mainly he said waste was the big problem in life and in his life from now on he wasn't going to waste much. He said waste was like moral rust. MR he said. Here he laughed. MR he said again. I think he knew he was ripping off Zu Zu.

Every once in a while my father would stop talking about waste and start whistling again. I didn't think I was supposed to leave. Before he quit his job he didn't talk to me much only on Saturdays and this wasn't a Saturday so I thought I should stay. I'm not like Zu Zu. I don't mind listening to my father. She's got no time for him. But I didn't mind. He's o.k. When he'd stop whistling he'd start talking about waste again.

He said baking soda was good for waste. You could use baking soda for toothpaste and you could use it under your arms. I knew about using it under your arms because I heard my father and mother get into a big fight about not buying Mennens anymore and my mother told him to go back to work and get a job and stop telling her what to put under her arms. Baking soda was also good for washing your clothes my father said. And if you ever spilled a poison on the floor you could clean it up with baking soda. I could also put baking soda in my tennis shoes which he said my mother ought to buy a size bigger for me and put clumped up paper in the toes until I grow into them. That's when he got going about how many shoes my mother has and how we only need three or four pairs and maybe some boots to get through life. All the rest is waste. He stopped for awhile. I think maybe I should go.

Then he wants to know if I know how many plates we have in the kitchen and I don't. He says we have 86 flat plates. That's what he calls them. Flat plates. And we have 52 forks. We have 102 sweaters if you count my grandmother's and Zu Zu's. He's been through the house since we moved and counted all kinds of stuff we don't need. We have 22 pairs of gloves and some of them only left handed. The reason he says we have such a big house is to store our waste. If we didn't have 86 flat plates we could have had a smaller house but oh no we've got to have this big house full of plates and shoes and sweaters. By now he's stopped swinging his legs and he's not whistling. He's still sitting on his freezer but he's not whistling.

Do you see this my father says. He pulls out a sheet of paper from his pocket. It is like a page from a magazine only it is folded. This is why I quit. He says quit. This is why I quit. Then he unfolds the paper and holds it out so I can see. There is this picture of a dog looking out at us. See what it says my father says. It says do less have more. This is what's wrong. Everybody wants to have more: 106 flat plates, 300 sweaters. Do you know what your uncle said when the stock market crashed a few years ago. He said that was the end of the American Dream. Do you know what he said the American Dream was. He said the American Dream was making a lot of money without having to work for it. That's what he said.

My uncle was in the same office with my father but I don't think that means you can figure out what they did. Then my father doesn't say anything again for awhile. Only he gives me the magazine page with the dog on it and do less have more on it. I kept it. I never understood why a dog would say do less have more.

Then my father asks me what I think. He says he wants to know if I think he's FO or not. He says that means freaked out like I wouldn't know that for myself. FO. What did I think. He sort of laughs like he's supposed to or something but it's not really a laugh.

I don't think much I guess. Not about stuff like waste or church or wars or my mother or father. Mainly I think about what I'm going to do. Like going to the pond. Or what I'm going to say in this free writing. Or trying to guess if Joel is going to have more than one smoke on the way home. I might think about what I'm going to say to the water in the pond but sometimes not. The other day I thought about good and evil because Bernie asked me if I'd do his free writing for him for a dollar. I don't think that's much thinking if you ask me. Anyway I don't know what to say when my father asks me what I think.

But then I think I don't know what I call him. I don't call my father anything. My mother calls him Ted because that is his name but I don't call him that. Bernie calls his father Pops and Joel calls his father Old Man but I've never called my father anything unless it was when I was young. Maybe I called him something funny when I was young because I was the one who called Zu Zu her name because one day she took me to the zoo and after that I just called her that because I wanted to go back so I'd pull on her skirt and say Zoo Zoo. That's what they tell me anyway.

So I don't say anything when my father asks me what I think. Maybe I should have said I think I don't know what to call you but I didn't. So instead I try to whistle but it doesn't come out very well and my father smiles and whistles some himself. It is not something I know. He says it is from a movie about Africa. Very famous. This woman whistles it. Or maybe hums it.

That's when my father says *don't let them outnumber you*. Maybe I should break my rule and put that in quote marks because my father said it a number of times. He has stopped whistling and he is just sitting on the freezer and each time he says *don't let them outnumber you* he either looks at me or he looks away from me like when my mother hits him with the *Foxfire* Woman and once after he says *don't let them outnumber you* he even puffs out his cheeks. But the last time he says it he's looking at me again. I don't know what he means but maybe if I write it out again it will come to me but I don't want to. Then my father said I could go to the pond. I didn't know he knew about the pond.

I've been thinking. About how you said when we wrote this we could write about anything at all just as long as it really happened only we didn't have to write it like a theme with a beginning middle and end. I've been thinking I'm going to end this before what really happened. I just wanted you to know. Also I've been thinking about the list you said we had to make. The list of five things we learned from free writing. I don't think I can get to five unless I remember all four things my father told me about life and then add something of my own. I don't know what I've learned from this. But maybe if I write about what happened before the end that I'm not going to write about something will come to me. I just want to get another *Excellent* because that's what I've always gotten in writing since we've been here even from Mr. Schwartz who always wants beginnings middles and ends. I know the third thing I am going to claim for free in free writing but I'm not going to tell you even though you've probably guessed it by now. I'll tell you anyway. I'm not going to use question marks. I don't know why it just seems like something not to use. I don't like a question so much if I have to answer it. Joel says in Spanish they are upside down.

Since this is due tomorrow by now I don't have time to write much about everything that happened after my father was sitting on the freezer and whistling and saying all that about not letting them outnumber you. Even if it is before the end of what happened. It is just that I went to the pond because my father said I could. When I got there I went over to the rock where my note to my girlfriend was but it wasn't there anymore. I don't think anybody took it I just think maybe I didn't remember the right rock or that it got washed away with the big rain we had over the summer and maybe now it was in the pond. Maybe the snapping turtle that was going to drag me under until my eyeballs floated up ate it. It was a pretty good note and I liked it because I wrote it. When I get another girlfriend I'll write another note and put it under a bigger rock so I can read it even when I get to the High School.

Anyway I am at the pond talking to the water about waste and trying to whistle. I also try out a few names for my father that I will not write here. I don't like any of them very much but I keep saying them to the water and then I see my mother's car go by on the road. She can't see me where I am. I don't think I have to go home because it's summer so I just stay where I am. After awhile I stop talking to the water and wait for the mud turtles to come out onto the log and they do. I like this because it means you have to sit very still and not do anything but look at them or look at the water or at anything else but you can't talk or move and every time you don't talk or move another mud turtle will come out onto the log like you are calling them by not saying anything. I like that. After awhile the log was full and that's when I heard something down at our house.

You can't really hear all the way from the house to the pond but sometimes you can. Like the time my mother went looking for me you could hear her slam the door to her car only it wasn't a slam just a noise. Then I could hear the car go. This time there was some yelling and I thought Zu Zu had come back the other way and that she was in SLOT. I'm not going to tell you what that means because I don't think free writing means I can use dirty words. Anyway sometimes Zu Zu gets into SLOT and my mother really yells at her and Zu Zu yells right back. I thought that is what it was. Then I hear the car door slam really hard and so do the turtles and they all go off the log. Or maybe they go off the log because I stand up to see if I can see who is leaving if anyone is. Only no one is and then I see Zu Zu's car coming down the road the front way from town so I know she's not in trouble. Trouble is one of the words in SLOT. Then it is quiet for awhile and I think I'll just stay where I am. Maybe the turtles will come back onto the logs or maybe I'll look under some other rocks for my note. I don't know what.

Pretty soon Zu Zu comes up the road just walking and then she comes across the field to where I am. She tells me she knows I come here but she didn't tell anybody. Just when she gets there I see my father's car go up the road not very fast at all.

That's all I want to write. I didn't think if you wrote about things that happened you'd feel like you did when they happened in the first place. Or at least you feel sort of like you did when they happened in the first place. I didn't understand that. Maybe I should have written Bernie's free writing for him then I could have felt like him for a change. Free writing isn't all that free if you come to think about it.

I'll read back over what I've written like you tell us to before we hand it in and maybe I can find some things I've learned even if it's not five. Or if I can't find anything maybe I'll think of something to put in a list just to have it. I don't much like lists because that's what you put in front of colons and I don't like colons because they are like road signs telling you to look both ways before you pull out.

The Man Who Sees Music

"What do you see?"

"He says he sees music," says Edna. "You can't see music."

"I see music," Sam Watkins says.

"What does it look like?"

"Music," Sam says.

"Do you see the notes?" And here Dr. Levine mouths the first four notes of Beethoven's *Fifth Symphony*.

"No. I see music."

"What did I tell you, Doctor?"

Sam Watkins picks up the *Cottonwood Good Deal* off Dr. Levine's office table, unfolds it, and, holding it to the ceiling light, reads: "*There will be snow in the Caucasus all week.*"

"He does that at home, too," says Edna. "He says it's in Russian. He can't read Russian. Who can read Russian?"

Dr. Al Levine and Sam Watkins both attend the Cottonwood Rotary's meeting noon-to-one every Thursday—noon in Cottonwood is signaled by a long blast on the town's emergency siren. Then a second blast when the hour is over. Many stores close noon-to-one.

Al Levine doesn't like Rotary, but with patients in and around Cottonwood and Whitewoman County, he thinks he ought to show up for some community events—and the churches were out of the question.

There is a short program at Rotary and once or twice a year Dr.

Levine agrees to make a presentation. It is never about medicine. He had grown up in New York, living with his parents and his older sister in a Bronx apartment off Jerome Avenue, and so became a Yankees fan. One program he did for Rotary was on the architecture of Yankee Stadium (using the word "shape") and pointing out where the various memorials are located. Another program was on the boroughs of New York, limited to their locations (each of which he pointed to on the map he used for the program—but not noting that he had grown up in the Bronx). As for Sam Watkins, he never gave a program, and had recently stopped coming to Rotary.

"What kind of music?" asks Dr. Levine.

"That's another thing," says Edna. "He bought this record player at Second Hand Treasures along with something to run it, and speakers all together with a milk crate of records. We got ourselves a radio for the livestock reports and we got a television for Fox News, and we've never needed anything more. Now we got Symphonies and Beethovens and Concerts and Quartets and Bachs. We don't need it. I don't want it. And in between he reads Russian from the newspaper."

Al had wondered what had become of his old stereo set and records (*Just put them in that metal milk crate*, the woman who runs Second Hand Treasures had said). He had replaced everything with CDs and a disc player, plus a receiver/amplifier. There were times when he thought he might want the records back, scratches and all. However, he'd have to reclaim the record player as well. And you can't play a record in your car.

"Perhaps," says Dr. Levine to Sam's wife, "I should talk to your husband by himself. Thursday morning at 11 is open. Will that work?"

"I'll drive him."

"I can drive myself."

"He's safe to drive," says Dr. Levine. "In the meantime, I'll get something he can take that might help with his..." He almost says *delusions*, but does not. Nor are the pills he gets from his office cabinet anything but a placebo. On the way out, with Sam Watkins ahead of him, Dr. Levine tells Mrs. Watkins that he wants to see her alone as well.

"I am worried," she says. "We don't need this. We bought cattle last spring to sell this fall and the price is low. And we got months of no rain for the pastures."

Al (Israel) Levine got his undergraduate degree at Fordham, where he majored in Russian, with a minor in biology. St. Petersburg (not Moscow) was on his bucket list; his favorite composers and writers were Russian and German: Tchaikovsky, Wagner, Pushkin and Dr. Chekhov. He also had a fondness for the geography of Russia: the great spread of the old country.

Later he earned his medical degree at The Albert Einstein Medical College not far from where he had grown up. Then he went to Boston General, where he took a rotating internship. He thought he might like to be a surgeon, but late one day he was left to close after a gall bladder operation so the chief of surgery could attend a Wagner/Tchaikovsky concert. It was the very concert for which he had bought a standing-room ticket and now could not go.

Closing after an operation is a tedious process, but it has to be done with care, the stitches tightly packed, the layers of fascia folded in with precision. Israel was too careful an intern to hurry. Nor, as it turned out, was it ever the case that such a confluence (and conflict) of medical procedures and music occurred again. So instead of surgery, he chose psychiatry. Not that he put that degree on the wall of his Cottonwood office, much less in his listing in the phone book. To the folk of Whitewoman County he was Dr. Al Levine, M.D. (*General Practice*).

Once a year in summer he returned to New York for two weeks. There he stayed in the Bronx apartment that he and his sister,

Rachel, had inherited. Between them they had decided to keep it with the idea that one or the other might make use of it now and then, just as Israel did to take in Yankee games, attend concerts, and see friends in the Village. He would drive the three hours from Cottonwood to Denver and stay overnight at the airport to catch an early flight to LaGuardia, leaving the car at the motel for his return trip to Cottonwood.

Usually Rachel would be there in the fall, flying in from San Francisco, where she, like Israel, practiced medicine. But unlike Israel, she had become a surgeon, and in fact the chief of surgery at Stanford Medical School, specializing in cardiovascular surgery.

Sometimes their paths would cross, and sometimes they would agree to meet over the holidays. Two weeks from when Sam and Edna Watkins showed up in his office, Al had planned to make his trip to New York. Rachel would be there during his final week. He would leave his patients (Sam Watkins among them) in the care of James Blankenship, Cottonwood's only other doctor.

"Do you see all music?" Dr. Levine asks at Sam Watkins' second visit.

"Not if it comes over the radio."

"Just classical music?"

"Yes."

"All classical music?"

"No."

"Do you know your composers?"

"I read them off the records."

"While they are playing?" Dr. Levine asks, then thinks to himself: *What a question. Of course not.*

"Yes."

The two of them sit looking at one another, then:

"And what's this about reading the paper in Russian?"

The *Cottonwood Good Deal* is again on the table. Sam Watkins picks it up, holds it to the ceiling light, and reads:

"*Yalta will be sunny and warm today.*"

Dr. Levine thinks to ask if it is always a weather report, but does not.

Of the hour they spend together much is in silence, there being long pauses between questions and answers, with the longest silence at the end before Dr. Levine asks if Sam will be going to Rotary, to which Sam says no—just as the noon siren runs its course.

A week after Sam's appointment Dr. Levine met with Edna, and unlike Sam, she did most of the talking—and plenty of it. She was worried about "this Russian business" because Russians were *Communists* and maybe somebody would find out that Sam was reading Russian and you know how gossip spreads and we don't need that. Then there was the question of the music.

Edna's sister was over when Sam was playing one of those records, first watching it spin like he was trying to read something on it then just standing in the middle of the living room, looking first this way and then that way—crazy as all outdoors, and no telling what her sister would say to half of Whitewoman County.

Then to beat hell, when the music stopped, Sam put his hands to his eyes and walked out the front door even though it was raining pitchforks from that rain we got a couple of days ago and I thought (God forbid!) that rain after all this drought is because Sam sees music and reads Russian. My sister told me once that crazy people have powers. And bringing the rain might make Sam a witch doctor because he has some tribe in his blood from when Dull Knife came through.

When Edna paused to catch her breath the town noon siren

went off and Dr. Levine told her he had a Rotary program to give, which was not true. Nor did he correct her by saying it was probably *medicine man*, not *witch doctor* that she meant.

"I have a patient who sees music," Israel says to Rachel the evening she arrived from San Francisco. He had been there a week and had a week to go.

"And I have a patient," she says, "who tells me over and over again that it's good for us to have our *heart-to-heart talks*. He thinks he's funny."

"Mine reads the local paper by holding it to the light, where it turns in into Russian: *Yalta will be sunny and warm today*."

"You win. With synesthesia we're tied, but there is no cure for reading Russian from the local paper. You win."

During his first week in New York Israel went to all three games of a Yankee hometown series with the Kansas City Royals—tickets he had bought in advance. He dined with friends in the Village, and took in one concert (Beethoven's *Sixth* and Bach fugues), saving a second set of concert tickets to use with Rachel.

"Still the same in *West Jesus Land* as you call it?" Rachel asks.

"Chicken fried steak on Fridays, Mexican on Tuesdays, pizza on Wednesdays, scalloped potatoes and ham on Thursdays, fried catfish on Fridays, bierocks on Saturdays, closed Sundays."

"My, my. What are bierocks?"

"Don't ask."

"And the wine?"

Israel laughed.

The other doctor in Cottonwood was James Blankenship. By training he was a pediatrician, and to Al's eye not a very good one. Beyond that he was lazy, a womanizer, and a drunk—at least at night when gossip had it that he'd hold forth at the country club's "Duck Blind Bar" on Obamacare, among other government intrusions into the practice of medicine. Nobody could understand how his wife could live with him.

One evening Al was called to the country club because Blankenship had passed out and fallen. Nothing serious but because Blankenship was the only other doctor in the town there were reasons (trips back to New York among them) to take care of him. Unlike Al Levine, James Blankenship was not gay. Nor Jewish.

"Do they still not know you're gay?" Rachel asks over dinner in the apartment a few nights after she had arrived.

"I am bisexual."

"Tell me about the women in your life. It will be the first I've heard of this. Are you in love with them?"

"I love the women I meet in songs," Israel says.

"Songs? What songs?"

"*Every time we say good-bye. For all we know. I'll be seeing you.* Others."

"Rod Stewart songs?"

"Yes. I am told I look like him."

"Now that I think about it, you do. Is that where you got the songs?"

"I got them from our father playing them on the piano in memory of our mother after she died. You had gone on your residency in California. I was still at Fordham and living here."

"How amusing. And not to know this about you."

"I could never understand," Israel continues, "how it was possible to love a woman until I heard those songs. It came to me from our father to our dead mother to Rod Stewart and in the process Rod became me, or I became him."

"The transmigration of notes," says Rachel. "And sexuality in the process. There's a disc player I bought around here somewhere. Do you have a disc of Rod Stewart being yourself?"

"No, and better you play them if you don't mind."

It was for Rachel they had bought the piano although their father played it as well, mostly Broadway show pieces they would sing together: *How are things in Glocca Morra? Oklahoma.* He had been in vaudeville as a young man. And he had wanted to name his son in honor of Irving Berlin. But his wife insisted on "Israel." That *Levine* would later become the conductor James Levine was much the same future of fate as Israel looking like Rod Stewart.

"Were there other songs that he played for her?" Rachel asks.

"*I'll be seeing you. It had to be you. The way you look tonight. They can't take that away from me*—which I must say, given my medical degree, seems a bit paranoid."

Rachel goes to the piano and starts a medley: *It had to be you. The way you look tonight. The nearness of you.*

"That last one also," says Israel.

"Is there a different woman for each song? Do they appear in your mind's eye?"

"Do I see women instead of music?" Israel says. "I hadn't thought of it that way. Very funny. Did you do a rotation through psychiatry? 'Tell me your fears and I'll tell you your phobias.' And the whole business about my mother and love songs. Sophocles and Freud would have a grand time with that."

"So?"

"So what?"

"Do you see a woman for each song?"

"Just one. But she has more faces than Eve. And Lilith."

"What about Lolita and Lorelei?"

"Those girls as well."

"Maybe you're not gay," Rachel says. "Gays don't watch baseball games. Gays don't see women in romantic songs. When I told Father that you said you were gay, he said that couldn't be because no one in the family had ever been gay."

"I've got late onset gayness," Israel says.

"Like onset diabetes? I suppose it's possible."

"I was teasing."

"Promise me something," Rachel says.

"What?"

"That if it gets too weird out there, you'll come back here."

The day before Al was to leave for Denver, Edna returned to the office in the morning without an appointment and a few hours before Sam was to keep his. Again she had plenty to say:

The horse had not been shod because the farrier missed coming and Edna was sure that was because he'd heard about Sam and wasn't about to work a horse that belonged to a witch doctor. You can't blame him. But the steers need to be moved to the north pasture and you can't use a horse doing that unless he is well trimmed. Not that Sam was safe to ride, and who knows that he might start spouting Russian on the way and somebody hears him from the country road that runs along there and turns him in to the sheriff. We don't need this. We might as well sell the horse, old as he is anyway, and get someone else to move the herd.

On top of that, Betty's got herself knocked up at the state college by some professor and she wants him to marry her. And it's my thinking that Teddy's queer. What they call *gay* these days, only it is not so gay to be *queer* if you come from Cottonwood and somebody finds out. He's at the college with Betty, two years behind. What's the use of going to a state college if you get yourself preggers and your brother gets queer? And now I've got Sam seeing music and reading Russian from the paper. Why can't everybody be normal? She left tapping the right side of her head with her right index finger.

At eleven Sam came, the weekly edition of the *Cottonwood Good Deal* tucked under his arm. He handed it to Dr. Levine.

"Read it," Sam says. "Go to the middle page, the one with the story about the wheat crop."

"I am there."

"Hold it to the light."

"O.K."

"Do you see that the 'Neva is frozen'? It flows through some city in Russia. It must be cold there."

Dr. Levine adjusts the paper to the light, moving it back and forth to see what he can see. In so doing the story of the wheat crop jiggles a bit, then a bit more. Then it vanishes and something else comes into focus. Al pushes the paper away, rubs his eyes with the back of his right hand, puts the paper (still unfolded) on the table in front of Sam. He is tempted to look again, but does not.

"The Neva flows though St. Petersburg," Dr. Levine says. "It's a city in northern Russia. It's too early for it to be frozen."

Sam picks up the paper, holds it to the ceiling light and reads: "*The Neva is frozen.*"

The next day Al drives to Denver, stays overnight, and then flies to New York to meet Rachel. Before he got on the plane he bought himself a copy of the *Denver Post*, and somewhere over Whitewoman County he held the national weather section to the sky out the window. It would be warm and sunny in New York. Nothing jiggled.

"Why do you stay out there?" Rachel asks.

She was again at the piano, this time playing the theme from *Alfie*. They were having a drink before going out to dinner. The next day Al was to catch a plane from LaGuardia back to Denver. It would be a three-hour drive to Cottonwood, but his car had a disc player and so Bachs (as Edna Watkins put it) and Beethovens would keep him company. It had been a good stay, but for reasons that he was not going explain to either Rachel or himself, he was looking forward to getting back.

"I want to continue treating my patient who sees music and reads Russian in the newspaper," Israel says.

"Do think he means patterns in music? Themes? Motifs?"

"He wouldn't know the words. And as his physician it is my duty to understand."

"Be serious," says Rachel. "Ten years of living in *West Jesus Land* can't be good for your own mental health. You could have stayed here. Lived in the apartment. There is plenty of work in New York. East Side matrons full of anxieties. Ripe for pill popping and couches at two hundred and fifty dollars an hour. 'Here, my dear, have a little Prozac with your martinis at lunch.' You had to put yourself through psychoanalyses to get your degree. It's time for a refresher round. 'Doctor, heal thyself.'"

"The Doctor in 'Ward Six' tried that and it turned out badly. It's a Chekhov story," Israel says.

"I've read it."

The night before Israel was to fly back to Denver, he and Rachel went to a concert, and by a bit of good luck it was more or less the same concert from years ago when he was a resident: Wagner's *Tannhäuser Overture* and the *Prelude and Liebestod* from *Tristan und Isolde*, followed by an assortment of Tchaikovsky—not the same assortment as in the Boston Concert to be sure, but ending as it did those many years ago with *Eugene Onegin*.

He had not told Rachel this and it somehow pleased him in much the same way it pleased him to join friends (Rachel included with them) after the concert at The Boiler Room in the Village, where they got the early-morning edition of the *Times*. And later riding uptown in a cab he saw Rachel catch him in the reflection of his window holding the weather page of the paper up against the lights of the city.

"Read any Russian?" Rachel asks.

"Rain in Urals," he says. Which was not true—and disappointing. Warm and sunny in the city the next day was more like it. Some jiggles to the text that faded on the west side of Central Park.

Al Levine had booked an afternoon flight to Denver and that meant he'd stay over at the airport motel where he had left his car. It was quicker back to Cottonwood on the interstate, but he much preferred the slow route on the state highways through the Front Range. He liked the silence of the land with its scattered and mostly abandoned houses. There was a buffalo ranch partway into the trip. This time he saw a herd of antelope to the south. By now he was out of range of the National Public Radio station. That was fine. The country through which he was driving was quiet enough.

Halfway to Cottonwood he stopped at the Western Café to get a cup of coffee. The *Front Range Gazette* was on one of the tables and he picked it up. First, he looked through the news: feeder cattle market prices; the wheat report; local sports news. He was stalling. Checking to see if anyone was watching, he held the paper to the ceiling light: nothing but classified ads. Then he held it to the outdoor sunshine coming through the window. Yes. Maybe. The waitress came up to refill his coffee and ask was he looking to find something special. Her husband had a horse to sell.

An hour into the final stretch he inserted a Bach disc: fugues. What someone he had read called "The Divine Sewing Machine of Music." Could that be what Sam Watkins meant? Is that what he saw? Bach as a sewing machine? Beethoven's *Sixth* as pastures like the ones in and around Whitewoman County? Wagner as Valkyries on horseback looking for fallen warriors? It didn't seem possible for Sam Watkins. For Israel, sure.

But now as he looked out the windshield coming into and going through Last Chance, Colorado, that was not a sewing machine in the glowing of the sky above the road ahead of Dr. Israel (Al) Levine. Looking again (and again): It was music. Yes. Yes.

He tried singing the lyrics of Rod Stewart songs to see if any woman with the many faces of Eve or Lilith or Lolita could blot out the music that was first just outside his windshield and now had come into the car itself. But that did not work. Nor could he see the Bach as "notes" or "motifs" or "themes" ... or even a sewing machine. It was music. Pure music. Now he knew what that looked like.

Al had given himself two days after returning to Cottonwood before seeing patients. In the meantime Blankenship had taken appointments for him: Tad Trayer, had a cough (*either bronchitis or the usual hypochondriasis*—as Blankenship's note put it). Others (flu mainly). And Sam and Edna Watkins (*nutsastheycome the 2 of them*).

On his first day back Al bought himself the most recent edition of the *Cottonwood Good Deal* and took it to his office. He unfolded the paper to the middle page, where, once again, there was a report on the wheat crop. Indeed it had been very good, but now the problem was too much of it and the price was poor. There was other news: The pheasant population was looking up. There might be two hatches. The milo was coming on strong. *Smoking on The Beaver* had been a huge success, with a local man (Harley Wickie) winning first prize for his beef ribs.

Holding the paper to the light, Al saw nothing, which somehow distressed him. He moved it so that it caught the outside light. Nothing.

Then he refolded the paper to see what he had missed on the front page: the lead story was that Dr. James Blankenship had taken a job in a clinic just east of Denver and would be leaving at the end of the month. A committee was being formed to find a new doctor. It was hoped that Dr. Al Levine would be chairman. There was a knock at the door. It was James Blankenship.

He said his wife had left him the week before and had gone to Texas to live with her sister until the divorce was settled. And the husband of one of the women he had been "boinking" found them out and arrived at the Duck Blind Bar with a pistol. There was a fight, no shots were fired, the cops came. The paper did not do a story, nor was it recorded on the police blotter: There were some advantages to being a doctor in West Jesus Land.

"You're gay, right?" Blankenship said to Al at the door before he left.

The next day Dr. Levine called Sam Watkins and asked him to stop by that afternoon. His copy of the *Cottonwood Good Deal* was on his office table when Sam came in. Edna was with him.

"I expect you heard about what happened when you were gone," she says.

"About Dr. Blankenship?"

"About Sam."

"What about Sam?"

"The fuss he created at Rotary. How they had to call me and all to come and get him."

Sam Watkins is sitting in the chair by the table where Dr. Levine has put his *Cottonwood Good Deal*.

"That one says it will be warm and sunny in the tundra," says Sam as he picks it up.

"That's not the same paper he brought to Rotary," says Edna. "It was last week's. Twenty-five copies. He took over the program from the sheriff. That's who called me to come up or he'd have to put Sam away somewhere but not the jail. I don't exactly remember. Nine-one-one someplace. When I got there they were all holding the paper up to the neon lights in the civic center and laughing while Sam was reading the weather report. Just like now. Something about rain in the urinals."

Dr. Levine told Edna he needed Sam to stay for some treatments and she should drive home and come back later in the afternoon. He would call her. After she left, Al picked up his copy of the *Cottonwood Good Deal* and held it to the light: letters jiggled in the wheat report. But nothing came into focus.

"Turn to the back page of last week's paper," Sam Watkins said.

"The classified section. Hold it steady. Both hands. Spread it out a bit."

Behind the Watkins' ad for their horse, there was something taking shape. Yes. The jiggles of previous papers in New York, Denver and the Western Café were becoming words: *Bitter cold in the Koryak Mountains*, Al Levine thought he had said to himself.

"Yes," said Sam Watkins. "Do you know where they are?"

"Just across from Alaska," Al says.

"See?" Sam said.

"Yes."

"What are you doing here?" Israel asked.

"The Super called," Rachel said. "She told me that..."

All through the apartment were copies of the *New York Times*, opened and not refolded: On the piano bench. On the piano. On the tables in the kitchen and in the living room. On the floor. In chairs. On top of one another. Bach fugues were playing on a loop. Rachel turned them off.

"It is snowing along the Stanovoy Range," Israel said.

The Skull Hunter

I call myself the Skull Hunter, and I guess I am. It's not painted on the side of my pickup or anything. And the guy I work for doesn't have any name for my job, only, "My man Wallace will take care of you." I work for Karl Ganz who owns Whitewoman River Floats and Motel. Karl doesn't know anything about the skulls. Neither does his wife. She left him last year and is living in Denver. I mean to go see her some day when I'm out there. I think I will.

I have a wife and I have this woman on the river. Sally Norton is her name. I like to mess with women. I like my wife. We don't have any children. *Nothing in the oven*, my wife will say and pat her belly. We live at the motel. Number 26. It's one of the cabins. The biggest one. We get it as part of our pay. My wife cleans for the motel. And she makes extra money by fixing picnic baskets for the floats. Karl knows about the picnics, but he doesn't want a cut. I let my wife keep it for herself. She buys flowers or plants. Spring through the fall. She makes 26 a home. It's nice.

Sometimes she'll go to Cottonwood and buy clothes. Pretty clothes she wears for me at night. It's always good to come home to her, even if I've been with Sally Norton, or sometimes with another woman I have in Cottonwood. It will be the same if I ever get with Karl's wife in Denver. I'll be driving back at night having nailed Karl's wife but looking to see mine. You have to know how I feel to understand.

What I do when I'm not working the river is keep the motel fixed. Plastic pipe made plumbers of us all, and a cordless drill makes you a carpenter. I put doors right when they've pulled off their hinges. Fix windows. Screens. Steps. In the summer between floats I paint. Inside and out. The motel is yellow, but not inside. Inside is white. I change light bulbs. Before I was a pen rider in Ogallala.

"My man Wallace will come right down, lady, and change that light bulb pronto." *Pronto* is one of Karl's big words. We do everything pronto at the Whitewoman Floats and Motel. The lady who wanted her light bulb changed, that's another story. She and her husband are regulars. Every July. The story's not like you think. It's more fucked than that. My wife and I have never told anyone. Like I've not told Karl about the skulls.

The deal with the skulls is this. We have these canoes that Karl rents to float the Whitewoman starting with this one group that comes from Tulsa in wetsuits the end of March. Then the summer floaters. Then all the way through early October when we get people who want to see how the leaves have turned along the river. It's warm here mostly through Thanksgiving. Winter is something else. But I like that, too. Ice in the wind.

Karl's made this deal with the ranchers along the river to clean up any mess his floaters leave. That way Karl doesn't have the ranchers down on the river yelling at the floaters to stay off their land. The river's not theirs but the land is. My job is to go down the river when a float's over and pick up after them. That's when I hunt for my skulls. Then, and other times as well. I was the one that came up with the idea about the fences.

Every time the river runs from one ranch to another, there's a fence. Even across the water. Which means the floaters have to slip under the fence, and it's barbed wire. What Karl used to do, he'd give everybody a pair of cheap work gloves to push up the wire as they'd go under. Only they'd get scraped anyway. Along their arms. And once this lady from the Plaza, Kansas City, got her hairdo caught in the wire and started screaming like she was on fire. She jumped out of the canoe and wouldn't get back in. At least that's what they said when the rest of them got to the end of the run where I was to meet them up at the Two Sleeps Bridge and drive them back to the motel. They said she was just sitting on the bank about a mile upriver and somebody'd have to get her by truck because she wasn't anymore getting into the canoe. Her husband said leave the bitch to walk out. The dizzy bitch.

After I drove everybody up the Oil Road to the motel, I went back to the Whitewoman and got her, only it wasn't easy because she was where Bone Creek comes in, and you can't get down to the river there by truck, so I had to walk the last part. That's when I thought about just cutting open a length of PVC pipe and slipping it over the bottom strand of wire so you could just hold it up with your hand when you took the canoe under. Even if it did drop down, it wouldn't get caught in your hair or anything.

I told my thinking to the Kansas City lady as we walked out, but she was still fucked from the fence getting caught in her hair, and I don't think she paid much attention. I liked her, though, and I took her hand a few times to pull her up banks. I opened the door to the truck and helped her in. If you're nice to women, they'll be nice to you. Maybe not right away, but sooner or later. Maybe it doesn't mean you'll nail them, but it's a start.

I think of things like that. I think that all women are related when it comes to how men treat them, so that the word gets around about you. Like the birds know when my wife starts filling up the feeders in the winter. Or animals will know where to find water in a dry year and tell one another. I've not worked the idea out all the way to the end, but that's the start of it. Ideas are like women because they're fun to think about when you're by yourself. On the river, I'm by myself a lot. Unless I'm with Sally Norton.

You can't see where Sally lives from where Bone Creek comes into the Whitewoman. Or even from where I had to park my truck to go down to get the lady from Kansas City. But where she lives is not far away. Upriver two bends. Near where I found my first buffalo skull. And my third. Across from the oxbow nobody knows about. Or the dugout with this guy's skeleton on his back with no head on his shoulders. Near there. All around are good skull-hunting pastures. The best.

What I do is sell the skulls. The cattle skulls. Other skulls. But not the buffalo skulls. I don't sell those. I sell the cattle skulls in Denver to this guy who cleans them up for his shop. It's called the High Plains Hangout. I also sell him wild turkey feathers. Rattlesnake skins. Coon tails. Arrowheads. Mainly I sell him cattle skulls and deer skulls. Hawk skulls. Horse skulls. Coyote skulls. Two bobcat skulls, both from the same year. But mainly cattle skulls. It's my specialty.

Every time I go to Denver with a load of skulls, he takes me to the Buffalo Exchange for lunch. The place is full of animal heads on the walls. He treats me to a buffalo burger and some Fat Tire beer. That's a name, now isn't it? Fat Tire beer. I think he should get a better name for his store, but I don't say so. Maybe *Skull Heaven*. Something.

"Do you ever find any buffalo skulls?" he asks me the other day.

"No," I say.

"They say sometimes they'll wash out of the riverbanks in the spring," he says.

"That'd be the time," I say.

"If you ever find one, I'll pay top dollar for it," he says. He buys me another Fat Tire.

I don't tell him I have seven good buffalo skulls from the river. I don't tell anyone. Not even my wife. Nobody. Seven. Only Sally Norton knows about them because that's where I keep them. At her double-wide up from Bone Creek. Then there's plenty I don't tell Sally, either. Mostly, I don't tell her much. There's more to me than I've ever told anybody. Especially women.

"I mean top dollar," he says. "If it's old. From the Indian days. Not one of Ted Turner's buffalo. And not busted up."

"Sure," I say. I tell him I'll keep an eye out.

We go back to his shop, and he pays me for what I've brought, and I look around and see what I've sold him before that's still on the walls and tables, and what prices he gets for the cattle skulls after he's bleached them out in a tub of Clorox so they look like they've been in the pastures half of history. Some of them he's had painted. I wouldn't pay what you have to pay to own one of my skulls, but I'm glad somebody does.

Then I head home. Four hours. I like the drive because most of the time it's sunny out here, and in the afternoon coming back across the Front Range you get these long shadows from behind, filling in the creek beds and draws and canyons like it was dark snow, and I like that.

"Sell everything?" my wife says.

"Five hundred and twenty-seven dollars' worth of everything," I say. She is dressed in this buckskin skirt and a red blouse with the top two buttons not done, and that means she wants some pleasure for herself. When she's like this, she doesn't like to wait until after supper. Karl says women always want to wait. They want some romance before they get nailed. Not my wife. Not tonight at least. She's got two beers in frosted mugs, and I can see her tits are trying to unbutton number three all by themselves. I take my pleasure; she takes hers. Afterward, we finish our mugs in bed.

"The man in cabin eighteen left me another note," she says when we're eating supper. To let me look at her across the table, she hasn't put her blouse back on. Only her buckskin skirt. That's to get me going a second time, and it might work. "It was under the pillow," she says.

The man in cabin eighteen is the husband of the woman who wanted me to change the light bulb a few years back, and that's when all this started. They're from Omaha. A pair of lawyers. Or something. Professional people is what they say for themselves. That's lawyers, we figure. Or college teachers.

"They're something," I say.

My wife has fixed meat loaf, and it's good. She puts egg in it and bread crumbs and onions and steak sauce on the top so she gets this deep-red crust. I can't have it any better. I drink my Coors out of the frosted mug she's fixed and look at my wife and think about my ride across the Front Range with $527 in the glove compartment all the time, coming home to her wanting to get nailed twice, and I say to myself I am one happy Skull Hunter. Maybe I should put that on the side of my truck. *One Happy Skull Hunter.*

"They want us tomorrow," she says. "After supper."

"Was there any money?" I say.

"Twenty bucks," my wife says. She points to it under a sunflower magnet she has on the refrigerator. It's one of those new twenty-dollar bills.

What cabin eighteen wants is for us to watch them while they do it. Sometimes it's enough they can see us at the back window looking through into the bedroom, but sometimes they want us in the living room. When they want us in the living room, they don't want us to watch, just listen. They are older than we are, but they can really go at it.

When they've asked, we've never not done it. It will be the same this time. We always spend the twenty on something special. Dinner out in North Platte, usually. Or Cottonwood. There's a good Mexican place in Cottonwood. The woman I have in Cottonwood is a waitress there. We try not to look at each other. Only, sometimes we do. She's younger than me. By a lot. When I'm with her, I show her some things she doesn't know about. It's fun.

"City people are weird," says my wife, as she gets up to clear the table. I look at her naked back and to tell the truth her back and her shoulders and all the way down to where her skirt is tight across her waist is just as beautiful to me as anything else she's got for a body. Just as pretty going away half naked as coming at me. You can't like a woman better than that.

"City people are weird," she says again, as she turns toward me after having put the dishes on the counter.

"That they are," I say. "Any other notes?"

My wife gets these other notes when she's cleaning the rooms, from guys looking to nail her.

"One," she says as she sits down. "From six. No money, though. You want to read it?"

She saves the notes. She keeps them for a journal she's writing about how we live out here. Like the guy does in *Dances with Wolves*. It's her favorite movie. I can't watch it. Not what happens at the end to the horse. Or to the wolf. I can't even watch it as far as when they find the buffalo all skinned. I just can't.

My wife wants me to keep a journal, too. About the floats. The skulls. She says I can't use the notes she gets, even though she lets me read them. Some are just shit-house notes. Most guys don't know how to write women. Some are pretty smooth. I left her one, myself, but she doesn't know that. She said it was the best one she ever got, and I still haven't told her. Maybe I should. Maybe not. I've been trying to figure out what you should tell women. Even your wife.

"I'll read it later," I say, because if it's a shit-house note, then it will spoil it for me with her for a second time. If it's good, I'd rather have written it myself.

"You hunting skulls tomorrow?" my wife says, with a smile on her face and tossing her hair back because she knows she's going to get me again. Then she touches her breasts with her fingers and watches herself do it.

"Yes," I say. I need another ten minutes or so.

"You going to take me along," she says.

She's poking me. But just for fun this time. She knows I won't take her on the river. Or to Denver. It's a scab between us. I have this theory that a man's got to have his own territory. Someplace where he's different from what he is when he's not there. Not that I'm not who I am when I'm with my wife. I'm me wherever I am. It's just that there is more than one me. Men are that way. Like my thinking about women, I haven't got it all lined out, but I'm working on it. Thinking takes time if you do it right.

"I'll take you someplace else," I say. "Florida." I don't mean it.

"How about we do it on the river sometime?" she says back.

I can tell she's just thought of it. And it sounds good. We did it once on a mattress in the pickup at night in the high school parking lot. It was her idea.

"Turn the canoe over," she says, as she gets up from the table and walks toward the bedroom, bending a little at the waist as she goes.

"Maybe," I say. I mean it. Only I'll take it back later. "Yes," I say and follow her into the bedroom.

Like I say, it's when I take a canoe down the river to see if the floats have left anything, I hunt for cattle skulls. Sometimes they wash over the bank. Sometimes they are in the water or on the sandbars. Mainly they are in the pastures, which means I get off the river to find them. Or stop by Sally Norton's.

Her husband was a trapper. He's still alive even after he shot himself, but he can't make it on his own anymore, so he's in Cottonwood at the home for cripples. I'm the one who saved him. I think maybe Sally shot him. I can sort of see it. Sally's a little fucked. The bullet went through his neck. He's a lot older than she is, and some people say he never was her husband. I found him by one of his traps. He was out, but he wasn't bleeding as bad as you'd think. I put him in my canoe and took him down to the Two Sleeps Bridge. Tom Bitters came by about then, and we laid out Sally's husband in the back of the truck and drove him into Cottonwood, where they said he wasn't dead. I hadn't been with Sally before he got shot, but I was afterward. That night, if you want to know.

I hunt my cattle skulls between floats during the summer, but I also hunt them in the spring before the guys with the wetsuits from Tulsa come out. That's when I go down the river to cut the logs out of it so the floats can get through. I fix the fences, as well. It's cold in March, but I like it better for hunting skulls because I don't feel rushed. I also like going down the Whitewoman after the last float in the fall, even if it's November or December and we've got some snow. With a good snow blowing on the river, you can't believe anybody was ever on it before you were, no matter how many floaters came through in the summer. There's something clean about winter out here.

It's in the spring when you find the buffalo skulls. Just like the guy in Denver says. They come out of the banks after a good rain. You've got to know where to look. You've got to know what you're looking for, also. I do. I know.

I look for a dark lump in the clay of the bank. Or for bones coming out. Ribs. Legs. Backbones. The skull will be along there somewhere. I've been lucky. The seven buffalo skulls I've found have all been good. Both horns. No eye sockets broken in. Noses all the way to the end. Big skulls. From *Dances with Wolves* days. I wouldn't know what top dollar would be in Denver for my seven skulls. But they're not for sale.

When I found number seven last fall is when I found my skeleton. But not his head. I call him Wallace. After me. He's all there. Feet. Arms. Ribs. All connected. On his back. Everything but the head. I've been the year up and down the river looking for it. No head.

I leave Wallace where I found him because nobody would know to look there. I check in on him now and then. He's in a dugout in a small oxbow. There are mud cats in it. It's big enough for that.

You can't see it from the river because of some plum thickets. I didn't know it was there myself until I came on it from walking the pasture behind it.

I don't think Wallace is old. Not like a buffalo skull will be old. But he's not young either. He's not like someone who came out on the river two years ago and got murdered or died and I need to tell the sheriff. Or somebody got left on a float like that guy from Kansas City wanted to leave his wife. Wallace has been around. I like to think that maybe he lived on the river and no one knew he was out here. A guy by himself. Who knows? I talk to him.

Sometimes, I imagine Wallace just packed it in one day from Chicago or Detroit during the Depression and found himself this oxbow and made his dugout and called it home. Other times, I think he was the last of the mountain men who wanted a place to live out his days where you can see the edge-of-the-earth morning, night and noon.

I got other ideas for him, as well. A hitchhiker from the highway who maybe had robbed a bank in Missouri. Some guy from Hays who went out for a pack of cigarettes on his wife and kids. Maybe an old Indian who escaped from the reservation in Oklahoma and came up here to this oxbow to die. I think I'll name the oxbow Wallace's Oxbow. In honor of him, not me. Wallace's Oxbow it is. Why not?

Every time I stop by, I add to his story about how he lived on the river. He's fishing with a taut line in the summer and setting snares for rabbits in the winter. I've given him my Model 12 so he can shoot prairie chickens. I'm thinking I should give him my 250 Savage so he can take a deer. Tan out the hides. Maybe one of the old deer skulls that washed out of the river last spring is one he shot. I make his stories with stuff like that in them. Maybe Wallace had a horse. A dog. But not a wolf. I don't want him to have a wolf. I tell him he doesn't have a wolf.

When I finish talking to Wallace, I go over to Sally Norton's double-wide. Her husband hauled it in over the Cody ranch about ten years ago. It was rough when he brought it in, and it's worse now. The roof is held down by tires, and some of the siding is starting to flap off. If the wind's up, I can hear it creak from the river. You can't use one room at all because the windows are out. That's where I keep my buffalo skulls.

I've got them all laid out on a big blanket, three down each side, and the best one at the top. I call him Bill. When Sally's not around, like she wasn't the other afternoon, and I'm waiting for her, I'll go into the room and lie down on my back so that the skulls are up my sides with Bill above my head. I like doing that. I like doing that and waiting for Sally and thinking about the way she likes to get nailed.

"I know where it is," Sally Norton says to me.

We're done and she's starting to come down. Right afterward she can't talk. She's pretty, but not as pretty as my wife. She makes different noises though. All along, she doesn't talk no matter how we go at it. But she makes these noises. First one kind of noise then another. Then at the end, all the noises at once. Like a lot of animals at once. After that is when she can't talk. You nail different women for different reasons.

"What?" I say. I pretend I don't know what she's talking about. But I do. The thing is, I didn't know she knew about Wallace. I never told her. Because she lives on the river, she might know about the oxbow but not the dugout. You don't know it's there.

"The head," she says.

"What head?" I say.

"I have it," she says.

"Where?"

"I'm not going to tell you."

I'm late getting home, and my wife has dinner on the table and she's got the candles lit, and she's been to Cottonwood to buy some new clothes with the money she's been saving up from the picnics, plus the forty bucks we got for watching the lawyers do it twice this summer.

She's wearing a yellow blouse with nothing on underneath. I'm not sure if I've got enough stuff left over from this afternoon, but I think if I can put her off until after dinner maybe I do. I've done it before back to back. It helps when the women are different. But I'm getting older. I can feel it.

"Let's eat first," I say as I sit down. "I've got a story to tell you." I don't, but my wife likes my stories and this might slow her down, although I can see she's breathing like she wants to do it yesterday, and that makes her tits shiver and I worry that they'll unbutton her new blouse from the inside out.

"What's your story?" she says. She's still standing, and I can see that she's bought this new skirt as well. It's yellow, too, only not so yellow as her blouse. I can see her legs through it. When she notices that I'm looking, she backs up some so I can get a better view. I'm in a tough spot here.

"Sit down and I'll tell you," I say.

"It better be good," she says, bringing a plate of baked chicken with her from the stove, and some corn and bread and potatoes as well. Two frosted beers.

I am trying to think of a story about some adventure I've had on the river or in Denver that she knows isn't true because it couldn't be. Like the story I once told her about sitting next to Jane Fonda in the Buffalo Exchange and how we talked about Fat Tire beer and buffalo burgers. My wife asked if Jane Fonda showed me some of her exercises that are on this videotape my wife has, and I say yes, she did. Then I say I did sit-ups with Jane Fonda right there on the floor in the Buffalo Exchange with the skull buyer and everybody watching and clapping. Then Ted Turner comes in. My wife said Ted and Jane have split, and so he wouldn't be there. But I say he is. That kind of story.

Or maybe I could go on with my white horse story. We've got this white horse out here that we like to think is wild. Some people have seen him and some have not. I've seen him, but not up close. On a ridge. Or down in Black's Canyon. On the river way up in front of me. He's around. Once at Bone Creek, just about where I parked the pickup to get the lady from Kansas City. You make the sign of the white horse when you see him. Or even when you talk about him. That's for good luck.

Anyway, I have this story I tell my wife about the white horse, which I make up as I go along. One story at a time. About how we are friends because he comes down to the Whitewoman to drink and doesn't spook when he sees me, because he knows I'm on the river like he is. How I talk to him. What he does. How he lays his ears back. Then forward. I put myself in his mind and have him think about me. He knows me, I tell my wife. He whinnies, seeing me in the canoe. Snorts low. Paws the ground. Rearing as if he's happy to see me. In my white horse stories, I haven't touched him yet. I thought I'd do that later. But I have him all white, although most everybody who has seen him says there's a bit of a gray blanket on his rump.

But with my wife sitting across from me in her new yellow blouse and this red ribbon in her black hair, I can't think of any stories like the ones from Denver or about the white horse because I hadn't set my mind to do it. After you've nailed a woman, the stories just go out of you. Not that I tell Sally Norton my stories. Or any other woman I'm with. Only my wife gets my stories. Just now, I'm a dry creek bed. So then I think maybe I should tell my wife the truth about something. Something she doesn't know.

"I found a buffalo skull," I say.

"No," she says. She knows I've been looking for one. She knows the man in Denver said he'd pay us good money for one. If good money is $500, she wants to go to Kansas City and stay on the Plaza when they've got the Christmas lights up.

"Yes," I say.

"Where?" she says. "Is it in the truck? Can I see it?" She knows this isn't a story I've made up. Right away she knows that.

"In Dull Knife's Cut by Bone Creek," I say. "On the south side." I don't know why I'm saying this. It's not good. I can feel something bad coming.

"Is it in the truck?" she says again. She's drained her beer so she gets up for another one and brings me one as well. I don't want to look at her because she's got nothing on but her new blouse and skirt, and I'm not ready yet. I don't say anything for a moment, and she asks again if it's in the truck, and she is about to go get it if I say yes. I hear myself say:

"I left it at Sally Norton's double-wide."

My wife drills me. She puts the mug down real slow. It doesn't even make a noise when it hits the table. She's still drilling me. Outside I think I can hear Ganz start his pickup. Maybe not. Maybe one of the cabins.

"I'll cut her gut button out with my Queen Steel," my wife says. "And shove it down her throat."

Sometimes in the early fall, you get these really warm nights with a moon to them. It's a good time to go down the river, and so I do. I'm not looking to go back to Sally's. I won't float that far. Just to the grain train bridge, then pull out and walk myself home. It's only about an hour's ride down, and if I cut across Lakin's pasture instead of taking the tracks, it's only twenty minutes. Maybe by then it will be better. I put the canoe in the bed of the pickup and go.

What I like to do on the river at night is mainly think. It's a pleasure to itself. Just like going down in the daytime looking for skulls is a pleasure. Only thinking is different from looking for skulls, and I do it best at night, even off the river. In bed with my wife twitching in her dreams beside me. Or sometimes coming back over the front range at night after I've been to Denver. I talk to myself, but not out loud. I keep it all in my head. You don't waste it that way.

What I'm thinking as I go down the river is about all the things I could have told my wife that are true that I haven't told her. That I've only told Wallace. About how I was married once before in Ogallala where I was a pen rider. Or how I was in the Navy just out of high school and that I might be wanted because I don't know how many years have to go by on an AWOL not to get busted. Or about my mother and how she died because of me. How I once was with Ganz's wife. But only once. Not that I wouldn't do it again if I could find her in Denver. Which maybe I can. Or about Wallace.

When his wife left him, Ganz told me that women have the most secrets, but I don't know. I am going down the river with the moon coming up in front of me, and I am thinking of all the stories about me I have kept secret from my wife. I am thinking that they are the stories I wouldn't want anyone to know but her. But I haven't told her any of them. Only bullshit stories about the white horse and Jane Fonda. Who wants to go belly up full of true stories he hasn't told anybody but a skeleton with no head in a dugout? I think that's what happened to Wallace. No stories for himself but the ones I make up for him. Not for me, I think. I have my wife. I can tell my wife everything. I have enough stories for her to last until we're dead.

I think what I should do is tell my wife something true once a week. On Fridays. Plus special days when we go out for dinner after the couple in cabin 18 have given us twenty bucks. Just take the heat from her until she gets used to it. Maybe I'll mix up my stories to start with. Tell her one of my Denver stories or something from the river. Then tell her one on me that's true. Not to fool her. Just to mix them up as if what's true about me is no different from what's not. I'll do it, I think. It's a plan. I'll go there. I feel good about it.

But coming around a bend in the river and out from under the bluffs, I think it's a bad plan. There's a lot of trouble waiting for you in the truth of things. At least with me there might be. What's the point? She'll get over Sally Norton. I've been caught before. Why set my own trap then step in it? Every Friday for a lifetime. Maybe I'll cut a deal whereby I won't see Sally anymore. Maybe drop the woman in Cottonwood, even though my wife doesn't know about her. Just find a woman in Denver because that's over the edge of the earth and news doesn't travel back across. Life is as good as it's going to get if I can smooth out my wife. Trying to make it perfect will just fuck it up. Then I see him. The white horse.

He's standing under this ash tree that dropped a big limb into the water last winter that I had to cut up and haul away so the floaters wouldn't have to get out of their canoes. He's standing right there. Because the wind's against me, he doesn't know I'm on the river. I break paddle and ease the canoe onto a small bar. It doesn't crunch. He's still standing there. This is no story. I can see him just like I've said I could. He lays his ears forward, then they go up. Then back. He's got no blanket. He's all white, like I tell it. I can see he's been to water. I can see the hoof prints in the sand where he's been. I'm that close. I can see his eyes. Black, like I make them. I wait for him to give me that low rumble I tell he has. He doesn't. His ears go up. He's thinking how the river is his every night. He's thinking about me and Wallace's Oxbow, and even Wallace, because he's been at the dugout, too. Which is true because I've seen his hoof prints. *I was Wallace's horse*, I have him think. *When Wallace went belly up, I went wild. I know where Sally Norton put his head. And where it was before she found it. I know about the skulls, and when I go belly up I want the Skull Hunter to have my head. But only for himself. Not to go to Denver. Only for himself. And his wife.*

Then he bolts. Not downstream but straight at me because he's heard something behind him. He bolts right up the riverbed, and in maybe three strides he's in my face. Then over the front of the canoe so close I get splattered with water and sand. I'd like to think he saw me, that we locked eyes and all that, but to tell the truth, I don't think he did. Only the canoe, which he probably took to be a log.

I can't turn around fast enough to see him leave the river, so I don't know if he went up the north bank or the south. He just wasn't there. Not even the sound of him going away was there. Only the breeze in the ash tree and water. Water coming around the bend and lapping against the canoe. Then I hear it. Something coming up the river. Deer, I think. It's in the middle of the river, whatever it is. Then I hear it talking to itself, and it's Sally Norton. The way the river lays right here, and because I'm in the dark of the bank under the ash tree, I can see her but she can't see me. Just like with the white horse.

She's walking along in her bare feet. I can see her that clear. It's a little late in the year for wading in the Whitewoman, but Sally's tough. She's naked like when I left her that afternoon. I see her tits in the moonlight. They're not as nice as my wife's tits, but they're nice. I'm going to tell my wife that. How her tits are better than Sally's. Maybe not. It's true, though. Sally's carrying my skull. She's got Wallace. In her right hand. Fingers in the eye holes. Swinging it as she walks. Just talking to herself about what I don't know.

Looking at her with Wallace's head in her hand, I don't think about Sally. Not even about how I nailed her earlier. Not about the noises she made or any of it. I couldn't get into my mind if I wanted to, and I'm not thinking of my wife that way, either. I'm not thinking about my wife. I'm not thinking about her yellow blouse. Although I could. I know I could. I'm thinking again about what I'm going to tell her when I get back if she's still there and hasn't gone down to Sharon Springs to stay with her brother and his wife. I hope not, because I've changed my mind again. I'm thinking, seeing the white horse is where I'm going to start with what's for real and what's not.

When I think that, then I start thinking about my wife in all kinds of ways with her tits moving under her yellow blouse and her legs and how good it is to nail her, and I can feel my trouser trout swimming in my pants. It's not just about nailing her. It's about how I'm going to take her down the Whitewoman, even now, late as it is, and show her where I found every one of the buffalo skulls. I'll get them out of Sally Norton's double-wide, and when my wife and I go down the river I'll put them back where I found them just so she can see. Maybe even hide one beforehand and pretend like she's the one who found it. I'll show her Wallace's Oxbow. I'll show her Wallace. I'll tell what I've made up about Wallace and let her pick the story about him she likes the best. After that we'll turn the canoe over like she wants to. And I'll nail her on the river. Then we'll go look for cattle skulls in the pastures together, and when we find enough I'll take her with me to Denver and I'll do sit-ups for her in the Buffalo Exchange and we'll have ourselves a Fat Tire beer. I'll ask the bartender if Jane Fonda's been in recently. I'll introduce her to Ted Turner when he shows up. *This is my One Happy Skull Hunter wife*, I'll say to Ted Turner. *Jane and me have made up*, he'll say.

I'm thinking all this as I'm looking at Sally Norton coming up the Whitewoman with my skull in her right hand, and then she's gone. Not there. Maybe I looked away for a moment like you do when you're thinking about something. I don't remember. I just know Sally's gone. Tits and skull and bare feet and talking and all.

There's nothing on the river but me. Me and everything that's inside me for having been out here. Now and before. Summer and winter. Floats. Seeing the lump of a buffalo skull coming out of the bank. Cattle skulls in the pastures. Looking for Wallace. Talking to him in his dugout. That woman from Kansas City. More. It's all in me. Sally Norton. The white horse. It's all me. I've filled up the river with me.

Then I feel myself going home to see my wife. It feels good. Not that I know what I'll tell her.

Afterword: Flowers

This collection ends with flowers for two short stories: "The War Eagle River Story" and "The Man Who Sees Music," both lost and lonely in their ways.

"The War Eagle River Story" was the first long story I ever wrote. It was for a fiction workshop at the University of Kansas, where I was an undergraduate. It was a third-person narrative of a trip down the War Eagle River in northwestern Arkansas, where a classmate of mine lived. He had invited me to go along on a "float trip" down the War Eagle, and I turned that friend into a hapless character (he was not). In the process I made the trip into one of misadventures and the death of my friend. I had used a technique of changing point of view, by moving out of the limited narrative to view things from the perspective of goats above the river, who were implied witnesses of the events on the War Eagle below. How I came to use this technique I do not know; it was the first time I used it. As a writer, I am a thief from other writers. Surely that device must have been somewhere in my literary reading as a young writer, but I cannot find it.

In those days in creative writing, you gave your stories to the professor (the novelist Edgar Wolfe in this case) a week or so before the workshop, and he (or she) would pass out one or two stories (mimeographed) at the beginning of the class to be read aloud. But before class, and after I had handed in my story, I happened to meet Professor Wolfe in the hallway and asked him if he had read my story, and if so, what he thought of it. He had indeed read it, and thought it was "a classic."

Somehow that praise found its way into an account of my literary life compiled by Tom Averill at Washburn University's Center for Kansas Studies, and over the years I have had queries from magazine editors offering to publish it. But the story got lost: I do not have a copy, and in the passing of time my classmates became lost to me as well, as did Professor Wolfe, who passed away in 1989. There might be a copy in Tom Averill's collection of Edgar Wolfe's papers in the Spencer Library at the University of Kansas, but I like to think the "War Eagle River"—and the goats—have found their place in hiding. Leave them be.

"The Man Who Sees Music" has a different fate: it has never been published. *The New Yorker* looked at it for about a month then passed. I especially like the story and didn't want its feelings to be hurt, so I set it aside (I know, a curious example of "the pathetic fallacy," but all my stories are like friends to me). Also, the story is set in West Jesus, Kansas, and would not be at home among the readers in the boroughs of New York City.*

In any case, by the authority given to me as their author, to both stories I bequest a very generous bouquet of "yellow flags"—as my mother called irises. Through her to her grandchildren: it is done.

---

* "The Man Who Sees Music" is in "Part Two: Men."

Appendix

Robert Day's Fictional Women

By Denise Low

Robert Day's first major literary work was the 1977 novel *The Last Cattle Drive*. It introduces many character types that have continued to engage this author's readers throughout the years. The novel's heroine, Opal Tukle, the rancher's wife, is a memorable archetype in Day's pantheon. This iconic Kansas woman—independent, plainspoken, practical, and tough—does not sit in the parlor of the farmhouse drinking tea. She manages the business end of the cattle ranch, sets the schedules, and sometimes bosses the men around. Today, Opal's western Kansas counterparts mend fence, drive tractors, bale hay, geld cattle, till gardens, and cook meals for threshing crews. I knew an old-time ranching widow who carried knitting in her saddlebags as she herded cattle on horseback. Opal is a fictional character, yet she rings true to my own experience as a fifth-generation Kansas woman. His female characters are realistic and independent; they exhibit maturity and a steely survivorship. These are traits of women in the old frontier West as well as in the new heartland.

The Opal archetype appears in most of Day's fiction. She can live on a cattle ranch or in the city. She can appear in the guise of a cosmopolitan Parisian painter or a suburban housewife in Evan Connell's Kansas City—Jane Austen and Evan Connell novels are touchstones for Day's fiction. Anne in Day's story "When the World Was Young and the Death of Bird Four" exemplifies this character type in an urban setting. In the opening scene, her husband directs her to create French titles for her Paris paintings so they can qualify for Internal Revenue Service travel exemptions (Schedule C). He trivializes her vocation. At the end of the story, after an epiphany, she leaves for Paris permanently without her boorish, adulterous husband. She contemplates new directions for her paintings beyond "cheeses on tables with wine titled in French." Anne's triumph as she extricates herself from the role of housewife creates a satisfying resolution to the drama. Fredericka, a minor character in the story, also resembles Opal. She pursues joint occupations as a fiction writer and a buyer of trappers' pelts from the High Plains. These she sells to a broker in Kansas City. She travels not just to genteel Paris, but also to rough country settings. Ranch country and Kansas City are the rural and urban poles of Day's cosmos, and the tough Fredericka can inhabit both. No men in these stories can do the same.

Day's fictional women are not ingenues. They are older women who have lost their innocence and gained maturity, if not always wisdom. The main character of "Chloe in the Canoe" is a middle-aged woman whose life as a prostitute has put her in a dangerous position. As the story opens, she is snowed in—and entrapped—at a western Kansas ranch. She does not submit to becoming a stranded sex employee and then household drudge without complaint and decent pay. Further, she persuades a humane newcomer into driving her to safety. Her imprisonment is more extreme than Anne's situation, and those of other unhappily married women in Day's fiction, but it is alike in kind. Enactment of the traditional women's roles is stifling at best.

Sallie French, in the story "I Am Lady Open," is another of Day's independent characters who rejects domestic servitude. Sallie dwells in a town similar to Atwood in northwestern Kansas, near the author's own part-time domicile. In this community adrift on the plains, she is a mechanical genius whose expertise is opening all the containers, wrappings, and plastic casings of commercial goods for her clients. She is a hero to the isolated elderly who no longer can unclamp the childproof bottles of their medicines. Sallie French does not suffer foolish lovers: her most recent paramour became a victim of her calculated revenge when she shot him in the foot as she escorted him out of the house. She dismisses the next potential mate as she realizes how much independence she would lose in the role of a wife, and she concludes by celebrating, "I am Lady Open. I am real. It feels good." She is complete without the encumbrance of a mate.

A fictional peer of Lady Open in the same town, "Bly," is the protagonist of "The One-Man Woodcutter." She is a widowed Christian farm wife who carries a terrible secret. She promises her dying husband she won't tell their family tragedy—details of their daughter's death. In the story the widow carries on her husband's business, cleans houses, and maintains her own household alone. She and her sister are among the diminishing population of this remote location, which has more people in the churchyard than in the pews. She has a gritty ability to survive psychological blows as well as the harsh setting.

Men in Day's fiction have their flaws, and also the women, often enacted in the situation of adultery. The narrator's parents in "Words Make a Life" both had lovers during their long marriage. Only after their deaths do the children explore this aspect of their parents' lives, and the narrator remembers his father's counsel about women: "If they break you can't fix them like cars." After his mother's funeral, the narrator notices in his mother's portrait how a sadness shadows the eyes. This suggests the breaks in the marriage, especially the father's admonition about women. It also acknowledges the mother's own lost love. The couple lived out a life of mechanical association, not a loving marriage. There is no happily-after-ever plotline in "We All Have Our Stories" either, which also centers on adultery. When a college-days affair continues after both participants are married to other people, this appears to stifle both the man and the woman as they continue to keep the secret. Neither can tell stories well, or remember them, and their ongoing affair mutes their ability to engage fully with their spouses. The most whole characters in Day's world, especially when it comes to the women, are single.

Edith of "Edith at the Eighth Street Tavern" is one of the more vibrant women in Day's fiction, and single. She has "missed her chances" of marriage and now owns a neighborhood tavern. She has her regulars, including one who is her lover, a married man. The local beaver trappers favor her with free meat during trapping season, which she makes into a savory stew. (This is literal, not literary innuendo; I have partaken of local beaver stew during winter months in Lawrence, where the tavern still stands on Eighth Street.) Edith's saloon is like this rich mix. Yet time passes, she ages, and the man quietly ends the affair as he also grows older. She remains alone, but not lonely, as she accepts another loss: "Eighth Street is silent again, save for the odd sound falling snow makes, which we all know but cannot describe." She has a lasting, intangible beauty in her life. Without flinching, she faces her own place in the natural order.

Day's women are not necessarily happy, and not all of Day's women are even heroic. In general, his fiction critiques social classes, and he reserves particular disdain for superficial wealthy people. In *The Last Cattle Drive*, this negative character type appears as the youthful Heather, a gold digger from the big city. She wants not true love, but to snare a wealthy mate. The sister in this collection's "Words Make a Life" is another exemplar of this type. She lives in an expensive house with a coffee table where she places her brother's art books for show. Day's narrator calls her a philistine, as she has no authentic connection to the arts:

There is a pleasing philistine sensibility about a well-designed, large-format book that features the flora and fauna from the French Impressionist period. The philistine sensibility is not in the book but in the plush homes and apartments where Monet's *Water Lilies* or Fantin-Latour's *Still Lives* languish.

The narrator is a book designer, and he laments that most of his oversized gift books are designed not to fit into shelves, but on coffee tables. Even more telling are the empty pages in the ornate blank book he gave his sister as a journal. She has no inner life and no stories of her own. Although well meaning, and not overtly evil, she represents the negative woman in Day's fiction. He also has a brotherhood of men who suffer the same ailments. Evan Connell's novels *Mr. Bridge* and *Mrs. Bridge*, set in the posh Country Club Plaza area of Kansas City like this story, are companions to Day's work.

Day takes the most radical of feminist positions. Women are discrete individuals not categorically different from men. In "We All Have Our Stories," two men ponder the riddle as old as Tiresias of Greek narratives: How do men and women differ? Day's answer is embedded in this dialogue:

"I've been thinking about the difference between men and women," says Rob.

"Why bother?" says U.S.

"Women can't tell stories," says Rob.

"Neither can I," says U.S. "I wish I could. Like you."

The issue here is voice, the power to create narrative. Day suggests in the story that such power is possible for both genders, as is failure.

Sometimes Day's women perform traditional roles, but most often they do not. Sometimes they are faithful in marriage, sometimes not. Some can tell jokes and stories, some cannot. After decades of reading these stories, I notice new dimensions. The proud, stubborn women who are my own mothers and grandmothers and greats—women who lived on farms and ranches and ones who grew up in Kansas City—all appear in these stories. They laugh, love, and survive. There are many reasons to read Day. Humor. Lyrical prose. Balanced plot and dialogue. Among the riches are women characters who come to life in the spell of fiction and beyond.

Denise Low, Kansas Poet Laureate 2007–2009, is winner of a Red Mountain Press Award for Shadow Light, *a book of poems (Red Mountain Press, 2018). Other recent publications are* Jackalope *(fiction, Red Mountain Press, 2018) and a memoir,* The Turtle's Beating Heart: One Family's Story of Lenape Survival *(University of Nebraska Press, 2017), a finalist for the Hefner Heitz Award. She founded the creative writing program at Haskell Indian Nations University. Currently she teaches for Baker University's School of Professional and Graduate Studies. She recently relocated to Sonoma County, California.*

"Barrel Heat": An Introduction

By Robert Stewart

The road to a short story can run through any terrain, if the story is reliable and thus specific to a place. In this case, the road to "Barrel Heat" careened through the High Plains of northwestern Kansas, up near but not into Nebraska, where Robert Day spends much of his time. It was there, in 2012, that Bob, my wife, Lisa, and I rode that terrain, slowly, in Bob's single-cab GMC pickup, which had been running those hills for a couple of decades. While we were not out to hunt on that trip, Bob was showing us where his yellow lab dog, Lullaby, would go to flush birds into the air.

There is a creek up that way called the North Beaver, and among the tall grass and wheat, one finds stands of briars and plum trees inhabited by pheasants in normal times. This was midsummer and one of those times. A house out there would easily be a mile from any other house; and from any given swell of the earth, a visitor such as I could see, through the windshield of a lumbering horse of a pickup, a hundred miles of golden landscape. One does not want such a tour to end soon.

As we were talking about pheasants and dogs—Lullaby being in the truck bed, looking in through the back window to where she normally would ride—Bob Day began to speak of his younger self as the trap-shooting champ of the state of Kansas and how it felt to smoke a skeet in competition. Did he talk about the Trap Grade Winchester Model 12, then? I think so, but my amateur, city-boy's mind easily could have missed such a technical and relevant detail. The next and crucial phase of the story's life belongs to my wife, Lisa.

"You need to write the story of your trap-shooting days, Bob," she said. "Or have you written it?"

"I've had it in mind quite a while," he said. "I have drafts and notes, but it's complicated."

"Finish it," she said.

Within a few weeks—maybe months, I am not sure—the story showed up in my mail at *New Letters* magazine, where we had published some of Bob's other fiction and essays. I read "Barrel Heat" in manuscript, somewhat trepidatiously, knowing that Lisa and I had at least urged Bob along in the effort, knowing also that there was a lot at stake. I was elated by the result, and the story came out in the winter 2013 issue of the magazine, alongside other important literary writers.

A reader of the story might notice, if I am not being too sure of myself, that among the sturdiest characters, the character of Lisa stands slightly outside of the plot, entirely motivating and self-contained. In classic Robert Day fashion, the first-person narrator does not offer up his own name, as the plot interacts with his identity in ways both surprising and powerful. The story revolves around—and is grounded in—the significant facts that come not from make-believe but out of the region and the trade of trap shooting. The speaker here begins his shooting on the circuit tentatively, as if beginning a narrative of some complexity, at trap clubs, he says, "in Eudora, Vinland, Overbrook...and once as far south as Centropolis."

I admire the courage of such writing to be both clear of time and place and also to employ the all-too-rare wit of implication (i.e., restraint) when needed. I could tell, as we rode in the pickup that day, that the writer himself was thinking about the challenge of putting together a complicated and rich story that demanded to be written, and which was contained in memory, all of its pieces, and yet—as any serious writer will understand—terrifying to begin for those very reasons.

Why had he not finished that story before? Because it mattered so much. This is fiction, yes, and some characters and dialogue rise from imagination and inspiration; at its core, however, "Barrel Heat" must be seen as among the most necessary and crucial stories not only of our time and of this region, Kansas, but of Robert Day's body of work and of his life.

Robert Stewart is the former editor of New Letters *magazine and BkMk Press and author of* Working Class *(poems, Stephen F. Austin State University, 2018) and* The Narrow Gate: Essays on Writing, Art & Values *(Serving House, 2014), among other books. He lives in Prairie Village, Kansas.*

Robert Day's "The Skull Hunter"

By Fred Whitehead

It seems forever that the adjective "Wild" has been affixed to the American West—as in Buffalo Bill's Wild West shows that famously "re-created" the cowboy and Indian fights. No one thought of the West as peaceable or calm: it was Wild. And so is this narrative, set along the valley of the fictional Whitewoman River somewhere in western Kansas. Though the river is a fiction, there is a White Woman Creek, now mostly dry, and I think never properly navigable, even for canoes. At any rate, Wallace, the narrator, supplements his small income by scavenging cattle skulls along the banks and selling them to a dealer in Denver. Thus, like Buffalo Bill, he serves a market in the cities for colorful souvenirs. In the nineteenth century, beavers were hunted almost to extinction for their pelts, made into elegant, expensive hats for gentlemen back East and even abroad.

Wallace calls himself a hunter, a much more romantic and dignified word than a scavenger. He takes unto himself the role and the lore of hunting so important to the Wild West. He sometimes finds buffalo skulls, which could command a good price in Denver, but he never sells them. He wants to keep that part of the West for himself.

This element of the skulls reminded me of the route taken up the Congo in Conrad's *Heart of Darkness*, where skulls are fixed on posts along the banks, grisly portents of doom ahead. We are brought into close proximity to mortality. Wallace discovers his doppelgänger, whom he names after himself: a headless, nameless human skeleton partially exposed in the bank of a river cove. As in Conrad, we enter a landscape of unease and fatality. My late novelist friend Truman Nelson observed that all great literature has a sense of menace, and so it is here as in Conrad.

"The Skull Hunter," however, differs from Conrad's novel and its somber mood in its humor and sensuality. Wallace is content with his wife, but also has intimate connections with other women. He has no guilt about these affairs, but reports them as simple facts of life. The word "pagan" is from Latin, and it referred to those who lived in the country rather than the cities. Similarly, "heathen" denoted those who lived on the heath. Without any religion, Wallace exists contentedly in the world around him.

Rivers and bodies of water are in traditional cultures places inhabited by spirits, especially female spirits such as nymphs. Some such spirits could be sinister and even deadly, like the sirens of the *Odyssey*, so memorably painted by John Waterhouse. And when Wallace encounters the naked woman holding the skull of his doppelgänger walking down the river at night, we have one of those unexpected, shocking moments of facing the truly Uncanny. The reader wonders if, indeed, it might have been "only" a dream.

A perceptive woman reader of my acquaintance offers this: "The prose has a pace to it which is almost a meditation, which adds to the notion that it is not a true story, but a dream or hallucination of some kind. The male ego seems to be in overdrive, which might suggest something of the opposite....I would suggest that Wallace is trying to come to terms with something. To me, the story is not the story."

Until that night encounter, the story has been mostly realistic, but suddenly we are transported to another world, or a world with new dimensions. To be convincing, a hallucination must be presented as real, so that it becomes to the reader the same as what the character experiencing it "sees." All great literature expands beyond the mundane and ordinary to the visionary. And so it is in this remarkable story.

Fred Whitehead is a retired independent scholar living in Kansas City, Kansas. He was coeditor of the pioneering anthology Free-Thought on the American Frontier *(Prometheus, 1992) and has authored many articles and books focusing on the Midwestern radical heritage.*

Acknowledgments

The author honors the publishing counsel of Walter Cummins, the design craft of James Dissette, and the studied and wise editorial advice of Kathy Streckfus. Finally, I want my fellow authors Denise Low, Robert Stewart, and Fred Whitehead to know that I very much appreciate their gifted "insight and advocacy" of my own writing.

Credits

"Edith at the Eighth Street Tavern" first appeared under the title "Beaver Dinners at the Eighth Street Tavern" in *Black Warrior Review* 4, no. 1 (Fall 1977) and was reprinted in Robert Day, *Speaking French in Kansas and Other Stories* (Topeka: Center for Kansas Studies / Woodley Press, 2005).

"We All Have Our Stories" originally appeared in *North Dakota Quarterly* 72, no. 4 (2005): 35–43 and was reprinted in Robert Day, *The Billion Dollar Dream* (Kansas City, MO: BkMk Press, 2015).

"When the World Was Young and the Death of Bird Four" originally appeared in *North Dakota Quarterly* 72, no. 4 (2005): 23–34 and was reprinted in Robert Day, *The Billion Dollar Dream* (Kansas City, MO: BkMk Press, 2015).

"Words Make a Life" originally appeared in *Little Balkans Review* and was reprinted in Robert Day, *Where I Am Now* (Kansas City, MO: BkMk Press, 2012).

"I Am Lady Open" originally appeared in *North Dakota Quarterly* 80, no. 3 (2015).

"The One-Man Woodcutter" originally appeared in *North Dakota Quarterly* 72, no. 4 (2005): 7–22 as "The One-Man Woodcutter Meets His Widowmaker" and was reprinted in Robert Day, *Where I Am Now* (Kansas City, MO: BkMk Press, 2012).

"Chloe in the Canoe" originally appeared in *Kansas Quarterly* and was reprinted in Robert Day, *Speaking French in Kansas and Other Stories* (Topeka: Center for Kansas Studies / Woodley Press, 2005).

"My Uncle's Poor French" originally appeared in *New Letters* 71, no. 3 (Spring 2005) and was reprinted in Robert Day, *The Billion Dollar Dream* (Kansas City, MO: BkMk Press, 2015).

"The Billion-Dollar Dream" originally appeared in *North Dakota Quarterly* 74, no. 2 (2007): 76–97 and was reprinted in Robert Day, *The Billion Dollar Dream* (Kansas City, MO: BkMk Press, 2015).

"Sometimes It Is, Sometimes It Isn't" originally appeared in *Numéro Cinq* 3, no. 8 (August 2012) and was reprinted in Robert Day, *The Billion Dollar Dream* (Kansas City, MO: BkMk Press, 2015).

"The Four-Wheel-Drive Quartet" was first published by The Galileo Press of Baltimore, Maryland, in 1986, and was reprinted in Robert Day, *Speaking French in Kansas and Other Stories* (Topeka: Center for Kansas Studies / Woodley Press, 2005).

"Speaking French in Kansas" originally appeared in *New Letters* 48, no. 2 (Winter 1981–1982) and was reprinted in Robert Day, *Speaking French in Kansas and Other Stories* (Topeka: Center for Kansas Studies / Woodley Press, 2005).

"My Father Swims His Horse at Last" originally appeared in *Tri-Quarterly* 79 (Fall 1990): 7–36 and was reprinted in Robert Day, *Where I Am Now* (Kansas City, MO: BkMk Press, 2012).

"The Mackinaw" first appeared in *Cottonwood Review* 1, no. 1 (1965) and was reprinted in Robert Day, *Speaking French in Kansas and Other Stories* (Topeka: Center for Kansas Studies / Woodley Press, 2005).

"Pan-Kansas Swimming Champion" originally appeared in *Kansas Quarterly* 23, nos. 1/2 (1991) and was reprinted in Robert Day, *Where I Am Now* (Kansas City, MO: BkMk Press, 2012).

"Where I Am Now" originally appeared in *New Letters* 76, no. 3 (Spring 2010): 73–100 and was reprinted in Robert Day, *Where I Am Now* (Kansas City, MO: BkMk Press, 2012).

"By the Light of the Silvery Moon" originally appeared in *North Dakota Quarterly* 78, no. 1 (2011): 74–87 and was reprinted in

Robert Day, *The Billion Dollar Dream* (Kansas City, MO: BkMk Press, 2015).

"Stealing" originally appeared in *The Summerset Review* (Winter 2014) and was reprinted in Robert Day, *The Billion Dollar Dream* (Kansas City, MO: BkMk Press, 2015).

"Notes on the Cold War in Kansas" originally appeared in *New Letters* 73, no. 2 (Winter 2007): 157–171 and was reprinted in Robert Day, *Where I Am Now* (Kansas City, MO: BkMk Press, 2012).

"It Puts Matters in Doubt Here in Two Sleeps" first appeared in *KS Magazine* and was reprinted in Robert Day, *Speaking French in Kansas and Other Stories* (Topeka: Center for Kansas Studies / Woodley Press, 2005).

"In My Stead" was published by Cottonwood Press in 1981 in book form and was reprinted in Robert Day, *Speaking French in Kansas and Other Stories* (Topeka: Center for Kansas Studies / Woodley Press, 2005).

"Barrel Heat" originally appeared in *New Letters* 79, no. 2 (Winter 2013) and was reprinted in Robert Day, *The Billion Dollar Dream* (Kansas City, MO: BkMk Press, 2015).

"Free Writing" originally appeared in *New Letters* 73, no. 2 (Winter 2007) and was reprinted in Robert Day, *The Billion Dollar Dream* (Kansas City, MO: BkMk Press, 2015).

"The Skull Hunter" originally appeared in *New Letters* 71, no. 1 (Fall 2004–2005): 135–153 and was reprinted in Robert Day, *Where I Am Now* (Kansas City, MO: BkMk Press, 2012).

Robert Day's novel *The Last Cattle Drive* was a Book-of-the-Month Club selection. His short fiction has won a number of awards and citations, including two Seaton Prizes, a Pen Faulkner/NEA prize, and Best American Short Story and Pushcart citations. His fiction has been published by *Tri-Quarterly, Black Warrior Review, Kansas Quarterly, North Dakota Quarterly, Summerset Review,* and *New Letters,* among other belles-lettres magazines. He is the author of two novellas, *In My Stead* and *The Four Wheel Drive Quartet,* as well as three collections of short fiction: *Speaking French in Kansas, Where I Am Now,* and *The Billion Dollar Dream.*

His nonfiction has been published in the *Washington Post Magazine, Smithsonian Magazine, Forbes FYI, Modern Maturity, World Literature Today, American Scholar,* and *Numero Cinq.* As a member of the Prairie Writers Circle, his essays have been reprinted in numerous newspapers and journals nationwide and on such Internet sites as *Counterpunch* and *Arts and Letters Daily.* Recent book publications include *We Should Have Come by Water* (poems), *The Committee to Save the World* (literary nonfiction), and *Chance Encounters of a Literary Kind* (memoir). Other publications include the novel *Let Us Imagine Lost Love* and *Robert Day for President: An Embellished Campaign Autobiography.*

Among his awards and fellowships are a National Endowment for the Arts Creative Writing Fellowship, Yaddo and McDowell Fellowships, a Maryland Arts Council Award, and the Edgar Wolfe Award for distinguished fiction. His teaching positions include the Iowa Writers Workshop, the University of Kansas, and the Graduate Faculty at Montaigne College, University of Bordeaux.

He is a past president of the Associated Writing Programs, the founder and former director of the Rose O'Neill Literary House, and founder and publisher of the Literary House Press at Washington College, Chestertown, Maryland.